THE MOON CHASERS

Copyright © 2003 Thomas R. Carey

ISBN 1-59113-387-4

All rights reserved. No part of this publication may be reproduced, stored in a retrieval system, or transmitted in any form or by any means, electronic, mechanical, recording or otherwise, without the prior written permission of the author.

Printed in the United States of America.

The characters and events in this book are fictitious. Any similarity to real persons, living or dead, is coincidental and not intended by the author.

Booklocker.com, Inc. 2003
Cover Design: Julie Sartain

THE MOON CHASERS

By Thomas R. Carey

To Linda: for all the years of happiness.

PROLOGUE

Long ago: long before cars and telephones, hospitals and computers, and everything else we take for granted, people lived difficult and perilous lives. A simple infection might spell death. Droughts and floods could mean mass starvation. And when tragedies struck, our ancestors would gaze skyward at the magical points of light scattered across the darkened heavens and cry why? There must be a reason why.

At first they were met with mute, cold indifference. Then they began to notice things: wonderful things. Groups of these points of light appeared to form images. Great bears, dragons, serpents, and other creatures slowly swirling overhead in a silent and seasonal dance. Images we now call the constellations.

They also noticed bright sky wanderers. Sometimes these wanderers appeared just before the dawn of a new day. Others plodded through the sky's nocturnal images for weeks or months at a time. Bright wanderers we now know as the planets.

And to the whole of it all they began to wonder. Did movement of the wanderers mean life? Life of a higher order? Were they winged servants of the gods? Or were they gods themselves? If so, could they be coaxed to intercede in worldly matters? Or were they already speaking through their movements? Trying to forewarn of disasters or foretell good fortunes?

To many of these questions the ancients ultimately concluded yes. In their quest to control their destinies, they studied what they saw and, after a time, some believed they had deciphered the messages of the gods twinkling overhead in the distant darkness.

Priest astrologers came to be consulted in advance of battles. Shamans would offer sacrifices to sky gods to help prevent droughts or cure the sick. Comets and falling stars might signal impending doom.

But of all the myths about the heavens, only one is reported to have had an actual earthly component. An old and cryptic tale which, if true, would seemingly have proven, once and for all, that the sky wanderers were indeed gods. An event some believe was witnessed near and far, and documented by the most celebrated sky watchers of all: the ancient Maya.

Chapter One: Parks's Destiny

"Mr. Parks," said Professor Warren, setting the typewriter-written thesis proposal aside on his polished, mahogany desk. "This is an interesting research topic; very interesting, indeed."

The walls of the Great Professor's office were mostly hidden from view beneath a jigsaw puzzle of framed diplomas, awards, and honors. A case behind him was crammed with books, some of which were quite old, clad in soiled cloth or cracked and faded leather. Others were new, or nearly so, with glossy, soft covers. Despite each one's age or condition, all dealt in one way or another with archaeology: Warren's field of study for the last thirty years. His was the office of a serious academician, at least from all outward appearances. But like many things in life, one must never judge a book by its cover.

"I think the approach has real promise, Professor," replied Gordon Parks, one of Blaine University's new graduate students for the fall semester.

"It's novel, to say the least," replied Warren, leaning back in his leather chair, which creaked miserably under his weight. He steepled his fingers and peered at Gordon over the top of his reading glasses. The young man looked more like a strapping athlete than a serious anthropology major, with his broad shoulders, longish, dark-brown hair, hazel eyes, and chiseled facial features. But his research proposal did show promise: perhaps *too* much promise. "You realize, of course, that a sizable majority in the archaeological community consider the Rome Codex a forgery—an elaborate hoax. I'm a bit surprised *you* apparently have no doubt of its authenticity."

"I'm fully aware of the controversy surrounding it," replied Gordon, bending forward in his chair to defend his proposal: the outline of an investigation he hoped would lead to fame and fortune, and perhaps even a graduate degree from the vaunted Blaine University. "My research might help establish whether or not the Rome Codex is authentic. You must agree that confirming hoaxes and revealing frauds are as much a part of archaeology as field work is."

Professor Warren frowned at Gordon's confidence. A long series of professional disappointments had shaken his own to the point he had to rely on stealing the successful research of others to maintain his status as chairman of Blaine University's Anthropology Department. It was a bitter feeling, but not one tinged with enough guilt for him to change his ways, especially at his age. Gordon Parks's research was fair game, just as much as the rest of his students' work. "I've discussed your proposal with the other faculty members," he continued in a serious tone. "In general, that is. I've omitted mentioning the Rome Codex and your search for the Mars Beast Ceremonial Center. Professor Jenkins is convinced the Rome Codex is a fake. Even so, he is still of the opinion your proposed research doesn't fit within the department's graduate thesis parameters."

"Really? How so?"

"Typically we like to see research involving historic archaeology where the student builds upon the established fieldwork of others. Jenkins thinks you might be trying to upset our academic apple cart with your high-tech ideas. He also thinks you'll be wasting your time." Warren leaned forward again, removing his glasses and studying Gordon with cold, gray eyes. "Will you be wasting your time, Mr. Parks?"

Fighting back the butterflies that had taken flight in his stomach, Gordon struggled to look undaunted. This was it. He would know in a moment whether his longed-for quest would ever get off the ground. "Not at all," he replied firmly. "Professor Jenkins is entitled to his opinion, but I'm not required to agree with it."

"Well, then," continued Warren, putting his glasses back on. "You'll be happy to know Professor Maitland doesn't think so either. She believes evaluating the use of aerial radar to look for Maya ruins hidden in the jungles of Central America is a marvelous thesis topic. Too bad she isn't the one who has to approve your work." He pinched the edge of Gordon's proposal and slowly drew it to his side of the desk. "Are you certain NASA will provide access to the radar images you refer to in here?"

"Yes," replied Gordon, sitting up straight and adjusting his tweed jacket: the kind with oval patches on the elbows. "I can obtain copies under their new technology transfer program, but only if the university approves of my research in writing. They require confirmation that I'm a serious student working under the auspices of Blaine's Anthropology Department."

Warren didn't respond right away. He simply stared at Gordon's proposal, drumming the fingers of his right hand on his desk as if struggling to come to an important decision which could go either way. It was an act. He *was* the Anthropology Department and had already decided to let Gordon have a crack at his proposed research. If the young man was successful, Warren would step in, flunk him out of school on some pretense, and send him packing. He'd done it to others before and would certainly do it again. Afterwards he could claim full credit for Parks's discovery. And such a discovery it would be! It would place Professor Carl C. Warren within the ranks of the most preeminent archaeologists in the world. He would be a Central American version of Howard Carter, the famous Egyptologist who discovered King Tutankhamen's tomb. If Parks was wrong, then another project could be selected or he could be flunked anyway. He finally stopped drumming and looked up at Gordon. The young man was staring anxiously back at him. "My initial inclination was to side with Jenkins," he began so as not to appear too eager, throwing in a couple of condescending *sniffs* for good measure. "However, given the novelty of your research and NASA's willingness to cooperate, I've decided to accept your thesis proposal on two conditions."

Gordon sighed inwardly with relief before fighting a knowing smirk. Professor Warren's reputation as an unabashed credit thief was well known across campus and elsewhere. Little did the pompous, fat, old man know that this time *he* would be the one taken advantage of. Warren was going to help Gordon get just what he wanted: access to NASA's radar images. "What two conditions?" he replied innocently, imagining the Great Professor was a talking fiddle about to be played.

"First, you are to begin your research immediately. I know most students don't start so soon, but I want you to submit a progress report to me three months from now—shortly after the start of the winter semester. If I determine your efforts are indeed being wasted, you'll have to come up with a new thesis proposal. You understand in either event you'll be required to complete your research by next spring or loose your credits."

Gordon nodded that he understood.

"Second, if your work survives my initial review and you do indeed locate the mysterious Mars Beast Ceremonial Center—or any other undiscovered ruins, for that matter—your research must be turned over to me and the department immediately. Don't take offense, but any significant finds will need to be addressed by greater minds than yours. You'll also be expected to keep the locations strictly confidential." He thumped his finger on Gordon's thesis proposal. "If word got out on the locations of lost Maya ruins before the sites could be secured by the appropriate authorities, the looters would have a field day. By the time we arrived, there wouldn't be anything left undisturbed!" Warren narrowed his eyes and closely studied Gordon's face. "And speaking of confidential, how many people have you shown your proposal to, anyway? How many copies are floating around out there?"

"There's only the original," replied Gordon, nodding towards the document on Warren's desk. "You're the only person I've given it to and I haven't had a chance to make a copy yet." (This last statement being a bold-faced lie to help him get what he wanted. He'd researched Warren's tactics well.)

"What about the folks at NASA? What have you told them?"

"Only that I'm doing some general research on Maya ruins in western Belize and northern Guatemala."

"Good. Listen, Gordon: I'll be honest with you. I don't seriously believe for a moment you're going to find the Mars Beast Ceremonial Center. My approval of your thesis proposal is based more on the potential use of aerial radar to help locate ruins in general. In that sense, your research is admirable and I commend you on your ingenuity. However, I have an open mind. In the event you locate anything interesting you must come to me first." He opened a drawer in his desk and placed Gordon's proposal in. "Rest assured, you'll receive all the credit and be included as part of a larger group effort. We would assemble a team and proceed though proper government channels. If you *do* find the Mars Beast Ceremonial Center, I might even tag along myself. I haven't been to Guatemala in ages, assuming that's where you find it." Closing the drawer he pulled a key from his suit coat pocket and locked it. "I also recommend you refrain from mentioning the real purpose of your research to anyone else. I'll keep your written proposal safe. No need for a copy. You wouldn't want anyone to steal your idea and beat you to the punch would you?"

"No, sir!"

"Good. That's the smart thing to do. Take it from me, even in the scholarly professions there are a lot of unscrupulous people. Well, what do you say to my conditions, Mr. Parks?"

Gordon stood and offered the professor his hand. "Of course I can live with your conditions," he lied again.

Professor Warren stood as well and the two shook hands. "I'll send a notarized letter to the NASA representatives identified in your proposal, confirming you are indeed a student working under our direction. A letter from New Hampshire's most prestigious university should provide them with all the proof they need. If they have any questions they can call me."

"Thank you, Professor."

Warren looked at his watch. "As much as I've enjoyed discussing your research, I'm afraid I'm running late for a meeting and must bid you good day. Good luck to you and let me know how things go. I look forward to your progress report."

Gordon said, "Thank you," a couple more times while quickly gathering up his things. Finally stepping into the hallway and closing the door to Warren's office behind him, he breathed a sigh of relief. For a while it looked like he might not pull it off. Since the discovery of the Rome Codex several years ago, archaeologists and fortune hunters from all over the world had searched in vain for the Maya ceremonial center referenced in the ancient document. If he could find it he would become famous. Obtaining Professor Warren's approval of his project had been necessary to gain access to NASA's radar images. Now that he had it, he would get the images and closely guard his findings. He had no intention of sharing the location of the Mars Beast Ceremonial Center with anyone until he was certain to receive full credit for such a significant discovery.

"Hi, Gordon," said Max Zenger, Gordon's tall and lanky roommate.

"I see I find you in your natural state," replied Gordon, closing the front door of the townhouse behind him. Max's "natural state" was being sprawled out on Gordon's sofa, reviewing reams of wide, tractor-feed computer printouts.

Max twisted around to sit up, carefully pushing printouts aside as he did. "You know I need to edit these programs for class. I always tidy-up when I'm done."

"Just kidding, Max," said Gordon as he strolled into the living room. Then, eyeing his friend, he gave a low whistle. "Why are you so dressed up?"

Max usually wore various combinations of denim jeans, corduroy sport coats, and T-shirts sporting the logos of computer companies. Today was no exception, except in place of his T-shirt he was wearing a brand new, blue polo shirt emblazoned with, "Pascal Rascal" in small, gold letters at its upper left. Max looked down at it and shrugged. "Oh, no reason," he replied, before carefully smoothing back his long, sandy-brown hair just so. After adjusting his glasses and looking at his watch, he began quickly and noisily folding up a long printout draped over the coffee table and stretching clear across the room. "How'd it go with the old claim-jumper?" he asked, finally finishing and placing the printout on a deep pile of others on the floor next to the sofa. "Was it yea or nay?"

"The proposal is approved," replied a now-beaming Gordon. He pulled a copy out of his briefcase with a flourish and held it up in the air. "You should have seen the old credit hound drooling over it. He wants me to keep my research 'hush, hush,' and hand him over my results. Ha! Does he think I was born yesterday?" He tossed the proposal on the coffee table next to where Max was seated. "By the time he figures out he's been had, we'll probably already be gone; taking pictures of my find deep in the jungles of Guatemala or Belize."

Max picked up the proposal and began thumbing through it. They'd been undergraduate students together before enrolling in graduate school at Blaine. Unlike Gordon, who had majored in Latin and ancient studies, Max had majored in physics and was now pursuing a graduate degree in computer science. Both young men were considered brilliant in their own right.

"It must be nice to have family money to engage in such risky pursuits," said Max, placing the proposal back down on the coffee table. "Graduate degree in anthropology! You're nothing but a treasure hunter and a thrill seeker."

"Me? What about you? Mainframe computers! Mainframes are a thing of the past. Haven't you heard of the new microcomputers?"

"They're toys. Mainframes are the future," quipped Max just as a knock was heard at the door. He jumped up to get it. "It's probably Holly. I forgot to tell you she's coming over. I'm helping her on a programming assignment."

"So *that's* why you're dressed up today, huh? It took a girl to get you to break down and buy a polo shirt."

"Ha. Ha. Very, funny, Gordo," said Max, looking out a peephole set within the townhouse's front door, beyond which stood Holly Graham, her brown eyes gleaming happily. She waved at the peephole.

Holly was a student Max had met while conducting a computer tutoring session for Blaine undergraduates. She was pretty, smart, and confident and seemed to genuinely like Max. He seemed to like her too, which, unbeknownst to him, was a point of contention with Gordon, who had developed a bit of a crush on her himself.

"Hello, Max," she said as he opened the door for her.

"Right on time," he replied, looking at his watch.

"I can't help it, being a military brat and all. Thanks for helping me out again. This computer programming can get confusing sometimes."

"Please come in; make yourself at home."

Holly walked into the large, high-ceilinged living room and said, "Wow" to the elegant furnishings: a tasteful mixture of antiques and custom furniture all resting pleasantly on a grand Persian rug bordered by gleaming hardwood floors and walls filled with original oil paintings. She was wearing a pair of designer blue jeans with a lot of fancy stitching on the back pockets and a pink Izod polo shirt—collar up—beneath an equally pink, and equally Izoddy, cashmere sweater. "Nice place you have here," she added before noticing Gordon. "Hi,

Gordon, how'd it go? Max said this was your big day. Was your research project approved?"

"It was approved by Professor Warren himself," replied Gordon. "But, was there ever any doubt it would be accepted? After all, what does Max know about anything? You really shouldn't listen to everything he says."

"Oh, shush!" she teased back. "Max said they'd be fools if they rejected your proposal; especially since he came up with the best part. Congratulations, Gordon! You really must tell me what this is all about, though. Max said it's top secret. I'm dying of curiosity."

"Well, I intend to keep the results secret until I receive proper recognition. Professor Warren is a blatant research thief; practically everybody knows it. If I find what I'm looking for, *I'm* going to get all the credit! He can flunk me if he likes, because I'll be able to get into any graduate school in the country." Then he remembered his manners. "Please come in and sit down," he said, taking her backpack and setting it on an end table in the living room. "Can I get you anything? Coffee? Soda? Tea?"

"No thank you," replied Holly, sitting down on an overstuffed chair. "Really, Gordon, tell me about your research," she pressed, brushing her long, brown hair back over her shoulder. And then she turned to Max, "You're in no rush to start in on my homework yet, are you Max?"

"My evening is yours, as is your grade," replied Max. "Besides, I haven't heard Gordon's proposal above a dozen times." He sat down on the sofa next to Holly's chair and kicked his feet up onto the coffee table. "It's really quite interesting, though. And I feel like I've contributed to it in my own small way. Fire away, Gordo. You can trust Holly."

"Well," began Gordon, "I'll tell you, but I'd prefer if you keep it under your hat."

Holly smiled. "Never a word, I promise." She motioned like she was zipping her mouth shut.

"Good. Have you ever heard of the ancient Maya?"

"Sure I have," replied Holly. "My folks and I went to Cancun last spring. It's a new tourist spot in Mexico. We took a day trip to a place called 'Tulum' where there's a big Mayan pyramid on a bluff overlooking the ocean."

"They constructed many such pyramids," said Gordon. "The Maya people had a highly advanced civilization which lasted for nearly two thousand years. We know that over time they developed a complicated social and religious structure requiring the construction of pyramids, temples, and ceremonial centers all over parts of what are now known as Mexico, Belize, and Guatemala. They were also great astronomers. Their religion was intimately tied to what they observed in the night sky. By the time the Spaniards arrived in the sixteenth century, though, the Maya had degenerated into small, mostly independent villages. No one knows what caused the decline."

"So you're going to do a research project on the ancient Maya?" guessed Holly.

"More like fortune hunt," said Max with a grin.

Grinning back, Gordon walked over to an enormous antique case and plucked out a glossy textbook. "Have you ever heard of the Rome Codex?"

"Codex?" asked Holly. "I don't know what that is."

"A codex is what archaeologists call a Maya book," said Gordon. "I first learned about them as an undergrad. The Maya had a detailed written hieroglyphic language made up of hundreds of pictures and symbols called 'glyphs.' Most haven't been deciphered yet. Their books were made of tree bark coated with lime paste and folded like accordions." He opened the textbook to a page and handed it to her. "This is a photographic copy of the 'Rome Codex.' It's called that because the original was found wedged between two ancient bookcases in a church in Rome, Italy a few years ago. Its discovery caused quite a stir in archaeological circles until some suggested it was a phony. I believe it's authentic."

"You hope it is," said Max. "Otherwise you've *really* been wasting your time."

Holly turned a few pages of the textbook before grimacing. "Some of these pictures are ghastly-looking! All these serpents and monsters; people being sacrificed. Ghastly."

"That's just what the conquering Spaniards thought," said Gordon. "They believed the codices were records of unholy rites and rituals. In order to help convert the descendants of the Maya, they ordered all their books be gathered up and burned. The Spaniards were very thorough in their work. Only four other codices are known to exist today."

"What's so significant about the Rome Codex?" asked Holly, looking up from the textbook.

"It appears to have been written as some sort of basic lesson for Maya children. The glyphs are less complex than those found in the other codices, while the images it contains are much more striking and frightening. Some think it was written to convey the seriousness of an important religious ceremony in a way that wouldn't be soon forgotten."

"I certainly wouldn't want to show this to little kids," replied Holly. "It would give them nightmares."

Gordon knelt down next to Holly's chair and turned a few more pages for her. "See this picture?" he said, pointing at a drawing of a hideously deformed beast with a long, curved nose. "It's believed this monster represents the planet Mars: the 'Mars Beast.' And this circle, containing a reclining woman cradling a rabbit over here," he said, pointing at a second picture. "She's believed by some to represent the Moon. She's called the 'Moon Goddess.'"

"Now she doesn't look so scary," said Holly, pointing at the picture.

"What follows next is a series of pictures and glyph sequences in which the Mars Beast flies beneath a two-headed serpent towards the Moon Goddess," said Gordon. "When it arrives, the Mars Beast commands her to hand over the rabbit. The two-headed serpent then goes to sleep, reclining over the head of the Moon Goddess, who now appears sleeping as well."

"You see all of that?" exclaimed Holly. "These pictures are so convoluted and intertwined it's hard for me to follow along."

"Trust me. If you study it long enough it jumps right out at you," replied Gordon, turning another page and pointing at another series of pictures. "The Mars Beast rides the terror-stricken rabbit down to an austere temple where several Maya priests and bound captives are assembled."

"Now this is the spooky part," warned Max before frowning in thought.

Gordon turned another page. "Here, the Mars Beast transforms into what appears to be a spherical object. It almost looks like a huge orb of white light. And in this next series of pictures the priests begin throwing the captives into it. See how they disappear while the rabbit looks on in horror? After they've all been thrust in, the object resumes its beast-like appearance, remounting the rabbit and riding it back up to the Moon Goddess, who wakes to accept it back. In this final series of pictures, the two-headed serpent stretches out again and the Mars Beast resumes its journey beneath it across the heavens. The Rome Codex ends with a glyph sequence which has been deciphered as follows," he concluded, pointing at a paragraph at the bottom of the page.

Holly began reading aloud as Gordon stood up. "The Mars Beast resides in the heavens and will return to the Maya people with the help of the Moon Goddess' rabbit; there to receive the offerings and tributes of the people to aid it on its journey across the belly of the Sky Serpent. Death awaits those who are unprepared for Mars Beast when it returns to the place known to all, but seen only by the gods of the heavens."

"This very final glyph—the ornate one set apart from the others over here," said Gordon, leaning over and pointing, "is believed to identify the place where the Mars Beast appeared to the Maya people. It has come to be known as the 'Mars Beast Ceremonial Center.' This glyph is very special because no other like it has ever been seen and the place it represents remains a mystery."

"This is where my theory comes in," said Max.

"I'll admit it was an astute observation," replied Gordon. Professor Warren thought so too, once I explained it to him."

"I'll need a prop to help me demonstrate," added Max, getting up and going into the kitchen. He returned a short while later carrying a large, round, silver platter upon which sat several pieces of fruit. He placed the platter on the coffee table before sitting down on the floor next to it. "After Gordon first showed me the Rome Codex, I began thinking," he said, arranging the fruit. "Most of the planets in our solar system travel around the sun on roughly the same plane or level. This level is called the 'ecliptic.' If this orange at the center of the platter represents the Sun, and these grapes and this cherry represent the planets, then the platter itself represents the ecliptic. Imagine the grapes and this cherry rolling counter-clockwise around and around the orange on the plate. The closer in they are, the faster they would travel. The same goes with our solar system."

Gordon stooped over and grabbed a grape from the plate, tossing it into his mouth.

"Hey, you just ate the planet Mercury!" shouted Max as Holly giggled.

"Sorry," replied Gordon. "I haven't had my supper yet."

"Anyway, suppose this grape is the Earth and this cherry is Mars—the Red Planet," continued Max, rearranging the fruit again. He selected a smaller grape and showed it to them. "Say this small grape represents the Moon. Once, in a great while, when it is lined up between the Earth and Mars like this," he continued, placing the grape on the platter and slowly rolling it between the two he had already positioned, "Mars will disappear from view behind the Moon for several minutes: to observers here on Earth, that is. In astronomy it's called a 'lunar occultation.' It's only possible because Earth, Mars and the Moon travel along the plane of the ecliptic."

Holly reached over and grabbed the grape representing the Earth, tossing it into her mouth. "I get it," she said between chews. "But what does that have to do with the Rome Codex?"

"I think the pictures Gordon just explained may actually depict a lunar occultation of Mars," replied Max. "According to Gordon, the Maya were keen on astronomy." He scooted over to Holly's chair. "May I?" he said, pointing to the textbook she was holding.

"Here you go," she replied.

Flipping a few pages he handed it back to her. "See how at first the Mars Beast flies under this stretched out, two-headed serpent? I believe this represents Mars traveling along its orbit in the ecliptic. The serpent represents the ecliptic. The weird part is when the Mars Beast actually reaches the Moon," he said, turning another page for her. "Instead of just disappearing behind it, as one would expect, the Rome Codex depicts a physical, earthbound apparition. Some sort of strange anomaly the Maya may have believed was the Mars Beast coming down from the heavens for a short while." He pointed at the pictures showing the Mars Beast transforming into what looked like a giant sphere of light. "This sphere appears just after the Mars Beast reaches the Moon. I did some research and found out a lunar occultation of Mars can last up to a couple of hours: that's more than enough time to offer sacrifices to whatever the anomaly depicted is." Turning a few more pages, he pointed again. "Afterwards the Mars Beast is shown to be returning to the heavens. See how it goes back to traveling under the stretched out serpent again? I believe at this point the occultation is over. As soon as Mars would reemerge on the opposite side of the Moon, the orb anomaly on the ground would disappear."

Holly looked skeptically at Max and then at Gordon. "So what you're saying is according to the Rome Codex, when the planet Mars is observed to disappear behind the Moon's disk, an orb of light would appear at a place called the Mars Beast Ceremonial Center? That the Maya thought this orb was a god or something and made sacrifices to it? And then it would disappear once the occultation was over? I know a little about astronomy, but I've never heard of anything like that!"

"Its impossible to say what the object depicted is," replied Max. "Lunar occultations of Mars are rare, but aren't known to cause any associated Earth-bound manifestations. Why would they, after all? It wouldn't make sense from an astronomical or gravitational standpoint—at least none we know of."

"While it looks like an orb of light, I believe it may represent a deep, circular, water-filled sinkhole called a 'cenoté,'" said Gordon. "The area where the Maya lived is riddled with them. Some of the bigger, deeper ones were used for human sacrifices. During major ceremonies, victims would be weighted down with stones and tossed in to drown. We'll never know what the object is for sure until the location of the Mars Beast Ceremonial Center is discovered, if it in fact exists."

"And that's where Gordon's research comes in," said Max, nodding towards his friend and standing up again.

"One of my old classmates did an internship at NASA last summer," continued Gordon. "He told me that at the request of some archaeologists from Essexbridge in London, NASA used a special kind of radar to map large portions of Guatemala and Belize from an airplane. Officially it's called a 'side scanning synthetic aperture radar.' It was designed to map the surface of Venus through its heavy cloud cover. The archaeologists wanted to see if the radar could be used to locate lost Maya cities, as well. Much of the lowlands in western Belize and northern Guatemala where the Maya lived are now covered by a dense rain forest. So dense, in fact, you could be standing next to an ancient Maya temple and not even realize it."

"Did it work?" asked Holly.

Gordon shrugged. "I haven't seen the images yet, but I understand the radar wasn't able to penetrate the tree canopy as much as hoped."

"Then how is it going to help you find *your* lost ceremonial center?" pressed Holly. "Do you know something they didn't?"

"For one thing, both these archaeologists have ridiculed the Rome Codex as a fake. I'm certain it didn't even enter their minds when they were reviewing the radar images. Second, I'm looking for a large, geometric design that can only be seen from a great height. The radar NASA used produces very detailed images of objects on the ground in a profile view: images showing even minute changes in surface elevations. I'm hoping the surface elevations associated with this geometric design will be visible even through the rain forest canopy."

"What geometric design are you looking for?" asked Holly.

"A large, four-pointed star," replied Gordon, kneeling next to her chair again. "As I mentioned before, a special glyph is located at the end of the Rome Codex." He turned a few pages in the textbook for her and pointed. "Archaeologists refer to these types of symbols as 'emblem glyphs.' Some of them represent specific Maya locations. It's believed every Maya ceremonial center has its own unique one. Tulum, the place you visited in Mexico, has its own. Most archaeologists agree that if the Rome Codex is real, then this is an emblem glyph for a place not yet discovered: the Mars Beast Ceremonial Center."

Holly studied the glyph Gordon had pointed to in the textbook. It consisted of a large, squarish-looking cell containing a simple, four-pointed star surrounded by two long-nosed beasts that appeared to be looking down towards it. Immediately to the left of the star cell was an elongated figure that kind of resembled a convoluted snake. On the top of the cell rested what looked like two, round eyes with distorted pupils. "I still don't get it."

"This snake-like drawing to the left means 'divine' in the Mayan language," said Gordon, pointing. "These two round pictures on top mean 'Lord of.' Divine Lord of... Every emblem glyph for a Maya ceremonial center starts pretty much the same way." He pointed at the cell containing the star. "Divine Lord of 'Mars Beast.' I believe this star symbol represents the place where the Mars Beast Ceremonial Center is located."

"But, how is that going to help you?"

"Remember the translation at the end of the Codex. I've committed it to memory. 'Death awaits those who are unprepared for the Mars Beast when it returns to the place known to all, but seen only by the gods of the heavens.' *Seen only by the gods of the heavens.*" Standing again, he held up his right arm while pointing his fingers towards the floor. "If this translation is correct, then the Mars Beast Ceremonial Center may only be visible from a great height. A height the Maya believed only their gods could see. Here, I'll show you." Gordon trotted into the kitchen and returned a short while later hiding something behind his back. "Please stand up and close your eyes, Holly."

Holly stood up and closed her eyes.

"Okay, now you can open them."

When she did she saw he was holding a red, plastic object just in front of her face.

"What's this?" asked Gordon.

"It's a cookie cutter."

"Not bad, Holly. She's already doing better then you did, Max."

"I've never baked a cookie in my life!" protested Max. "How would I know what that thing is?"

"Okay, smarty-pants. What shape is it?"

"I can't tell. You're holding it sideways—on its edge."

"Now suppose this was a wall at ground level. Still wouldn't be able to tell, right?"

"I guess not."

"Now you're flying overhead and the perspective changes completely," said Gordon, slowly stepped back and twisting the cookie cutter around.

"It's star-shaped!" exclaimed Holly. "A star-shaped cookie cutter! I see what you mean now! The Maya may have built a series of long walls or trenches that might not look like anything on the ground, but would appear as a four-pointed star from the air. That way the Mars Beast could always see where to land!"

"That's what I think," said Gordon, setting the cookie cutter on the coffee table. "Only problem is nowadays most of the lowlands where the star might be located is covered by rain forest. No way of seeing structures beneath it from the air anymore. I'm hoping at least a portion of the star will be visible in NASA's side scanning radar images as corresponding indentations or ridges in the rain forest canopy. If I'm able to find it, Max and I are going to hop on a plane during spring break and confirm the location on the ground." He winked at Holly. "As a couple of tourists, of course. I've got family friends in Central America. Access to guides, pontoon planes, and ground transportation isn't a problem. We should be able to get just about anywhere we like. Then I'll take some pictures, make some measurements, and whip up an article for publication. At that point there'll be no way Professor Warren can claim the discovery for himself."

Holly shook her head and frowned. "I don't know about this you guys. Looking at radar pictures is one thing, but crawling around in a jungle in a foreign country sounds like it could be dangerous. Heat. Bugs. Snakes. Don't you think so, Max?"

Max secretly agreed, but had decided to wait to reevaluate his offer to accompany Gordon until after his friend's review of the radar images. After all, Gordon probably wouldn't find anything anyway. He simply shrugged. "We're just going to take a few pictures. There's nothing wrong with that. So long as the location isn't too remote, we should be okay."

"That's the spirit, Max!" said Gordon, picking up his proposal and shoving it back in his briefcase. "I know you two have to study. I'm going to grab a bite to eat and head over to the library to pick up some topographical maps of Belize and Guatemala to help me with my research. See you later. And remember, Holly, mums the word!" he called out as he left, slamming the front door to the vintage townhouse behind him.

Max shook his head and sighed before looking over and smiling at Holly. "See what I mean? He's like a pit bull when he decides on something. He'll find what he's looking for or die trying," he added, looking at his watch. "I just remembered. I need to make a quick call to reserve some mainframe computer time at the lab. Would you excuse me for a moment?"

"Certainly," she replied. After Max disappeared into the kitchen, she got up and slowly wandered about the living room, gazing at the oil paintings and other antiques. Everything looked very expensive.

"Want to study in the dining room?" asked Max, emerging from the kitchen again. "The table is huge and great for looking at program printouts."

"Anywhere is fine," she said, stopping to look at a bronze statue of a cowboy riding a horse. The cowboy's rifle was drawn and he was aiming it at some unseen target in the distance. Stooping, she read a little plaque attached to its base, which read, "Commissioned by the Parks Arms and Ammunition Company–1886." Standing straight again, she walked over to retrieve her backpack. "Can I ask you something?"

"Sure."

"I hope you don't think I'm prying," she continued, following him into the opulent dining room. "But how in the world can you guys afford this place? Are you house-sitting for a rich person or something?"

Max laughed as they sat down. "Don't you know?" he asked. "I thought you knew."

"Know what?"

"Gordon owns this place. He rents me a couple of rooms on the cheap because we're friends. Gordon Parks: doesn't his name sound familiar? I thought as an 'army brat' you'd recognize it right away."

"Gordon Parks, Gordon Parks," she said, pulling a pencil out of her backpack and lightly tapped its eraser end against her cheek. She stopped tapping and pointed it at Max. "You know, he kind of looks like a young, muscular version of James Mason: that old Hollywood star."

Max chuckled. "You know, come to think of it, he does kind of look like James Mason, only with a rounder face and without the beard. He's not movie star, though. At least I don't think he is."

Holly resumed her thoughtful cheek tapping again before remembering the name on the bronze cowboy statute, a look of disbelief flashing across her face. "Is he related to the Parks family that owns the 'Parks Arms and Ammo Company?'"

"Not only is he related, but he's one of the few remaining heirs to the Parks family fortune—at least for the time being. His parents were killed in a plane crash when he was six. It was big news at the time. Afterwards his Aunt Dorothy raised him. She's a complete pacifist and managed to turn Gordon off to guns. He hates them. When his grandfather found out he was furious! Can you imagine, a pacifist running one of the largest arms manufacturers in the world? The old man has threatened to disown and cut Gordon out of the family fortune unless he changes his ways, but Gordon doesn't care. He still has a considerable fortune from his parents' estate.

"Poor, Gordon. It must be awful growing up without your folks, even if you are rich. Still, it must be nice to have lots of money. If I were him, I'd be traveling around the world enjoying myself. I wouldn't be spending my time struggling through graduate school."

"Believe me, Gordon has done his share of traveling. His aunt is a complete jet-setter. Every summer vacation, school break, or holiday since he was a kid, she'd drag him along with her to some spot on the globe. When he was older he would strike out on his own or with friends. He's been all over Europe, Asia, Central and South America—even Africa and the Middle East. Traveling is in his blood; he's fascinated by other cultures and their histories, and the more exotic or remote the location, the better. He's just as happy slogging through a mosquito-infested rain forest as he is dining in a four star hotel. He also has a lot of connections everywhere—people gravitate towards money, I guess. That's why Gordon doesn't think its any big deal to hop on a plane to some third world country and go exploring. He's used to it and knows the ropes."

"I see. That's why he's interested in anthropology."

"That's part of it. I think the real reason he's in school is to find a way to distinguish himself without manufacturing and selling weapons. Gordon hates the fact the name 'Parks' is practically synonymous with the word 'gun.' He also believes his discovery of the Mars Beast Ceremonial Center will be a great start at what he refers to as his 'family name rehabilitation.'"

"Well, he seems awfully confident he's going to find it. I hope he won't be too disappointed if things don't work out the way he expects."

"Don't worry about Gordo. He's the kind of guy who throws himself into his work. As long as he feels his premise is sound and gives it his best shot, he considers whatever he does a success. The word 'failure' is not in his vocabulary. If these NASA radar images don't pan out, he'll consider it a learning experience and move on to the next project with equal enthusiasm."

Despite his friend's opinion and a promising start, two months later Gordon was seriously considering adding the word "failure" to his vocabulary after all. Professor Warren had come through with his notarized letter to NASA confirming the legitimacy of Gordon's research, and the space agency had reciprocated, as promised, by turning over a large box containing hundreds of aerial radar images of the rain forests of Guatemala and Belize. But his research soon became problematic and continued to be a complete letdown.

For starters, the radar images were contained on long, unwieldy rolls of positive transparencies which hadn't been cataloged or organized due to the space agency's recent budget cuts. To figure out exactly what area was shown on any given one, Gordon had to look for landmarks such as rivers and towns, and then compare them to those depicted on regular printed maps.

Furthermore, the transparencies were similar to x-ray films and could only be viewed properly by holding them over a back lit surface in a darkened room. Since neither the university's library or the anthropology department had a compatible viewer, he had to make his own, and the final result was less than user-friendly. The jury-rigged spindles he'd constructed to hold the images while viewing them over an old x-ray reader borrowed from the medical school would often pop loose, allowing the slippery rolls to unwind and tangle maddeningly in the dark. The whole process had become time-consuming and frustrating.

But the worst part was he wasn't finding anything. The radar images themselves were extremely impressive, as one would expect from a project undertaken by NASA. They showed the densely-packed treetops of the rain forest, as well as swamps and rivers, known Maya ruins cleared of vegetation, and other surface features in near three-dimensional detail. They were much clearer and more vibrant than any aerial photographs he'd ever seen. Despite these attributes, however, the radar obviously couldn't see through the rain forest canopy to reveal any Maya ruins hidden below.

After two months of searching for any subtle signs that might reveal the location of the four-pointed star he was looking for, Gordon was losing hope. Staring at back lit images in darkened rooms for hours on end had also taken its toll. His eyes were now constantly burning and each image was starting to look like the next. He was also beginning to believe Professor Jenkins had been right all along.

Then, as with many scientific discoveries, an unexpected event occurred which changed everything. Gordon was comparing one of the radar images to a topographical map in the dark, using a small flashlight to illuminate the map, when a stack of tracing paper haphazardly placed on a shelf over his desk cascaded down over him and his improvised viewer with a *swoosh*. Tired and agitated, he cursed his bad luck and began sweeping the paper out of the way with his hands. Just as he was about to pick up the last piece that had fallen onto his viewer, he noticed something strange. As he studied the image through the sheet, he saw faint lines emerging from the rain forest: faint lines forming geometric grids and patterns.

"The tracing paper must be obscuring some of the smaller surface features appearing as dots and speckles on the transparency," he muttered to himself in disbelief. Absent this visual background noise, he could now make out what were obviously surface features beneath the rain forest canopy. It was like magic! When he would remove the tracing paper, the grids and patterns would disappear. By adjusting the number of sheets placed over the transparency, more or less faint lines would appear. "These lines might be the remnants of ancient Maya agricultural or drainage canals," he speculated, continuing to study the image. "If *they're* visible through the tracing paper, then the Mars Beast star might be as well!"

Filled with a renewed enthusiasm, Gordon decided to cut all his classes and pour non-stop over the radar images through the tracing paper lens he had accidentally discovered. For the next three days he rarely left the small meeting room he had taken over in the basement of the Anthropology Building to do his research. Starting all over again with the first roll of transparencies, he concentrated on quickly scanning each radar image for anything looking like a four-pointed star through the tracing paper. While he couldn't seem to locate any hidden Maya ruins, the canal gridlines were clearly visible in many of them.

By midnight of the third day of his marathon research session, however, he had scanned nearly three-quarters of the radar images and was again losing hope. His other homework assignments were piling up and he was running out of excuses to skip class. He was exhausted, his eyes were sore, and just when he thought he couldn't go on he spotted it.

The radar image he was looking at was of an area of dense rain forest located somewhere in the northern Guatemalan lowlands. At first he hadn't seen any of the telltale lines he was looking for and was about to call it quits; perhaps even for good. Then, just as he was getting up to turn on the room lights, he noticed two faint lines near the image's right-hand side. The lines were connected at one end, with their free ends diverging away from each other until they disappeared off its edge; forming a perfect, triangular notch.

"This notch appears to have the same dimensions as one of the star points on the Mars Beast emblem glyph," he muttered lowly, "only on a much larger scale; maybe a half mile across at its open end." He could barely believe his tired eyes. Rubbing them gingerly, he sat down again to study the image more closely. As he did his heart began racing at the sight of the lines and their apparent match to his recollection of the star depicted on the emblem glyph: a recollection burned into his memory after so many months of research and anticipation.

"This may be it. This may be it," he whispered to himself over and over again, slowly rolling to the next transparency in the sequence; taking care so as not to upset his fragile viewer. He centered the image before closing his eyes to say a little prayer. Opening them again he took a deep breath. "Here we go." He placed a piece of tracing paper over the image, closely studied the edge of the frame opposite where the notch was located on the previous one, and clearly saw the remaining three star points revealing the location of the Mars Beast Ceremonial Center. He stared at it in disbelief for a moment before leaning back in his chair and saying, "Thank you" to the ceiling. "Gordon Parks, you've just made one of the greatest archaeological discoveries of the twentieth century," he congratulated himself. "And you did it without ever setting a foot in the field."

"Where've you been, Gordon? You look terrible!" cried Max as Gordon strode into his townhouse for the first time in days. "I tried to report you missing, but the campus police said you hadn't been gone long enough. What's going on? Is everything all right?"

"I've never felt better in my life!" beamed Gordon through bloodshot eyes framed with dark circles. He set his briefcase on the kitchen table, opened the refrigerator, pulled out two cans of Coca-Cola, and handed one to his friend. "Here you go, Max. What do you say to a toast?"

Max took the can, giving Gordon a significant look before cracking it open. Then he pointed his finger at the grin slowly spreading across his friend's face. "You did it, didn't you? You lucky dog! And just when you were about to give up, you did it!"

Gordon cracked open his soda and offered it up. "Here's to the Mars Beast Ceremonial Center: a mystery no more." The cans clanked together and they took a drink.

"And here's to the Rome Codex: a forgery no more." The cans clanked again and then Max motioned towards the table. "Sit down. Sit down. You've got to tell me all about it. I can barely believe it! Where is it? How did you find it?" After weeks of hearing about failure after failure, Max had all but concluded his friend would never find the object of his quest.

"Listen Max, you're my best friend," said Gordon as they sat down. "You know that, but I want to keep the details to myself for the time being. The way I found it turned out to be so simple, anyone who has access to NASA's radar images could find it in a few days time. A team of people might be able to locate in a matter of hours! I can't risk letting anything about it out until I publish my results. I hope you're okay with that."

"Come on," pleaded Max. "You've got to tell me something. This is big!"

"Don't worry, Max. You'll be the first to see it. As soon as we land in Guatemala City I'll tell you more. We should be able to hire a guide and make it to the location in a few days time. It's not too far from a river I think is wide and slow enough to land a pontoon plane on."

"Guatemala. Just where you thought it might be! Congratulations, Gordon. Wow. I can't believe it. Wait until I tell Holly." Then, recalling something, he snapped his fingers. "I almost forgot. I have something for you." He got up and trotted out of the kitchen, returning a short while later holding a gift-wrapped package. "I was holding off on giving you this until you were fairly certain you'd found what you were looking for. For awhile I thought I'd never be able to give it to you." He smiled, handing Gordon the package. "Here's some icing for your cake. Congratulations, Gordon."

"What's this?" asked Gordon, opening the package and studying the thick stack of paper it contained. "Why this looks like a computer program printout. How very thoughtful of you. I don't know what to say."

"Very funny, Gordon. Read the title."

"'Computer Program to Predict Lunar Occultations of the Planets, By Max Zenger.'"

"It's an assignment I completed for my advanced programming class. Your Rome Codex gave me the idea. You'll be happy to know I got an 'A' on it. I thought you might be interested in lunar occultations of Mars."

Gordon paged through the thick document. "I didn't know you knew so much about astronomy. This looks really complicated."

"I took a class in celestial mechanics once. It's not as bad as it looks. According to my program, there should be a lunar occultation of Mars observable from Guatemala about a month from now. Look at the table on page fifty-two. We may still have enough time to get down there to meet your Mars Beast in person," he concluded with a wink, knowing it was a mere legend and nothing more.

"No kidding," replied Gordon, quickly turning to the page. "January 7th: a little over a month and a half from now. According to this table there won't be another lunar occultation of Mars visible from Central America for another twelve years. We've got to get down there! I intend to include your theory on the Rome Codex in my article. Imagine being smack dab in the middle of the Mars Beast Ceremonial Center at the precise moment the Mars Beast is supposed to appear. It will make great copy! What a story. What a coincidence: a once-in-a-lifetime coincidence. It's even more perfect than going during spring break, because the whole country of Guatemala pretty much shuts down from Christmas though January. We'll be able to get around without attracting much attention. I feel like destiny is calling me, Max. I can't thank you enough." He offered his hand and Max shook it.

"And who knows, Gordo," said Max. "Maybe the Mars Beast really will come down from the heavens to meet and let us take its picture. Now *that* would be a story! I just hope it's not as hideous in real life as it is in the Rome Codex."

The next two weeks were a whirlwind of activity, much of which was not aimed at Gordon's best interests—at least from Holly's and Max's parents' standpoint.

Upon hearing of Gordon's discovery and their plans to travel down to Guatemala during the university's scheduled Christmas break, Holly had unexpectedly frowned. "I never in a million years would have thought Gordon would actually find anything," she had said. "Now that he has, I think you should seriously reconsider your offer to go with him. I've been reading up on the political situation in Guatemala. I bet you didn't know they're in the middle of a civil war. Downtrodden people fighting a ruling elite supported by the police. It's dangerous and I don't like it. You also promised to meet my parents over the holidays," she added, revealing the real reason for her reluctance to see him go.

At first Max tried to assure her they'd be all right. "Plenty of tourists still go there," he argued to calm her fears. He also promised he would meet her parents as soon as he got back.

It was no good. Day after day she persisted. While Gordon was simultaneously studying for exams and coordinating the detailed preparations for what was essentially a mini-archaeological expedition conducted on very short notice, Holly had mounted an all out campaign to get her new boyfriend to back out of the trip. She simply, flat-out, did not want Max to go.

Worse, his parents were also dead set against the trip. They were big on holiday get-togethers and could hardly believe Max would even consider spending Christmas and New Year's away from home.

Moreover, Max and Holly had just started dating and he liked her very, very much. He hated the thought of hurting her feelings so early in their relationship. But deep down he believed she might be right. He was no adventurer—not like Gordon, anyway—and the more he thought about it, the more he dreaded the thought of traipsing around in a bug and snake-infested jungle when he and Holly could be snuggling around a warm fire with family and friends.

Max was also worried about his upcoming final exams. At this point in his academic life he preferred concentrating on them rather than on helping Gordon prepare for the trip. While he hated to disappoint his friend—after all, a promise is a promise—he hated the thought of flunking even more and in the end contrived a scheme he believed would satisfy both Holly and Gordon.

"I can't believe you're going to back out now," fumed Gordon, raking his hand through his hair in a gesture of disbelief. "After all the planning and work! Everything is ready to go. Plane tickets, hotel reservations, gear, cameras, travelers checks, everything. How can you possibly back out at the last minute?"

"I'm not backing out," replied Max sheepishly, getting up from the sofa in Gordon's living room. "I told you that. All I'm asking is to postpone the trip until the end of February like we originally planned. I talked to my professors and they won't let me miss the first two weeks of winter semester unless I have a good excuse. Since I can't tell them where I'm going or why I need the time off, they said they might flunk me if I decide to go. You know how tough Blaine University is."

"Make up a lie and stick to it," shouted Gordon, raising his arms in frustration and pacing about in a circle. "Just like I did. Tell them you've got a sick relative at Death's door. Tell them you need an operation or something. They'll never check up on you!"

"I can't afford to take that chance. I'm not a great liar, not like you—no offense. I don't have piles of money sitting around in banks collecting interest either. Attending Blaine is costing me every penny I've got. And that's on top of what I've had to borrow. I need this degree!"

Gordon stopped pacing and pointed his finger at Max. "I said I'll pay your way! And don't forget it was *your* computer program that predicted the lunar occultation for January 7th. I can't help it if that's the first day of the winter semester! There won't be another occultation visible from down there for another twelve years. By then the Mars Beast Ceremonial Center will be old news."

Max put his hands on his hips and shook his head. "You're obsessed, Gordon. Do you know that? Who cares whether or not there's a lunar occultation of Mars when you visit the site? Nothing's going to happen and you know it. You said it yourself: the orb object in the Rome Codex is probably a sinkhole or something. You just want to include an interesting tidbit in your article. Something like, 'We watched the Planet Mars slowly slip behind the Moon's horizon, patiently awaiting the arrival of the Mars Beast who, in the end, never appeared.'"

"Don't you want to test your theory?" replied Gordon, his blood rising in anger at his friend's last-minute defection. "That was your idea too!"

"Believe me, Gordon. I want to go, but I can't. Not until spring break."

"You're making a big mistake, Max, because I won't wait. I'm going with or without you. I can't believe you're going to miss out on one of the greatest archaeological discoveries of all time over one lousy semester of graduate school. If you do, I promise you, you'll regret it for the rest of your life."

"That's not the only reason!" Max snapped back, growing angry at his friend's stubbornness. He never dreamed Gordon would consider going it alone. "Don't forget, there's a civil war going on in Guatemala. It's not safe."

"Baloney! There's always a civil war going on in Guatemala. It hasn't affected travel." Then Gordon's eyes narrowed as he studied his friend's face. "It's Holly, isn't it?" he accused, pointing at Max a second time. "She's gotten to you, hasn't she? *She's* the real reason you don't want to go. You're a better liar then you think, Max."

The words hit home.

"You're a fool!" shouted Max, his face flushing red with guilt and anger at being found out.

"And you're a coward! A lovesick coward!"

"You should talk. I've seen how you look at Holly. I wouldn't be surprised if you were forcing the issue to try to break us up. If you can't have her, nobody can, right?"

Gordon's jaw clenched. Although he kind of liked Holly at first, he hadn't thought about her at all since he started reviewing NASA's radar images all those weeks ago. "You're dreaming, Max. I could care less about Holly Graham. Really."

"Right," grumbled Max, stooping and grabbing textbooks and papers off the coffee table and cramming them into his backpack. "I'm going over to Holly's place for a while. I've got my last final exam in the morning and I don't need this. Frankly, I'm sick of hearing about *your* project and *your* fame and *your* glory. Have at it and leave me alone. I don't need this."

It was clear he'd hurt his friend's feelings and Gordon wished he could take back his rash assessment of Max's intestinal fortitude. Since he couldn't, and since he was still angry himself, he simply bit his tongue, fished around in his tweed sport coat's breast pocket, and produced an envelope. "Here are your plane tickets," he said, tossing the envelope onto the coffee table. You're still welcome to join me, but if you don't I'll understand. If you do change your mind, let me know. We can hook up at the airport next week like we planned. I'll be leaving for my aunt's house in New York tomorrow afternoon. I'll leave you her number."

Max pushed the envelope aside before grabbing the last of his computer printouts. "I've already made up my mind," he replied coldly, still quite angry himself. "Holly had nothing to do with it either," he added, zipping his backpack shut and slinging it over his shoulder.

"Right. Suit yourself. See you later," replied Gordon, absently picking up a camera from an end table and pretending to inspect it. "I'll send you a postcard."

Max slept very little that night. He had studied late into the evening and when his alarm finally went off the next morning he awoke so tired and nervous it felt like he hadn't slept at all. He was also exceedingly guilty about leaving his friend out on a lurch at the last minute. Holly *had* been the one to convince him not to go to Guatemala and last night—in anger and frustration at his friend's stubbornness—he promised her he wouldn't. There was no turning back now. Gordon was right. Max Zenger *was* a lovesick coward.

Max showered and shaved with a heavy heart, trying to find words for an apology. But when he finally dressed and emerged from his room, Gordon was already gone—probably rushed out to the store for more, last minute supplies. He lingered for a while, started writing apology notes three times, then balled each one up in turn to throw away. With his biggest exam looming over his head he couldn't think about anything else. He decided to apologize in person afterwards.

Max returned later that afternoon, feeling much better now his last exam was finally over. It hadn't been nearly as tough as he thought it might be. As he entered Gordon's townhouse, however, it was clear his friend had already left. Gordon's numerous bags and supplies were gone and despite its splendor the house seemed empty and lonely. Looking around for a note, he found one on the kitchen table. In addition to a telephone number, all it said was Gordon was sorry about last night and promised he would try to call Max before his scheduled flight back to New York on January 14th to let him know how his meeting with the Mars Beast went.

Max thought about Gordon a lot over the days that followed: all through the Christmas holiday, spent at either his or Holly's parents' houses; and all through the New Year's celebrations. Early on, he had called the hotel in Guatemala City where Gordon said he would be staying, but his friend had already checked out. It would be up to Gordon to initiate any further communications from his end. Yet day after day he saw or heard nothing from Gordon Parks, not even the promised postcard.

Finally returning to Blaine University for the start of the winter semester, Max eagerly waited for what was certain to be a celebratory telephone call from his friend. January 14th came and went without a word, though, and Max was getting worried. The next day, just as he was about call the airport to see if Gordon's flight had arrived on time, his telephone rang. It was Gordon's Aunt Dorothy and she sounded worried as well.

"Hello, Max," she said with a slight East Coast accent. "I sent the limousine around to the airport yesterday afternoon to pick Gordon up, but he wasn't on his scheduled flight. I called the hotel he was supposed to be staying at in Guatemala City, but they said he checked out some time ago. I've called all our friends down there, in fact, and no one has seen him recently, just Señor Carlos Rojo who recommended an airplane pilot to him a few weeks ago. Have you heard from Gordon at all? He told me you two had a bit of a falling out."

"I haven't spoken to Gordon since before the holidays. When was the last time you heard from him?"

"He called me on New Year's morning. I still can't believe he had to spend the holidays in Guatemala, of all places, rather than with his family and friends; although he's quite an adventurer, as you know. It's in his blood, I think. He was very excited and said he'd found what he was looking for and had taken a lot of photographs. Gordon said he was going back to the site on the 7th to make some sort of special measurement or observation, though he wouldn't say what. He wanted the whole thing to be a surprise. Gordon promised to call me when he was back in Guatemala City. He never did call and now he has missed his flight. I was hoping he may have called you."

"I haven't heard from him at all. Maybe their phone lines are down. We are talking about Guatemala, after all."

"Well, if he telephones you, please have him ring me immediately. He never would tell me exactly where he was going. His grandfather and I are a little worried because Gordon promised he'd call and he hasn't. Gordon always comes through on a promise."

The words stung Max deeply like a slap in the face. "Of course I will, Aunt Dottie," he replied meekly. *Gordon must have mentioned my shameless, last-minute backing out to her*, he thought. "And I would appreciate it if you would do the same for me."

"I will, my dear," she replied, followed by an awkward pause. "Max, Gordon was very, how shall I say, 'vague' about why he had to go running off to Guatemala on such short notice. I know he said he might be going, but not so soon. Not until spring break, if at all, I believe. He said it was due to a new deadline on his thesis project. It seems strange his professors would require him to make the trip over the holidays. I called one of them this morning—an irritating fellow named Warren. He seemed quite upset when I asked him why Gordon had to go and he said he didn't know anything about it. Do you?"

Max gulped. He was tempted to tell Gordon's aunt the whole story, but his loyalty to his friend's wishes overcame his urge. "I don't know anything more than what you just said. All he told me was he was under the gun to take photographs of some Maya ruins in order to prove something: some theory or hypothesis he was working on. He said it was no big deal; not much more than an exotic tourist trip."

"That's also what he told me," replied Gordon's aunt, her voice reflecting a hint of relief. "Well, let me know if he calls and I'll do the same for you. Goodbye, Max."

"Goodbye, Aunt Dottie."

There were no further communications from Gordon Parks, from Guatemala or anywhere else for that matter. It was as if the young man had vanished off the face of the Earth.

There were the police inquiries, of course, both in the United States and in Guatemala, with all their routine questions. What were Gordon's travel plans? Did he have any enemies? Why hadn't Max used his ticket? But amazingly, the real reason for Gordon's trip never came up, at least in much detail. Max suspected the police probably believed Gordon was some eccentric, rich kid who stumbled onto a group of guerrilla fighters somewhere along the highway leading into northern Guatemala, only to be robbed and murdered.

Whatever the reason for Gordon's disappearance, Max's own guilt at abandoning his friend at the last minute grew day by day. At times it felt like an enormous weight hanging around his neck.

And Holly, the girl Max thought he might marry someday, increasingly became the object of his disdain. He blamed her for turning on Gordon at the last minute, and after what seemed like an endless mantra of her saying, "I told you so, I told you so," he finally *told* her he never wanted to see her again. He resented the fact her meddling may have prevented him from helping his friend in a time of need.

Then there was Professor Warren the credit thief: the man responsible for Gordon's almost paranoid desire for secrecy. Max disliked him even before the Great Professor showed up at the door to Max's much smaller and drearier apartment all those weeks later looking for Gordon's research notes and the radar images borrowed from NASA. According to Warren, Gordon must have stored them somewhere for safekeeping, as they couldn't seem to be located anywhere despite rigorous searches at the university. Moreover, those incompetent fools at NASA had mistakenly sent the original images without making any back-up copies.

Max replied, saying he hadn't seen any of Gordon's notes or research work, and that his friend's grieving aunt had picked up the rest of his things some time ago.

At this, Professor Warren—looking quite agitated—asked, "Did Gordon say he was looking for anything in particular in Guatemala? Anything about a place called the 'Mars Beast Ceremonial Center?'"

Warren's question triggered a fond memory of Gordon's enthusiasm and certainty of success. Despite whatever had happened, his friend had indeed succeeded in his quest—of this Max had no doubt. And here, standing before him, was the remorseless, credit vulture in the flesh: trying to steal Gordon's work away. That would never happen, but Max couldn't resist. He simply nodded, smiled knowingly, looked Warren straight in the eye and said, "Yes, he did, Professor. He mentioned something. He also said he found what he was looking for." And before the clearly shocked Professor Warren could reply, Max smirked and slammed the door shut in the old man's face.

What no one knew, or even suspected—not even Max—was that in addition to discovering the jungle-covered ruins of the mysterious Maya Ceremonial Center built all those centuries ago, Gordon Parks *had* come face-to-face with the Mars Beast that warm and misty January evening—at the precise moment predicted by his friend. And much to Gordon's surprise, and ultimate destiny, it certainly wasn't a sinkhole.

CHAPTER TWO: THE MYSTERIOUS ARTIFACT

Thirty-Five Years Later.

Porter Smith slowly coasted his bicycle along the last few yards of sidewalk leading to North Kendell High School. It was your classic late-summer morning. Just a hint of fall's approaching coolness in the pleasant morning air. Tree leaves beginning to flag in anticipation of their brilliant yellow, red, and rust-orange autumn coats. Little, gray squirrels busily foraging for acorns across neatly-trimmed lawns. Rolling to a stop and hopping off, he could sense the excitement and anticipation of a new school year in the voices and laughter of the assembled teenagers. Excitement and anticipation which crackled like a low electric current as everyone waited for the first bell to sound. He jostled among several other riders as he locked his bike to a rack, then slung his backpack over his shoulder and headed towards the school's entrance.

"Hey, Porter!" someone called out over the din.

Looking about, Porter saw Henry Dundridge—one of his friends from last year's freshman class—waving at him from within a small circle of Kendell's techno-geeks. Henry had recently achieved hero status among them by defeating their former master's champion in last spring's locally televised robot battle contest. Porter waved back, turning and walking towards them. "Hey, Henry!"

"How's it going?" asked Henry after Porter had joined the group.

"It's going, Dundridge," replied Porter with a smile, noticing his friend had grown even pudgier over the last few weeks, despite the baggy, green, button-down shirt Henry was wearing to hide the fact. "How was your job at computer camp?"

"It was all right. Tutoring little kids can drive you crazy sometimes, but the food was good and I was able to save up enough money to finish the 'Project.' The camp people let me work on it in their lab."

"Wait until you see it!" cried little Michael Morrison, a fellow camp instructor and another one of Henry's new, geeky admirers. "He replaced the original processor with three connected in parallel! I helped him with the programming upgrades too."

To Porter the words were nearly meaningless. "Are you going to take on Robby Lee again?" he asked Henry, craning his head about to see if their mutual enemy was within earshot. Robert T. Lee, the former master of the techno-geeks, hadn't taken his battle robot defeat graciously. In fact, it was Lee whom they suspected of sending the email-borne viruses which had nearly destroyed both Henry's and Porter's personal computers just before Henry had gone off to camp. While his friend was the obvious target of Lee's revenge attempt, Porter was certainly fair game by reason of association. It was only through Henry's near-genius computer skills they were able to salvage the machines and all their files.

Henry crinkled up his button nose and scratched his head through his wavy, brown hair. Although flattered at first, he was finding his fame and the techno-geeks' admiration to be burdensome, especially considering his somewhat shy and bookish nature. "I don't think so. The Project is intended for more constructive purposes. Besides, we don't need any more grief from Robby Lee and I can't afford the modifications necessary to convert it into a battle robot."

At this the techno-geeks began to protest loudly in favor of battle conversion, but before they could talk some sense into their new master the first bell rang and the groups of teenagers began dissolving into streams flowing towards the school's entrance.

"How was your summer, Porter?" asked Henry as they walked up the steps of the ancient, gothic-style building. "Get to do anything fun while I was away at camp?"

"It was great. I spent most of my time working at the marina: learning how to fix yachts and taking more sailing lessons. My instructor knows a lady who competes in the Chicago to Mackinac race every July. If I'm good enough by next spring, he said he'd recommend me to her as a crew member."

Henry's stomach flipped at the thought of stepping aboard a boat, or any other floating object for that matter. He was prone to extreme seasickness and avoided boating at all costs. Even ice-skating made him queasy sometimes. His doctor said it might have something to do with the astigmatism in his left eye. "That's great," he said to be polite. "I hope you get to be a crew member. What's the name of her boat?"

"*Fléche*—that's French for 'arrow.'"

"What a great name for a racing boat," admitted Henry out loud.

Porter smiled. "I agree. Let's see what homerooms we've been sentenced to."

As they stood on tiptoes, straining to study the homeroom lists posted on a wall near the cafeteria over the bobbing heads of their schoolmates, Porter suddenly felt someone very close, deliberately pressing up against his side.

"Hi, Porter," came a familiar, sultry voice in a breath that caressed his cheek like a gentle kiss. It was Kelly Martino, far and away the prettiest girl at North Kendell High School.

Henry glanced over at Kelly and her entourage of designer dress-clad fashion model friends and shook his head in disapproval. Kelly was the budding leader of Kendell's sophomore class popularity clique. She had blond hair and the kind of glossy, deep blue eyes which could make a boy's heart jump and then melt—usually in that order. She was extremely smart and charming, but also spoiled, mean-spirited, and egotistical. In short, she was a neat, tidy, beautifully-wrapped package of adolescent cruelty: the poster girl for both "things dreams are made of" and "casual heartbreaker." Astonishingly, it seemed like only Henry, and the other computer and science geeks—and those other unfortunates who fell within that cruelest of categories known as the "unpopular"—who seemed to realize it.

Porter's heart nearly stopped at the sound of her voice and he spun around. "Hi, Kelly," he stammered, falling back a few steps. "How've you been?"

"You're looking good," she replied, pursuing him before reaching up to squeeze his upper arms through his blue and white striped polo shirt. "Look at those muscles and what a nice tan." She gently stroked her hand across the side of his head. Is your hair blonder from the sun? Even your eyes look bluer than I remember! I thought you were going to call me this summer."

"I did call. Twice," he stammered again, suddenly love-stricken to the point of near paralysis.

"Only twice!" she teased as several of her friends giggled. "Only twice! You expect me to return only two phone calls?" Tossing her head in mock indignation, Kelly stormed away with her entourage in tow. After a few steps the girls turned around, gazed at poor, paralyzed Porter, burst out laughing, and hurried away in obvious merriment. A school of female sharks in search of more defenseless, male prey. Sharks which absently pushed past Henry one after another like he was a bothersome clump of seaweed, unworthy of a bite, much less a nip.

Henry sniffed in indignation and wondered whether ill attention was better than no attention, gazing after the girls until they disappeared around the corner at the end of the hall—after all, he appreciated beauty as much as the next guy. When they were gone he judiciously cleared his throat. "I think you and I are in the same homeroom again," he said, pointing at one of the postings. "Room 221. Let's get going."

It took Porter a moment to shake himself free of the hypnotic spell Kelly had cast over him. "She's so beautiful," he finally said, returning to consciousness. "Did you see the dress she was wearing?"

"I was standing right here, Porter."

"She's a goddess. Do you think she likes me or was just horsing around?"

Henry wanted to say, "Are you nuts?" but thought better. He'd been warned it was dangerous to wake a sleepwalker and he certainly wouldn't be the one to try to shake someone from a delusional fantasy, even if that someone was his friend Porter Smith. Instead, he simply shrugged. "Let's get going or we'll be late for homeroom."

The rest of the day went much as could be expected. Figuring out schedules and remaking acquaintances. Classes and roll calls. Lunch: a tasteless array of hot and cold health food selections loving trowelled out by Mrs. Flynn, the cafeteria lady. And then it was time for the dreaded anatomy class. It was Porter's last class for the day.

He went into the formaldehyde-smelling room and said, "Hi" to a couple of kids he kind of knew before strolling down the single, center aisle separating two parallel rows of gleaming, wood-topped lab tables. The walls all around were covered with posters of frogs and other animals laid wide open at their seams, showing their guts in graphic and disturbing detail. At the end of the aisle Porter selected a table near the windows—just in case he'd need some air when the gruesome class was underway in earnest—and sat down. He unloaded a pad of paper from his backpack and had just started skimming through one of the beautifully illustrated dissection manuals piled on the table—the one on cat anatomy—when he looked up and saw Kelly Martino walk into the room followed by Robby Lee. *His love and worst enemy together?* It was a disturbing sight, which evoked a sudden flood of conflicting emotions. They were chatting pleasantly as they selected a lab table near the front of the class on the opposite side of the room. Stunned, Porter quickly looked down at the dissection manual again and pretended to be intensely interested in how a cat's musculature was separated by interconnected layers of fascia.

"Yuck!" squealed Kelly as she began thumbing through one of the manuals. This caused a chorus of laughter and giggles to erupt throughout the room. Kelly had a knack of maneuvering herself to the center of attention under almost any circumstance.

Robby pointed at the book she was holding and cried, "Meow!" This got even more laughs. Grinning at his own droll humor, he was about to embellish it even further with, "Nine lives my foot!" when he noticed an unmoved Porter Smith sitting stoically at the back of the classroom in apparent deep study. Robby frowned. He disliked Porter Smith for being so straight-laced, but positively hated Smith's chubby, little, friend Henry Dundridge for stealing away Robby's battle robot crown. *Time to assert a little authority,* he thought. *Remind Smith it was a big mistake to hang around with the likes of Dundridge.* "Hey, Porta Potty! Get any interesting emails lately?" he called out in a threatening tone.

At this the laughter and chatter began to die away. Everybody knew that one of Robby Lee's special, untraceable, virus-containing emails was a virtual death sentence for any computer system unlucky enough to receive it, regardless of the sophistication of the virus scan software used.

Porter flinched from a sudden rush of adrenaline at this sudden and blatant confirmation of his and Henry's suspicions, as well as the fact that honor now required he do something about it. But what? Robby Lee was a lean, hawkish-looking fellow who always wore black or dark gray clothing clearly intended to help maintain his "evil genius" persona. This had earned him the nickname, "The Undertaker" from his classmates: a nickname Lee despised. Up to now, Porter felt fairly confident he could take him in a fair fight. Seeing Robby for the first time since the spring, however, he wasn't so sure anymore. The Undertaker had shot up at least six inches and was now a good head taller than Porter. Lee was also known to be a dirty fighter and, although generally regarded as a geek, had endeared himself to the school's jocks and well-known bullies on account of doing their calculus homework for them. Therefore, he was considered a well-connected and dangerous geek: the sort of person who can ruin one's life in high school.

"I thought his name was 'Porter,'" mocked Kelly innocently in her pretty voice.

Porter could now feel every eye in the room upon him. *That's it!* he thought. *I'm not going to let myself be intimidated by a wanna-be bully, especially in front of Kelly, and everyone else for that matter. Especially after he tried to damage my property and is now openly bragging about it!*

"Hey, Smith. I'm talking to you!" threatened Robby again.

Porter composed himself before calmly looking up. Then he raised his hand and cradled his chin between thumb and index finger, like he was trying to recall some uneventful piece of information. "Oh, yeah. I received one infected with some sort of virus," he replied matter-of-factly. "It must have been the work of an amateur, because my scanner deleted it before it could damage my computer."

Robby's eyes narrowed and he almost said, "That's impossible," but caught himself. Writing computer virus code was one thing he absolutely excelled in. It was also one thing that could get you kicked out of school, or worse. While he had no doubt that the only use Smith's computer could now be put to was as an expensive doorstop, he would have to call this transparent bluff in a way which wouldn't implicate himself too much as the culprit. After all, his reputation was now at stake!

But before Robby could think of anything, Porter pressed on, now in his own threatening tone. "Anyway, I know who the little weasel was who sent it. He's just lucky his feeble *undertaking* was a failure and the virus ended up in my computer's email *graveyard*. Otherwise he'd be sporting a black eye to match his clothing. He still might if he doesn't pipe down."

This counter-threat and clear reference to Lee's clothing and hated nickname caused an immediate tangle of voices calling, "Yeah" or "Wow," over a chorus of low snickers throughout the room. Kelly looked at Porter in disbelief at first. She had never seen this fearless side of him before and made an effort to catch his eye, smiling at him with newfound admiration.

Robby's face flushed red with anger as he struggled to come up with an equally threatening parry to Porter's verbal thrust when Mr. Bauer, the anatomy teacher, walked in and deprived him of his chance. All he could do was silently glare at Porter and grumble under his breath as he hunkered down into his seat. *Porter Smith is dead meat*, he vowed.

"Good afternoon, everyone," said Mr. Bauer, walking down the aisle and back again towards his desk at the front of the class. "Welcome to Sophomore Anatomy. My name is Mr. Bauer and I'm your teacher this semester. I hope you all the like the smell of formaldehyde, as our ongoing assignment will be to perform detailed dissections of *feline domesticatus*—a familiar mammal you will all recognize as the 'domestic cat.'" Turning, he nodded towards a big, black plastic barrel sitting at the back of the room next to Porter's lab table: a container filled with at least two dozen, formaldehyde-soaked cat carcasses patiently awaiting dissection.

All heads in the classroom simultaneously glanced at the ominous-looking barrel. Some grimaced. Others giggled nervously. Kelly said, "Yuck" again, this time with much more conviction.

Mr. Bauer looked down, attempting to conceal a grin. He had a reputation of being somewhat of a ghoul, but was in fact a promoter of the old school of anatomy instruction: closely supervised dissections of carefully prepared specimens. This year it was cat carcasses injected with blue and red latex to help distinguish vein from artery. After the initial shock of dealing with a dead, embalmed animal, he was certain his students would find his class interesting and, perhaps, learn a little basic anatomy. A useful end to an otherwise unwanted pet or stray. He took role, noted a couple of absent students, handed out a class syllabus, and began explaining what his course goals and expectations were.

Porter, still a little wound up from his encounter with Robby Lee and his annoyance with Kelly Martino, was trying to refocus and follow along when a knock resonated from the classroom door.

Mr. Bauer stopped his droning lecture and all eyes turned towards the source of the sound.

Slowly, tentatively, the door opened and in walked a raven-haired girl dressed in a mid-riff, sleeveless, yellow blouse and a green, ankle-length skirt. Her hair—blacker than Porter imagined possible—was set in a ponytail which drifted down her thin, straight back. And her eyes: such eyes! They shimmered green like back-lit emeralds. In an instant it was clear her beauty matched, or perhaps even surpassed, Kelly Martino's.

Every boy in the classroom shot up straight in his seat at the sight of the new girl, especially Robby Lee. Kelly Martino eyed the newcomer coolly, while the other girls in the classroom either shook their heads or rolled their eyes at the boys' untoward behavior.

Mr. Bauer surveyed his students and a look of amusement bloomed across his face. He'd never seen such a response to a new student before. Turning, he addressed the young lady. "Can I help you, miss?" he asked kindly.

"Yes," she replied with a clear English accent. "I'm dreadfully sorry for being late. My name is Sarah Weston and I believe I am in your class."

Reaching down, Mr. Bauer picked up his class roster from his desk and studied it. "Why yes you are, Miss Weston. I see you're the new transfer student from Felixstowe, England. Welcome to the United States and North Kendell High School." For a moment he considered scolding the girl for being late, but something about her made him reconsider. "Here you go," he said, handing her a syllabus before scanning the room for an open seat. "Please take the seat next to Mr. Smith," he said, absently nodding towards Porter's lab table.

Sarah bit her lip and craned her head about, looking around the room in vain.

"Porter, please wave your hand. There you go, Ms. Weston," said Mr. Bauer, pointing at Porter's hand raised on high. "He's the tan, good-looking fellow near the back of the room."

Robby Lee's jaw clenched as Sarah walked down the aisle away from him and towards the unbelievably lucky Porter Smith.

Sarah said, "Hello," giving Porter a pleasant smile as she sat down. Fortunately, his tan from spending most of the summer outdoors helped conceal a significant blush.

Mr. Bauer waited until Sarah was seated before continuing. "We'll be pairing up students two to a cat as lab partners. I'm preparing a list of pairings and will post it before our next session." He then went on to discuss the highlighted items on the class syllabus, before explaining the purpose of the tools contained in the dissection kits they would use to perform their grisly tasks. He'd made it through most of the introduction in the dissection manual when, looking up at the clock, he noticed his class was drawing to a close. "Well, that should do it for today's lesson. Please read Chapter One in the anatomy textbook for tomorrow. If you have any questions about grading you can look at the school's web page or I'll address them next time." A simulated school bell over the public address system finally cut him off, signaling the end of class and the end of the first day of school. Mr. Bauer tried to make a few last closing remarks, but was generally drowned out by the sound of books slamming shut and the loud, deliberate skidding of chairs. He gave up after a few moments, sighing and sitting down at his desk.

Kelly Martino and Robby Lee were now completely forgotten as Porter closed his textbook and reorganized his handouts a few times while trying to think of something witty to say to the new most beautiful girl in the world sitting next to him. Just as he decided on, "Where is Felixville?" he felt a hand on his arm. It was Sarah and she looked frightened.

"Don't go yet," she pleaded under her breath. "That boy over there with the pale skin and slicked back hair is giving me the creeps. Will you wait here with me for a moment until he leaves?"

Porter eased back in his chair, glancing in the direction Sarah had been looking. He should have guessed. It was Robby Lee, unabashedly leering at Sarah as if trying to place a hypnotic spell over her.

Lee finally noticed Porter's gaze. "What are you looking at Smith?" he growled.

"I'd watch it, Lee. Someone might mistake you for one of the dead cats in this barrel."

Sarah squeezed Porter's arm and giggled.

"Class is over boys," clipped Mr. Bauer without looking up from notes he was scribbling away at. "It would be a shame for me to send you both to detention on the first day of school. What kind of display would that be in front of Ms. Weston?"

Robby looked down, fighting the urge to deliver another disparaging remark. Then, grabbing his book bag he stood up, gave Sarah one more significant look, and slowly walked out of the classroom. "Don't waste your time on that loser," he called over his shoulder as he passed through the threshold of the classroom's door and Mr. Bauer's jurisdiction.

Mr. Bauer's face shot up from his scribbling and for a second it seemed like he might go after Lee. Then he just sighed before shaking his head. "I expect such behavior from the likes of Mr. Lee," he said to Porter, "but not from you. I will not tolerate disruptions or disturbances in my class. I suggest you ignore Mr. Lee in the future and concentrate on your studies." He looked over at Sarah. "I apologize for such a scene, Ms. Weston. Mr. Smith is usually a gentleman who refrains from name calling and comparing his classmates to dead animals." Then, glancing furtively from side to side to make certain no one else was listening, Mr. Bauer leaned forward towards them a bit from his desk. "Although in this instance," he said in a subdued tone. "I may have to agree with Porter's assessment. Now good day to you both," he concluded with a wink and a smile before returning to his scribbling.

Sarah smiled back. "And good day to you, sir," she replied before turning to Porter. "That boy is quite a scary-looking fellow," she whispered, gathering up her belongings into her book bag. "Did you see the way he was staring at me? I do hope there are not a lot more like him around here."

"Better steer clear of Lee," suggested Porter as they stood up to leave. "Everyone calls him 'The Undertaker' and he causes a lot of good kids a lot of grief. I should have warned you. If he bothers you again let me know and I'll take care of it." (This last sentence being totally self-serving, of course.) Collecting himself he offered Sarah his hand. "My name's Porter Smith. It's very nice to meet you."

She shook it with a firm grip and smiled. "Sarah Weston. Stranger in a strange land."

Porter smiled back. "I'm supposed to meet my friend Henry after class. Want to come along? We can walk you home if you'd like. He's the smartest guy in school."

"I'd like that very much. My mother dropped me off this morning, but has an appointment this afternoon. I'm so turned around I don't know how I shall ever find my way back home. It's dreadful feeling lost."

"Don't worry about that. Where do you live?"

"We live near the university on Forest Street. "1435 Forest Street."

"I know right where that is. It's near the marina where I work. It's a little bit of a hike from here, but not too far if you don't mind the walk."

Sarah smiled again. "The English love hiking, I'll have you know. Especially on beautiful days like today." Their eyes met and she blushed, looked down, and back up at him. "Especially with nice people like you."

"You can't imagine my excitement when I heard you were in the United States, Dr. Weston," gushed Morton Hargraves, head curator of the Kendell University Field Museum. "I'm so glad you called when you did. Our Board of Trustees has accepted your gracious offer to assist us during the final stages of our recovery efforts. We can hardly wait to have the artifacts cataloged and moved to their new home at the museum."

"The pleasure is all mine, Dr. Hargraves," replied Elizabeth Weston as they walked down a winding footpath surrounded by towering oaks and elms. "This is an ideal way to accent my research sabbatical at Kendell University," she added, adjusting her briefcase's strap over her shoulder.

"Please, call me Morton," he replied before pointing to her briefcase. "May I help you with that?"

"No. No. I'm fine. It seldom leaves my side."

"I know the feeling," replied Morton, testing the weight of his own briefcase in his hand. "Academics and all their important papers." He glanced quickly at her again before forcing himself to look along the pathway they were walking. What a fool he would look like if he tripped and fell in front of her like an enamored, middle-aged, stuffed, pinstripe suit. Everyone said Dr. Elizabeth Weston was beautiful, but he never expected really how much. In person she was simply radiant. He'd never seen such poise before. Her movements reminded him of a cat. And her silky, raven hair and those emerald green eyes. They almost seemed to glow from within. Even though she was casually dressed in khaki pants and a pale green blouse to visit the excavation, he couldn't seem to keep his eyes off her. *Am I acting like a giddy teenager?* he dreaded. He hoped not, but he just couldn't seem to help himself. "And speaking of homes, how are you and your daughter settling in?"

"Quite well; thank you for asking. Sarah is having her first day of American high school today. I do hope she is all right."

"I'm sure she's fine. My wife is a history teacher at North Kendell High," he added, attempting to check his strange, growing feeling of glee. "If you'd like, I can ask her to look in on Sarah from time to time."

"That is kind of you to offer, but my daughter detests any kind of special treatment."

"Well, let me know if you change your mind."

They proceeded over a small hill and past an old, oval fountain hissing white plumes of water to a pleasant collection of ducks and sea gulls basking quietly in the mid-afternoon sunshine. This time of day the park was always nearly empty of people.

"Well, here we are at last," said Morton as they came upon a large, brick building situated on a man-made bluff overlooking an enormous lake stretching away towards the horizon. Two grand, bronze lions—green with decades of oxidation—greeted them with frozen roars at the steps leading up to its wide, columned entrance.

"What a wonderful view!" exclaimed Elizabeth.

"Indeed it is," replied Morton, looking out over the pale blue water. "And the Kendell Park District can't wait to get their building back. That's another reason we're so glad you're available. We never dreamed we'd get an archaeologist of your reputation to help us." He put his hand in his suit coat pocket, pulled out a key, and in his giddy state promptly dropped it. It hit the stone footing with a *cling*, then made a weird, almost controlled bounce right into Elizabeth's hand. "Nice catch," he said. "I wouldn't want to loose a master key. We'd have to get all the building's locks changed."

She simply nodded in agreement, handing it back to him.

As he reached out to take it, a spark of electricity leapt from one of her fingertips and gave him a good zap on his palm. "Ouch!" he cried, quickly pulling the key back. "That felt like more than just static."

She just shrugged, smiling prettily at him. "Some people say I have an electric personality."

"I believe that you do," he replied slowly, gazing into her green eyes. Was he feeling dizzy? He shook himself and looked away before quickly strolling up the steps leading to the building's entrance, where he went to its front door, unlocking it as Elizabeth caught up from behind.

She followed him into its large lobby and looked around. "Classic Art Deco style of the 1920s."

"Right you are. This building was constructed in the late-1920s, just before the Great Depression," replied Morton, leading Elizabeth towards a descending staircase. His giddiness was gone, but now he felt strange: almost lightheaded. *What's wrong with me?* he wondered. He stopped at the staircase and shook his head, clenching his eyes shut and rubbing his left temple.

"Are you all right?"

"Fine. Just a bit of a headache, that's all," replied Morton as he started down the staircase. "They were removing an old fuel oil tank in the basement six months ago when they discovered a large void beneath the floor where the tank was situated," he continued, now starting to feel a little better. "At first they thought it was a sinkhole of some sort. The engineers say they can't believe it wasn't discovered during the building's original construction."

Their footsteps echoed eerily as they proceeded down the worn, granite steps. At the bottom they came upon a short hallway lined with lockers crammed full of coveralls and workmen's boots. Several hardhats hung on nearby coat hooks. Morton plucked one off and handed it to her. "Here you go," he said, placing another on his own head. "The excavation is shored up and there's nothing to worry about. These are just a standard precaution. The other scientists are working at the museum today."

"Believe me, Morton. I've seen my share of excavations," replied Elizabeth, putting the hardhat on.

They proceeded along the hallway and Morton unlocked a large, steel door at its end. Giving it a good push, it creaked wretchedly on rusty hinges as it swung into darkness. "Watch your step," he cautioned as they navigated a second flight of steep, metal steps. "We're almost there." At the bottom landing he searched around on the wall with his hand before flipping a couple of light switches. Several ancient florescent lights flickered and buzzed slowly to life overhead, revealing a large, deep, rectangular excavation carved into and through the floor of the basement, which was surrounded by temporary safety railings and several high intensity work lamps. They strolled over to the nearest railing and Morton turned on a couple of the lamps as well.

"My word, it's much larger than I ever imagined," said Elizabeth, studying the excavation. It spanned nearly the entire length and width of the basement, which was filled with a wet, musty, tilled soil smell. The building's original supports, scattered here and there, were skillfully shored up with beams and jacks to prevent it from caving in on itself.

"The void was at the far end from where we're standing," continued Morton, now feeling almost normal again. "That's where they found the main stone artifact the papers are calling 'the altar.' The engineers hauled a lot of dirt out of here, and after we have everything removed they'll have to haul it all back in again. An expensive undertaking to be sure, but immanently worthwhile. There's never been another find like it in the Midwest."

The excavation sloped downwards at a fairly steep angle until it reached a depth of about twenty feet below the original floor grade, at which point it flattened out for another hundred or so feet towards the basement's far end. Across it were scattered worktables, roped-off dig areas, chairs, charts, and camera equipment supported by tripods. The main artifact was draped with a blue, plastic tarp. Next to it sat a drab-green, canvas-sided shed with a wooden roof.

"Would you like to take a look?" said Morton, realizing he was avoiding making eye contact with her. *Why am I acting so strangely?* he wondered.

"I can hardly wait," replied Elizabeth, quickly grabbing a rope railing supported by a line of stanchions leading down into the excavation. "From what I've heard, it almost seems impossible such artifacts could have been found in the Midwestern United States."

Using the rope to steady themselves, they carefully made their way down the sloped surface. At the bottom he led her to the far side of the excavation.

"We might as well start with the altar," said Morton. "It is by far the most interesting artifact." He bent down and with Elizabeth's help they carefully removed the tarp before stepping back to have a good look.

"This is truly an amazing find, Dr. Hargraves. Amazing! I don't quite know what to make of it. What on Earth is it doing here?"

"We were hoping you might be able to tell us. It has everybody stumped."

They walked around the artifact, studying it closely. It consisted of a large block of stone with steps carved up one side. Its surface, which was about four feet above the ground, was adorned with a large, bias-relief carving of a muscular, angry-looking, toga-clad man with long, flowing hair, sideburns, and beard. In his hand he dangled a tiny, featureless man by the legs over a liquid-filled cauldron. Bowl-sized depressions were located at each corner of its surface. On the opposite side of where the steps were located was an extension of stone jutting out and away like a little plank. Around the sides of the artifact were more carvings of line after line of tiny shield and club wielding warriors marching steadily upwards towards the artifact's top.

"At first we thought it might have been dumped here as fill material," continued Morton. "If you go down to the boat launch you can find several partially-carved stone monuments from the old cemetery mixed in with the breakwater wall. But this level of strata was undisturbed," he said, flattening his hands and waving them back and forth at waist level. "Very unlikely it was dumped here. We also carbon-dated some charcoal embers found at this level and they dated approximately twelve hundred years old."

"That may or may not mean anything," replied Elizabeth, studying the crude carvings on one side of the artifact. "If we can indeed rule out other explanations as to how this may have gotten here, then this really is a mystery. The Native Americans who originally inhabited this area are known to have constructed large, earthen ceremonial mounds—like the Cahokia Mounds near St. Louis—but nothing even close to this. What about the other artifacts?"

"Mostly pottery shards," replied Morton, pointing to and walking over to the canvas-sided shed. "They're being cataloged in here. Would you like to take a peek?"

"Yes. Very much so!"

They went inside and Morton turned on the lights. The shed contained a metal shelf, three tables, and several chairs. The largest table was covered with neatly arranged fragments of broken pottery and little plastic bags containing small lumps of mud-caked charcoal. The second table contained an assortment of brushes, metal probes, rulers, magnifiers, and measuring calipers. The third supported a computer work station and several data storage disk containers. The shelf held an expensive collection of cameras and other recording equipment.

Setting their briefcases aside near the door, they walked over to the table containing the pottery fragments, where they donned pairs of disposable latex surgical gloves. Once properly glove-clad, Morton selected one of the fragments, carefully picking it up and handing it to her. "Most of these are consistent with Native American pottery techniques from the time before Columbus. Note the tempering material mixed in with the clay. Microscopic examination indicates it's probably crushed mollusk shell."

Elizabeth plucked a magnifying glass from the instrument table and studied the fragment through it. "Now this I would expect to see in this area of your country. The Cahokia and other ancient tribes of the Mississippi River Basin commonly used ground up shells to help strengthen pottery during the fire-hardening process. As you say, these would be consistent with twelve hundred-year-old Native American pottery from this area. Perhaps it's a confirmation of your carbon-14 dating results."

"Yes," said Morton, selecting another fragment from a different section of the table. "These other shards were found at the same level. What do you make of this?"

They swapped fragments and Elizabeth studied the second one. It still possessed a few wisps of pigment on one side. "There must be some mistake," she said slowly, peering at it though the magnifying glass. "This fragment is obviously from pottery which was spun and kiln-dried. It almost looks like it's from a small, third or fourth century Roman amphora vessel. The potter's wheel and the kiln were unknown to Native Americans until after the time of Columbus! And as far as I know the Romans never set foot in the New World. What a mystery. This simply can't be right. The area must have been disturbed." She carefully returned the fragment to the artifact table.

"I wish I could agree with you, but there was no evidence of disturbance." Morton pointed at the fragments again and then towards the door of the shed. "Just for the sake of argument, say you saw these artifacts in a museum in England. Without knowing where they were recovered, what would you make of them?"

Elizabeth pretended to mull over Morton's question. She'd already heard a lot about the artifacts and had a strong suspicion as to their origin, but that was something she would never share. Who would believe her anyway? Besides, she was there for her own reasons: reasons which had nothing to do with archaeology or Dr. Hargraves's museum. Reasons which had to do with power: power only she and other witches of her own, high-order coven could physically absorb for later use. Witches with genetic mind control abilities who could trace their lineage back to Ancient Egypt itself!

"I've gone through the exercise myself. So have the other recovery team members," pressed Morton. "Everyone seems to have their own unique theory."

Elizabeth looked up at him and he quickly avoided her glance. *Poor, weak-minded fool*, she thought. *Looking away shall not save you.* Then she smirked inwardly. It might be fun to toy with Morty a bit. After all, he was nothing more than an unlucky guinea pig she would use to test her theory. Once the artifacts were removed and the site was covered up again no one would ever discover the secret, at least not at this location, or unless the hapless Gordon Parks returns from wherever it is he disappeared to all those years ago. The place she would send Morty to see and report back about in a few weeks if everything went as planned—assuming, of course, he survived. "These pottery shards," she finally said, pointing towards a section of the table. "Again, I would suppose these are of Roman origin. Perhaps seventeen hundred years old." She walked over to the door of the shed and looked out. "As for the main artifact itself, the bias-relief carvings are crude, but the large figure with the flowing beard and sideburns is very similar to ancient depictions of a Celtic god the Romans called Teutates. Teutates is the Romanized version of the name 'Tout,' the Celtic God of War associated with the planet Mars. The lines of smaller warriors around its sides also suggest a Teutates connection. I bet if you count them up you'll find they total 780. That's the number of days in the Martian synodic year."

"Amazing! They do total 780!"

"And note the scene on its top," continued Elizabeth, now on a roll. "Teutates is often depicted sacrificing victims into a cauldron of water. While there is a dispute among authorities, Teutates' cauldron is believed by some to represent the Moon."

"Interesting. Very interesting. Several others have made the Roman connection, but you're the first to mention Teutates and Mars. What about the altar's size and configuration?"

Good question, thought Elizabeth. *Perhaps Morty isn't as dumb as he looks.* "There you have me," she replied. "Its size and shape are all wrong from a Roman or Celtic standpoint. It almost looks like a small version of a Cahokia pyramid mound. Note the slope of the sides and the broad, flat top. Take away the carvings and I'd say it's Native North American: definitely pre-Columbian and definitely from a Mississippi River Basin tribe."

Morton smiled. "That's what I hypothesized as well! I believe this find may represent proof of contact between the Old and New Worlds more than a thousand years before Columbus! Can you imagine? A Roman delegation somehow finding its way to the Midwestern United States and interacting with the local Indian tribes! I know it sounds fantastic, but think of the implications from an historical standpoint."

"Let's not get ahead of ourselves, Dr. Hargraves," replied Elizabeth. "Such a theory would require much more proof than you've discovered here, but it is intriguing. You're documenting your artifact chain-of-custody I take it? To satisfy all the Doubting Thomases there will *undoubtedly* be?"

"Of course. Such a mystery requires special efforts. We've also filmed and recorded all our recovery efforts for future study."

"Good. Excellent, in fact. I would like to review them as soon as possible to get up to speed."

"I'll have copies made. In the meantime you can use this computer station during the day to look at them." Morton picked up a data disk from a table and showed it to her. "Each disk is labeled with the date and time the particular record was made. They're arranged chronologically from left to right." He set the container back in its place among the others and was about to suggest heading back to the university when he felt an electric shock on the back of his neck and flushed lightheaded again, staggering and just barely catching himself. *What's going on?* he wondered, groggily shaking his head and pressing his fingers against his temples. It suddenly felt like something was trying to get into his head: something evil trying to hijack his mind. *I've got to get out of here before it's too late!* Thinking quickly he looked at his watch. "I hate to cut this short, Dr. Weston," he stammered, struggling to avoid her gaze. "I just remembered. I have a board meeting this afternoon. If I leave right now I'll just make it."

"I don't think so, Dr. Hargraves."

He staggered again before turning to face her. "What do you mean, 'You don't think so?'"

And there they were. Those eyes: those beautiful, glowing, green eyes. Larger and larger they loomed, slowly filling his field of vision. Growing pools of green. He was swimming in warm pools of green light. Pools...

Elizabeth laughed out loud, but Morton never heard her. He just stood there completely frozen; caught in her spell like a primitive insect suspended in amber.

Grinning, she removed her latex gloves with a couple of *snaps*, flinging each one away in turn like rubber bands. "You naughty boy, Morty," she chided, wagging a finger at him. "It's not nice to lie, is it? Don't take this the wrong way, but for being the director of the Kendell University Field Museum, you have an exceptionally weak mind."

"Exceptionally weak mind," slurred Morton slowly from his deep trance.

Elizabeth laughed again, taking off the silly-looking hardhat and tossing it to the floor, where it bounced noisily away. This was going to be much easier than she imagined. She fluffed up her hair and flicked it back over her shoulders as she walked over to the door of the shed. "Time to verify my suspicions," she said, picking up her briefcase and placing it on the instrument table. Unclasping it, she reached in and pulled out a small box. "No need to go any further if I'm wrong about this place." She opened the box and carefully removed a pair of glasses with cobalt blue lenses. Putting them on, Elizabeth walked back over to the frozen Dr. Morton Hargraves. "How do I look?" she said, pouting her lips, placing her hands on her hips, and tilting her head from side to side like a fashion model before a camera. "Are they me?"

"You look beautiful, Dr. Weston," slurred the wide-eyed Morton as a droplet of drool oozed from the edge of his mouth.

"Thank you, Morty. Do you know what these are?" she continued, pointing at her face. "These are very special glasses. The lenses were ground from the rarest of the rare ever to be yielded up from the bowels of the Earth. Lenses made from a dousing crystal itself! Have you ever heard of a dousing crystal?"

"Dousing crystals are pure fantasy," slurred Morton in reply.

"Then you have heard of them?"

"Legend has it that dousing crystals will glow when they come into contact with mysterious lines of supernatural energy called 'leys.' Some believe leys are conduits of magical power generated from forces deep within the Earth: conduits springing up and crisscrossing the Earth like a great, gossamer veil. It is said while alone they are too weak to be meaningful, nodes of elevated supernatural energy are formed where three or more happen to cross—nodes of energy which can be harnessed and absorbed by high witches to help them with their evil endeavors. Some even suggest that ancient peoples throughout the world sought out these ley nodes and constructed their temples, churches, and ceremonial centers upon them to control the supernatural energy they generated. Modern science has disproved such nonsense. There are no invisible lines of supernatural force. Dousing crystals and ley nodes are pure poppycock." Even in his paralyzed state, Morton was able to emphasize this last point with a scholarly *snort* of disapproval.

"Oh how I wish that were true for your sake. But, alas, these nodes *do* exist. They are exceedingly rare, but if I'm right, your precious altar is sitting right next to a big, powerful one. You'll excuse me for a moment while I confirm my suspicions. Close your eyes and don't move a muscle," she added, patting him on the cheek. "I'll be right back."

"Won't move a muscle," slurred Morton, closing his eyes as commanded.

Elizabeth removed the sunglasses and walked out of the shed and over to the large stone artifact again, where she gingerly set them down on its top before taking a slow, deep, breath. Stretching out her arms and fingers at her sides, she drifted for a moment in an elevated state of consciousness. "Yes," she whispered as a low, almost imperceptible electrical sensation barely tickled her highly-developed sixth sense. "It's here, I can feel it. And it's mine. All mine to absorb until the time comes." She jumped for joy. "Finally!" she shouted. "Now let's just see where it is." Picking up the glasses again, she carefully put them on and let her eyes adjust to the cobalt blue color for a moment. Then, looking around, she spotted it almost immediately. It was hovering a few feet away from the little plank jutting out from the stone artifact: a spherical hub of shimmering blue light with eight, equally-spaced spokes radiating outwards in perfectly straight lines that shot across the excavation before disappearing into its walls. An intact ley node made from the precise crossing of four ley lines!

What incredible luck, she thought, slowly walking over to the node—which was about three feet in diameter—and reverently reaching out to touch it. As her fingertip breached its surface she felt a fleeting wave of coldness pass through her body, followed by an intense feeling of inner energy. For a moment she felt so powerful she thought she might fly. Collecting herself, she quickly withdrew her hand again. "I need to go slowly," she muttered. "I need to acclimate myself to so much power." She took the glasses off and returned to the shed, where she placed them back into their box. Once they were safely secure in her briefcase again, she walked over to the frozen Morton Hargraves and commanded him to open his eyes.

Morton blinked a couple of times at the light before returning to his steady, wide-eyed gaze. "Hello, Dr. Weston."

"Hello, Morton," she replied happily. "The node is here, just like I thought it would be. And such energy! If your mind wasn't so weak you could probably feel it too. After so many disappointments I've finally found an intact ley node!"

"Disappointments?" slurred Morton.

"Yes, dear Morty: disappointments. Many, many disappointments. The direction of ley lines of supernatural energy are intimately tied to the Earth's geology. If this geology is disturbed the lines can be redirected. Earthquakes are especially disruptive and can cause nodes which have existed for thousands of years to become unfocused and disappear completely. Remember the Mars Beast Ceremonial Center I helped discover in Guatemala two years ago?"

"Yes," replied Morton. "I understand you were on that dig. That's where they found the backpack of that fellow who disappeared all those years ago—that wealthy fellow who owned the gun company. What was his name?"

"Gordon Parks," replied Elizabeth, strolling back over to her briefcase and removing a deeply weathered book. "This is his journal. We found it in his backpack, but the other members of my team seem to have forgotten all about it." She gave Morton a wink and a sly smile. "Just like you'll forget all about our little conversation here, Morty, old chap. I decided to keep Mr. Parks's journal as a little souvenir. You wouldn't believe what's written in here," she added, carefully thumbing through its fragile, old, handwritten pages. Walking back over to Morton, she held it up to his face. "It appears Mr. Parks rediscovered the large ley node the Maya built their Mars Beast legend upon. Only he didn't know it. By the time the ceremonial center was rediscovered by my team the node was gone; likely destroyed by that strange Guatemala earthquake of a few years ago. What a disappointment. The ley lines were still there, but they no longer crossed at precisely the same point. No crossing, no node. No node, no power. Do you understand?"

"I think so."

"Do you know what else I gleaned from Mr. Parks's work? Something even I didn't know? Something his friend the great Max Zenger theorized?"

"Max Zenger the computer mogul?"

"One and the same. He and Parks were roommates in college. Zenger believed a sequence of Maya glyphs in the Rome Codex indicated the Mars Beast would actually appear at the Ceremonial Center during lunar occultations. The Maya thought it was their Mars god coming down from the heavens for a visit and to feast upon human sacrifices. Do you know what a lunar occultation of Mars is?"

"I'm an anthropologist, not an astronomer, Dr. Weston."

"Don't get smart with me, Morty. A lunar occultation is a celestial event in which the Moon passes between another planet and the Earth."

"What does all this have to do with the altar?" slurred Morton.

"Patience, Dr. Hargraves. According to his journal, Gordon Parks discovered the Mars Beast Ceremonial Center on some old NASA radar photographs and timed his expedition to the ruins to coincide with a lunar occultation of Mars. When Zenger backed out of the trip at the last minute, Parks decided to go it alone. He wanted sole credit for such a big archaeological discovery—silly, secretive, foolhardy man. Guess where we found his backpack?"

"Where?"

"Precisely where the ley node must have existed before the earthquake! You can tell by how the ruins are situated and where the ley lines are now located."

"I'm still not following you."

"I believe a lunar occultation of Mars over a large ley node causes it to expand, making it visible to the naked eye. It probably has something to do with subtle gravitational perturbations unknown to modern science. The glyphs in the Rome Codex suggest this, as well as traditional Roman renditions of Teutates. In the Rome Codex the expanded ley node is shown as an orb of white light. In the case of Teutates it's depicted as a cauldron of water. In both instances human sacrifices are made. I believe Gordon Parks witnessed just such an event back in 1980 and was somehow drawn into the expanded node. They never did find a trace of him, you know."

"He was probably eaten by a jaguar, Dr. Weston," slurred Morton. "I believe you've lost your mind."

"Have I?" chuckled Elizabeth. Turning, she pointed forcefully at the shed's door. "Lunar occultations of Mars over this area through the years are probably what produced the void discovered beneath the floor of this building! The node expanding from time to time and sending the dirt to the place Gordon Parks disappeared to."

"Disappeared to?"

Elizabeth grinned again. "That's where you come in, my dear. When a ley node of the size and power of the one hovering before your precious altar expands it may create some sort of doorway. Perhaps a doorway to the past. Perhaps a doorway to other places. How else can you account for third or fourth century Romans ending up in the ninth or tenth century Midwestern United States? I believe that long ago a Roman delegation passed through an expanded node somewhere in Europe, traveled 500 years into their future, and ended up here. Then, with the help of the local natives, they built their altar and prayed to

Teutates and waited years for the next lunar occultation of Mars to occur. When it finally did, they used the re-expanded node as a gateway to travel back again through time: back to their home in third or fourth century Europe. Witnessing such a horrendous event, the natives who helped build the altar ran off—never to return. It's well known that local tribes avoided the area around the City of Kendell. They considered in an unholy place inhabited by long-bearded evil spirits."

"Poppycock," slurred Morton.

"Just like my spell on you, right Dr. Morton? Anyway, we'll be testing my theory soon enough. Local astronomers are predicting a lunar occultation of Mars will occur over your fair city on October 22nd at precisely 9:43 p.m. That's about five weeks from now. You're going to meet me here at nine on that auspicious evening and walk into the expanded node when it appears—like a supernatural explorer, if you will. I want you to return if you can to report what you find. The lunar occultation is expected to last about an hour, so that won't leave you much time to look around. Once it's over the node will contract again, closing the doorway. If you don't make it back before it does, then I'm afraid you're going to be stuck wherever it is Gordon Parks disappeared to." She smiled, batting her pretty eyes at him. "You *do* want to help me, don't you, Dr. Hargraves?" she said with a pout, petting his arm.

Gulping, Morton refused to reply.

Elizabeth raised a finger to his forehead and a spark of electricity leapt from its tip and sizzled against his brow.

Morton winced in pain, blinking a couple of times before returning to his wide-eyed stare.

"Let's try it again. I said, 'You do want to help me, don't you, Dr. Hargraves?'"

"I'll do anything for you, Dr. Weston. Anything! Just name it."

"That's better. For starters, how many master building keys do you have in your possession?"

"Two: the one in my pocket and another back in my office at the museum."

"Good." Smiling, she patted him gently on the cheek again. "You want to give me the one in your pocket, don't you? Since I *am* a member of the recovery team now."

"Yes," he said, placing his hand in his pocket and pulling out a key. "Here you are, Dr. Weston. Here is your building key, since you're a member of the recovery team."

"Thank you, Morty." She plucked it from his hand. "I'm honored. But I wouldn't tell anyone else about this, at least for the time being. You wouldn't want to make any of the other recovery team members jealous. You know how the littlest of things can upset people."

"Let's just keep this key business between ourselves for the time being, Dr. Weston," he slurred back.

"You can count on me, Morty. I'm a pillar when it comes to being discrete. By the way, when is the altar scheduled to be moved?"

"That decision is Dr. Young's. He's heading up our recovery efforts. The final phase of our work is expected to be completed about two weeks from now and the artifacts moved shortly thereafter. Then the engineers will start filling up the excavation."

"That will *not* do. We'll miss the occultation! And I certainly need more than two weeks to absorb energy from the node. I don't think the final phase should be completed for at least another month and a half. Not until after the October 22nd occultation date at the very earliest. Maybe Dr. Young is being a bit too ambitious. Maybe he should be replaced by someone a bit more thorough; perhaps by someone more like me."

"I think Dr. Young is letting people at the Park District hurry him along too much," slurred Morton. "I'll raise the issue at our museum board meeting tomorrow night. He'll need to be replaced immediately. Would you be available to lead the last phase of the excavation for us, Dr. Weston?"

"Me? I'm flattered. Of course I'll take over. Since it's so sudden, and since it may impact my duties at the university, I'll need to be compensated accordingly."

"Anything. Name your price. Whatever I can't squeeze out of the board I'll pay for out of my own pocket."

"That's very generous of you, Morty. Let me sleep on it. I'll let you know once the board makes me an offer officially." She grabbed his arm and started leading him towards the door of the shed. "Listen to me carefully Morton. This is what I want you to do. I'm going to pull you out of the green soup now, but you're still mine for the time being. You like being mine, don't you?"

"I love you, Dr. Weston."

"Why, Morton. Don't be foolish. We only just met!"

"I meant to say I like you, Dr. Weston."

"That's better. When you leave this cozy, little shed, you're not going to recall anything we've spoken about since you fell into the green soup. There are no such things as ley lines or nodes. Dousing crystals are indeed pure poppycock. But what you will do is wake up and think to yourself what a good idea it is for Dr. Weston to have a master key to the building and stay behind this afternoon to review the artifact recovery recordings. You're going to run off to your board meeting, but halfway there you're going to remember the meeting is actually tomorrow night. That will be good because it'll give you time to think about all the reasons there are to fire Dr. Young and replace him with me. You'll feel no regret. In fact, until I tell you otherwise, you're going to feel fantastic. The best you've felt in years!"

"I feel fantastic."

"I'm happy for you. Meet me here tomorrow morning at nine to introduce me to the other recovery team members. And one more thing, from now on, every time I say, 'Morty, my dear,' you'll find yourself back in the warm, green soup."

"I love warm, green soup."

She pulled a handkerchief from her pocket and mopped the drool away from the sides of his mouth before retrieving his briefcase, hanging its strap over his shoulder. "Now get going," she said, giving him a good shove out the door with her foot.

Morton fell forward, just barely catching himself and his briefcase. "I need to be more careful," he thought as his spell-spun mind turned back on. "Sorry about this, Dr. Weston. I completely forgot about my meeting."

Elizabeth followed him outside and smiled. "Are you certain it's all right for me to stay a while to get started on the recordings?"

"Of course it is! You're on the recovery team now." And to himself, "If I have my way, you'll be leading it once I get rid of that scoundrel Dr. Young." He pointed to a clipboard hanging next to the shed's door. "Just sign in and log out when you leave. The front door to the building is always locked from the outside. Make sure you push it shut behind you when you go," he added, looking at his watch before trotting away. "Sorry I must run," he called out over his shoulder. "Meet me here tomorrow morning at nine and I'll introduce you to the rest of the team."

"Thank you, Morton. I'm so excited about working with you and the others."

"Watch your step when you leave!"

"I will!" called Elizabeth, waving goodbye. "And you as well!" She watched him for a bit as he climbed out of the excavation, then returned to the shed. Sitting down at the computer table, she stretched like a satisfied cat. "You are such a little witch, Weston," she whispered to herself, cocking an ear towards the door and quietly listening to Morton's steps echoing away and up the metal exit stairway. Listening to the door to the basement clanging shut behind him, followed by more fading footsteps and the distant *clack* of the front door to the building slamming closed. "We wouldn't want anything to happen to you, would we my little guinea pig—at least not before October 22nd."

"Your friend Henry is quite a fellow," said Sarah as they slowly walked along the sidewalk leading towards her new home near Kendell University. "He certainly likes to talk about his robots and computers. I do hope his tongue will be all right."

Porter chuckled at the thought of his friend's inadvertent, self-inflicted wound. "He'll be okay," he said, pushing his bike along by its handlebars. "It serves him right for talking so much. This weather must have gone to his head." He closed his eyes and took a deep breath. It was one of those impossibly beautiful late summer afternoons: the kind where blue skies, puffy-white clouds, scented breezes, and special company blended together so perfectly that everything seemed right with the world. "I love this time of year," he added, opening them again. And then to himself at the thought of his new companion: *I must be the luckiest guy in the whole world.* He stole a glance at her and she caught him and smiled. He smiled back before blushing and quickly looking away. "So, what brings you to Kendell?" he asked. "Did your folks get transferred to the United States or something?"

Looking down, Sarah frowned for the first time since they'd met. "My father died when I was quite young," she said, twisting a lock of hair which had worked its way loose from her ponytail.

Porter frowned as well, imagining slapping his forehead with his hand. *Nice going, Lunkhead*, he thought to himself, and then to Sarah, "I'm sorry."

She brightened to show him it was okay. "Don't be silly. No need to apologize. I can hardly recall father at all, but my mother has told me all about him. He must have been wonderful, because she still adores him. She doesn't say as much, but I can tell."

They reached a corner across the street from a large, tree-filled park, which gradually rolled down to the shore of a pale-blue lake stretching away as far as the eye could see. Stopping, they both admired the serene view in silence.

"She's the real reason we're here," continued Sarah after a quiet sigh. "My mother is an anthropology professor. She's on sabbatical at Kendell University."

Porter wondered what the word "sabbatical" meant, but didn't ask for fear of looking stupid. He'd look it up in the dictionary later. "KU is a great university. I've heard it's tough to get accepted there. Your mother must be pretty smart."

"Indeed she is. She's also helping the museum with the artifacts found at the old field house," she added, pointing to a large building nestled within a stand of trees in the park. "I believe she's over there right now discussing it with some of their officials."

"That stone slab thing they call the altar? I saw a few stories about it on the news a few weeks ago. There were a bunch of archaeologists arguing over what it is and where it came from. My dad thinks it's some kind of hoax. What does your mother think?"

Sarah shrugged. "She doesn't know what to make of it yet, but I'm certain she'll figure it out. All her colleagues say she's quite a gifted archaeologist."

"I think archaeology is fascinating," said Porter. "I love to watch shows about it on TV. I sure would like to meet her someday."

"Oh, I'm certain you will, and quite soon. My mother insists on meeting all my new friends to make certain their hearts are pure."

Porter shot her a questioning glance. "To make sure their hearts are pure?"

Sarah giggled at first before looking thoughtful. "She likes to know who I acquaint with, that's all. If she doesn't approve of their character, I'm forbidden from seeing them anymore. She says she can spot a bad influence a kilometer away."

Porter gulped. He never thought of himself as a bad influence, but what if Sarah's mom got the wrong impression of him?

"Don't worry, Porter," she said as if reading his mind. "I couldn't before, but now I can spot a bad influence just as easily as my mother can—just like I spotted that dreadful Robby Lee boy. You've got nothing to worry about."

A man appeared on one of the footpaths leading up from the field house across the street from where they were standing. He was wearing a silly-looking hardhat and whistling and skipping along like a child. When he noticed Sarah and Porter he stopped and waved. "Wonderful day, isn't it?" he shouted.

They smiled and waved back.

"I feel fantastic! Best I've felt in years," he declared loudly, pounding his chest a few times with clenched fists.

"We're happy for you!" called Sarah.

The man looked at his watch. "Got to run!" he shouted, adjusting his briefcase's strap across his shoulder before speeding off down the path again, skipping as he went and singing, "Goodbye, Youngeee. So long, Youngeee. Goodbye, Youngeee. Tomorrow's your last day!"

"It looks like this beautiful weather has gone to his head too," said Porter.

"He certainly looks like a happy fellow," added Sarah as they watched the man skip out of sight.

Another lake breeze, strangely cold, rustled nosily through the trees and past them.

Sarah shivered at its touch, pulling her short, yellow half-jacket tighter around her shoulders.

Porter noticed and said, "It's starting to get a little cold. It's always cooler by the lake. Want to get going?"

She nodded and they started walking north towards her house again.

"So, Mr. Porter Smith, tell me. What kind of things do you like to do?"

"You mean like hobbies?"

"Sure."

"In the summer I like to go sailing. I work part-time at the marina and get free lessons. Do you like to sail?"

"I've never been, but I'd love to try."

"I'll take you before the season closes if you'd like. Do you know how to swim?"

"I'm a capital swimmer!"

"Great. You can save me if I fall in."

"You are pulling my leg, Porter Smith. Everyone knows all Americans can swim."

"Not all, but most," he replied, briefly imagining a mouth-to-mouth resuscitation scenario with his new friend.

They continued on, enjoying the weather and getting to know each other. Their mutual love of music. Porter's guitar playing. Sarah's piano and voice lessons. Porter's pursuit of a varsity letter in fencing. Sites to see in Chicago—Porter promised to show her them all. Her grandparents in England—he would love Felixstowe in the fall. On and on they talked until they finally realized they must have been standing in front of Sarah's house for quite some time: an old, vintage row house owned by the university. It was her miniature portacom phone which finally shook them from there reverie.

Plucking it from her pocket, Sarah put the device to her ear without looking at its display. She knew who it was. Quickly glancing at Porter, she raised her finger to her lips and made a "shush" gesture before answering. "Hello?"

"Hello, Darling," said Sarah's mother over the tiny phone. "How did your first day of school go?"

"It was fine; so very different from schools in England. I don't know where to begin."

"We can talk about it when I get home. Sorry to say I'll be spending a bit more time at the field house getting aquatinted with the artifacts. They're quite a mystery."

"I can't wait to hear all about them."

Then there was a short pause. "Darling, who are you with?"

Sarah quickly turned away from Porter and clapped the phone between her mouth and free hand. "I hate it when you do that!" she hissed under her breath. "How in heaven's name do you always know when I'm with someone? Can you see through my portacom or something?"

"Someday you'll find out my dear," replied Elizabeth coolly. She'd been subtly coaxing Sarah's inner magical powers along over the years, just as her mother had done to her, and her grandmother to her mother, and on and on, generation after generation for thousands of years. It was her ancestors' time-tested method of developing their female children's powers to the point they could not easily refuse becoming high witches once they were told who they really were.

Sarah was quickly approaching that point. The young woman's inner light was developing quickly, and while Sarah probably suspected by now she was different somehow—able to read the thoughts of weak-minded people and influence their emotions with mere thoughts—she lacked the necessary skills to control her growing powers: skills only formal instruction in witchcraft could provide.

This lack of control had led to problems back in Felixstowe in recent months. All those weak-minded boys hanging around the house, peeking through windows and stalking poor Sarah wherever she went: influenced into pure, uncontrollable love by so much as a single, innocent smile from her little girl. That was the real reason for her new—and seemingly cruel—rules about who Sarah could make friends with. Until her daughter was able to control her powers, Elizabeth would make certain Sarah would only associate with the strong-minded: those who could not be accidentally influenced so easily.

"You know the rules, Sarah," she continued. "No striking up

friendships willy-nilly anymore. Remember all the trouble we had back at home?"

"I remember," replied Sarah miserably.

"Who is he? Where did you meet him?"

Turning, Sarah glanced over at Porter, who looked back at her questioningly. She mouthed the word "mother" at him before returning to her conversation. "He is a boy from school. His name is Porter Smith and he rescued me from a scary-looking boy in class today. He has walked me home like a gentleman."

"You don't say," replied Elizabeth. "Be honest. Is he fawning all over you like that annoying Hanson boy? Remember how much trouble *he* turned out to be. They had to practically administer shock therapy before he finally gave up and left you alone."

"No, Mother. Porter is not fawning over me," replied Sarah. *Well, maybe just a little*, she added to herself hopefully.

"Put him on," ordered Elizabeth. "I would like to speak with this knight of yours."

"Mother!"

"Sarah, do as I say. I just want to say hello to your new friend."

Sarah looked at Porter again, who had been following along with her and her mother's conversation. He now appeared quite pale despite his tan. She lowered the portacom from her ear and offered it to him. "My mother would like to say hello."

Porter gulped as he took the phone. He wasn't used to speaking to girls' parents, and Sarah's look made him think this wasn't likely to be a promising start. Raising it to his ear he bravely continued on. "Hello? Mrs. Weston?"

"Hello, Porter. Thank you for walking Sarah home today. Now please hold the phone close to your ear. I want to make certain you hear me and that we understand each other."

His mouth became so dry at the sound of Elizabeth's cold, malevolent voice his tongue began sticking to its roof and sides as he helplessly pressed the phone to his ear as commanded. "Okay," he croaked nervously. "I'm listening."

Now able to sense Porter's mind through her own phone, Elizabeth grinned. *Now let's see if I have to nip this in the bud.* Pointing at the tiny device, she rolled her eyes back in concentration and a spark leapt from her fingertip.

Simultaneously, at Porter's end, a spark crackled out of Sarah's portacom and sizzled against his ear before rebounding back into the phone. Wrenching it away from his head in pain, it slipped from his hand and he dropped it.

At Elizabeth's end—at nearly the same instant—the spark leap back out of her portacom and into her fingertip with a vicious and painful electrical *snap*.

Porter thought he heard Elizabeth cry, "Ouch" as Sarah's phone tumbled out of sight into a hedge next to the sidewalk.

"Porter, are you all right?" shouted Sarah, grabbing him by the arm.

Rubbing the side of his head, Porter quickly bent down and began fishing through the hedge with his hand. "Your phone just gave me a nasty shock. I hope your mother is still there. She'll think I'm an idiot." He found it after a few, crunchy-sounding gropes, then stood and raised it warily to his ear again, this time holding it a few inches away. "Hello? Mrs. Weston? Are you still there? Sorry. I dropped Sarah's phone."

Elizabeth was still there all right. She had quickly recovered from a dose of her own electricity, but not from her surprise at Sarah's new friend. The young man's mind was so strong it could apparently deflect a pretty good dose of her magic. He would be the perfect companion until Sarah's formal training in witchcraft would begin! Her daughter had done well in selecting her first friend in the New World. "I'm still here Porter," she replied happily. "What happened? Is everything all right?"

"Sarah's phone gave me a little shock, that's all. There must have been a static build-up from the dry air." Elizabeth's tone had softened so much he unconsciously drew it a little closer to his ear. "You were going to tell me something?"

"Oh, just that I'm *so very glad* Sarah has met such a nice young man. She said you rescued her in class today. I hope it's nothing serious."

Porter smiled, looking over at Sarah. "Just one of the school bullies. Nothing I can't handle."

"Indeed. Well, thank you again and I hope you can stop by this Saturday afternoon for tea. Sarah has unhappily told you of my strict and utterly draconian acquaintance rules, I'm sure."

"Yes, she has."

"Good. Would you please put her back on. And good day to you."

"Goodbye," said Porter before handing the phone back to Sarah.

"Hello, Mother?"

"Your friend seems like a very nice young man. I've invited him for tea on Saturday. I'm certain there'll be no trouble at all."

Sarah brightened. "Thank you, Mother."

"Good. That's settled, then. Oh, and I've decided to bend my rules a bit. Even though I haven't met him in person yet, I don't see why you can't spend time with Porter at school this week—within reason, of course. Let's call it a probationary period until he receives my final blessing."

CHAPTER THREE: INTRODUCING SOLARITRON

"So, you were paired up with Sarah in your anatomy class," said Henry in a voice filled with more than just a hint of jealousy. He would have given his right arm to spend an hour a day, five days a week, with such a lovely, young lady. He sighed wistfully at the thought of her as he pressed a button on a remote control operating the door to his dad's workshop: a converted barn completely renovated inside. The locks responded with soft, but competent, *clicks* and the door swung open. "You lucky dog. She's so pretty and polite. Half the guys in school already have major crushes on her, and it's not even the second week of school!" They stepped through into a large room and Henry turned on the lights. "She's nice too," he added, grabbing a long, stained lab coat—pockets sagging with hand tools—from a hook on the wall and pulling it on over his blue, short-sleeved shirt and light-gray trousers. "She's not stuck up like Kelly and her crew. Does she have any sisters?" he asked, grabbing a second, clean lab coat from another hook and offering it to his friend.

"Only child," replied Porter, taking and putting it on to protect his varsity fencing T-shirt and blue jeans from whatever nasty chemicals had stained Henry's. "Sorry." Ever since they'd walked her home the Monday before, Porter could tell his friend was within the ranks of the "crushed" over Sarah Weston. Henry had jabbered away so excitedly upon first meeting her he accidentally bit his own tongue, causing him to lisp for couple of days. "Besides, Sarah and I are just friends."

"Friends? Now I *know* you're crazy. Everyone can tell she likes you and you like her. I wish I were in your shoes."

Porter blushed. He did like Sarah—a lot, in fact, but he wasn't as certain as his friend about how much she really liked him. After all, they'd only known each other for a few days. He hoped Henry was right, though. And he still had to meet Sarah's mother tomorrow afternoon—to pass her strange approval test, whatever that was. "Well, let's have a look at it," he said to get his mind off the dreaded meeting with Elizabeth Weston. "Let's see the mysterious 'Project.'"

"Follow me and prepare to be amazed."

They walked past workbenches, tables, and shelves filled with tools, bottles of chemicals, and incomprehensible devices in various degrees of construction or disassembly. Henry's dad, Paul Dundridge, was an engineer who worked for Zenger Enterprises: a large, multinational company specializing in computers and advanced robotics. Paul also liked to tinker around in his spare time—taking things apart to try to find ways to make them work better, or inventing new gadgets outright. He'd been pretty successful too and held several patents. Once he invented a golf ball which would jump up and down on command so its owner could find it in the rough. Another time he came up with a fast food wrapper which would warn customers when catsup, mustard, or any other part of their order was about to fall on their laps.

"This is my workshop," said Henry as they came to another door located on the opposite side of the room. "This is where the important work around here goes on." He opened it and they went in.

"Wow," said Porter, putting his hands on his hips and looking around. There were dozens of computers and computer screens everywhere, taking up every useable shelf and workbench space. Some looked quite old—almost like antiques. Others were the very latest models, consisting of tiny cubes and paper-thin viewing screens. And everywhere snaked cables and bundles of cables and fiber optic connections. Each piece of equipment was interconnected in ways Porter would never be able to comprehend. For a moment he thought he'd have to suffer a long-winded explanation of how everything worked. His friend had a tendency to become quite verbose when it came to topics near and dear to his heart, especially computers and robots—naturally. Porter's fears were unfounded, though, as Henry simply motioned towards the equipment with his hand as they passed by, saying, "Don't even ask."

They went through another door into a garage-like area at the back of the barn and Henry turned on the lights. The space was filled with all kinds of lathes, drill presses, grinders, saws, and carts filled with hand tools and electrical diagnostic equipment. "That's it over there," he said, pointing at a roughly five and a half-foot-high cylindrical object covered with a green, canvas tarp. They walked over to it and, stooping over, Henry grabbed the tarp's edge. "Ready?"

"Ready!"

Henry stood again before quickly jerking the tarp away with a flourish—like a magician revealing the climax of an elaborate trick. "Ta da! Meet the 'Project!'"

Porter tried to stifle a laugh with his hand at the sight of the strange-looking contraption. Then, biting his lip, he struggled to appear awestruck as he slowly walked around it.

The upper portion was a greenish-gray, two-foot-wide cylinder topped off with a clear crystal dome. Within the dome was a tightly-packed cluster of lenses and little, odd-shaped antennae. The largest two lenses were located centrally above the rest on an assembly which kind of made them look like big eyes. Evenly-spaced around the outside of the cylinder were vertical recesses filled with brushed titanium bars topped off with different kinds of folded up claws. The upper part sat on a wider, flying-saucer-shaped carriage, which seemed to balance magically on a single, bowling ball-sized rubber roller nestled below it in a centrally-located recess. The flying saucer was also ringed with vertical recesses filled with the same titanium bars and folded-up claws.

"You built this?" exclaimed Porter, suddenly realizing how very intricate the machine actually was.

Henry pointed at his friend. "You were going to laugh, weren't you? I knew you'd laugh. I just knew it! What is it they say? Pearls before swine?"

Porter smiled at his friend and motioned towards the machine with his hand. "Well, look at it. You should've warned me it was so goofy-looking."

"Goofy-looking?" replied Henry—astonished by his friend's choice of words to describe his creation. "Goofy-looking? I would have preferred the term, 'radical design.'"

"Does it really work?"

Henry grumbled something under his breath about, "All brawn and no brains," before saying, "You bet it works. Come on, I'll show you." He grabbed a bar with a T-handle sitting nearby and attached its hooked end to a recess under the machine's saucer. Once the bar was secure, Henry plucked a remote control from his lab coat pocket and pressed a button on it with his thumb, signaling one of the garage doors to roll open. "I had a few mishaps during my original programming," he continued, tucking the remote back in his pocket and pulling the machine outside with the T-handle. "Last week, before I finally worked out all the programming glitches, it went berserk and smashed some of my dad's equipment. Now my folks will only let me turn it on outside and well away from the house."

Porter bent down and looked under the machine as Henry towed it out across the large backyard. It traveled easily along on its single ball roller. "Why doesn't it fall over?"

"Gyroscopes. Lots of gyroscopes," replied Henry as they finally reached the minimum distance his dad had established for Project testing purposes. He removed the T-handle and tossed it aside. "Okay, Porter. Stand back." He pressed his thumb onto a small circle painted on the side of the machine's upper assembly and it replied with a couple of *beeps*. "This is my access protection. Solaritron will only activate if it reads my thumbprint first."

"Solaritron? You named it Solaritron? What kind of name is that?"

"It's retro. It kind of sounds like the way they named machines and robots a long time ago. It's totally solar powered and it's a robot. 'Solar–tron,' get it? What would you have named it?"

Porter shrugged. "I think 'Solaritron' is a great name. I just wondered, that's all."

"I'm glad you approve of something I've done," replied Henry, pulling a second, sleek-looking remote control from another pocket. "Goofy-looking, my eye." He looked over to Porter, who had stepped back a few paces from the sleeping machine. "Ready?"

Porter shook his head that he was.

Henry raised the remote control to his mouth. "Solaritron: full activation!"

In a flash, long, metallic legs shot out from the recesses along the sides of the machine's lower saucer section and it sprang up on them like some giant, aggressive spider about to seize its prey.

Porter shouted in surprise, falling down backwards at the sight.

The robot bobbed up and down menacingly for a moment—servos and electric motors roaring—as the two large lenses in its dome spun back and forth before fixing on Henry. "Good afternoon, Mr. Dundridge. I hope I find you well," it said in a tinny, old-fashioned, movie robot voice.

"Very well, Solaritron. Thank you." He pointed at his friend, who was still lying on the ground; staring drop-jawed and speechless at Henry's creation. *That's more like it*, thought Henry. "This is my good friend Porter Smith. It appears he has fallen. Would you please lend him a hand?"

The machine's lenses followed the direction where Henry had pointed and focused on Porter. "Certainly," it replied. "It is nice to meet you Mr. Smith." Turning, the robot walked smoothly towards Porter on its articulated, insect-like legs. There wasn't even a hint of jerkiness to its gait. As it approached, a titanium arm with a rubber-covered claw unfolded from one of the recesses on its upper cylinder and reached down towards him. "May I lend you a hand?"

Porter looked over at Henry. "This is incredible! You're a genius, you know that?" he said before looking back up at the machine and its outstretched arm. "It won't hurt me will it?"

"Of course not; I've gotten all the bugs out of its programming. Only thing Solaritron will hurt are other battle robots. Isn't that right, Sola?"

"You are correct, Mr. Dundridge."

Porter grabbed the robot's claw and the machine's servos whined ever so slightly as it pulled him to his feet. "Battle robot? I thought you said your battling days were over."

"I just said that because I didn't want Lee's old gang hanging around here any more. I don't trust them—probably a bunch of spies. Robby would do anything to regain his title back from me. He's been spouting off at school about how his robot malfunctioned and that I never should have won the last time. Boy will he be in for a surprise when his robot 'Rock Crusher' is dismantled by Solaritron here with three arms tied behind its back."

"I hope you're right," said Porter, dusting himself off. "I've heard Lee has rebuilt his robot from the ground up. It's rumored to be as big as a refrigerator now. He's definitely gunning for you."

"We're not afraid, are we, Solaritron?"

"No," it replied, this time in a deep and menacing metallic voice. "Perhaps a demonstration is in order."

"Good idea, Solaritron. I told Mr. Smith he should prepare to be amazed. Let's go over to our testing arena."

The robot quickly retracted its legs into their recesses and settled down again onto its single roller, assuming its original configuration, and began following the boys as they walked towards a metal shed next to an old, wooden-fenced corral in an overgrown field at the back of Henry's parents' property. The lawn within the corral had been recently mowed.

Porter glanced over his shoulder a few times as they walked along, certain the one-rollered machine would topple over any second. To his surprise it never did. Instead, the robot bounced easily over ruts and around stones without the least hint of waver or instability. "How in the world did you ever manage to construct such a thing?" he asked as they approached the corral.

Henry shrugged. "The mechanics weren't too difficult, really. Most of its components consist of salvaged machinery or inventions my dad started, but lost interest in. Solaritron's lower assembly with the roller and retractable legs, for example, was taken from my Uncle Philip's all-terrain wheelchair. He had it custom made just before he passed away. Uncle Phil had been an avid rock climber before a fall left him paralyzed from the waist down. The wheelchair's roller could be used on relatively flat surfaces, while its legs would deploy to cover rough terrain as well. Uncle Philip hoped to use it to at least go hill climbing again, but died in a car accident before he ever had the chance. Poor, unlucky, Uncle Phil. My aunt tried to donate it to several charities, but nobody wanted it, so she gave it to me, and I used it to help create Solaritron."

"That's awesome!"

Henry stopped at a gate leading into the corral and opened it. "The real trick lay in the computer processors and programming," he said, tapping the side of his head with his finger. "I know you're not interested in computers so I won't bore you with the details. I will say I used some human mimicry programming so it would appear somewhat intelligent, but as you can see it didn't work very well. No matter how hard I've tried, Sola's verbal responses and intonations always seem to come off, well, a little wooden."

"It makes him seem more scary," replied Porter before saying in his best imitation of the machine's voice, "Crush, kill, destroy!"

Henry laughed. "I never thought about it that way, but I think you're right. Anyway, this is where I test my battle robots." He pointed towards the grassy area within the corral. "I use some of my old ones to spar with Solaritron. It helps me fine-tune its tactics and weapons array." He turned to his latest creation. "Proceed to the center of the corral and prepare for minimally-destructive sparring."

The machine silently complied, rolling through the gate and over to the center of the corral, where it stopped and waited, its lenses turning to and fixing on the door to the metal shed.

"Wait here," said Henry, trotting over to the shed and disappearing inside. He emerged a few moments later with a bow and a few arrows tucked under his arm and holding a new remote control. He walked back and exited the corral, closing the gate behind him. "I'll use these arrows to mix things up a bit. Solaritron will be sparing with Thunderer. You remember Thunderer, my champion that defeated Lee's robot last spring?"

Porter remembered the wicked-looking machine well. Thunderer was a fast, agile robot which kind of looked like a low-slung crab with a spike-covered carapace sitting on a rectangular, six-wheeled carriage. It was equipped with two huge claws which could snip through metal like scissors cutting through toothpicks. It had reduced Robby Lee's battle robot into a pile of twitching, chipped-up, scrap metal and Porter couldn't imagine Solaritron had a ghost of a chance against it. "Are you sure you want to do this?" he said, thinking his friend might have overestimated his new robot's fighting abilities.

Henry grinned. "Don't worry, both robots are programmed to score hits without doing a lot of significant damage to each other." He turned on his new remote. "Ready?"

"I guess so."

Henry raised the remote to his mouth. "Thunderer, attack Solaritron!"

Looking over, they saw movement at the shed's door and then Thunderer appeared—bristling and angry-looking—giant metal claws snapping fearlessly. It rolled slowly into the corral and began circling Solaritron like a prizefighter sizing up its opponent.

Solaritron just sat placidly, while the lenses in its glass dome followed Thunderer along.

Then Thunderer made its move, shooting directly at Solaritron at high speed.

Porter fought the urge to cover his eyes, seeing no way Henry's new robot could avoid being rammed.

Then, just before certain impact, Solaritron's legs flashed out and it jumped into the air. And what a jump! Thunderer passed harmlessly underneath it with a few feet to spare.

Thunderer's wheels locked as it skidded to a stop, quickly turning back and forth; searching for its opponent.

By now Solaritron had also deployed the six, titanium arms on its upper cylinder. Each one was topped off with a different kind of claw, pincer, or cutting blade as it began following behind Thunderer—bobbing and weaving like some kind of giant weird insect.

"What's it doing?" asked Porter, no longer so certain of the outcome of the robots' duel.

"Solaritron has analyzed Thunderer's field of view and is trying to sneak up on it."

Suddenly Thunderer detected its opponent again, spinning around and rushing it a second time.

Again Solaritron jumped, only this time it landed right on top of Thunderer's spike-covered carapace.

Thunder made a loud squealing sound as it raced wildly about, stopping, turning, and accelerating; desperately trying to shake free of its opponent, but it was no use. Solaritron's legs had clamped on tight between the spikes and its six arms had gone to work. Sparks flew and the air was filled with the sickening, high-pitched whines of drill bits and saw cutters on metal as Solaritron strategically attacked Thunderer's armor and front sensor array.

"Thunderer will be disabled shortly," said Henry as the crab-like machine slowed to a stop; its claws still clacking and flailing wildly at Solaritron, which pitched to and fro to keep out of reach. "Now watch this."

Porter turned and saw Henry had nocked an arrow and was holding the bow drawn, string to eye.

Then, aiming directly at Solaritron, Henry let loose and the bow sprang open with a *twang*, launching a rubber-tipped arrow, which whistled through the air as it sped straight and true at its target.

Porter followed its flight and just before impact the arrow was plucked from the air by a blur which turned out to be one of Solaritron's claws. The claw snapped the arrow in half like a twig, tossing it to the ground.

By now, Henry had nocked another arrow, only this time he was aiming high above the dueling robots. The bow released with another *twang* and the second arrow arched skyward above the machines at a forty-five degree angle.

At the same instant a thin, tube-like arm appeared from Solaritron's upper cylinder and its end erupted with several, *pufft! pufft! pufft!* sounds. At almost the same instant the second arrow burst into pieces in mid-flight, which lazily rained down to the ground.

"What was that?" exclaimed Porter.

"Compressed air gun. Solaritron's a pretty good shot, isn't it?"

Porter nodded, now watching poor Thunderer give up its mechanical ghost. Its claws now hung at its sides, twitching wretchedly as Solaritron hopped off its back and began retracting its numerous arms and legs. After a moment the victorious machine sat placidly on its single roller again.

Smiling, Henry pulled Thunderer's remote from his pocket and spoke into it. "Thank you, Thunderer. You may return to standby mode pending completion of repairs."

Immediately the disabled robot stopped twitching and its giant claws fell lifelessly to the ground with a couple of heavy *thuds*.

Even though he knew Thunderer was just a machine, Porter still felt a tinge of sadness for the fallen champion. "Do you enjoy destroying all your toys?"

"Can you think of a better way to test battle robots? Besides, don't you worry about old Thunderer," he added, as if reading his friend's thoughts. "It's equipped with one of my dad's latest creations: 'micro-repairbots.' It'll be good as new in a few minutes."

"Micro-repairbots?"

"Come on, I'll show you," said Henry, opening the gate.

Porter followed him into the corral and they walked over to the disabled robot.

"Micro-repairbots are tiny robots my dad invented to perform automatic repairs on larger machines. They're sort of like the robotic versions of white blood cells and platelets. I've equipped both Thunderer and Solaritron with them. They're stored in little internal containers and automatically deploy when damage or a malfunction is sensed." Kneeling next to Thunderer, Henry pointed at the areas Solaritron had damaged. "See how the little devils are swarming to make repairs."

Porter studied the areas where Henry had pointed and saw what looked like dozens of tiny to medium-sized silver insects crawling about. They seemed to be poking and prodding deliberately at the robot's internal workings and every so often their actions would produce sparks and hissing sounds. "Unreal," he muttered under his breath.

"When the repairs are complete they'll return to their container. Obviously they can't fix major damage, but they can't be beat when it comes to wiring and circuitry. My dad says they'll probably never see widespread use because they'd put too many people out of work. Let's see how they're doing. Stand back."

The boys stood and moved a few paces away from the robot.

Raising Thunderer's remote, Henry spoke into it again. "Thunderer, diagnostic activation. Can you move yet?"

Thunderer's claws sprang up to its sides and snapped deliberately a few times. Then it rolled from side to side, testing its renewed mobility, before saying, "Repairs are progressing in accordance with system parameters."

"Good. Very good," replied Henry. "You may proceed to your power hookup in the shed and return to standby mode while they are completed."

"Yes, sir," replied the wicked-looking machine as it turned and began rolling slowly towards the shed's wide, metal door.

Henry placed the remote control back in his pocket. "Well, enough about Thunderer. What do you think of Solaritron?" he said, fairly beaming with pride.

Grinning, Porter looked over at the machine which seemed to magically balance on a single ball roller and pointed at it. "That thing is a marvel, an unbelievable marvel! Lee's robot hasn't a prayer against it. Who would have guessed something could be so lethal, so dangerous, and at the same time be so goofy-looking. It looks like a giant top with eyes when its arms and legs are folded up. When you first showed it to me I thought you might be trying to laugh Robby's robot to death."

Henry's smile faded and he crossed his arms in indignation. "Very funny, Porter. Robots don't laugh, not really anyway. And I still prefer the term, 'radical design.'"

Over the next few weeks, Porter, Henry, and the rest of the teenagers at North Kendell High School slowly settled into their respective routines. Sports teams and clubs were joined. Friendships and rivalries were either started or renewed. And as Henry had suspected, despite the attention lavished on Sarah Weston by most of the school's male students, it soon became clear she preferred Porter's company best; although Henry couldn't imagine why. Porter had easily met with Elizabeth Weston's approval after the first week of school and ever since then he and Sarah had become nearly inseparable.

Elizabeth Weston. Henry had to meet her approval as well before officially being allowed to be friends with Sarah. An approval which consisted of nothing more than a static-filled handshake—Henry would never forget the weird jolt of electricity which had leapt from her fingertip—followed by pleasant conversation over tea, during which it became clear where Sarah had gotten her own looks, poise, and charm. Sarah and Elizabeth could almost pass for sisters and at first he thought Porter had lied to him about Sarah being an only child.

After that, Henry was free to hang around with Sarah as well, and he and Porter did, often enough—being in the presence of Sarah Weston was a pleasure even if you had no chance in the world of dating her. She'd also pushed all the right buttons, saying she thought Solaritron was simply "grand," and Henry eventually came to regard her as a good friend in his own right. He was still jealous of Porter, though, and the passage of time didn't seem to remedy this unhealthy feeling.

What was even worse, from Henry's standpoint, was—rightly or wrongly—he felt like he was slowly being excluded from Porter's growing circle of friends. From the start, Sarah's popularity seemed to rub off on Porter, but not on himself. Maybe it was because their fellow students believed any boy who could attract such a beautiful girl must be special in his own right and worthy of favorable attention and Henry was a mere hanger on. Maybe it was because she was drawing Porter out of his shell. At her urging, the two had auditioned for and gotten the starring roles opposite each other in the high school play. There were even rumors they might actually be voted in as the sophomore class courtiers to this year's homecoming dance. While Henry thought such an honor was childish at best, he suspected it was only a matter of time before Porter's newfound popularity went to his head and their friendship would cease altogether. What Henry didn't suspect was the seething resentment and jealousy Porter and Sarah had unwillingly unleashed in Robby Lee and Kelly Martino.

In Robby's case it was due to his intense attraction to Sarah and the sheer disbelief she would prefer a mediocre character like Porter Smith to Robby himself. He also bristled at the fact she was clearly avoiding him, concluding it was due to some lie Porter had told her.

Kelly Martino, on the other hand, had no real interest in Porter—none she would admit, anyway—apart from the fact she thought he was moderately cute and had once been within her stable of admirers. It was Sarah Weston she despised. Despite clear offers to join Kelly's clique—as a subordinate member—Sarah had politely refused. Even worse, the new girl from England was quickly garnering her own loyal following by simply being honest and nice to her classmates. To Kelly this simply wouldn't do. Furthermore, she was convinced if things kept going the way they were, Sarah Weston would dethrone her as North Kendell High's most popular female sophomore. Kelly vowed she would do everything in her power to prevent such a disastrous event from happening and set out to either shake the new girl's confidence or discredit her outright in the eyes of their fellow classmates. And now, as she sat in the dreaded anatomy class again, discreetly paying more attention to Porter and Sarah than to the unlucky cat carcass she and her dissection partner were butchering, Robby Lee leaned over and whispered into her ear.

"Don't those two lovebirds just make you want to hurl? She must need glasses or something if she likes Porter Smith."

Kelly drew away a bit. Although she liked to use Robby for her own math assignment needs, she didn't want to be too closely associated with anyone who was referred to as "The Undertaker" by her classmates. It wasn't her fault she'd been paired up with him as dissection partners. "Porter's kind of cute," she finally whispered before nodding her pretty, blond head towards her rival's lab table across the room. "It's Sarah Weston I can't stand. She's so high and mighty. Little Miss Manners from England. Little Miss Perfect Student. What a phony. I just can't stand her."

"Want to cause some trouble?" whispered Robby as he hacked mercilessly away at their cat's thoracic musculature. "Pour some rain on their parade?"

Mr. Bauer appeared out of nowhere and the two automatically clammed up. He studied Robby's dissection technique for a moment, shook his head in disgust, and wandered away again.

"What did you have in mind?" replied Kelly after Bauer had moved on.

"You'll see. Stop by my folks' house tonight. Say half-past seven. We'll talk."

She shot him a suspicious glance.

"Don't worry. I'm not going to hit on you. My parent's will be home and you can bring some of your friends if you would like, so long as you can vouch for their discreteness."

"And if I decline?"

Robby glanced subtly towards Sarah and Porter. Kelly followed it and saw Mr. Bauer had stopped by the two's lab table and was nodding approvingly at their dissection work.

Robby grinned. "Then rumor has it that in addition to stealing your part in the school play, you're looking at the two *new* sophomore class homecoming courtiers."

A wave of jealousy washed over Kelly at Robby's obvious jab. Loosing the coveted part of the princess in the school play to Sarah Weston had been bad enough. Losing her spot on the homecoming court to the new girl would be unbearable. "Never. No way," she hissed under her breath, even though she suspected The Undertaker might be right. "I know for a fact Bradley Masterson and I will be elected to the court."

"I wouldn't be so sure," said Robby. "If I were you, I might start preparing myself to attend the dance as a mere, mortal student. Unless, of course, you stop by my parents' house tonight."

Kelly and her friends Paulette Summers and Larry White neared Robby Lee's house at around eight that evening. It was cold for mid-October, and their breath formed jets of vapor as they walked along the dimly-lit street bordered on each side by large, deep yards and near-mansion-sized homes.

"I can't believe we're actually going to Robby Lee's house," said Paulette, looking nervously around. "What a creepy guy. Are you sure about this?" She rubbed her hands together a few times before thrusting them back into her coat pockets to keep warm. "And it's creepy around here too. All these spooky, old houses and gnarly, old trees. Who would ever want to live in Kendell's Historic District, anyway?" As she spoke a breeze rustled down upon them through the twisted branches of an ancient oak towering overhead. An owl hidden nearby hooted at the same instant and Paulette jumped in fright, yelping out a little scream as she left the ground.

"Rich people, that's who," said Kelly. "And we're going because I think he's got something on Weston the Witch."

Larry offered Paulette his elbow and she gripped it tightly. "Come on, chicken."

"Robby's not so bad," continued Kelly as they walked along. "He just has a few issues when it comes to his clothing preferences. He thinks the 'all black, all the time, look' will be back in fashion soon. Besides, why do you think we brought Larry with us?"

"Lee's a weasel," piped Larry. "If he didn't help me and the other guys with our math homework he'd be smacked around on a daily basis just for dressing so weird." He pounded the clenched fist of one hand into the palm of another to emphasize the point. "Freak."

Kelly glanced at Larry's blond dreadlocks, distressed varsity jacket, and red and white striped trousers. "You're one to talk," she said with a laugh as they reached their destination. Raising a piece of paper towards the nearest street light, she read it before turning to look at the address on a plaque situated at the end of a long driveway. "This is it. 1320 Lake Avenue." They went up the street a little further and turned onto the walkway leading to the house's front porch.

"I should have guessed," said Larry as they approached the large, brooding, Italianate-style house: the kind which was popular with the wealthy at the end of the nineteenth century, with long, narrow windows, rounded turrets at each corner, and at least three floors. "Looks like something out of one of those old horror flicks."

Except for a couple of windows, the house was completely darkened. Not even the porch light was on. They quietly crept up the creaky, wooden steps leading to its entrance, then stopped and waited.

Paulette gripped Larry's elbow even tighter and began pulling him back towards the stairs. "Come on, let's get out of here. If he's got something on Weston he can tell us at school on Monday. There's nobody home."

"Let's just make sure," said Kelly, pressing a glowing button set within an ornate bronze fixture next to the house's massive front door. "I don't know about you two, but I'm freezing. And I didn't come all this way just to turn around again. He better be home."

A bell could be heard echoing somewhere deep within the bowels of the house, followed by some heavy, approaching footsteps, which stopped at the opposite side of the door. With a muffled click light streamed out of a peephole set within it. The peephole dimmed.

"Too bad," griped Paulette, stamping her foot in disappointment.

There were a couple more clicks before the doorknob turned and light from within the house flooded the porch. "You're late!" snapped Robby. "I've got people waiting. You should've called."

"Aren't you going to invite us in?" asked Kelly in her sweetest voice, ignoring Robby's remark completely. How could he not expect them to be fashionably late?

"Of course I'm going to invite you in. Come in. Come in," replied Robby testily. "It's just that we've got everything set up and Jimmy has to go home in a little while." He opened the door and hustled them in. "Hi, Paulette. Hi, Larry," he said in turn. Once they were all inside he seemed to brighten a bit. "I'm glad you all stopped by." Then he raised his finger to his lips. "Shush. My folks are entertaining some of my dad's clients in the dining room. We need to be quiet until we get upstairs. Follow me."

Kelly, Larry, and Paulette were practically in shock as they followed Robby up the gleaming, twisting, carpeted staircase leading up and up to the third floor of the mostly darkened house. They had never seen him like this before. He was dressed in blue jeans, tennis shoes, and a *Swampy KLOMP* rocker T-shirt. The Undertaker actually wears regular clothes! Wait until the kids at school hear about this. Everyone thought that at home Robby probably wore a funeral shroud. At the top of the stairs he led them to a door beyond which was a second, even steeper stairway. "This is the way to my playroom," he said, starting up it.

Their footsteps echoed loudly in the narrow, wooden passageway at first, but as they climbed the sound of their own movements was quickly drowned out by the strains of screeching Rip Rap music.

Robby cursed under his breath and quickly jogged up the final few stairs. Flying across the top landing, he wrenched open a door on its opposite side and loud, painful, music immediately blasted out. "Hey! I told you guys to keep it down!" he shouted as he went inside.

Paulette immediately clapped her hands over her ears. "I hate Rip Rap music!" she shouted to be heard over the high-pitched, poorly articulated, noise.

"What?" shouted Kelly, now shielding her ears as well.

The music stopped.

Paulette breathed a sigh of relief and lowered her hands. "I said I hate Rip Rap music," she repeated, this time in a more subdued tone.

Robby poked his head out from the door and waved at them. "Come in; this way. Don't be shy."

They walked through the door and found themselves in a large, modern-looking space which was undoubtedly a finished attic. Race car and rock group poster-covered walls angled oddly upward towards a flat ceiling in a reverse image of the house's roof. With the exception of some skylights the room was completely windowless—which made it feel closed and cramp, despite its size. Jimmy Luntz and Martin Wooten, two of Robby's scrawny, braces-clad, computer geek friends were there. Both were wearing identical outfits: red and white-stripped polo shirts and black cotton jeans. They were ribbing each other and giggling as they adjusted a digital camera resting on a tripod in front of a green, plastic screen supported upright by ropes attached to the ceiling. A cable from the camera snaked down to and across the floor to a multileveled desk supporting several different sized monitors and an array of neatly positioned modular computer components. The setup looked like the control console of some futuristic spaceship. An old fashioned, folded-up, white laminate drafting table and some chairs sat on the opposite side of the room—pushed out of the way to make room for the screen, tripod, and camera.

Robby turned to his guests. "Take off your coats. Make yourselves at home. You know Jimmy and Martin, right?"

The two boys stopped what they were doing, looked over, and waved. "Hi guys," they said. Jimmy then gave Kelly a particularly long, leering look before returning to whatever adjustments they were making to the camera.

"We've seen them around," replied Kelly coolly, now suspicious of whatever it was Robby had in mind.

"Where's Bradley?" asked Robby. "I thought you never left home without the Big Man on Campus."

"Recovering from football practice," replied Kelly.

"What's with the screen?" Larry cut in rudely, taking off his coat to reveal a sleeveless Kendell wrestling sweatshirt. "I didn't come over here to see a movie." He tossed it on a chair and helped the girls with theirs. "Start talking, Lee," he growled, cracking his knuckles before stretching out his large, muscular arms in a dominance display.

Robby ignored Larry's thinly veiled threat, muttering, "Dumb jock." Then, looking over at Kelly and Paulette, he gave a low whistle, beaming at what he saw. "Wow. You girls shouldn't have dressed up just for me." he said, smiling broadly at them. "Are those designer outfits?"

Paulette, a doe-eyed beauty with long, reddish-brown hair, was dressed in a black, knotted, knit blouse and dark-golden leather pants sporting a red and gold floral pattern at the waist.

Kelly, on the other hand, was accentuating her beauty this fine October evening with a long-sleeved, Champaign-colored blouse which puffed out at the wrists, and black Venetian crepe pants. Both girls would have looked nearly as beautiful wearing sackcloths and ashes.

"We didn't," clipped Paulette, rolling her eyes.

"And they are," added Kelly, with a flip of her pretty, blond head.

"All the better, my lovelies! All the better. Come on, Kelly. Follow me." Walking over to his control center, he scooted a single chair next to his specially wired throne, then sat down before pointing at Kelly and then to the chair. "Have a seat, gorgeous." His imitation of Humphrey Bogart would have been laughable had it been at all recognizable.

They followed him and Kelly sat down.

"Okay, Jimmy. Get ready!" called Robby over his shoulder. "Martin, turn the digital camera on." He placed the palm of his left hand on a metal pad on his chair's armrest. As he did, a mental command was transmitted from his brain, through his palm, past the metal pad interface, and into his computer's processor.

The largest of the computer monitors flashed on, displaying Jimmy standing in front of the green screen. After a moment the image rippled and Jimmy appeared to be standing in a classroom at North Kendell High School. "How do I look?" he said, waving at them through the camera lens. His voice could be heard emanating both from within the room and through a speaker buried somewhere within Robby's equipment.

"Like a mope," muttered Larry, leaning over Kelly's chair to watch, before craning his head around over his shoulder, where he saw Jimmy standing in front of the green screen, waving at the camera.

Kelly and Paulette looked back and forth a couple of times as well. It was obvious the waving Jimmy in the video classroom and the waving Jimmy behind them were one and the same. "How did you do that?" exclaimed Kelly.

"Old fashioned Hollywood special effects technique coupled with modern computer technology. It's really quite simple so long as you're a genius like me. Now watch this."

The image on the computer screen split. On the left stood Jimmy, now making faces at Martin. On the right was a candid, still photograph of Porter Smith walking down a school hallway at roughly the same scale.

"Notice anything?"

They studied the split screen for a few seconds before Paulette blurted out, "They're wearing the same clothes! Red and white stripped polo shirts, black jeans, and white tennis shoes."

"Anything else?"

"They're about the same height, except Porter is built better and is much cuter," said Kelly.

"He's a mope, too," added Larry.

"I'm afraid I must agree with you on that one," said Robby. "What's worse, he has stolen my girl and with Kelly's help I intend to get her back."

"Your girl?" chuckled Larry with amusement. "Since when was Sarah Weston ever your girl?"

"She is. She just doesn't know it yet."

"What do mean, 'My help?'" cried Kelly. "I thought you had some dirt on her!"

"Dirt?" Robby turned his head and shot Kelly an incredulous look. "Dirt? Sarah's perfect I hope you know, except for her current choice in boyfriends."

Kelly's jaw dropped in disbelief. Weston even had Robby Lee mesmerized! This can't be happening. She fumbled for the right words to let Robby know what a fool he was, then in frustration simply huffed, "Lets go!" before forcefully shoving her chair backwards to stand up.

"Wait!" cried Robby. "What I have in mind will serve both our purposes. Sit. Watch," he pleaded, pointing at the computer screen.

"Yeah," added Larry. "Let's hear him out."

Kelly glared at Larry, who stood back a step and folded his arms. "You said it yourself," he added. "We didn't come all this way for nothing."

"Oh, all right," she huffed back when it was clear Larry wouldn't blindly obey her command. *What's the world coming to?* she added to herself, sitting back down again. "Show me what you have in mind." She crossed her arms and pouted.

Robby nodded appreciatively towards Larry for his help and returned to his demonstration. "The lovely Ms. Martino will not be disappointed."

As they all watched, the split screen disappeared and the image of Jimmy filled it again. Then his face blurred over and reappeared after a moment as the spitting image of Porter Smith.

Larry, Paulette, and Kelly all leaned forward in amazement. Larry pointed at the monitor and laughed. "He's turned Jimmy into Porter Smith! Too radical, Lee. *You Rad*."

Robby grinned. "You ain't seen nothing yet, brother. Okay Jimmy, I've got the image and voice modulation stabilized. You may begin your performance. And this time don't ad lib. And no clowning around either! Martin, give us a close-up of poor, lovesick Porter's face."

Jimmy stopped clowning around and looked into the camera's lens. On Robby's screen the view closed in and fixed upon the face of Porter Smith—the mask Robby's computer had created. After assuming an expression of pure longing the mask began pleading to Kelly. "Oh, Kelly. You know you're the one I love. Sarah Weston means nothing to me. She's just a friend. You're the one I want to go with to the homecoming dance. Please, oh please, won't you go with me. I promise I'll never speak to Sarah again." While the words were in Jimmy's voice in the background, they emerged from the hidden speaker as that of Porter Smith's. It sounded like the two boys were performing a duet.

Kelly blushed as Larry and Paulette craned to get a good look at the computer-generated image.

"This is too weird, Robby," said Paulette. "It looks just like Porter Smith. Same sandy-blond hair and blue eyes. Same nose and dimples. Same high cheek bones and round chin. It sounds just like him too. But, why do you have him asking Kelly out? Everyone knows he's going to the dance with Weston."

"Why? Because jealousy and scorn are very powerful emotions, that's why. How would you feel if you found out Larry was about to dump you for another girl?"

"I'd kill him and never speak to him again!" declared Paulette without hesitation.

Larry patted her reassuringly on the shoulder. "You're the only girl for me."

"I'm certain you're using the word 'kill' in the pejorative and not the literal," said Robby. "I would hate for anyone to get killed. Wounded in the heart, perhaps. I only intend to use my fake Porter Smith recording to drive a wedge between the two lovebirds right before the homecoming court election. It's for Sarah's own good. If I'm successful she will be so angry and hurt she'll never want to see Smith again. She'll withdraw her nomination and neither one will be going to the dance. Both our problems will be solved. I'll get Sarah and you and Beefy Boy will be elected to the homecoming court."

"I don't see how you are going to use that recording for anything," said Kelly. Sure, Porter looks real and if anyone could make another girl jealous it would be me, but it's just him looking into a camera lens."

Plucking a sheet of paper from a printer tray, Robby offered it to her. "That's where you come in. What you've seen so far is a demonstration of my equipment close to its maximum processing capacity. It's good, but I can't generate the school background *and* two faked images at the same time and still have everything look absolutely, 100 percent real. I need you to perform a little skit with Jimmy in front of the green screen. On the recording it will look like you and Porter Smith have been caught on camera in, how shall I say, 'An awkward moment.'"

Kelly took the short script and began reading. It started with the lines Jimmy had just delivered. When she got to the next part she screamed and laughed. "No way, Lee!" she shouted in disbelief, tossing the paper back down on Robby's desk. "There's no way in a million years I'm going to kiss Jimmy Luntz, especially on camera."

At this, Jimmy and the image of Porter said, "Hey!" in unison. Maybe they wouldn't be planting one on the girl of their dreams after all.

Robby picked up the paper and offered it back to her. "You won't be kissing Jimmy Luntz, Porter Smith will be kissing you—on camera, anyway. It's only a little peck on the cheek. Read the end. You get to give the forward, presumptuous dog a good slap in the face before you reject him."

"Yeah, come on," pleaded Larry, now caught up in Robby's scheme. He didn't hate Porter Smith or anything, but thought he might have a shot at dating Sarah Weston if Smith was out of the way.

"You're in the drama club," pressed Robby, appealing to her sense of professionalism. "It shouldn't be too difficult. You kissed Alan Holmes in last year's school play."

"Yeah, but Alan Holmes is cute," she grumbled, grabbing the script back from him. She read through it again and considered the alternatives. Something had to be done about Sarah Weston, and soon, or it might be too late. If Kelly lost the homecoming vote she'd have to play second fiddle to the new girl from England for the rest of the year; maybe even for the rest of high school. She'd never played second fiddle to anyone or anything in her life! And the election was on October 15th—about a week away. The homecoming dance was a week later on the 22nd. If Robby's scheme worked, Weston probably would withdraw her nomination, English pride being what it is. She certainly wouldn't discover she'd been tricked until after the election, if at all. The more Kelly thought about it, the more she believed Robby's plan might actually work. It would certainly send Weston for a loop, and might actually draw her into Kelly's clique—as a subordinate member, of course. "If I agree to do this, how will you get Weston to look at it? She avoids you like the plague."

Robby seethed at the truth of Kelly's statement for a moment before collecting himself. "*She* will ask me to show it to her. Curiosity killed the kitten, you know. First I'll show the recording to her new, but devoted friend Lisa Collins on my portavid." He plucked what looked like two pens from a container on his desk and pulled them apart. As he did, a paper-thin video screen unrolled and stretched taught between them. He pressed a virtual button on the screen and held it up for all to see as a *Scream'n Demon* Rip Rap video roared painfully to life.

The girls clapped their hands over their ears again. "Turn that noise off," cried Paulette.

Robby grinned, shaking his head and pressing another button on the device. The music stopped and the screen scrolled closed again. "You no like *Scream'n Demon*?" he asked, placing the closed portavid back down on his desk. "Anyway, Lisa and I are friends from grade school. After I show her our faked video, she'll run to Sarah and tell her of Porter Smith's betrayal. Lisa is quite a busybody you know. Sarah will seek me out to confirm it with her own pretty, green eyes. I can't wait to see them well up with tears of heartbreak when she sees it. I'll be there to console and comfort her in her hour of need."

"You're evil and ruthless, Robby, do you know that?"

"Evil? Perhaps. Ruthless? Definitely!" He looked at his watch. "Well, Kelly. What do you say? We don't have much time. Jimmy has to leave soon."

Kelly studied the script again and stood up. "I'll do it under conditions."

Robby smiled, standing himself. "Name them."

"You do not copy the original recording. No emails. No back-up computer files. Nothing."

"Certainly."

"I want the original destroyed after you show it to Weston."

"Done."

"If anyone asks, I'm going to say I don't know anything about any vid recording or Porter Smith making a pass at me."

"Good. That'll make you look discreet. Just because you slapped and rejected the cad doesn't mean you have to advertise it."

Kelly pointed at Jimmy and Martin, who were standing nearby and closely listening to her negotiations with Lee. At the moment she agreed to participate in the elaborate hoax, the two geeks had done a high-five hand slap followed by some sort of goofy victory dance. "Not a word of me ever letting Jimmy Luntz kiss me. From any of you," she added, her eyes meeting Jimmy's and then Martin's. "If I find out either of you are bragging around school about it, Larry is going to see to it you spend some quality time in the hospital. Right, Larry?"

Larry's face became a mask of stone, cold brutality as he quickly advanced to within arm's length of the boys. He pointed the finger of his right hand and jabbed it forcefully into Jimmy's chest. He turned and did the same to Martin. "Not a word. Swear it!"

Jimmy and Martin fell back fearfully, rubbing their chests before quickly raising their right hands as if taking an oath.

"Not a word. I swear!"

"Never, never. So help me!"

"Anything else?" asked Robby, frowning at what he considered an unnecessary show of force.

"That should do it," replied Kelly. "Let's get this over with." Tossing the script into the air, she turned towards the green screen.

"Hey, my script!" shouted Robby. "You promised."

"I don't need your script. I'm a method actor. Just let us know when we're in position. Paulette, you can direct. Larry, you keep an eye on Robby's computer so he doesn't try anything funny. Come on guys," called Kelly to Jimmy and Martin as she and Paulette strode confidently towards the green screen and camera set up. The boys obeyed immediately, falling in behind the girls like lovesick puppies.

Robby looked at Larry. "Method actor?"

Larry shrugged. "They're taking an acting course. Don't ask me." He motioned towards Robby's command chair. "Sit down and fire up your machine again. I can't wait to see this." And then under his breath and out the side of his mouth as Robby sat down, "You better never even think of pulling a stunt like this on me or the guys."

"Never in life, my good fellow," replied Robby as he activated his equipment again. After a few moments the main computer monitor flashed to life again, revealing Kelly, Paulette, and Jimmy standing in front of the green screen. Paulette began nudging Kelly and Jimmy back and forth, trying to get them into the right position. Jimmy looked like he was enjoying himself immensely.

"Jimmy doesn't get out much, does he, Lee?" asked Larry, sitting down in Kelly's chair to watch.

Robby ignored Larry's comment and issued another mental command to his computer equipment, which beeped in reply as the image on the monitor's screen rippled and Kelly, Paulette, and Jimmy appeared to be standing in one of the locker-lined hallways of North Kendell High School.

After positioning Kelly and Jimmy just so, Paulette looked into the camera's lens. "How's that Robby?"

Robby studied the screen. Both Kelly's and Jimmy's faces would be visible during their performance. Paulette, in fact, had done a much better job of positioning them than he had been able to accomplish during his trial rehearsals with Jimmy and Martin. "That's perfect," he called out. "She's really good," he added to Larry.

Paulette disappeared off camera and Jimmy and Kelly were left alone in the imaginary school hallway. Kelly looked confident. Jimmy, for the first time, looked nervous.

Robby issued another command and Jimmy's head fogged over on the screen and reappeared as Porter Smith's. After stabilizing the image and voice modulation, he started his data recorder and called out over his shoulder again. "We're rolling. They're all yours, Paulette."

Paulette, who was now standing behind Martin as he peered into the camera's eyepiece, shouted, "Action!"

As Robby and Larry watched, Porter Smith delivered his opening lines, confessing his love of Kelly, his antipathy towards Sarah, and his begging invitation to the homecoming dance. Kelly simply looked back at him pitifully, like he was some poor, misguided soul. Then, immediately after he said, "I promise I will never speak to Sarah again," Jimmy sprang like a tiger, grabbing Kelly in a one-sided embrace and mashing his lips onto hers like a big, hungry suckerfish; planting an awkward kiss right on her mouth.

Kelly's eyes bulged in surprise for a fraction of a second before she began beating on Jimmy's shoulders; twisting and struggling to break free. They wrestled around for a bit and when Jimmy finally let go she hauled off and slapped him so hard across the face his head snapped sidewise and he nearly fell over.

Robby and Larry stamped their feet in merriment, watching the act unfolding on Robby's computer screen; struggling mightily to keep from howling in laughter.

Paulette's jaw dropped in disbelief at the force of Kelly's blow to poor, Jimmy's face.

Jimmy, now holding both hands over his blooming, cherry-red cheek, bravely recovered himself, standing back up again to confront a fiery-eyed Kelly.

"How dare you grab me!" shouted Kelly, rubbing the sides of her arms and the painful palm of her right hand. "You hurt me. And how dare you kiss me! Sarah's my friend and I would never do anything to hurt her feelings."

Jimmy and his Porter Smith-generated counterpart hung their heads in silence and shame.

"I won't go with you to the homecoming dance," fumed Kelly. "Not now. Not ever. And don't you ever lay a hand on me again! Ever!" She then softened a bit at the sight of the injured and dumbstruck Jimmy. "I'm not going to mention this to anyone, Porter. If you're smart, you'll come to your senses and stick with Sarah. She's the best thing that ever happened to you." Tossing her head, she turned and stormed off camera.

"Cut!" cried Paulette.

Larry, Robby, and Paulette all burst into applause at the conclusion of the performance.

"That was perfect Kelly and Jimmy!" declared Robby. "Perfect on one take. Come and see it. Come and see the recording. Porter Smith is doomed! Doomed, I say!"

Martin abandoned his camera, but instead of going to watch Robby's recording he ran over to Jimmy and pulled him out of earshot of the others. "Was it worth it? Was a kiss with Kelly Martino worth the slap?"

Rubbing his sore cheek, Jimmy glanced over to make sure none of the other conspirators were listening before looking back at his friend and smiling broadly. "You bet your life it was!"

Clash! Clang! Clash!

"I see your sword no longer sleeps in your hand, Sir Falcon," chided Kevin Horner, parrying a series of thrusts from Porter's blunt theater prop sword. His face, hawkish and lean, was working up into a healthy pink color from the exertion of battle.

"Aye. It is not easily stirred," shouted Porter as they practiced the sword fight scene for the school play. Both boys were dressed in loose-fitting cotton sweatpants and baggy "N.K.H.S." athletic T-shirts, which swirled over their wiry limbs as they fought. *Clang!* Parry. Thrust. More quick, precise movements and the thump of sure feet. "But once awakened in defense of true love, it shall not sleep until it vanquishes those who would dare try to rend such love apart!"

Their blades clashed again as they began an elaborate and noisy series of thrusts, parries, and counterattacks back and forth across the stage, all of which was punctuated with shouts of the play's rehearsed dialogue.

"Rend apart?" cried Kevin, trying to keep from laughing as he delivered the mushy lines in a rather poor French accent. Porter had talked him into auditioning for the play because they were sparring partners on Kendell High's fencing team. Porter thought the two of them could really spice up the fight scene climax at the end of the second act—since they were so used to each other's fencing moves and techniques. They were really hamming it up and having a blast. "Ha! The only thing that shall be 'rended' is thy head from thy body!" Kevin made a roundhouse swoosh with his blade and Porter jumped back out of the way just in time.

"Oh! Be careful, my love!" cried Sarah, bolting up from her chair on stage and raising her hands to her mouth in fear. Her English accent and poise had made her an easy choice for the part of the play's beautiful, lovelorn princess. Although this wasn't a dress rehearsal, her long, blue skirt and sleeveless, white blouse made her look like royalty, anyway. She had her hair twisted up in the back in a way that added to the effect nicely.

"Your choice of words is wise, for they could apply to either knight, my dear," declared Kelly Martino coldly from a director's chair set up on a small platform in the center of the stage. Kelly had to settle for the role of the evil, contemptuous queen in the play. And while today, like most days, she looked more like a runway model than aged royalty— being dressed in a sleeveless, black cashmere top, zebra print Ottoman pants, and black patent leather pumps—her obvious enmity towards Sarah made her own performance so powerful that had she been on Broadway, she'd probably be nominated for a Tony Award. "I would advise additional caution, for professions of love to the wrong person can serve to sour one's reputation in the House of Kendell."

It suddenly dawned on Kelly that the lines were prophetic. In a short while Robby would hatch his scheme to drive Sarah and Porter apart and tomorrow was the homecoming court election. She pursed her lips at the thought, smirking inwardly. If things went as planned, neither would be attending the dance. Instead, Porter Smith and Miss Goody Two Shoes would be history and Kelly and her date, Bradley Masterson, would once again be slated as the undeniable class homecoming courtiers. At least her problem would be solved. The likelihood of Robby Lee ever convincing Weston to date him, she believed, was still less than a degree above absolute zero. She wondered why such a calculating, observant—albeit evil—person like Robby couldn't see it. It was almost as if Weston had unknowingly cast a spell over The Undertaker. In reality, Porter's bookworm friend Henry Dundridge probably had a better chance of hooking up with Weston. *Robert Lee*, she thought. *Poor, delusional fool.*

As Kelly gloated over what she hoped was the looming demise of the Smith and Weston relationship, Porter and Kevin continued dueling to and fro across the stage. Between the flashes of blades under the bright theater lights and the clanging of metal they recited their lines and traded barbs which their schoolmate Randall King, the play's young writer, had crafted in an attempt to pay homage to the spirit of the Great Shakespeare. An attempt which, although well intended, had come off campy and, well, sophomoric. King was standing in the wings, silently mouthing dialogue along with the boys and grimacing every now and then as his precious lines were poorly or incorrectly delivered.

On and on Porter and Kevin fought, and just when it looked like the evil French knight might actually prevail, Sir Falcon engaged in some incredible sword play and vanquished his opponent with a single, quick, rather fake looking, blade stroke beneath Kevin's left armpit. The astonished Sir Duard dropped his sword, gave out an, "Ugh!" and rolled his eyes back in mock agony as Porter mercilessly shoved him off his own sword with his foot. Kevin, trying not to laugh, fell heavily to the stage floor, where he began rolling around: twitching, moaning, and dying a slow, equally unconvincing, death.

As called for in the script, once Sir Duard gave his last death rattle, Porter hung his head, flinging down his sword and falling to his knees at center stage; trying to look anguished and exhausted. *Now for the best part*, he thought as he started to catch his breath.

Sarah bolted from her chair again and ran to Porter's aid. "Sir Falcon! Sir Falcon!" she cried, carefully kneeling next to him and tenderly helping him to his feet. "You've won! You've vanquished the evil Sir Duard!" She looked over at Kelly, whose angry frown was ever so convincing because it was real, and back over to the victorious Porter. "Now you can rightly claim your title as King to the House of Kendell. Oh, Edward. Sir Edward Falcon. Now we can be together, always."

They held hands and looked searchingly into each other's eyes—just like Mrs. Lawrence, the drama teacher, had rehearsed them—and Porter said, "Aye. And you shall be my queen, Princess Serena," embracing her as the theater lights slowly faded into darkness, signaling the end of the second act.

Unseen by anyone else, Porter and Sarah continued embracing on that silent, pitch-black stage. She was holding him tighter than she had during prior rehearsals and he responded in kind. And it was in that fleeting moment—that rarefied instant in which it felt like they were alone in the universe—his memory of this day became indelibly etched in his mind under the heading: "Perfect." The warmth of her breath on his neck. The rhythmic *thump, thump, thump* of their hearts beating together. Just the two of them. The smell of her hair. This was a day he would always remember. A memory which would help sustain him through the turmoils of life which would certainly come. Then, just before they reluctantly parted, as they both knew they must, Sarah gently pushed him away, stood on her tiptoes, and gave him a quick kiss on the cheek. "You were wonderful!" she whispered in his ear just as the theater lights came back up again. She blushed beautifully and ran off stage before anyone else could see.

"Very nice performance, everyone!" shouted Mrs. Lawrence, clapping and standing up in the front row facing the re-lit stage.

Porter barely heard her. He had never kissed, or been kissed by, a girl before and suddenly realized that, despite his recent workout on stage, his heart was racing in a way he'd never experienced before. Blushing, he looked down in confusion for a moment, then back up again to see where Sarah had ran off to when he felt a slap on his shoulder.

"You're one lucky devil," said Kevin, now completely resurrected from his theater death.

Porter looked over at him. *Had Kevin seen?* he dreaded, still quite shy of having a first girlfriend. "How do you mean?"

"Being in this play. How else would you ever beat me in a sword fight?"

Porter breathed a sigh of relief.

"Very nice performance, boys," called Ms. Lawrence. "Very nice. Very realistic. Only Kevin, you must try not to smirk and giggle so much. It distracts from the severity of the performance. It almost looks like your character, Sir Duard, actually enjoys being killed by Sir

Falcon. As I've told you time and time again, this play is a tragedy, not a comedy."

"I'll try to remember that," replied Kevin, stooping over to pick up his prop sword.

"Good. Okay everyone, that's all for today!" she shouted, clapping her hands again. "Keep practicing your lines and I'll see you all back here again tomorrow afternoon. And good luck to all the homecoming court nominees."

Porter's heart leapt at the sudden mention of the homecoming court election. All he wanted to do was go to the dance with Sarah and have a good time. He would kill whoever it was who had nominated them as the sophomore class representatives to the court and secretly hoped they wouldn't be elected. All his friends had taken to good-natured teasing over the nomination, calling him the "Homecoming Sissy." Porter didn't like to be teased, even if it was good-natured.

Sarah, on the other hand, was simply thrilled over the election. "Quite an honor just to be nominated," she had said.

Sarah Weston. He glowed at the thought of her and touched his cheek where she had kissed him. He could still feel its warmth and hoped the sensation would never go away. "Is this what love feels like?" he wondered, searching for her again among the young actors who were chatting in the wings or slowly wandering away. He finally spotted her standing off to the side of the stage near the theater curtains; talking to a couple of kids who were sitting on the floor painting the background scenery. She glanced up at him and beamed a radiant smile before returning to her conversation.

"Yes!" he concluded as a wave of giddy happiness and youthful energy swept over him. He joyously retrieved his prop sword and brandished it at Kevin, who was standing nearby and saying something to Richard about Sir Falcon probably being a homecoming court sissy too. "Lucky, huh? I'll have you know Richard's play is remarkably accurate in its portrayal of the better swordsman. On guard!"

Shaking his head, Kevin raised his own sword and crossed it with Porter's. "You'll never learn, will you, Smith," he replied, assuming a defensive fencing stance. "On guard!"

Richard jumped out of the way as the two boys resumed their noisy sparring back and forth across the stage, blades flashing and clanging.

Kelly, still atop her jury-rigged throne—her real one still under construction in the school's wood shop—silently watched the boys before glancing over to where Weston the Witch was standing in the wings. *Robby must have shown that busybody Lisa Collins his faked recording by now!* she thought. Where was she? Kelly looked at her watch and when she finally looked over again she saw Lisa running up to Sarah. "Bingo!" she exclaimed under her breath as Lisa pulled on Sarah's arm to get her attention before frantically speaking with her, pointing every now and then towards the stage. Soon Sarah was shaking her head no. Kelly thought fast. Maybe she could help things along. "Porter Smith!" she shouted so everyone in the theater could hear.

The boys stopped dueling and looked over at her.

"Yes?" replied Porter.

"Be a gentleman and help me down from this platform. I'm wearing heels."

What's she up to? wondered Porter. Ever since he and Sarah started hanging around together, Kelly had barely spoken to him. "Come on, Kevin, let's help Kelly down."

"My pleasure," said Kevin. "She's fantastic," he added under his breath. "And will you look at that outfit! No wonder I can't remember my lines. I can barely concentrate on the play."

Kelly glanced over at Sarah and Lisa as the boys approached from across the stage. Her rival was watching the unfolding drama closely. "Keep watching, girls," she murmured. "Keep watching."

Poor, dumb, Porter—oblivious to the trap he was falling into—walked over to Kelly and offered her his elbow.

Kevin bowed with a flourish and offered his as well. "May we assist your highness?"

Kelly ignored Kevin altogether, gripping Porter's arm tightly. Then, rising from her chair, she faked a trip and fell straight at him.

Porter quickly cast his sword aside and caught her by the waist, while she pressed herself into his chest. "Hey! Be careful, Kelly. Are you okay?" he said, gently pushing her away and steadying her on the stage floor.

"Thanks," she said, brushing her hand through her hair and batting her pretty blue eyes at him. Smiling, she reached over and squeezed the sides of his upper arms. "You're a lot stronger than you look."

Porter blushed, looking down bashfully. "You're welcome," he replied. "Try to be more careful."

"I will. You are a sweetheart, you know that?" she added, before walking off stage. After passing by Sarah, she turned around and called out to him again. "And sorry about the other day, but you should have asked me sooner. Maybe next year." She then caught Sarah's eye and gave her an "I know something you don't" smirk before quickly disappearing off stage.

Kevin looked at Porter, who simply shrugged. "I have no idea what she's talking about," said Porter, picking up his sword again as the two renewed their loud, raucous dueling.

"See? See? I told you!" implored Lisa, tugging on Sarah's arm again. "He asked her out to the homecoming dance. He tried to kiss her! I saw it with my own two eyes on Robby's portavid. Now Kelly's having second thoughts. I told you she and Bradley are having a fight. I told you Porter had a major crush on her last year."

A look of concern and hurt flashed across Sarah's face, followed by a stoic frown as she collected herself, showing that famous English stiff upper lip. "I do not care what you think you saw, Lisa. I know Porter and I know he would never do such a dreadful thing to me. It's unthinkable and I will not see Robert Lee or his fake recording. I don't care if you two do go way back. I appreciate your concern, but let's not speak of this further. Porter and I are going to be elected to the homecoming court tomorrow. We're going to go to the dance next week and we're going to have a fabulous time together. Now good day to you," she concluded, turning her back on Lisa.

"I know what I saw, Sarah," said Lisa flatly. "That recording was real. Porter doesn't deserve you!" she added, hurt that Sarah had practically accused her of being a liar.

"I said good day to you," repeated Sarah sternly over her shoulder.

Frowning, Lisa quickly walked away.

"What do you mean she won't see it!" cried Kelly as the group of coconspirators paced back and forth in the late-afternoon sunshine next to the bleachers ringing North Kendell High's athletic field. "You said she'd come running to see it. The election is tomorrow!"

"What are you going to do now, Lee?" grumbled Larry White. He'd been trying to flirt with Sarah all week—discretely, of course—so he could make his move when the time was right. He had his heart set on consoling and ultimately hooking up with Sarah once Smith was toasted by Robby's scheme. The Undertaker would get a fat lip for his efforts and Paulette—well Paulette would just have to get over him. It would be difficult, but she would get over Larry.

"Do you think I am not disappointed as well?" said Robby, tugging nervously at the collar of his black silk shirt. "It's obvious Sarah Weston is more devoted to Porter Smith than I realized. It's obvious that drastic measures are required!" He stopped his pacing, turned towards Kelly and Paulette, and pointed at Kelly. "I guarantee you she *will* see the recording and that you, Ms. Martino, will be on the homecoming court."

"How? How can you guarantee it?" shouted Kelly angrily.

"You leave that to me," replied Robby.

Larry gave Robby a good shove in the shoulder and pointed his finger at him. "You better not mess this up Lee," he threatened.

Robby glared at Larry, rubbing his shoulder. "Jimmy and Martin, you come with me," he finally said to the two computer geeks sitting silently nearby in the bleachers, who sprang up and ran over to his side. "There is much to do before tomorrow morning."

CHAPTER FOUR: A WITCH'S SCORN

Porter was fidgeting. He never fidgeted, but couldn't seem to help himself, waiting for the homeroom session to begin. "Stupid homecoming court election," he grumbled under his breath so no one else could hear. "I'll be glad when the whole, stupid thing is over with."

Noticing his friend's nervousness, Henry leaned towards Porter from his adjacent desk in the rather Spartan room: beige floor tile, beige cinderblock walls, rows of smartly-dressed students sitting at small, wood-topped desks made of twisted, brown, metal bars, facing the teacher's somewhat larger one, also beige, and a wide, rectangular blackboard hanging centered on the wall facing all, except for the teacher's, which faced those of the students. "Don't worry," he said lowly. "If you win, you win. You'll go to the dance and have a great time. The guys know you're not a sissy. If you lose, you still win, because you'll be with Sarah, who's probably the most beautiful girl on the planet. Your in what they call a 'win, win' situation. The catbird seat, as they say."

"I know," replied Porter, looking down at his red shirt, smoothing and adjusting it just so. "I never was one for popularity contests. I just wanted to go and have a good time. What a dilemma."

Henry straightened in his seat. "If only *I* were to be faced with such a dilemma," he said, running his hand through his wavy, brown hair, before looking down at his own, nondescript beige shirt and realizing if he stood next to the wall he would disappear like a chameleon. "I couldn't even find a date. I'll be spending the night at home," he griped. "Why is it the girls around here just don't appreciate brains?"

"You're too picky."

"Too picky?" exclaimed Henry in astonishment. "Too picky? I..."

Henry's sentence was cut off by the sound of the public address system beeping, followed by the room lights dimming and the blackboard lighting up inside to form a large television screen. All the kids moaned at the sound because it heralded the start of the Thursday edition of *What's Happening*—a short, student-produced broadcast everyone had to suffer through at precisely quarter-past eight every morning. The program's kettledrum intro-music blared as the screen filled with the smiling faces of Ted Corinth and Carrie Letterman, sitting like two shiny, new pennies behind the news anchor desk in North Kendell High's very own TV studio.

"Good Morning," beamed Carrie, always way too chipper for such an early hour. "Welcome to *What's Happening*. As you all know, Kendell High's homecoming dance is only one week away. The Student Committee is holding the courtier election today, so remember to fill in and return your votes to the ballot boxes located in the cafeteria." As she spoke she twisted her head up, down, and to the side in a little triangle, trying to imitate the professional news anchors on real TV. "The results will be broadcast during tomorrow's program. Good luck to all the nominees! Ted?"

"Thanks Carrie. Good morning everyone. For all you astronomy buffs out there who *won't* be attending the dance," he added with a wink.

Henry moaned, leaning forward and bouncing his head on his desktop a couple of times.

"The heavens over Kendell will also yield a rare celestial event next Thursday night," continued Ted. "At precisely 9:43 p.m., a lunar occultation of the planet Mars will be visible from parts of the Midwest. Our own Henry Dundridge has prepared a computer simulation demonstrating what a lunar occultation is. Let's have a look."

The smiling faces of Carrie and Ted faded away to be replaced by a vivid picture of a nearly full Moon suspended in a clear, starlit night. Underneath the image was a logo reading, "Dundridge Productions."

Porter glanced over at Henry. "I didn't know you were working on this."

Henry shot him a dirty, *pipe down* look and said, "Shush," before pointing at the screen. "Watch now; talk later."

"A lunar occultation of Mars is predicted for next Thursday evening at 9:43 p.m.," began Henry's narration from the blackboard screen. "In order to understand and appreciate what this is, a few basic astronomical considerations are in order. To begin with, the right and left sides of the Moon are called 'limbs.' The Moon will appear as a seventy percent waxing gibbous next Thursday. This means that seventy percent of its visible disk will be illuminated: practically a full Moon approaching the middle of its lunar cycle. Only a portion of its left limb will be darkened, and that's where the occultation will commence."

Suddenly a bright, red dot appeared at the middle, upper-left-side of the Moon. A white arrow shot across the screen, then pointed at the dot and flashed a couple of times before disappearing again.

"This is the planet Mars as it will appear to the naked eye next week," the narration continued. "Once in a great while, the path of the Moon positions it between the Red Planet and observers here on the Earth." As he spoke the red dot closed with the darkened left limb of the Moon and disappeared behind it with a spectacular, crimson flash. "This celestial event is referred to as a 'lunar occultation of Mars,' and is only possible because most of the planets and the Moon travel roughly along on the same plane as the Earth in our solar system. In astronomy terms, this plane of travel is called the 'ecliptic.'"

At this, the screen filled with a planetary orbital schematic as Henry explained how the ecliptic worked. At the end of his explanation the image of the Moon reappeared.

"The term 'occultation ' is derived from the word 'occult,' which comes from the Latin 'occultus' or 'occulere' which means 'to conceal.' The word 'occult' also refers to supernatural influences, agencies, or phenomenon." A silhouette of a witch riding a broom zipped across the Moon and into darkness.

Someone in the room shouted, "Scary!" Another cackled like a witch, while several others made loud, snoring sounds.

"Astronomers in the early part of the last century timed lunar occultations in order to obtain important information on the structure of the Solar System. Although current observations of such planetary occultations can reveal little additional information of scientific merit, they're still interesting to amateur astronomers, especially since many can be seen with the naked eye. The lunar occultation of Mars predicted for next Thursday will last for approximately one hour." The red dot finally emerged again on the Moon's right, brightly-lit limb.

"The next one won't be visible from this area for another ten years, so get out and enjoy it." With this the image faded and was replaced by the smiling faces of Carrie and Ted again.

"Thank you, Henry," said Carrie. "That was very interesting and enlightening."

"Yes," added Ted. "Even if you're at the dance, take a peek outside at 9:42 and see if you can get a glimpse of this unusual celestial event. And now…"

Suddenly the blackboard screen rolled with interference and blinked a couple of times. The sound of the broadcast distorted wildly into static before ceasing altogether with a loud, electronic *pop!* Carrie and Ted looked back and forth at one another before their images rippled away; replaced by that of a repulsive, horned cartoon demon with waves of multicolored light pulsing behind it. It was Mephisto, the music video mascot for the rip rapper group *Scream'n Demon*. His arrow-capped tail swished back and forth to the beat of *Scream'n Demon* music that began blaring out of the school's public address system. The music's volume quickly diminished and Mephisto began addressing the entire faculty, staff, and student body of Kendell High in a watery, unidentifiable, and decidedly evil synthetic voice. "We at *Scream'n Productions* interrupt your regularly-scheduled, boring programming to bring you a truly *unusual event* which occurred three weeks ago here at Loser High."

Each and every head in each and every homeroom stared either in awe or dumb struck at the hideous cartoon image. Someone had finally done it. Someone had actually hacked into the school's computer system! What nerve. What brazen, steely nerve!

There was a drum roll as Mephisto held up its right hand with empty palm open for all to see; pointing at it with its left to confirm it was indeed empty. Then, like a magician performing a card trick, it clenched its right hand into a fist, shook it up and down quickly a couple of times, and with another *pop* it contained a photograph stuck between two fingers. Looking at the photo as a devilish grin sank across its face, Mephisto tossed its ugly head, jerking quickly to look back into the camera lens and shouting, "Boo!," flicking the photo away at the same instant. Everyone jumped in their seats at this, before watching the photo tumble through the air in slow motion, growing and growing until it finally stopped, filling the entire blackboard screen to the clash of cymbals. It was a candid, still photograph of a young man and woman in a locker-lined hallway facing each other.

Henry studied the image on the screen. "Hey, that's you and Kelly Martino," he said, looking over at Porter.

"Yeah," replied Porter slowly, trying to recall a solitary meeting with Kelly. He couldn't. Whatever was going on, he didn't like the looks of it.

In her homeroom, Kelly Martino gasped at the sight of the photograph and buried her face in her hands.

In his homeroom, Larry White bit his lip to stifle a grin before glancing over at Sarah, who was seated two rows over. He could tell she was clenching her teeth and her normally pleasant and inviting face was quickly clouding over with a look which can only be described as a mixture of deep hurt and dark scorn. *This is going to work*, he thought. Robby might be a geek, but he's going to pull this off. What guts! And then under his breath to himself, "I wouldn't want to be Porter Smith right now."

"This photograph and the visual recording to follow were captured recently after a rehearsal for the school play," continued Mephisto, now in a voice-over. "I'm certain you all recognize these students and know who their significant others are. One and all are nominees to the homecoming court. Watch carefully, as you are about to witness the back stab, big grab, and face slap of the century. Enjoy."

With this the image on the screen sprang to life and when the recording was finally over, and after the laughs and gasps at what had apparently transpired finally subsided, every head in Porter's homeroom turned towards him, and each set of eyes reflected a either a look of amusement or sheer disbelief. Porter just sat there, silently staring wide-eyed at the screen with his jaw dangling open.

The duel use blackboard screen rippled once again, returning to Mephisto's dreadful, grinning face floating over pulsating waves of colored light. "Since the lovely Ms. Weston will look the complete fool if she attends the dance alongside 'Pucker' Smith," it gloated in its garbled, modulated voice, "we have taken the liberty of removing both their names from today's election ballots. This is for Ms. Weston's own good. All school computers have been disabled until she withdraws her nomination officially to enforce our decision in this regard." The image pulled back a bit so the demon's hairy upper torso and wretched arms were visible. "We now return you to your regularly-scheduled, dopey programming," it concluded, and with a snap of its finger the image rolled back to the confused faces of Carrie and Ted sitting behind their *What's Happening* anchor desk.

"We…We apologize for that," stammered Carrie, trying to compose herself after being informed by someone off camera they were back on the air. "The recording you just saw was *not* part of our intended broadcast and we apologize to Sarah Weston: poor girl. Our hearts go out to you. We also sincerely apologize to Kelly Martino."

"Yes," added Ted. "Our equipment has been tampered with." He turned to Carrie. "Although the recording was obviously real," he added before looking back into the camera lens. "We'll try to get this mess straightened out by tomorrow; until then, good morning from all of us at *What's Happening*. And remember, all assaults, unwanted touching, and incidents of harassment must be reported to Principal Norman's office immediately."

The image of Carrie and Ted faded as the room lights came back up and the back lit screen darkened into a blackboard again.

Porter, still in shock, stared dumbfounded at it as a palpable and awkward silence lingered over the entire room. He finally blinked a couple of times, shook his head as if waking from a weird dream, and slowly gazed around at the disapproving faces of his classmates.

Henry, his face flush red with anger, bolted up from his desk. "How could you do this to Sarah?" he demanded, pointing a finger of accusation. "Have you lost your mind?"

"Yeah!" called several scattered and angry voices. With a few notable exceptions, Sarah Weston was uniformly liked, and in many instances much cherished, throughout the entire school.

"Kelly Martino over Sarah Weston?" exclaimed an incredulous Richard King. "Forsooth! I'm going to demand you be kicked out of my play!"

"That wasn't me!" shouted Porter, bolting up from his small homeroom desk as well, which tipped over and crashed noisily onto the floor, sending his books and papers flying wildly about. He didn't see or care as he pointed at the blackboard. "That wasn't me, I swear it! This must be some sort of joke." He tried to feign a laugh, but it came out sounding more like a gravelly, dry-throated, croak of guilt.

"It certainly looked like you, Mr. Smith," said Mrs. Huttleson, the homeroom monitor. The tone of her voice was cold severity tinged with pure disapproval. "It also looks like you attacked Ms. Martino. I would call that assault and battery in my book," she added, glaring at him. "I believe it's called that in the school's conduct code as well. What a terrible display, attacking a poor, defenseless girl. Whoever made that recording has done Kendell High a service. If I were you, I'd prepare myself for expulsion."

Porter's face turned as pale as kindergarten paste at the mention of the word "expulsion." Both his parents were FBI agents who had drilled notions of high character and personal responsibility into him since he could walk. If he was expelled he would disgrace them. He would be disgraced. His life would be over. He gulped at the disturbing thoughts, which were now streaming into his head in quick succession. "I swear to you, Mrs. Huttleson, on my honor, that wasn't me. Ask Kelly Martino. Ask her!"

"Me thinks thou dost protest too much," cut in Richard, quoting the Great Shakespeare. "Who could fake something like that, anyway? It'd take a small army of programmers weeks to come even close. Why would anybody even want to?"

Practically the entire class agreed with a sudden, loud, overlapping chorus of, "Yeah!"

Sensing the tide was quickly turning against him, Porter pleaded with his classmates and Mrs. Huttleson. Most of them were his friends to one degree or another. They could be reasoned with. They had to. "You all know me. You know I'd never do anything like that," he said, pointing at the blackboard again. "I never laid a hand on Kelly Martino!"

"It certainly looked like you did," repeated Mrs. Huttleson, even more coldly than before. "Poor Kelly Martino. What a shameful display. If left unchecked, such behavior can only lead to much, much worse. It must be nipped in the bud, and soon."

"Bud, nothing! Wait until Bradley Masterson gets his hands on him," mocked Jason Aaron, one of Bradley's friends. "You're toast, Smith."

Suddenly the door to the homeroom burst open and in stormed Principal Norman, followed by the equally-beefy football and wrestling coaches. All three men were wearing arresting police officer frowns as they pushed past Henry, surrounding Porter to prevent any attempt at escape. "Let's go, Smith!" he commanded. "In my office: now! You're in a lot of trouble," he added to emphasize the seriousness of Porter's apparent attack on Kelly Martino to the other students.

Porter suddenly felt the room spinning around him. *This can't be happening*, he thought, pointing at the blackboard again. "I swear to you that wasn't me," he croaked weakly, realizing his goose was already dressed and on its way to the oven.

"Save it," clipped Principal Norman as his two goon coaches grabbed Porter's shoulders on either side and began marching him out of the room.

His eyes now glazing over in shock, Porter absently motioned towards his pile of books and papers scattered about the floor around his toppled desk. "What about my stuff?"

Norman stopped and looked over at Henry. "Dundridge, pick up his belongings and bring them to my office. Come on Smith, you know the rules."

Porter hung his head and, with drooped shoulders and feet which felt as if they were encased in cement, was led away like a common criminal. A common criminal everyone was firmly convinced he was.

As the horrendous events at North Kendell High School were about to unfold across town that morning, Elizabeth Weston was sitting in the den of the wonderful, old row house the university had provided as part of her ever-sweetening compensation package. Having taken the day off to meditate and reflect upon their very good fortune since arriving in the United States all those weeks ago, she had her long, black hair tied in a loose ponytail and was comfortably curled up on a cozy, overstuffed chair in her favorite green bathrobe. The morning sun had crested the roof of the house across the way and was now streaming its rays through an ornate stained glass window, which tinted them with color and cast them about the room to form patches of red, green, and blue illumination. She picked up an antique tea cup from an end table, raised it smoothly to her lips, and took another leisurely sip of tea while Wicca, Sarah's beloved calico cat, yawned, stretched, and purred contentedly in a puddle of sunshine warming the hardwood floor at the foot of her chair. Elizabeth smiled at the cat, stretching out a slender leg to pet it with her toe. "Dear Wicca."

Wicca rolled over quickly, sitting up and staring at Elizabeth with its intense owl-like, golden-green eyes.

"Things couldn't be going any better, could they?" she continued, carefully setting the teacup down again, which met its matching saucer with a pleasant *clink*. "I'm heading up the artifact recovery team. I have Dr. Hargraves and the other university officials eating out of my hands and the lunar occultation is only one week away. Only one week! Oh how I do hope Dear Morty will survive his stroll into the expanded ley node to return and tell us what secrets lie at the other side. Under my spell he'll be like a human recorder."

Wicca blinked a couple of times, beaming Elizabeth a telepathic message in its curious visual feline language: Dr. Hargraves walking in a wide-eyed trance off a cliff into a bottomless abyss.

Elizabeth studied the image in her mind's eye and sighed. "I know. It is indeed unlikely he shall return; but it's worth a try. Nothing ventured, nothing gained, as they say. Even if he doesn't, my daily immersions within the node have yielded results even *I* would never have imagined possible." Uncurling, she rose from her chair and walked over to a mirror hanging on the wall to peer into it. And from within it peered back the face of Elizabeth Weston from fifteen years ago. Elizabeth tilted her head from side to side, admiring her newfound youth, before smiling. "I look and feel like I'm twenty-five years old again!"

Wicca beamed another telepathic message: Elizabeth and the shimmering blue orb of light separated by a high fence.

"Not to worry, my dear. Not to worry. I've stopped immersing myself within the node's supernatural energy. If I start looking *too* young, people might start getting suspicious." She touched her face as a look of thoughtfulness flowed across it. "Sarah and I really can almost pass for sisters now."

Wicca purred at the mention of her master's name and beamed Elizabeth an image of a radiant Sarah holding a lovely bouquet of flowers which magically bloomed over and over again.

Elizabeth glowed at it. She'd never seen her daughter so happy before, or felt Sarah's emotions so clearly: another unexpected side effect of the ley node's strange power. Like other high witches of her pedigree, Elizabeth had always had a somewhat telepathic connection with her daughter. Until recently, this connection was limited to general impressions or sensations of Sarah's moods and whether or not the girl was in trouble or the company of others. The node's cold energy had somehow strengthened this connection by at least fifty-fold! Now Elizabeth could reach out with her mind and secretly see what Sarah was seeing. Feel what Sarah was feeling. Pick up and read her daughter's thoughts; share the young lady's emotions as if they were Elizabeth's own, and lately Sarah's strongest emotion was a Porter Smith-induced happiness bordering on glee.

Wicca beamed Elizabeth the message again. Wicca did not like to be ignored.

"I agree. I've never seen her so happy before either," she finally replied. "I think Sarah is falling in love for the first time." At this, an image from deep within Elizabeth's mind unwillingly surfaced: an image of her long-departed husband, George Weston. A handsome and young George Weston of years and years past. George Weston: her first and only love. "Nothing like being in love for the first time," she said, quelling a sudden, strong feeling of loss and repressing the image deep within her mind again. "Real love, that is," she added, forcing herself to brighten, which she did. "What do you think of the 'dashing' Porter Smith?" she teased, knowing perfectly well Wicca was quite jealous of Sarah's new friend.

Wicca growled lowly before jumping on the overstuffed chair and curling up into a big doughnut of fur.

"Oh don't be jealous. Sarah will always love you best—silly beast." She looked in the mirror again before walking over to the stained glass window; absently touching a few of its cut fragments of red and blue. "Anyway, this is Sarah's big day. It's the homecoming court election, you know. Sarah was so very excited this morning." Elizabeth turned and looked at Wicca again. "And what a lucky coincidence she'll be away at the dance at the precise moment of the occultation. I won't have to make any excuses about going back to work so late in the evening. I'm fairly certain she can tell immediately when I'm lying." Closing her eyes, Elizabeth raised her arms and held them perpendicular to her body. "Let's just have a peak at how things are going at Kendell High this auspicious morning." She drifted in concentration until a wave of coldness flowed through her, followed by a sensation of flying through a darkened tunnel speckled with points of light and then pleasant warmth as she emerged, initiating a secret telepathic connection with Sarah. As it became firmly established, Elizabeth found herself awash with her daughter's senses, thoughts, and emotions. Happiness and anticipation over the election. Porter Smith: a dreamy, wonderful knight. The homecoming dance. Lot's of good friends. This afternoon's play rehearsal. Another kiss for Porter. Elizabeth gasped at this last thought and quickly dropped her arms to terminate the link. All the images and sensations from her daughter's mind quickly faded, as if Elizabeth was waking from a deep daydream. When they had swirled away, she put her hands on her hips and glared at Wicca. "Another kiss for Porter!" she shouted. "Another kiss for Porter? Sarah is entirely too young for such behavior! Wicca, you knew about this, didn't you?"

Wicca covered her head with her bushy tail and hunkered down deeper into the chair. Unlike Elizabeth's newly amplified telepathic abilities, Wicca's own mental connection with Sarah had always been quite strong. The cat always knew precisely what her master was thinking or doing at any moment of the day, despite any great distance separating them.

"Wicca?" repeated Elizabeth, wagging her finger at the cat. "You know better than to keep such important life events from me. Sarah is entirely too young..."

Wicca swished her tail back from her face and made a subtle cat frown at Elizabeth, then beamed another message: Elizabeth's mother Emily lurking in the shadows while an extremely young Elizabeth snuck a kiss from George Weston while the two sat together on a bench in the garden behind the house she grew up in Felixstowe.

"That's not fair, Wicca. I recall I was much older than Sarah at the time. And I've warned you over and over again not to beam images of George. They cause me too much pain."

Wicca stubbornly beamed a quick series of images in reply. A young Elizabeth at home. Elizabeth at school. Elizabeth and George Weston holding hands. Elizabeth with her schoolmates. And in each and every one Emily was lurking in the shadows. Then the final blow: an image of Emily reading Elizabeth's secret diary.

Elizabeth gasped inwardly, realizing Wicca was right. Tuning into her daughter's thoughts was just as bad as—and perhaps even much worse than—reading Sarah's own diary. That was something she had never ever considered doing, and the more she mulled over it the more her stern look faded until her face projected thoughtfulness again. "I am dreadfully sorry, Wicca. You're absolutely right—for a change. Sarah's privacy is as at least as sacred as my own; within reason considering her age. I've decided that from now on I shall only make secret contact with her mind in emergencies: when I sense something is amiss. There, does that make you feel better?"

Wicca uncurled, quickly sitting up and beaming Elizabeth an image of a dead redbird: the universal feline language symbol for 'thank you.'"

"You are quite welcome. And, truth be told, Sarah's choice of a first love, if indeed that's what Porter Smith is, could have been much, much worse. His mind is so very strong and organized. It's quite refreshing to sense. In fact, I've never seen anything like it from a mortal before; only George's mind was stronger! I am convinced that, like Sarah's father, Porter is descended from high witch stock: so much so I've undertaken to investigate his genealogy. Too bad the male descendants of high witches are physically incapable of possessing any supernatural powers. It makes it so difficult to establish a clear lineage since only female descendants are recorded in the Great Book."

Wicca beamed Elizabeth a question: Porter standing on a shore, sadly waving as Elizabeth, Sarah, and Wicca sailed off in a little wooden boat. Now boats Wicca could understand. Riding away back to their home in England in the belly of a big, noisy, metal bird was simply too much for the cat to comprehend.

"Oh yes. I know we will not be in America forever."

Wicca beamed the same question, only this time Sarah was weeping and waving goodbye to Porter as he drifted off into the distance.

"As for that, I intend to reveal to Sarah who she really is on her seventeenth birthday. If she's still interested in him after her formal training in witchcraft begins, we'll make arrangements for Porter to come back to England with us. He will benefit greatly from attending college in London. I'm certain his parents will agree," she added with a grin and a wink. "After that, and after college, it will be Sarah's decision alone as to the ultimate fate of Porter Smith."

Wicca started to beam Elizabeth another mental image when it abruptly stopped and made a loud, completely unexpected, "Yeowoo!" call of panic. Springing from the chair like a cornered tiger, the cat landed hard on the wooden floor, then jumped wildly again as if in great pain before running around and around the room making the same awful call.

"What is it, Wicca?" shouted Elizabeth. "What's wrong?"

Wicca howled again before wedging herself underneath the sofa.

Then Elizabeth felt it: an intense surge of distress emanating from Sarah's end of their ever-present telepathic link. "Oh, my goodness!" she gasped. She had never sensed such a dreadful mixture of emotions from her daughter before. Calming herself, she stood straight and raised her arms. "Here I come," she muttered, concentrating on establishing a strong telepathic connection with Sarah. She had to find out precisely what was going on. "Hang on, daughter." Closing her eyes, she felt a wave of coldness followed by the dark tunnel of lights. Warmth. Opening them again, she found she was sitting in a dimly lit room full of young men and women facing a large, rectangular TV screen. Then, as Sarah's thoughts started streaming through, Elizabeth watched Porter Smith humiliate her little girl in front of the entire student body of Kendell High School. And for several awful minutes, her daughter's heartbreaking thoughts, senses, and emotions were impressed upon Elizabeth's memory as intensely as if they'd been her own. Such feelings of scorn and betrayal she had never experienced before. She finally lowered her arms to terminate the link. "Dump Sarah for a mere mortal?" she shouted, her face flushing red with anger. "A mortal dumping *my* daughter for another mere mortal?" Sarah's heartbreak was now being filtered through the psyche of an overprotective mother who now also happened to be the most powerful high witch on the planet, thanks to the ley node's supernatural energy. She ran out of the den and down the hallway to her bedroom to get dressed. "Come on, Wicca. We're going to get Sarah!"

A glossy-eyed, but now somewhat composed Wicca, peeked from beneath the sofa before crawling out and slowly padding over to the door of the den to wait.

Elizabeth continued shouting as she dressed; only now it was a series of potential fates that awaited the doomed Porter Smith. "I'll have my revenge! No one shall cause such distress to my daughter and get away with it. I'll hypnotize him into thinking he is a pig! Ha. That's what I shall do. No…a rat: better still. A scrabbling, little rat. A mere mortal over Sarah? It is utterly incomprehensible. Or I could fry his brain with a super jolt of magic. His mind is strong, but not that strong." Once dressed, she emerged from her room and ran back into the den. "Let's go, Wicca!" she roared. "We're driving over to Sarah's school to pick her up. I'll just grab my coat." As she was trotting back towards the hallway she received another telepathic image from Wicca: an image of a wide-eyed, hypnotized Dr. Morton Hargraves morphing into a wide-eyed, hypnotized Porter Smith.

Elizabeth skidded to a stop and studied the image in her mind's eye. "Yes," she hissed lowly, like a slithering cobra looking for prey to strike at; her scornfully pursed lips stretching into a wide, evil grin. Turning, she looked Wicca in the eye before pointing forcefully at the cat. "Of course. Excellent idea, Wicca. Excellent! That's just what we'll do. We'll use Porter Smith as our guinea pig next week instead of Dr. Hargraves. After all, Dear Morty does have a family to support."

Wicca made another subtle cat frown before beaming an image of an entranced Porter slowly disappearing into a large orb of intense, white light and reemerging a few moments later.

"As for that, if the rat is lucky enough to return, we'll learn what he knows and I'll cast him back into the expanded node just before it closes. It's best Sarah never be troubled by the sight of him again. Rest assured, after next Thursday no one will ever see the 'dashing' Porter Smith again."

The next few days were far and away the worst of Porter's young life. He was expelled from school for two weeks for maintaining his innocence and refusing counseling. His parents—mortified after being shown the recording in Principal Norman's office—not only grounded him indefinitely, but also took away his computer and portacom phone. Henry, Kevin, and the rest of his friends had seemingly abandoned him to his fate. But the worst thing was Sarah refused to speak to him any more. If there was any way life could look lower, or if there was any way he could feel more down, he couldn't think of it: that is until the date of the homecoming dance finally arrived. Unable to get Sarah off his mind, he laid on his bed practically the entire day, imagining over and over again the dreadful vision of his girl at the dance with someone else. His heart physically ached at the horrible thought. His only relief was an alternating series of fantasies, the first being Sarah throwing herself into his arms after he proved his innocence. Interspaced between these were escalating scenarios of the revenge he would visit upon whoever it was who'd set him up so spectacularly. He'd just finished devising another version of his vengeance plot, which consisted of the unspeakable, when he heard a soft knock at his bedroom door. "Yeah," he replied miserably to the ceiling.

The door opened and his mother, Kimberly Smith, looked in. "Your friend Henry is here," she said. "Would you like to see him?"

"I thought I was grounded."

"You are," replied Kimberly. "Boy *are* you ever grounded. He says it's important. Do you want to see him or not?"

Porter sat up and twisted around to sit at the edge of his bed. Maybe Henry had figured out who'd done this to him. If anyone could figure out his mess, it would be Henry Dundridge. "Sure," he replied. "I'd like to see him if it's okay."

"I'll get him." Her head disappeared from the door and after a brief while she walked back in followed by Henry. "Porter is grounded," declared Kimberly in a flat, level voice. "You've got half an hour, Henry. *Capisca?*"

"I understand, Mrs. Smith," replied Henry, walking over to Porter's desk, taking off his brown leather coat and sitting down. He then looked absently away, clamming up until the door closed shut behind her. When she was gone he looked over at Porter. "How's it going?"

"Terrible. Have you seen Sarah? My folks took my portacom and computer away. They're so strict; I hate them. I tried to call her last Thursday before I was grounded, but she wouldn't pick up. She hasn't tried to call me all week. How is she?"

Henry sighed. "It's hard to tell, Porter. Her mother showed up at school a little while after they took you to Norman's office. It was the weirdest thing, because I don't think anyone called her and Sarah seemed surprised but glad to see her. They left school that morning and Sarah didn't show back up again until last Monday. She's been quiet, but she doesn't seem too upset."

"Not upset? How can she be not upset? I feel awful. Have you talked to her?"

"Not until this afternoon. I think she's been avoiding me. I called her house after school, just before I came over here. I needed to get my…'our,' ducks in a row first. Boy have you been set up, Porter. I'm sorry I didn't believe you at first."

Porter stood and faced his friend. "Finally someone believes me!" he shouted, throwing his hands up in the air. "Who did this to me, Henry? Who did it and why?"

"From what I've been able to learn, I'm pretty certain Robby Lee and Kelly Martino did this to you. I think Jimmy Luntz and others were involved as well. There's a rumor floating around that Robby Lee showed Lisa Collins some sort of video of you the day before the incident. She tried to get Sarah to look at it, but Sarah refused. Everybody's pretty tight lipped about it, especially after how much trouble you landed in. If anyone involved came forward now, they'd probably get kicked out of school too: for not coming forward sooner."

Porter flopped back down on his bed. "But why? I've never done anything to Robby or Kelly. Lee hates me because you and I are friends, but why would he go to such an effort? And I've never done anything bad to Kelly, except ask her out a couple of times last summer. What's so wrong with that?"

"Think Porter. Have you been so wrapped up with Sarah and school you couldn't see it? Who else was nominated for the homecoming court? Kelly and Brad, that's who. Kelly had the perfect motive to try to sink your chances of winning, and what better way to do it then to trick Sarah into breaking up with you the day before the election. Sarah also beat her out for the part of Princess Serena in the school play. Losing the election too would have been a double whammy to Kelly's giant ego. By the way, Kelly and Brad did get elected to the court."

"Who cares," moaned Porter, thinking about the dance and the fact he wouldn't be there with Sarah. "But what about Robby Lee? Why would *he* go after me? We haven't had any run-ins since the first day of school."

Henry shrugged. "He's probably got a crush on Sarah, too. Practically every other guy at school does. Maybe Lee thought he'd have a chance of dating her if you were out of the way, which leads me to my next point. We've got to prove your innocence, and soon. The guys at school are circling around Sarah like hungry, lovesick vultures. Larry White even dumped Paulette to ask Sarah to the dance tonight. I think Sarah was actually considering going, because Larry's been telling everyone he's going to meet Elizabeth Weston this afternoon."

"What?" shouted Porter, bolting to his feet again. The thought of Sarah and Larry White together made his blood boil. "Larry White?" he growled, his face turning red and clouding over with rage. "I've got to get out of here! I'll go to the dance and punch his lights out. I'll knock Lee around for his efforts as well."

"You'll do no such thing. If you go to the dance tonight and pick a fight with Larry or Robby Lee you'll get kicked out of school for good. We've got to do this the right way; the smart way."

"But, how?"

"Don't worry just yet," replied Henry. "I think I've derailed Larry White's train—at least for a little while, anyway. When I called Sarah, I told her you were set up and that I'll be able to prove it—if given a little time. I've convinced her it would be totally unfair if she went to the dance while you—an innocent man—languished like a prisoner in his own home: never even given an opportunity to defend himself. Sarah said her mother wanted her to go to the dance, even if she went alone, but she agreed she won't. She also said she doesn't believe I can clear your name, but promised me one week to try, beginning today. I hope Larry White doesn't find out. The big goon will murder me."

"Thanks, Henry," said Porter, sitting down at the edge of the bed and looking at his friend hopefully. "But can you? Can you prove I'm innocent? Nobody believes me because that Mephisto video looks so real. And it *does* look real! Even after seeing it three times I can hardly believe it's not me. Can you prove it's a fake?"

"It's being worked on as we speak. Robby Lee isn't the only computer genius at Kendell High, you know. I hacked into the school's computer system a few days ago and downloaded a copy of it. My dad and I are analyzing it in our computer laboratory at home. If the video was faked, he's confident we can show it. Once we do, I'll send Principal Norman and the local newspapers an anonymous email message from one of the school library terminals with our findings. Norman won't be able to ignore that, especially if it proves they kicked an innocent kid out of school and pretty much ruined his life. In the meantime, Kevin and I are trying to convince Lisa Collins to tell us what she knows. The problem is she's old friends with Lee and doesn't want to get him into trouble. We think she may be starting to crack, though. If we can get enough evidence in front of Norman to connect Lee with the original hacking incident, you can bet all his fellow conspirators will start spilling their guts to keep from getting kicked out of school. Lee's and Martino's gooses will be cooked." Henry stood and put his hand on his friend's shoulder. "It may not look like it, Porter, but you've got people in your corner, and I'm working on Sarah." He plucked a portacom phone from his pocket. "Since I tried to call you and your portacom was turned off, I figured you were grounded. When I talked to Sarah this afternoon, I told her I was coming over here. She said there's something she wants to say to you and promised she'd pick up a message flagged from this number. She didn't sound very pleased, though. Do you want me to call her?"

"Yes!" shouted Porter. "If I can just talk to her I *know* I can get her to believe me!"

Henry dialed Sarah's number into the miniature phone and put it to his ear. After hearing a ringing sound, he quickly offered it to Porter, who snatched it away and clapped it against the side of his head. After a few rings there was a soft *click*, followed by Sarah's voice.

"Hello? Henry?"

"It's me, Sarah. It's Porter. I swear to you that video of me and Kelly Martino was a fake! You've got to believe me," he pleaded. "And Henry and I are going to prove it! Are you okay? I miss you so much."

At the other end of the connection Elizabeth Weston grinned like a hungry spider watching a moth flying straight into her web. She'd tricked Porter's pudgy, little friend Henry into thinking he was speaking with Sarah when he called a little while ago. Now she would do the same to that rat, Porter Smith. Henry's call only made things easier, since she wouldn't have to place a traceable one from her end. The boys' pleas of innocence were ludicrous and it was time to set the hook. She knew what she saw on that terrible morning a week ago and Porter Smith would pay with his life, while Sarah was forgetting all about him at the homecoming dance with that nice—though rather dull-minded—Larry White. "I don't have long, Porter," she finally said in an exact imitation of her daughter's voice. "My mother has forbidden me from ever seeing you again. You know her rules."

"I'm innocent!" replied Porter quickly, glancing over at Henry, who had removed himself a discrete distance away and was pretending to read a dictionary pulled from a bookshelf.

"Look, Porter. Henry says you are too, but frankly I do not see how he or anyone else can possibly prove it. I know what I saw last Thursday, but I need to see you one last time. I need to look you in the face and tell you how I feel. It's far more than you deserve."

"I swear to you, Sarah," Porter started to say before the voice of Sarah Weston cut him off.

"You can't come here—my mother would never allow it. School is off limits because I don't want to be seen in public with you. So if you want your one and only chance to tell me your side of the story, meet me at the old Kendell field house in the park at nine-thirty tonight. I've stolen my mother's building key and we can talk in private."

"But, I'm grounded. I'm not supposed to leave the house."

"Do you want to see me or not?" demanded Sarah's voice in a tone of severity Porter had never heard from her before. "Yes or no? It's as simple as that."

"Yes," replied Porter quickly, suddenly feeling like he was talking to Elizabeth Weston. "Yes. Yes. I want to see you. I will meet you. I don't care if I'm grounded or not."

"Then nine-thirty at the old field house it is," the voice concluded, followed by a sharp *click* of disconnection.

"Hello? Hello?" called Porter into the portacom. No reply. Turning it off, he walked over to Henry and offered it back to him.

"What did she say," asked Henry, placing the dictionary back on its shelf and taking back his portacom.

"She said...She said she wants me to meet her at the field house tonight at nine-thirty; to give me a chance to tell her my side of the story."

"The old field house in the park? The park closes at dusk. Why the old field house?"

Porter shrugged before hanging his head in misery. "She says she doesn't want to be seen with me in public."

"Well don't give up hope now!" exclaimed Henry, trying to lift his friend's spirits. "She wants to see you. You're half way there!"

A firm knock resonated at Porter's door. "You've got five more minutes, Henry," called Kimberly. "Better start wrapping it up."

"Okay," replied Henry, and then in a subdued tone to Porter, "This is your lucky night, friend. My dad has lent me the pickup truck to take Solaritron to the Robot Battle qualifying trials. They should be done by eight-thirty or so. I'll swing around afterwards and pick you up at nine to drive you over to meet Sarah. Act like you went to bed early and sneak out. I'll park around the corner on Oak Street. If you can escape without detection, I might be able to get you to the park and back without your folks ever realizing you've left. There's a risk you'll be caught and punished even further, though."

"That's a risk I have already decided to take," declared Porter. "Thanks for your help, Henry. I'm really going to owe you one after all this is over."

"What are friends for?" asked Henry as they shook hands. "Good luck, Porter."

"I'll need it. Boy, will I ever."

Porter and his reflection studied each other through the mirror hanging above his dresser. He'd put on a simple outfit Sarah was quite fond of: a long-sleeved, royal blue, button-down shirt and black jeans. He combed his sandy-blond hair one last time before looking at his watch: one of those highly accurate military jobs with some sort of lifetime, radioactive power source. Its luminous dial indicated 8:55 p.m. "Time to move out," he muttered to himself. He clicked off the lamp on his dresser and crept over to the door, locking it as quietly as possible before pressing his ear up against it to listen. After a moment he could recognize the muffled sound of the TV in the family room downstairs, where his mom, dad, and sister Sally were undoubtedly assembled. Strolling quickly back to his bed, he donned his black leather coat before slinging his lace-tied tennis shoes over his shoulder. Sock-clad feet would be much quieter on the roof of the house as he made good his escape. Tiptoeing to the window, he slowly opened it and then crawled out onto the pitched roof of the attached garage below, closing it again behind him—except for a narrow crack so he could sneak back in again later.

The gritty asphalt shingles tingled the soles of his feet as he padded silently across the roof to a maple tree at its opposite side. After selecting a pathway of branches that would hold his weight, he carefully climbed down. Once on the ground he looked from side to side, making certain the coast was clear. Seeing no one, he hunched forward and ran down the block and around the corner to Oak Street like a wanted fugitive, where he straightened and walked along the sidewalk, looking for Henry's pickup truck among the line of cars bordering the street. A darkened vehicle parked half way up the block flashed its headlights a couple of times. "Good man, Henry!" he said aloud, running over to the truck and hopping in.

"Hi," said Henry, starting the truck's engine. He turned on its headlights and signaled before pulling out onto the street. "How'd it go?"

"So far, so good," replied Porter. "I don't think anyone heard me leave." He un-slung his tennis shoes from across his shoulder and untied them, hiking one foot up after another to put them on. "How did Solaritron do?" he asked, tying each one up in turn.

"Unlike you, the judges were very favorably impressed with Sola. It passed their qualifying standards with flying colors. They didn't use colorfully-descriptive terms such as, 'goofy-looking' or 'top with eyes.'" Henry turned, pulling open his leather coat. The beige dress shirt he'd worn to the qualifying trials was unbuttoned down to his waist, beneath which he now wore a bright, red shirt. "They even gave me an official T-shirt. I couldn't wait to put it on." It was adorned with big, white letters that read, "Robots Rule."

"That's awesome," said Porter, studying what was certain to be his friend's new, most popular article of clothing. Sitting up again, he looked over his shoulder, where he saw Solaritron tethered secure in the truck's bed under a tarp. "And don't lie. I never said I wasn't impressed with Solaritron," he continued with a grin, recalling his first sight of the weird-looking robot. "I think that Sola is great. So does Sarah."

Henry signaled and turned left onto Forest Avenue. "I've been thinking about our plan. I forgot I'm to film the lunar occultation of Mars tonight for *What's Happening*—a follow-up piece to my last one."

"That certainly brings back a memory I'd just as soon forget."

"Sorry," replied Henry. "Anyway, it's apples and oranges. I had nothing to do with what Lee and Martino did to you."

"I know. I know. But it still triggers a vivid recollection of the worst day of my life. What about our plan?"

"You are supposed to meet Sarah at nine-thirty, right?"

"Right."

"The lunar occultation is predicted to start at 9:43 and my folks want me back by ten-thirty to avoid Kendell's student driver curfew. Mars reemerges from behind the Moon at approximately 10:43; an hour after the occultation begins."

"So?"

"I'm going to turn Solaritron on when we get to the park and have it record the start of the occultation. To make it home to beat my curfew *and* record the end, we need to leave the park by quarter-past ten at the latest."

"Henry! That only gives me forty minutes or so to talk to Sarah!"

"That's plenty of time to patch things up. If I'm not back by ten-thirty, I'll never get to use my dad's truck again. How will I get Sola to the Robot Battle Contest next month? This year it's all the way in the city."

"Your dad wouldn't do that to you, would he?"

Henry glanced over at Porter. "You think *your* parents are strict. My spare portacom is in the glove compartment. Take it and put it in your pocket. I'm going to call you at ten past ten to remind you."

Porter's face bent into a look of extreme disappointment as he opened the glove compartment. Reaching in, he searched around and found the tiny phone, then pulled it out and shoved it in his coat pocket. "I thought you were trying to help me out," he grumbled, slamming the compartment shut.

"I am. Believe me Porter, I'll send Solaritron in to get you if you don't answer when I call. You've got to be back at the truck in time so I can make it home before ten-thirty. We'll be cutting it close anyway. Sarah will understand. You're taking a big risk as it is."

They drove the rest of the way in silence. Upon reaching the park's closed entrance, Henry turned off the truck's headlights before driving over a curb and around the gate to get to its long, narrow parking lot, where they continued quietly on again under the illumination of the stars and a near-full Moon. When they reached the pathway leading to the old field house, Henry rolled to a stop and turned off the truck's engine. As soon as he did, Porter opened the door and jumped out, slamming it behind him. "We're a little early," he called out over his shoulder, trotting towards the path. "I'll see you back here at quarter-past ten. Thanks, Henry," he added in a hopeful voice.

Once Porter was gone, Henry got out of the truck and looked around. It was a silent, spooky, late-fall evening. The ancient, towering oak and elm trees scattered across the park had long since shed their fall colors; their twisted bare branches now scratching skyward as if trying to capture the Moon, which hung high in the eastern sky like a brilliant, bluish-white lantern. And just like on his last *What's Happening* feature, to its upper left, darkened limb crept a bright, red dot: the planet Mars. Shivering in the cold, dry air, he quickly buttoned his shirt and zipped up his brown leather coat before walking around to the back of the truck, where he opened its tailgate and climbed in to un-tether Solaritron. After removing the tarp and tossing it aside, Henry pressed his thumb within a little red circle painted on the robot's upper assembly and the sleeping machine responded with a *beep*. Climbing out again, he pulled a remote control from his pocket and walked clear several good paces before turning and raising it to his face. "Solaritron: slow activation. Carefully deploy yourself to ground level south of the truck."

At Henry's command, the legs on the machine's lower saucer section slowly emerged, unfolding as it stood up. Then with one great leap it sprang from the truck's bed and noisily onto the asphalt parking lot, where it bounced a couple of times, steadying itself before folding its legs into their recesses again and settling back down onto its ball roller. "Good evening, Mr. Dundridge. It is good to see you again."

"Hello, Sola," replied Henry, looking up at the Moon and back down at his wristwatch. "The lunar occultation we spoke about this afternoon will commence in about eighteen minutes. Please follow me and prepare to begin visual recording."

"Camera lenses and recorder are ready. Recording will commence at 9:41 p.m., Central Daylight Time."

Henry started walking along the tree-lined path leading towards the field house: the path Porter had taken, Solaritron whirring quietly along behind him. "We'll get a better view from behind the field house on the bluff overlooking the lake. There'll be less background light too." After a while they reached the steps leading up to its darkened entrance, where they stopped in front of the first, creepy-looking lion statue they came to and looked around. There was no sign of his friend or Sarah. "They must be inside," he said to before glancing at his watch again. "Come on, Sola. It's almost 9:35. Eight minutes to go." Looking up he saw Mars was now practically next to the upper left darkened limb of the Moon. They quickly proceeded along another path leading around to a bluff behind the building, past which was a steep, tree-less slope which rolled down to the water's edge. Selecting a spot, Henry sat on a nearby bench. "Okay, Solaritron, its show time. Prepare to commence recording."

Solaritron's main lenses swung skyward towards the rare celestial alignment which was about to unfold. At precisely 9:41 the robot became completely motionless. "Recorder on."

Gazing up in silence, Henry watched as the bright red dot and the Moon's left limb neared each other. Closer and closer they drew together, then they were touching and Mars disappeared with a little, red flash. He looked at his watch. "9:43, right on time. Solaritron, please record for another couple of minutes."

"Recording to cease at 9:45 p.m., per your command."

Afterwards, Henry continued gazing into the heavens, absently wondering at Porter's predicament. *How unfair life can be!* he thought. One moment you can be on top of the world and the next right at the bottom of the trash heap. From there his mind wandered to the homecoming dance underway across town and how much fun was being had while he was sitting alone in the dark, staring at a celestial event few people even cared about with a robot that might very well be destroyed in a few weeks time. Destroyed simply to provide computer and engineering geeks like him with a little entertainment. Maybe he would withdraw from the contest after all. Even though its human mimicry programming didn't work, he was still quite fond of the machine. At the notion of fondness he thought of Sarah Weston. "She is so wonderful," he muttered. "But *why* is she so wonderful? Is she really so much nicer and more beautiful than the other girls at school? Or is it something else? In time I may find the answer." *Time!* Suddenly the time popped into his head and he looked at his watch. It was already 10:11! "Oh, no, I'm going to be late," he groaned, as he bolted to his feet. Pulling his portacom from his pocket, he quickly keyed in a number and raised it to his ear.

After several rings the phone's pleasant, female computer voice said, "That number does not respond."

Setting his jaw in a hard line, Henry jammed the phone back into his pocket. "Porter forgot to turn on my spare portacom. Either that or he's ignoring me. Come on, Sola," he shouted, "lets go!"

Boy and machine quickly wound back up the path leading to the front of the field house. Once there, Henry crept up the steps leading to its darkened entrance, where he found the building's front door propped wide-open with a brick. *They must still be inside*, he concluded, quietly peering through the door's threshold and seeing light shining up from a staircase. "Porter?" he called out, his voice echoing away.

He waited for a few seconds, but there was no answer.

Stepping back from the door's threshold, he turned and called down to Solaritron. The machine had stopped and was waiting for him at the stone footing at the bottom of the steps. "I don't want to eavesdrop on Sarah and Porter, but we've got to get going." Glancing at his watch again, his heart sank with dread. "My dad will kill me if I'm late. Sola, I want you to deploy your walking legs and go find Porter. He's somewhere in the lower level of this building. Follow the light and bring him back here. Do it as quickly as you possibly can and do not, I repeat *do not*, return without him. Understand?"

"Understood," replied the robot, quickly unfolding and extending its six legs before effortlessly walking up the steps, where it weaved itself through the door like a huge spider and trotted across the building's lobby and down the staircase—metal feet clacking loudly on the old marble floor and steps.

Henry pulled Solaritron's remote control from his pocket. He would give the machine five minutes to retrieve his friend, which came and went as he counted away the seconds. With no sign of Porter or his robot he finally raised the remote control to his face. "Solaritron, please transmit status report. Have you found Porter yet?"

Nothing but pure static hissed back at him.

"Solaritron?"

More static.

"Uh oh," muttered Henry, tucking the remote back into his coat pocket. "Maybe Sola has malfunctioned! Just great," he groaned, running into the building and down the stairway towards the light. On the landing below he found himself in a short, dimly lit hallway lined with lockers crammed full of dirty coveralls and muddy boots. At its end he spotted an old, metal door cracked open a bit, through which streamed a flickering, pulsating light accompanied by a weird buzzing noise.

"What the?" exclaimed Henry, stepping over to the door. Giving it a push, it creaked loudly on ancient, rusty hinges as it swung open. Walking through he found himself on a small, metal landing ringed with a handrail, where, looking about, he noticed the light was streaming up out of an enormous excavation carved into the basement's floor: casting eerie, dancing ghost shadows across the ceiling and walls of the otherwise darkened room. Although he couldn't see its source from where he was standing, a scene from a horror movie popped into his head: a scene in which a ghostly, white light bubbled up from the bottom of a grave being robbed. Yes. The excavation did look like a giant, open grave! And in the movie the ghost light had drawn the helpless, screaming grave robbers to unspeakable deaths in a pool of quicksand that had stirred up from beneath them. His heart leapt at the recollection. Forcing the dreadful vision from his mind, he cupped his hands around his mouth. "Porter! Are you in here?" He had to find his friend and get out of there.

"Henry, is that you?" shouted back the voice of Sarah Weston from within the grave.

"It's me, Sarah! What's going on? Where's Porter?"

"Henry, come quickly. We need you!"

"I'll go get help!" shouted Henry, terror struck again. The ghost shadows were spinning and flickering faster now; the buzzing noise slowly increasing in pitch.

"Henry! Come to us now!"

The eerie light and terrible buzzing was chilling to behold and Henry's sense of self-preservation was screaming for him to run away, and he almost did before a rush of adrenaline gave him enough courage to steal himself. "Here I come, Sarah!" he shouted, hurrying down the old, corrugated, metal stairs—his shoes clanging away. "Hang on, Porter!" At the bottom he sprang from the last step and ran purposefully to the nearest side of the excavation like a reluctant superhero, where he immediately tripped on a cord and fell face first down a steep, earthen ramp. Henry cursed as he began to topple foreword, trying desperately to break his fall with his hands, but he didn't get his arms up in time and slammed forcefully onto the tilted ground before tumbling wildly downward, knocking the wind out of himself before finally rolling to a stop.

"Henry," cried Sarah's voice over the terrible buzzing. "Get up! Come quickly! Hurry!"

Henry lay there for a moment, gasping musty-smelling air through a mouth full of dirt; clenching his eyes shut in pain.

"Henry!"

Sarah's desperate cries for help triggered another rush of adrenaline and Henry spit a wad of mud from his mouth before rolling onto his stomach and struggling to his hands and knees. As he did, he noticed a nearby metal stanchion supporting a rope railing. Still dazed, he crawled over and grabbed it, then slowly pulled himself to his feet. Finally steadying himself, he slowly looked in the direction of Sarah's voice and gasped in disbelief and awe at what he saw, chill after terrible chill running up his spine. There, hovering in the air just past a big stone slab at the far end of the excavation was a huge, round orb of pulsating, white light, streaking here and there with random flashes of cobalt blue lightening; buzzing like a giant beehive about to burst at its seams. "Good Lord," he muttered, before shouting again. "Sarah! Where are you? What is that thing?"

"Over here!" she called back. "I'm standing on the altar. Hurry! Come quickly."

Henry shielded his eyes with flattened hands and through the glare could just make out the darkened silhouette of a person standing atop the slab. It was like trying to look at someone in front of a great, brilliant spotlight. Overcoming another powerful urge to flee, he forced himself to start walking towards Sarah and the hovering, buzzing orb, passing charts, tables, and camera equipment as he went. With each heavy, fearful step his urge grew; but every time he stopped or hesitated, or turned to run, Sarah would coax him along with her desperate cries and pleas for help. There was something about her voice. Her voice: he was being drawn towards it—drawn against his will. When he finally reached her he was practically numb with fear. Trembling, he stopped and looked up, where he saw the darkened silhouette quickly starting down some steps carved into the slab towards him. "Sarah?" he croaked weakly, as a static charge began combing through the legions of goose bumps flowing out from his stomach and across his arms, legs, and neck.

"Hello, my dear," replied the silhouette, bending down and thrusting out a shadow arm towards him like a viper about to capture a paralyzed prey it had long since bitten. "Take my hand."

Unable to resist, Henry slowly reached up towards the shadow's hand, felt a terrific spark of electricity sizzle against his palm like a sharp fang, and slowly drifted into warm, green unconsciousness.

CHAPTER FIVE: WELCOME TO BORIKEN ISLAND

Flashing to consciousness, the warm, green light in Henry's eyes was replaced by shocking, cold waves of white all around. "Where am I?" he cried, barely able to hear himself over the loud, buzzing noise tearing away at his eardrums. At the same instant he realized he was falling forward, as if someone had given him a good kick from behind. Just catching himself, he tripped to stop and stood motionless as an intense tingling sensation began enveloping his body: as if he was standing in a warm cloud of electrified gas. He twitched all over at the sensation and everywhere he looked he saw the same shimmering, white light. It was beginning to hurt his eyes. Then, without warning, he was seized by a terrible, invisible force—like some great, unseen tentacle had lashed out and wound itself around his arms and chest. He had just enough time to gasp before it began pulling him deeper and deeper into the white, buzzing light. Terrified, Henry clenched his eyes shut and instinctively fought back, digging in his heals and struggling to break the force's monstrous grip. It was no use. The more he resisted the harder and faster it pulled him along. After a few seconds he was in a flat out run. The white light—now intense beyond belief—stabbed painfully through his clenched eyelids and soon his legs were windmilling wildly to keep up. Breathing hard and nearing exhaustion, his head began spinning and he became disoriented. "Let me go!" he shouted in desperation. "Let me go!"

As if in reply, the field of white dissolved and Henry pitched headlong into darkness: his legs shooting out from under him as he flew forward. With one last surge of energy he thrust his arms up just in time to break his fall, landing hard on his hands. At the same instant his elbows buckled and he began tumbling down what felt like an endless ramp of logs lined up next to each other. Luckily his leather coat acted like a cushion, protecting him from the more serious bruises and abrasions which would normally accompany such a fall. He finally came to rest after colliding with something that replied with a muted, metallic *clang*. Violently gasping for air, he tried standing, but collapsed to his knees instead, toppling over sidewise and quickly passing out.

"What happened?" groaned Henry, finally stirring from a deep stupor. How long he had been lying there was anybody's guess. His hands were numb with pain, his left elbow smarted terribly, and there was a strange, tingling sensation crawling all over him. And his eyes felt blinded and burned: like he'd been staring at a bright light for a long time. Hard as he tried, he couldn't remember what had happened. The last thing he *did* remember was walking into the old Kendell field house. "I must have stumbled onto a live wire somewhere," he groaned woozily to himself as his wits began to return. "I must have been electrocuted. That would explain things." When he finally came to and was fairly certain he hadn't broken his neck, he slowly sat up and bumped into something. Still barely able to see past the bright spots dancing before his eyes, he groped around with his hands before concluding he was sitting next to his robot. "There you are, Sola."

The machine didn't reply. It just sat there, silently resting in cold shutdown mode: its robotic version of deep sleep.

"I better call for help." Fishing around in his pockets, he couldn't find his portacom, just his remote control for Solaritron and some change. Had he dropped it? He vaguely recalled handing it to someone. "I better get home," he muttered, slowly standing up. Staggering, he nearly collapsed before catching himself, then wobbled to keep his balance. He felt exceedingly weak and his vision was still quite blurry. Closing his eyes, he rubbed them gently through their lids until the burning sensation had subsided a bit. Thankfully, when he opened them again, some of his sight had returned.

The first thing he noticed was a clear, starlit sky framing a near-full moon less radiant than he remembered, and far to its right hung the Planet Mars: a blurry, red dot. *The occultation must have been over hours ago*, he thought before noticing it was warm out: much warmer than before, in fact. He realized he was sweating underneath his coat. "How did we get…" he started to say before gasping in shock.

The field house was gone, as well as the leaf-covered sidewalk leading up to it. Everything he fully expected to see—the fountain, bike paths, lake, and marina—was gone: all vanished as if part of some magician's grand illusion. He stood motionless, his groggy mind trying to piece together what had just happened. He found he was in a clearing at the bottom of a large, five-foot-tall platform constructed of rope, thatch, and ornately carved wooden beams. The front of the platform was accessed by a wide, shallow ramp of logs expertly lashed together and painted with strange red, green, and yellow symbols. This is where he must have fallen, but how did he get here? He looked about, but couldn't remember anything. The ground around him was littered with upturned baskets, trampled fruit, dried fish, and clay figurines.

He absently shed his coat and placed it on the ramp. "This is crazy," he said, studying his surroundings. "This can't be happening."

The platform was at one end of a wide clearing bounded on two sides by rows of what looked like tall, thin gravestones lined up side-by-side and forming three-foot-high walls. The clearing between the walls was dotted here and there with fires burning in shallow, clay vessels. Their flames cast flickering shadows which danced eerily across the stone walls and dense, tangled vegetation further out. All around the grass was freshly padded down, as if hundreds of people had recently been crowded there.

Henry listened for a moment, but heard nothing. Nothing but a light breeze rustling gently through the tops of unfamiliar-looking trees and the rhythmic *co-kee* chirping of some sort of night creatures. A chill ran up his spine as he suddenly felt he was being watched. He studied the edges of the clearing as his sight slowly returned and began catching glimpses of what looked like faces. Each would disappear into the shadows and vegetation so quickly he couldn't be certain his eyes weren't playing tricks on him. Maybe this was all part of the dream he was obviously having. A vivid dream, to be sure. The most vivid one he'd ever had. He tried to will himself awake, but it was no use. He would just have to let this one run its course until morning.

Dream or not, his feeling of being watched continued. Finally mustering his courage, he took a deep breath and cupped his hands around his mouth. "Hello!" he shouted. "Can anybody hear me?" He waited and called out again, this time even louder.

No reply; just momentary pauses in the night creatures' chirping.

The pain in his left elbow stabbed at him, raising serious doubts as to his dream theory. Wincing at it, he took a deep breath and rubbed it away gingerly. The air was warm and flavored with a pleasant incense smell. He heard some rustling sounds not too far off and stopped to listen, but they didn't return.

Then he remembered Solaritron. Maybe his robot could provide some answers! Still quite dizzy, he carefully made his way back over to the sleeping machine, where he pressed his right thumb into the little red circle painted on its upper assembly. The machine replied with a couple of *beeps* and Henry backed away from it a few steps, pulling a remote control from his pocket and raising it to his mouth. "Solaritron: full activation!"

Solaritron's dome lights flared to life and in a flash it quickly sprang up on its insect-like legs, bobbing and whirring menacingly for a moment.

At the same instant, a chorus of screams erupted at the edges of the clearing all around, followed by the sound of legs crashing and churning wildly through the undergrowth: frightened people running headlong away.

"Wait!" cried Henry over the screams of horror and rush of stampeding feet. "Wait!"

It was no use. Their cries slowly receded into the distance and in a short while all was quiet again.

Henry shrugged. *Haven't they ever seen a robot before?*

Solaritron bounced a few times, testing the firmness of the ground, before retracting its legs and settling down onto its roller again. "Good evening, Mr. Dundridge."

"Good evening, Solaritron," replied Henry, rubbing his left temple with his free hand to try to slow the spinning in his head. "Access your global positioning system and tell us where we are."

A central processing unit or "CPU" light within the robot's dome glowed green for quite a while before fading. "Current location cannot be ascertained. Global positioning system does not detect the presence of any orbiting GPS satellites."

"No satellites? That's impossible!" cried an incredulous Henry, tucking the remote back into his pocket. "You know that's impossible. Try again."

"Confirmed," replied Solaritron after a few moments. "Exact location cannot be ascertained," it added, when all of a sudden its dome lights flashed a few times and it quickly began repeating, "Ascertained, ascertained, ascertained..." over and over again, before tipping forward and wobbling around in a circle on its ball roller like a lazy top.

"Solaritron, what's wrong?"

Slowly righting itself again, the robot's dome lights dimmed and buzzed before returning to their steady glow. "Wrong? Nothing's wrong. I feel fine. If you would be so kind as to allow me to finish, I was about to say that a comparison of current celestial observations with seasonal astronomical data indicates we are located somewhere in the Northern Hemisphere between latitudes twelve degrees, twenty-eight minutes north and twenty-three degrees, eight minutes north."

"Just great," groaned Henry, rubbing his temple again. "*Now* your human mimicry programming decides to kick in. Where did you say we were?"

"I *said* a comparison of current celestial observations with seasonal astronomical data indicates we are located somewhere in the Northern Hemisphere between latitudes twelve degrees, twenty-eight minutes north and twenty-three degrees, eight minutes north."

"What does that mean?"

"That depends on our longitudinal coordinates."

Henry raked his hand across his head in frustration. Why hadn't he paid more attention in his geography class? He made a guess. "What about the longitudinal coordinates for, say, North Kendell High School?"

Solaritron's CPU flashed. "In that case, we would be located somewhere between Managua, Nicaragua and the northern-most tip of Mexico's Yucatan Peninsula."

"That's impossible!" shouted Henry. "Do a systems diagnostic right now."

Solaritron complied, ticking off system after system, and insisting that each one was functioning at its highest level of efficiency and performance.

"Well, if that *is* where we are, how do you explain how we got here?"

"I have no explanation. My data files do not include any information that could account for this situation. Perhaps my recording of the events which occurred immediately prior to my automatic shutdown would be of help."

"What recording? What events? What are you talking about?"

"You programmed me to record all unusual events I observe, did you not? The orb-like phenomenon in the excavation beneath the old field house clearly constitutes an 'unusual event' for recording purposes."

"Phenomenon?" exclaimed Henry, remembering the weird, frightening light. "Good Lord, I remember now! I saw that light thing too, whatever it was. What happened?"

"As instructed, I proceeded to the lower level of the Kendell field house to retrieve Mr. Smith from his relationship negations with the lovely Ms. Sarah Weston. And you can't fool me, Mr. Dundridge. I know you have a secret crush on her. Anyway, at the bottom of the first flight of stairs I noticed a strange light and buzzing sound emanating from beyond a metal doorway. I proceeded through and down a service staircase into the building's basement, where I came upon a rather extensive archaeological excavation. Searching for Mr. Smith, I finally located him down at its far end. He was standing on a carved stone slab between me and the unidentifiable phenomenon: a large, spherical orb of light hovering in the air. He appeared to be in a trance. I needed to use several light filters before I was able to spot him through the glare. Ms. Weston was no where to be seen, although I did catch a glimpse of a cat running into a small, canvas-sided shed. At that point I activated my recorder pursuant to program parameters."

"Porter," muttered Henry lowly, looking about. He'd completely forgotten about his friend. "Sola, what happened to Porter?"

"As I approached Mr. Smith from behind to request his hasty departure, he jumped into the orb and disappeared. You told me not to return without him, so I tried to retrieve him."

Now Henry's memory came rushing back—sort of. His recollection of what had happened was choppy and disjointed. He too had seen the terrible orb, but what about Sarah? He kind of recalled her crying out for help, but for some reason his mind seemed to be blocking things out. Whatever had happened, Solaritron had ended up wherever *here* was. Porter must be nearby as well. "Solaritron, we need to find Porter. He may be hurt. He may need first aid."

"Stand back," replied the machine, the lenses within its domed top beginning to rotate slowly.

Henry could see Solaritron had activated its recently-installed night vision unit: lenses and circuitry salvaged from an old pair of army surplus binoculars his dad had given him. He nodded in approval.

Solaritron's lenses stopped, reversed a bit, and stopped again before whirring back and forth, focusing and refocusing.

Henry looked in the same direction, but couldn't make anything out in the darkness.

"Positive identification. Mr. Porter Smith is over there," declared the machine as it spun around, lurched forward, and sped across the clearing—dodging through the clay fire pots like a professional soccer player.

Henry stumbled after it and in a moment he saw his friend lying motionless on the ground.

Solaritron reached Porter first, and as Henry caught up the machine thrust out one of its articulated arms to restrain him. "It appears Mr. Smith has suffered a mild concussion. Observe the bump on his head. It is probably best not to move him until he wakes up."

Studying his friend's forehead, Henry noticed a goose egg-sized lump. "He must have fallen off the platform, hit his head, and staggered over here before collapsing. Porter, can you hear me?"

No answer, just the rise and fall of the young man's chest in what appeared to be an easy sleep.

"Do you think he'll be all right?"

Solaritron's CPU light flashed a few times indicating it was accessing one of his data files. "According to the 2014 edition of *Compton's Encyclopedia*, the main concern with any head trauma is when the injury is accompanied by internal bleeding. Such bleeding may occur even if the skull looks normal. An accumulation of blood may put pressure on the brain, eventually causing neurological damage."

Henry gulped nervously at Solaritron's diagnosis.

"Most head injuries, however, are not serious and a full recovery can be expected," it continued. "The person may sleep after the injury occurs and typically is back to normal within eight hours, except, of course, for any swelling in the area of the trauma."

Henry breathed a sign of relief. "What should we do?"

"Apply ice to the bruised area to minimize the swelling and observe the victim carefully for the first twenty-four to seventy-two hours. Symptoms of bleeding within the head usually occur during this time frame."

"I don't think we're going to find any ice around here," replied Henry, looking around in vain. "Not until morning, at least. What symptoms should we look for?"

The machine recited a laundry list of symptoms, most of which were quite unsettling. Visual problems, bleeding from the eyes, ears, or mouth, fluid draining from nose, repeated vomiting, seizures and, of course, the most serious symptom: death.

"Well, let's try to make him as comfortable as possible," said Henry. "Would you please fetch me my coat?"

As the machine sped off back towards the platform, Henry knelt down next to Porter, then carefully unzipped his friend's coat and unfastened the first couple of buttons at the collar of his shirt.

Stirring, Porter muttered something about his head hurting before falling fast asleep again.

"This whole thing is crazy," said Henry, looking around again. "Where are we? How did we get here?" He stood to meet the returning robot. Thankfully his dizziness was almost gone.

In addition to his coat, Solaritron had retrieved two of the baskets from the base of the platform. One contained some fruit; the other dried fish. It held them up towards Henry. "I thought you might be hungry. This basket contains several nice, ripe pieces of 'chrysopyhllum cainito.'"

"Chryso...? Chryso...? Awe, come on, Sola. What are they in English?"

"Chrysopyhllum cainito! They're commonly called 'star apples.'"

Henry plucked one from the basket and looked at it. It appeared to be purple in color, but he couldn't be sure in the dim light cast from the fire pots. It was about the size of an apple, but not nearly as firm. Raising it to his nose he gave it a sniff. "It sure smells good," he replied, before placing it back in its basket. Why are they called star apples?"

"Because when cut in two, the cores are star-shaped. According to my files, the pulp is soft and sweet, although the rind is reported as bitter and inedible." It then presented the second basket for Henry's inspection. "The small fish in this one are dried dorados. Both star apples and dorado fish are common to the West Indies. Assuming we are within the longitudes of those island groups, we are likely to be somewhere between Barbados in the east and Cuba in the west."

Henry studied the little, shriveled fishes staring lifelessly up at him from the second basket. While he had no explanation for what had happened, he still doubted his robot's estimation of where they might be, although its human mimicry programming was now functioning at 110 percent. "Thank you, Sola. Maybe I'll eat something a little later. I don't feel so hungry right now."

The machine handed Henry his coat before carefully placing the baskets on the ground.

"Sola, you said you recorded that light thing. 'Orb,' I think you called it."

"The record begins from the time I observed Mr. Smith in the field house using my glare filters until a voltage surge triggered my automatic shutdown. The record is approximately four minutes and thirty-seven seconds in length."

"Would you play it back please?"

"Your wish is my command."

A rectangular section on a smooth portion of the robot's upper assembly turned a milky white color before filling with a still image of Porter standing before a ten-foot-diameter sphere of white light, streaked here and there with bolts of cobalt-blue lightning. Henry shuddered at the sight as the picture sprang to life. Apart from sounds he recognized as Solaritron's inner workings, all that could be heard was a loud, buzzing sound emanating from the orb, like it was filled with thousands and thousands of angry bees. As Solaritron approached Porter from behind, it soon became clear his friend was in some sort of hypnotic trance, gently patting the orb's surface with his right hand; sending growing circles of light out from his touch like ripples expanding across a smooth pond. Then, without warning, Porter lowered his arm, stepped back a couple of paces, and lunged forward again, jumping straight into the orb where he disappeared in a flash of blue lightning.

Solaritron's recorder lens focused on the area where Porter had vanished. Larger and larger the orb loomed as the robot rushed towards it, trying to retrieve Henry's friend. A few bouncing camera jerks and the slab's steps disappeared from view; then in a bright, blue flash the room was gone—replaced by shimmering, white light all around. It was obvious the machine had plunged into the orb after Porter without hesitation.

As he watched, Henry found himself feeling nauseous, like the early pangs of seasickness were beginning to tug at his stomach. The shimmering light of the orb, he realized, reminded him of waves of water. "Please advance recording past these images," he gagged, looking away. "I feel like I'm getting seasick."

"Done."

Looking back at the screen after his stomach settled down, Henry noticed the image was in freeze-frame again. The white light had dissipated to mere wisps and people and torches could be seen. A red bar at its bottom indicated the robot's safety shutdown sequence had been triggered.

"This is where I exited the orb," said Solaritron matter-of-factly. "Its electric field rendered most of my sensors inoperable, causing my legs to retract shortly after I entered it. As you can see from the recording, it also caused a polarization discontinuity which triggered my automatic shutdown."

"I can see that," said Henry, studying the image. Solaritron had obviously emerged at the top of the nearby platform, upon which stood several handsome, bronze-skinned, black-haired people dressed in bright feather capes and elaborate headdresses. Some were holding baskets of fish or fruit. Others held torches. All were looking down and away: at something hidden from the recorder's view. Each and every one of them looked terrified and confused.

"Shall I resume playback?" asked Solaritron after a few moments.

"Please do."

The image sprang to life again and the people in it grew quickly as Solaritron hurled towards them. Almost immediately they jerked their heads around towards the recorder's lens and began screaming, running, twisting, and jumping to get out of the wayward robot's path. Torches and baskets were flung in every direction as they scrambled to escape. Then the view pitched downwards and for an instant he could see Porter near the bottom of the ramp. His friend looked dazed and was being supported by two young women. Then the image began wobbling violently as the machine's forward momentum carried it down the bumpy ramp on its ball roller. Now more shouts could be heard, followed by a general roar of panic. As Solaritron finally came to a rest at ground level, the view stabilized, showing hundreds of terror-stricken people running wildly in every direction. Many were pointing at the robot. Others were screaming something which sounded like, "Kulkon! Kulkon!" Some were dressed in exotic costumes made of animal skins and feathers. Most, however, were nearly naked: wearing only body paint, necklaces, and large, spindle-shaped earrings. The image abruptly stopped and faded away as the red bar, shrinking throughout the recording, disappeared.

"This is where my automatic shutdown occurred," concluded Solaritron. "It appears that somehow the orb transported us from the old Kendell field house to our current location."

Henry looked around again. Maybe this was some sort of elaborate joke Robby Lee was playing on him. But how could Solaritron have been tampered with? He thought the machine's security system was foolproof. Lee was a computer genius, though. Or maybe the answer was simpler than that. Maybe he'd been hypnotized and was at this very moment providing side-splitting entertainment to Lee and the rest of his cronies. No. If he was hypnotized he would never suspect it until after he was awake. This line of reasoning led him back to his theory that he was in the middle of a vivid dream. "Or maybe," he gulped. "Maybe I was electrocuted and died and this place is..." He shook the dreadful thought from his head. This place was obviously somewhere between heaven and hell. He just needed to figure out where they were and how to get home.

"Perhaps Mr. Smith's portacom would be of help," suggested Solaritron. "You tried to call him on it back at the field house, remember? I have also noticed he almost always carries a tiny radio receiver with him for entertainment."

"Of course!" shouted Henry, trotting over to his sleeping friend. He knelt down and carefully began searching through Porter's coat pockets. "Yes," he said upon finding the tiny phone. "That's right. I remember lending it to him now." His hands shook as he turned it on. "Oh please let it be charged."

After a moment the device said it was ready for dialing instructions.

"This is a medical emergency!" shouted Henry. "Please locate and contact the nearest available assistance."

The phone beeped acknowledgment and began dialing number after number, but after a few moments it stopped and delivered the following impossible message: "Unable to establish a connection with 911; unable to establish a connection with the operator; unable to establish a connection with the local police department; unable to establish a connection with the local fire department; and on and on down the list. And in each instance the portacom would conclude, "Unable to establish a connection."

Switching off the phone, Henry hung his head in disbelief. It was unheard of not to be able to establish a connection in this day and age. The whole world had been wired to the gills as far as portable telephones went. You'd have to be standing on the North Pole during a major solar flare to get the message the little phone just delivered.

Shoving it in his coat pocket, he knelt down again and searched Porter until he found the little, disk-shaped radio.

Standing, Henry told Solaritron to shine some light on it as he studied its controls. After figuring out how it worked, he clipped an earphone to a lobe and switched it on, praying he'd be rewarded by the sound of a familiar radio station. Instead, raw static blasted painfully into his head, causing him to wince. "Ouch!" *I'll have to warn Porter again on the dangers of loud-radio-induced hearing loss*, he thought, quickly lowering the volume and tuning from station to station. As he did, nothing but pure, uninterrupted static hissed back into his ear. He shook the radio and tried tuning it again, only to experience the same result. How could they possibly be out of range of any radio stations? Turning it off, he returned it to Porter's pocket. "I'm getting nowhere," he grumbled. "Either these things don't work or we're *really* in trouble."

"Perhaps an explanation will present itself in the morning," offered Solaritron diplomatically. "In the meantime, I suggest you eat something and try to get some rest. I will stand guard and wake you if anyone or anything approaches. My fuel cells are still sixty percent charged. That is more than enough energy for me to make it through to the morning. If it is sunny tomorrow I can recharge to full capacity in a few minutes."

"Thanks, Sola," replied Henry wearily. The physical and mental strain he had recently endured, coupled with their strange predicament, had finally taken its toll and he felt extremely sleepy. Rolling his coat up into a pillow, he lay down on the ground, placing it under his head before staring up at the stars twinkling above. "I think I will take a little nap," he said, closing his eyes. "Wake me if you detect anything that might pose a danger. Hopefully Porter will be better by morning and the three of us can figure out what's going on. Things never look quite so bad in the morning," he added slowly, before falling fast asleep.

Cacique Caguama, High Chief of the Island of Boriken, was sitting on a low, ceremonial chair as he prepared to address a hastily-gathered assembly of grim men—all sitting in a circle around a small, crackling fire to discuss what must be done, and Chief Caguama's decision might either doom or save his people. He was frightened, but as a leader had long ago learned to control his emotions. Empty seats immediately to his right and left were reserved for the spirits of his mother and father, and he hoped they would come to his aid in this time of crisis.

Not since the war and subsequent expulsion of the Spaniard invaders some years earlier had the Taino people faced such a dilemma. A few hours ago, during the ceremony to honor the long-awaited visit of Kulkon, something terrible happened. Kulkon appeared bathed in white as predicted—whisked down from heavens by the Moon Goddess. All was in readiness. Offerings had been prepared in accordance with the old ways. Prayers had been recited. Then, just as the first offering was being made, the Great God of War began disgorging spirits: three in all. At first everyone thought the second, metal-clad spirit was Kulkon himself, but then the white light disappeared and Kulkon, red as ocher, appeared in the heavens again on the opposite side of the Moon Goddess as foretold.

The arrival of the spirits had shaken everyone badly. While many of his people had run off, he and his elders and warriors, and several of the local sub-chiefs and priests, had retreated to Otoao, a village near the center of Boriken Island not far from the ancient ceremonial center of Ku' Karaya, the holy place dedicated to Kulkon, for the Great God would appear nowhere else. It had been Chief Caguama's home during the Spaniards' occupation of the coasts of Boriken and he knew it well. And as he had done back then, he would have to act decisively to save his people, for word was spreading fast that Kulkon was angered and had sent evil spirits to destroy them. But what course of action should he take? How should the spirits be dealt with? He turned to Mucaro, his trusted advisor seated to his right. "You were with us when Kulkon descended from the heavens a short time ago. Two of the spirits spat from his mouth look much like the evil ones who tried to conquer the Taino people."

"It is true, Highness," replied Mucaro, tracing an imaginary circle around his face with his hand. "They look much like the Spaniards. One is also apparently injured. The last runner who returned from Ku'

Karaya said it was still lying motionless on the ground. What sort of spirit can be injured so?"

"What of the other two spirits?"

"They are still speaking with each other in a strange tongue—neither Taino nor Spaniard-speak. They have finally found the first fallen spirit, but have refused to come to its aid."

"What of the girls who touched the first spirit? Do they still live?"

"Yes. Cajaya is tending to them."

"Bring them to me."

At this, an attendant standing silently behind Chief Caguama ran towards the door of the nearby village lodge: a large, well-built rectangular building made of wood and thatch, returning a few moments later with the girls in tow. They were clutching each other and sobbing uncontrollably as several priests—following closely behind—took turns blowing blue smoke on the girls through long wooden tubes; trying to purge any spells or curses the injured spirit may have placed over them.

Chief Caguama motioned for the girls to sit. They were nieces of his and he knew they could speak freely to him.

The girls, still clutching each other, sat down as commanded. Their sobbing subsided with the departure of the smoke-blowing priests.

"Listen carefully and answer truthfully, my children," said Caguama kindly. "The priests have rid you of any spells and you have nothing to fear."

The girls nodded in unison before staring meekly at the ground.

"When the first spirit spat from Kulkon's mouth appeared and collapsed in your arms, did it burn your flesh?"

They shook their heads no. Ginhua, the older of the two, held out her hands and arms to emphasize the point.

Mucaro leaned over and studied them for a moment. "I see no burns, Highness."

Chief Caguama nodded. "Did the Spirit's touch make you feel ill or dizzy?"

Again they shook their heads no.

Yimea, the younger one, spoke out. "Its clothes felt thick and heavy, yet very smooth. Not like this," she added, touching the hem of her woven, cotton skirt.

"Bring me the cloak of the dead Spaniards' chief!" commanded Chief Caguama.

One of his servants ran to a nearby basket and removed a folded up garment. Returning, he bowed respectfully and handed it down to Caguama. Although smooth and brown, it was stiff and badly cracked with age.

"You were very young, but do you remember the evil men who came to our island and tried to enslave us?"

"Yes," replied Ginhua. "The tale is sung near the end of every areyto ceremony." And in a sweet voice she began singing. "The Spaniards came in great ships pushed by the wind. They were kind at first, but tricked the Taino, showing their evilness. After stealing our gold, they whipped the Taino. Then they made us their slaves and cursed the Taino gods. Angered, Kulkon appeared and breathed new hope and great strength into his people. First, he conjured a great storm which destroyed the Spaniards' fleet. Rising up, the Taino defeated the remaining Spaniards and their dogs and horses. Those who did not escape were sacrificed and consumed in honor of Kulkon."

The assembly nodded approvingly at Ginhua's recital as Chief Caguama turned and offered the girls the folded garment. "This is a cloak that belonged to the Spaniards' chief. I carry it with me always. Do not be afraid. His spirit cannot harm you for I killed him with my own hands. It, and others like it, are made from the skin of strange beasts which live in Spaniards' faraway birth land. Beasts whose milk and flesh the Spaniards feed upon. Touch it and tell me: does it feel like the one worn by the injured spirit?"

The girls felt the garment for a few moments, before withdrawing their hands away in fear.

"It is old, but feels the same!" cried Ginhua.

"The same smoothness!" added Yimea.

Chief Caguama looked at Mucaro, who responded with a knowing nod. "Ginhua. Yimea," he continued. "Was there anything else you noticed about the spirit? Think carefully."

Ginhua looked bashfully at the ground. "He was very handsome," she said quietly.

Yimea gave Ginhua a good nudge with her elbow.

Chief Caguama shot Yimea a stern look, holding up his hand firmly towards her. "Stop that. Continue, Ginhua. There is nothing to be ashamed of. The truth is the most important thing now."

"He was hurt and I felt for him," replied Ginhua quickly. "I was not afraid until the priests started speaking of spells and curses. I felt nothing evil from the spirit. Only flesh and bones beneath his strange cape."

"And you, Yimea," continued Chief Caguama, handing the garment back to his servant, who trotted off to return it to its basket. "Do you feel this way as well?"

Looking down, Yimea shook her head that she did.

"You have done well to speak the truth, my children," said Chief Caguama before bidding them to go and stay with Cajaya for the night. When they were gone he called out to Natiao, the priest who had presided over the preparations for Kulkon's arrival. "Natiao, was it not because of Kulkon's last visit the Taino people found the strength to defeat the Spaniards?"

"Just so," the priest replied nervously, still quite shaken over the evening's events.

"And you are certain all preparations were the same? Nothing to anger him?"

Natiao fell forward, throwing himself face down onto the ground within the circle of men. "Everything was in accordance with the old ways!" he cried. "I swear it. Strike me dead right here if you believe it will make the spirits go away!"

"Get up, my friend," said Chief Caguama, motioning towards Natiao with his hand. "Return to your place in the circle." Caguama had witnessed how Natiao had struggled to make certain everything was ready for Kulkon's visit.

Natiao, still sobbing, pushed himself up and crawled backwards to resume his place among the others. When he was seated again, sub-chiefs sitting nearby patted him reassuringly on his shoulders.

Chief Caguama, his jaw set in a serious line, slowly looked from face to face of the men seated around him. Their eyes, glossy with fear and dread, twinkled back gravely at him in the reddish firelight. "I do not think they are spirits," Caguama finally declared in a firm and convincing voice.

This caused a palpable stir. "What about the second spirit?" cried one voice. "The one with many legs? It speaks, yet it has no mouth! It sees, yet it has no eyes!"

Standing, Chief Caguama walked over to a post next to the door of the lodge, upon which sat a down-turned, rusty, metal bowl. "Remember the Spaniard soldiers?" he said, plucking it off and holding it up for all to see. "They wore these metal vessels over their heads to protect themselves. They wore metal plates over their shoulders and chests as well. They called it 'armor.' Is not the second spirit encased in metal as well?"

Some members of the assembly began looking at each other, nodding their heads.

"The injured one is wearing the same strange animal skin garment worn by Spaniards, is he not? And Mucaro said it himself: 'How can a spirit be injured so?' After hearing the girls and seeing the injured one, I believe they are men, not spirits. I believe one is wearing armor, all three are mere, mortal Spaniards, and that Kulkon has brought them to us for some reason. Perhaps they were captured to tell us of the Spaniards' plans. Perhaps these three have been selected to be sacrificed and eaten in honor of Kulkon. In any event, they are unarmed and Kulkon honors us with them," he added, tossing the helmet back onto the post and turning back around to address the assembly. "All rise, my brothers," he commanded. "I have decided."

The seated men quickly rose to their feet, placing their right hands over their hearts and staring silently at their leader.

"Mucaro!"

"Yes Highness!" replied Mucaro, stepping forward as he adjusted his blue, feathered cape.

"You are to gather twenty of my swiftest official messengers and send them to each and every village on the island. They are to calm the people by declaring—in my name—that the Great Kulkon has delivered to us three of our mortal enemies: three unarmed Spaniards. The messengers are to summon all the sub-chiefs to Abacoa, my village on the northern coast of the island for a meeting to be held in one week's time. All must be present to question the Spaniards why they have been brought here and to determine their fate. Tell the messengers what I have said and make them repeat it back to you twice before they are dispatched. Hurry, now! Time is short."

"Yes Highness!" shouted Mucaro, before running out of sight.

Turning, Chief Caguama next addressed Natiao. "Natiao, you are the high priest closest to Kulkon. You know his ways best. You are to return to Abacoa and prepare yourself for the cohoba ceremony. If these Spaniards refuse to tell us why they have been delivered to us, I may invoke my divine right. You may be called upon to travel in the fifth direction to communicate with the Great Kulkon himself: to find out what he intends for us to do with them."

"I must fast for ten days," said Natiao quickly. "Prayers must be said or Kulkon may be angered."

"Prepare carefully," replied Chief Caguama. "I know it is difficult, but you must do your best. In the meantime, I will send a delegation to meet the Spaniards in the morning," he added before turning to the other high priests in the assembly. "Go now. Journey with Natiao to my village and purify yourselves in isolation. If the Spaniards refuse to tell us why they have been delivered by Kulkon, in ten days, when Natiao is ready, you may be called upon to conduct the cohoba ceremony. You must not speak of this to anyone until I say so. Do you understand?"

The priests, relieved by Caguama's certainty and fearlessness, nodded quickly before hustling Natiao out of sight.

When they were gone, Chief Caguama turned to the leader of his warriors: a muscular, middle-aged man who had been an interpreter during the dark days of the Spaniards' occupation of Boriken. "Boba, you speak the language of the evil ones."

"Yes, Highness," replied Boba with a look of extreme distaste. "I have not spoken it in many years, but I believe I can still recall much."

"Good. You shall lead my delegation to the Spaniards in the morning. I will send Ginhua with you. Her presence may lessen any hostility they may possess against us, since she came to the fallen one's aid. My bravest warriors will be sent as well; placed under your command. Greet and inform the Spaniards that although we are technically still at war, they are my guests and will be guaranteed safe passage for the time being. Request they return with you to Abacoa to meet with me and my sub-chiefs one week from now. You must force them if they refuse, but I do not want the Spaniards injured or officially taken prisoner until we better understand Kulkon's will."

Henry was dreaming he was late for a test. It was one of those vexing dreams: the kind that seems to repeat itself over and over again without resolution. First he couldn't find his classroom, and when he finally did, the test was written in a strange language he couldn't understand. Then he was lost again, only to end up in the same classroom facing the same incomprehensible test. Over and over again it went. It was a relief, therefore, when he finally awoke to someone tugging on his arm. At first he thought it was his mother waking him for school. His relief quickly dissolved upon recognizing Porter's voice and recalling last night's strange events.

"Henry, wake up!" shouted Porter again, giving another tug. "Where are we? How did we get here?"

Henry slowly sat up, rubbing the sleep from his eyes before looking around. The sun was already well above the eastern horizon; nestled pleasantly against a clear, blue sky. He studied their surroundings, but couldn't recognize anything revealing their whereabouts. They were still in the clearing bounded by the stone monoliths: square stones standing on end next to each other like long rows of big, gray teeth. In the daylight he could see each one contained primitive-looking carvings of people and animals. A few of the clay fire pots were still smoldering, giving off thin plumes of transparent, blue smoke which drifted lazily away. And all around them loomed mountains covered in dense, green, tropical vegetation. A flock of green parrots flashed overhead, squawking noisily before disappearing into a tangle of trees past the brightly painted platform and ramp where they'd emerged the night before. He finally noticed Solaritron sitting at the opposite side of the clearing. The machine had deployed its umbrella-like solar collector and was quietly replenishing its fuel cells. "How's your head?" he asked, standing up and dusting himself off.

"I must have banged it pretty hard," replied Porter, gently fingering the lump on his forehead. "I feel okay now, but I can't remember anything after you picked me up last night. I woke up a little while ago and found you sleeping and Solaritron sunning itself over there. What happened? It's so warm out I feel like we're in Florida. Where are we? How did we get here?"

Henry frowned, before recounting the events of the last twelve hours or so—as best as he could remember—including a narration of Solaritron's video recording. The blow to Porter's head must have wiped out most of the young man's short-term memory, though. While Porter listened attentively, he simply couldn't recall any of it.

"Charging complete," interrupted Solaritron during a lull in the boys' conversation, quickly speeding over from across the clearing. "I suggest you two eat something as well," it added, its solar collector snapping closed and disappearing into a rectangular compartment. "The fruit and dried fish in those baskets are edible. Afterwards, perhaps we can proceed down the path I have spotted at the far end of the clearing to look for help."

"Sounds like a plan to me," said Porter, stooping over and plucking one of the round, purple and green pieces of fruit from the basket. "Even though I'm confused and completely out of sorts, I'm still starving." He raised the fruit to his nose. "Smells delicious. What is it?"

"It's called a star apple," replied Henry quickly, beating Solaritron to the punch. "It comes from the West Indies. You better peal it first, because the skin is inedible."

"Is there anything you don't know?" asked Porter as he pealed a piece before taking a bite.

"As I have said on many occasions, it helps having a photographic memory."

Solaritron gave a low whistle, twisting its primary lens assembly skyward as if to say, "Oh, brother."

Henry shot the machine a disapproving glance and considered how much effort it would take to tone down its newly-acquired human mimicry ability. *Not too much*, he concluded, realizing how very hungry he was and stooping to grab a piece of fruit as well. Carefully pealing it and taking a bite, he found its flesh tasted like mild strawberries. "This is really good," he said, before quickly eating it and grabbing another from the basket.

Porter and Henry had finished several pieces—despite their hunger neither had a stomach for the little, dried fishes—when Solaritron beeped loudly a few times to get their attention. "Mr. Dundridge, I hate to interrupt your breakfast, but a group of people have gathered at the far end of the clearing. I recognize several from my recording last night, including one of the young ladies who appeared to be aiding Mr. Smith. Extreme caution is advised, as many are armed with clubs, bows, and arrows."

"Clubs and bows?" repeated Porter, looking over and studying the group of people assembling at the opposite end of the clearing—about fifty yards away. Most were naked, or nearly so, wearing only skirts or loin cloths—and a lot of body paint in the form of squiggly red, yellow, and green lines over their chests and around their upper arms. A man wearing a bright-blue feathered cape—the group's obvious leader—was flanked on either side by several, capable-looking men. Some were cradling what appeared to be wooden clubs. Others held bows and arrows poised for action. "Maybe this is one of those theme parks."

The group ceremoniously proceeded to the center of the clearing, where the man wearing the blue cape walked a few steps further before bowing slightly and reaching his arms out towards the boys.

"I think they want us to meet them half way," said Porter. "What do you think?"

"What choice do we have?"

Porter quickly looked around for an escape route, noting the edges of the clearing all around consisted of walls of dense vegetation. Seeing none, except for the pathway now blocked by the grim gathering beckoning to them, he squared his shoulders and tossed a half-eaten star apple to the ground. "This is what I think," he said, bending over and grabbing his coat. "I think we should play along—at least for now. This may be some sort of joke, but I don't think so. Solaritron, do you think this is some sort of joke?"

"I would hazard to guess. However, I do not see what the motivation would be. The cost involved to stage such an elaborate deception would, in my opinion, far outweigh any associated entertainment value either you or Mr. Dundridge could provide."

A look of amusement flowed over Porter's face. "I think we've just been insulted."

Henry shrugged, tapping his head. "The orb thing triggered its human mimicry programming."

"Great! I like Sola even better, now. Anyway, come on—let's play along. Henry, I think you should be our chief. Solaritron would vote for you anyway, so it would be two against one."

Glancing over towards the far end of the clearing, the man wearing the feathered cape motioned towards them again. If Henry suggested Porter play the part of the chief, it would look like Henry was chicken. "I'll be chief if you promise to treat me like one, at least in front of these people."

"You've got it, Henry."

Henry picked up his coat and turned to face the strange gathering. "Solaritron, you line up to my left," he said, pointing to a spot behind him. "Porter, you line up to my right." After they all were in as regal a procession the three of them could muster, Henry took a deep breath and began walking slowly towards the man wearing the blue, feathered cape—Porter and Solaritron following solemnly along a couple of paces behind. When they reached the center of the clearing, most eyes were locked warily on the robot; a few of the men raising and pointing their weapons at it. Trying his best to ignore them, Henry stopped and nodded towards the man wearing the cape.

Boba nodded back. This Spaniard was paler than the ones he remembered: so pale and white, in fact, it was as if the young man possessed little, if any, blood. For a moment Boba thought the three might be evil spirits after all and a chill ran up his spine. Remembering Caguama's certainty they were men, however, helped quell his misgivings. Moreover, if young Ginhua could survive the spirit's touch, Boba certainly could face them. Just in case, he decided to address them first in his native tongue. If these three were Taino spirits, they would understand him. Most Spaniards, on the other hand, had never bothered to learn much of the Taino language. "My name is Boba," he began. "Official representative of His Highness, Chief Caguama: Unifier of Boriken. You are undoubtedly Spaniards. As a state of war still exists between our peoples, you would normally be considered enemies and executed immediately. Since much time has passed, and since Kulkon has seen fit to deliver you to us, His Highness welcomes and invites you to accompany us to Abacoa, his village at the northern coast of the island to eat, rest, and meet with him and his sub-chiefs. You will be guaranteed safe passage for the time being and should consider yourselves Chief Caguama's guests: a great honor."

Henry studied the man addressing them, who was muscular in the extreme, with bronze-colored skin and jet-black hair pulled tightly over the top of his head in a short ponytail or topknot. In addition to his fine, feathered cape and blue cotton loincloth, the man wore a large, golden disk hanging from a strap and centered over his chest. A polished, red-colored wooden club—carved into the shape of a wide-mouthed shark—hung at his side, and every now and then Henry noticed strange gaps in his teeth as he spoke. Though unfamiliar in the extreme, the man's words were delivered in an unmistakably harsh and threatening tone. After he had finished his introduction, and was clearly looking for a response, Henry leaned slightly to his left side. "Did you get any of that Sola?" he said lowly out of the side of his mouth. "What did he say?"

"With the exception of, 'Boriken' and 'Spaniard,' his words do not correspond to any listed in my language or lexicon programming. The word 'Boriken' is what the ancient inhabitants of the Greater and Lesser Antilles called the Island of Puerto Rico."

"'Puerto Rico' and 'Spaniard,' huh?" muttered Henry, who had already taken two Spanish courses his freshman year and was active in his school's Latin American Club. "Sola, back me up if I need it," he ordered, looking down and cradling his chin with his hand; frowning in thought for a moment before addressing the man. "Estoy apesadumbrado. No entendemos. Usted habla Español? I am sorry. We do not understand. Do you speak Spanish?"

Boba's delegation breathed a collective sigh of relief. Chief Caguama was right. These were not spirits. Kulkon *had* delivered them three, unarmed Spaniards!

Boba grinned broadly at Henry, revealing rows of front teeth ground down at the edges into ghastly, sharp points. Several other members of the delegation were now grinning as well—many of who also had two or more sharpened teeth.

Henry and Porter gasped aloud at the sight, falling back a few steps.

"Si! Si!" replied Boba, noting the boys' anxiety with inner pleasure. He hated the Spaniards, as did most of the Taino people. "Yes! Yes! I speak the Spaniards' tongue well."

"Very good," continued Henry, trying to compose himself from the sight of such hideously sharpened teeth. He suddenly felt like a wounded deer surrounded by hungry wolves. Then, in a wavering Spanish, he introduced himself, Porter, and Solaritron—the latter as "Juan."

Boba nodded to each in turn before delivering his original message again, this time in Spaniard speak, but in the same harsh tone.

"What did he say?" asked Porter. Like Henry, the sight of all those sharpened teeth had clearly shaken his earlier confidence. "He sounds pretty angry at us."

"I didn't catch all of it, but his name is Boba and they think we're Spanish. He said we were brought here by something or someone called 'Kulkon.' They've invited us to their village on the coast to meet with their Chief: a guy named 'Caguama.'"

"In what tongue do you speak now?" interrupted Boba. It was more of a command then a question.

"We are speaking a language called 'English,'" replied Henry. "It is spoken in many lands, like England and the United States. Have you heard of the peoples of England and the United States? They are powerful friends of Spain."

Boba shook his head no. Was the Spaniard boasting of new allies? Allies who would also try to enslave the Taino people? Was this the reason Kulkon had delivered them? As a warning? He must tell Chief

Caguama of this! "Does this one, the one named 'Smith,' speak Spaniards' tongue?" he finally said, pointing at Porter.

"Only a very little," replied Henry. *Porter barely passed his Spanish class*, he added to himself. "He is from the land called the United States and speaks mostly English. He is a great sailor."

"And this one, the one named 'Juan,'" continued Boba, pointing his shark club at Solaritron. "The one in armor. Where is he from? What language does he speak?"

"He is my servant and protector," replied Henry, attempting to rekindle some of the fear he'd witnessed in the Taino people the night before: fear which might make Boba rethink any aggressive action he was contemplating against them. "He speaks many languages."

"Does he speak the language of my people? The Taino people?"

"No, not yet, but he is a quick study."

Solaritron had, in fact, already compared Boba's two greetings, the first in native Taino and the second delivered in Spanish. Several more translations would give the machine enough linguistic cross-references to form a working knowledge of the Taino language.

Boba, now emboldened by the fear *he* detected in the boys' voices, strolled over to Solaritron. "You say he is your protector," he continued, walking around the machine and studying it closely. "He has no weapons I can see. Where is his musket? Where is his sword? The Spaniards always fight with musket and sword. Did Kulkon take them away?"

"He did not," replied Henry in the coldest voice he could muster. "Perhaps a demonstration is in order."

"Excellent!" exclaimed Boba, calling what he thought was an obvious bluff. "What do you have in mind?"

Boba had taken the bait.

"A challenge: three of your warriors with any weapons they choose against my champion."

Boba was tempted, but he shook his head no. His orders were clear. The Spaniards were not to be harmed, at least for the time being; but he admired young Chief Henry's nerve. "No, no. I was only curious about his weapons, for I see none, only armor."

"Ah," replied Henry. "His weapons? Of course! May I borrow a bow and some arrows?"

Boba eyed Henry suspiciously for a moment before calling out a series of commands in his native tongue, after which one of his warriors trotted over, drawing his bow tight and pointing an arrow directly at Henry's chest. For a moment Porter looked like he might lunge at the man.

"Easy, Porter," gulped Henry. "Take it easy, man."

Once they had the drop on Henry, a second warrior walked over and handed Porter a bow and a couple of arrows.

"Forgive me," said Boba. "Our history with the Spaniards demands caution. I hope you are not offended."

Henry looked at the warrior aiming the arrow at his heart. The man's face was stone cold and full of hate. "I assure you, Boba. This is not necessary. We mean you no harm. But if it makes you feel better, we're not offended. Just tell your warrior over here to be careful."

Grinning back with his shark-like teeth, Boba said nothing. He had no intention of hurting any of them, not just yet anyway. That decision would be Chief Caguama's.

"He wants a demonstration of Sola's capabilities," said Henry out the side of his mouth towards Porter. "I asked for a bow and some arrows so we could perform Solaritron's little trick: the one I showed you last month. That ought to give them second thoughts about messing around with us. He obviously doesn't trust us with a bow and arrow, though. He's afraid we might use it on them."

"I can see that," replied Porter under his breath before smirking at his recollection of the robot's arrow tricks. "Solaritron," he said, pointing away from the gathering. "Proceed twenty-five yards in that direction and…"

"I heard him, Mr. Smith," the robot interrupted. "I know the drill, follow me."

Porter shrugged, shaking his head before following Solaritron away from the group. After reaching a safe distance, they parted, proceeding away from each other before squaring off at opposite sides of the clearing, perhaps twenty yards apart.

Porter tested the bow's tension a couple of times. It was smooth and well balanced: an artwork in its own right. The arrows, long and well balanced as well, were tipped with sharpened, metal shards. "These arrows have metal tips," he called out to Henry. "They look pretty sharp too. Are you sure you want to risk this? They might damage the robot."

"I have full confidence in Solaritron's capabilities," called Henry quickly, wishing his friend would get on with it. At the moment he was more worried about the arrow pointed at *his* own heart.

"Ready, Solaritron?" called Porter.

"I'm always ready," replied the motionless machine. "Fire away."

Nocking one of the arrows, Porter raised the bow, pulled back on it—bowstring to eye—and aimed. Then, exhaling slowly, he tipped it up slightly, estimated the distance to his target, and let loose. The bow sprang open forcefully with a *twang* and the arrow raced in a slight arc directly at Solaritron's midsection.

Then, as before, just before impact there was a blur of motion as one of Solaritron's articulated arms lashed out, catching the arrow in flight less than an inch away from its gray-green chest. Spinning around to face Boba, it held the arrow up for all to see as a second arm appeared holding a spinning, metallic blade. The robot slowly pressed the arrow through the blade, which made a loud and satisfying *burrrrrap* sound as it reduced the shaft of wood into so much sawdust. The spectacle caused a tangle of frightened shouts among Boba's people.

Before Solaritron had a chance to turn back around, Porter nocked the second arrow, aimed directly over the robot at a high angle, then pulled back mightily on the bow and let loose.

The robot immediately detected the second arrow racing skyward overhead. Spinning around, a third, tubular arm appeared which followed the arrow's flight for a second before erupting with a quick succession of *pufft! pufft! pufft!* sounds accompanied by little jets of vapor spouting from its tip. At nearly the same instant the arrow exploded into a cloud of tiny pieces, which arched and fluttered down lazily away towards the edge of the clearing. This caused an even greater stir among Boba's delegation.

Frowning at the robot's apparent fighting abilities, Boba eyed Solaritron warily for a few moments before shouting another series of orders. *These Spaniards would not be so easy to subdue if they refused Chief Caguama's invitation*, he thought.

The warrior with the drop on Henry lowered his bow and trotted back to his original spot among the delegation.

"Remarkable," Boba finally said, turning to Henry and forcing a smile. "I have never seen anything like it."

Now it was Henry who could detect some fear in Boba's voice. How long would it last, though? Hopefully long enough for them to figure out what was going on and how to get out of there. The hostility of Boba and the rest of his people towards them had been evident from the start. Only their fear of Solaritron seemed to have kept it in check.

Returning with Solaritron in tow, Porter offered the bow back to its owner. "Sorry about the arrows," he said, biting his lip to keep from grinning.

Snatching it back, the warrior wiped it on his loincloth as if it had been soiled by Porter's touch.

Porter and Solaritron then walked—in Solaritron's case rolled—back over to stand with their chief, taking up their original positions behind Henry.

"I must discuss Chief Caguama's gracious invitation with my men," said Henry in Spanish. "Would you please excuse us for a moment?"

"Yes. Mull it over if you would like," replied Boba, "but not for too long. My people will gather the offerings meant for Kulkon. You have until they are finished to decide." Turning, he shouted a few more incomprehensible commands to his delegation and—except for his warriors—its members began dispersing towards the wooden platform and ramp of lashed logs.

"Good job, Henry!" congratulated Porter as they walked off to the side of the clearing followed by Solaritron. "That put the fear in him—at least for now. I hope Solaritron doesn't break down any time soon. Maybe I'm wrong, but I get a strong sense these people hate us. What else did Boba say? I could barely follow along."

"This is serious," said Henry, wiping away beads of sweat from his brow. "They think Solaritron is a man in armor and that we pose a threat to them. You saw how Boba reacted when I asked for a bow and some arrows. There was also something he said at the beginning I couldn't make out. It started with, "Pues un estado..."

"Pues un estado de la guerra existe entre la gente de Boriken y los Españoles, normalmente le considerarían los enemigos y fueron ejecutado sumario," interrupted Solaritron, quickly recalling the exact sentence. "As a state of war still exists between the people of Boriken and the Spaniards, you would normally be considered enemies and executed immediately," it added, completing the ominous translation.

"Enemies? But we're not enemies. We're not Spaniards," objected Porter, looking at Henry and waving his hands in the air. "Why didn't you tell him we're not Spanish? I've never even been to Spain."

Henry shrugged. "I never said we were, either. I told him you were from the United States. Besides, you told me to play along."

"It probably doesn't matter at this point," said Solaritron, nipping a pointless argument in the bud. "Since you have spoken to Boba in Spanish, it may be impossible to convince him otherwise at this point. Furthermore, if you take him at his word, you have nothing to fear. Boba said we were guests of Chief Caguama for the time being."

"Yeah, but for how long?" said Porter lowly, looking over his shoulder and seeing several of Boba's warriors busily gathering the remnants of the shattered arrows. "I don't trust that guy."

"Me either," said Henry. "But we need information. Boba said we were brought here by Kulkon. We need to figure out who or what this 'Kulkon' is. I say we accept Caguama's invitation. Boba's people are gathering all the food from around here, so what are we going to eat? If they wanted to kill us, they could eventually overcome Solaritron. At some point we've got to run into somebody who can help us."

"I don't think we're going to run in to anybody who can help us," said Porter grimly. "Can't you feel it? Everything seems funny or different somehow. You know what I mean? I think somehow we've been transported back in time. How else can you explain no radio signals or satellites? They haven't been invented yet."

Henry shook his head and crossed his arms. "That's crazy, Porter. Time travel isn't possible, is it Solaritron?"

"Various theories have been presented over the years discussing both the possibility and impossibility of time travel. No such theory has yet been proven or disproved. Mr. Smith's statement is based upon our inability to establish radio or telephone contacts with anyone, despite the fact his radio and your portacom appear to be in good working order. I have been unable to make contact with any global positioning satellites; despite the fact my communication equipment is fully operational. Nor was I able to visually observe any orbiting satellites last night. All these factors, coupled with the orb phenomenon, would indicate we have experienced a significant, how shall I put it, geo-positional *shift* of some sort. A nearly instantaneous transportation from where we were to where we are. I cannot rule out a temporal shift as well: time travel as suggested by Mr. Smith."

"Suppose for the sake of argument we *have* been transported to a different time and place," continued Porter. "Can we estimate where we are *and* when we are?"

"Assuming Boba is to be believed, we are on Boriken," replied Solaritron. "Boriken is the ancient name of the Island of Puerto Rico. So somehow we have been transported to Puerto Rico. My celestial observations, as well as the local flora and fauna, support this conclusion. During the time of Columbus, Puerto Rico was inhabited by native peoples who called themselves the 'Taino.' Assuming we have traveled back through time, and these are in fact Taino people, then they have already had contact with the Spanish. This would place us somewhere between 1493, the year the island was discovered by Columbus during his second voyage to the New World, and 1511, the year most indigenous peoples of Puerto Rico had either died or left the island."

"Died or left?" exclaimed Henry.

"My historical data files do not include much information on the subject, but the arrival of the Spanish explorers exposed the native peoples of Puerto Rico and the rest of the West Indies to diseases like small pox which decimated their populations. The Spanish also subjected the Taino to extremely cruel treatment. At first they demanded tribute in the form of gold, cotton, and tobacco. When the Taino could not keep up with these demands, the Spaniards made slaves of them, subjecting the people of these peaceful islands to such harsh working conditions that many died of overwork and exhaustion. In 1511 the Taino people of Puerto Rico led an unsuccessful rebellion against their tormentors. After it was crushed, thousands of Taino prisoners were either shot or hanged. The rest fled to the mountain ranges in the central areas of the island or left altogether. It is believed that most the remaining Taino and Arawak Indians of the West Indies were dead by around 1544."

"Wow," replied Henry after a significant pause. "No wonder they hate the Spanish."

"If we have in fact traveled back to early-sixteenth century Puerto Rico," continued the robot, "extreme caution is advised. It is a time which marked the beginning of significant turmoil between Old and New World cultures."

"I agree with Henry," said Porter. "What we need is more information. In order to get it, I vote we accept Boba's invitation. I hope I'm wrong about this time travel stuff."

"Me too," said Henry. "If we *have* traveled back in time, we need to learn as much about this 'Kulkon' as we can. It may be our only way back home."

Then they heard Boba calling to them in Spanish. All the food and other sacrifices had been gathered up and it was time to go. "Have you made up your minds yet?"

"Yes," replied Henry. "We accept Chief Caguama's invitation."

With this, Boba uttered a few quick commands to a lean, young man in his group, who immediately began running towards the path leading away from the clearing: a messenger sent ahead to inform Chief Caguama of the Spaniards' decision.

CHAPTER SIX: A WEEK IN PARADISE

By the time Porter and Henry finished their negotiations with Boba—if the ferocious-looking man's one-sided statement of their options could indeed be called as much—the relentless rise of the sun in the eastern sky had long since burned away any remaining morning coolness. It now beamed its rays, oppressive and hot, down upon their bare heads: heads which just twelve short hours ago had been acclimated to near frigid, late-fall Midwestern temperatures. The boys couldn't imagine anything but a slow and leisurely procession to Chief Caguama's village in such heat and humidity. They were foreign dignitaries, after all—at least in the minds of the Taino people—and certainly wouldn't be driven too hard until they got used to Boriken Island's tropical climate.

Wrong. Porter and Henry had made a significant blunder in Taino foreign relations protocol by failing to offer Boba a gift in appreciation of Chief Caguama's generous invitation. Even the first Spaniards to visit the island had not been so crude and arrogant! Boba took the boys' mistake, innocent and uninformed though it was, as a personal affront both to himself and to Chief Caguama and decided that until they rectified it, the term "visitor" as applied to Porter, Henry, and Juan would be a half-notch above the term "prisoner." When it became clear no gift was indeed forthcoming, Boba angrily called out a series of orders and the members of the Taino delegation quickly started forming two parallel lines in the clearing between the rows of carved stone monoliths.

"Hey, watch it!" cried Porter as four of Boba's club-wielding warriors poked and prodded them into position towards the middle of the double-file lines. Since the members of the delegation were still clearly afraid of Solaritron, the machine was left un-harassed and only joined the procession in front of the boys at Henry's order. Afterwards, they barely had time to tie up their meager belongings into bundles made from their coats; slinging them over their shoulders just as a drum began beating somewhere up towards the front of the line. At the sound the delegation started trotting, two-by-two, out of the clearing and down a narrow, dirt path into the jungle. The drum continued to beat cadence as they went.

"I feel like we're in boot camp," huffed Henry after a few minutes, struggling to keep pace. "I hope Chief Caguama's village isn't too far."

Solaritron's lenses spun around beneath its glass dome and focused on Henry as the robot bounced along in front of them on its roller. "If Chief Caguama's village is near the northern coast of the island, and we are indeed in Puerto Rico, then at this rate the journey will take approximately one day, estimating the number of switch backs through the mountains and assuming only a few stops to rest are made."

"For once I hope you're wrong," Henry huffed back. "At this rate I'll be dead from exhaustion within the hour. I wonder what the rush is."

"Who knows," replied Porter, trotting easily next to his pudgy friend. "But did you see the way Boba was looking at us after we accepted his invitation? It looked like he was waiting for us to do something. Did you notice that?"

"I didn't notice anything," panted Henry.

"Hey, Sola! Did you hear what I said? Any insights?"

Solaritron bounced over a rut. "Watch your step," it warned, as its lenses turned and focused on Porter. "I did not notice it. However, my historic data files make mention of early explorers placing a premium on carrying gifts to present to native peoples as signs of good will."

"Gifts? Of course! He was waiting for a gift: a token of good will. Why didn't you give him a gift, Henry?"

Henry replied with an unintelligible grunt as he panted and puffed along.

"What kind of gifts?" asked Porter.

"Beads, mirrors, medals, hawks bells, magnifying glasses, axes, and similar items."

"Well, we don't have anything like that." Then, thinking of something, Porter put his hand in his pocket and pulled out a coin. "This is an old silver quarter my grandfather gave me," he said, holding it up for the robot to see. "I carry it around for good luck. And boy could we use a little right now. Would this serve as an appropriate gift?"

One of Solaritron's articulated arms shot out of its recess, unfolding and plucking the coin from Porter's hand, before quickly pulling it back to hold before its lenses. "1917 Standing Liberty quarter: fair condition," it added as its lens twisted to focus on Porter again. "I believe I can make a very appropriate gift out of this—with your permission."

"Go for it. And make it snappy! Our own Chief Henry isn't looking too good."

It was clear Henry was not paying attention to them as he struggled to keep up. His face was turning beet red and his shirt was soaked through with sweat.

Solaritron placed the coin in a slot that drew open on its lower saucer assembly. "Give me about ten minutes," it said, folding its arm back into its recess.

They continued trotting down the path as it wound its way through tangled walls of lush, green vegetation, following the beat of the cadence drum ahead. Then, as predicted—and well before the hour was up—Henry collapsed in exhaustion just as they reached a little clearing. Porter shouted, dropping his bundle as he tried to catch his friend, but missed and tripped himself. Both boys came crashing to the ground in a heap, landing on top of some soft, broadleaf plants that snapped and squished beneath them, breaking their fall nicely.

Suddenly the air was filled with loud squeaks and squawks of frightened birds and shouts all up and down the line as the drum beat stopped and the delegation ground to a halt. After a few moments several warriors came running and pushing their way through the other members of Boba's delegation along the path in front of them. Seeing this, Solaritron quickly circled back and took up a defensive position to protect Henry and Porter, unfolding three of its titanium arms and swinging them back and forth while menacingly snapping metal claws.

The warriors skidded to a halt at the sight of the robot before glaring at the fallen boys in obvious disgust. To Porter's surprise they didn't look the least bit winded. "It's okay, Solaritron," he said, standing up and dusting himself off. Tell them Henry needs a few moments to rest. Tell them our chief is still tired from his journey with Kulkon. Ask for some water."

"We will need to wait until Boba arrives. I have not yet learned the Taino language," replied Solaritron, retracting and folding up its arms again.

"That's right. I forgot." Porter turned towards the path and cupped his hands around his mouth. "Boba! Boba!" he shouted before kneeling down next to his friend; pulling a broad, thick leaf from a nearby plant and fanning it in front of Henry's face. "Are you all right?"

Henry didn't reply. He just lay there with his eyes clenched shut; sucking air with heavy, rasping breaths.

"Take it easy. You're going to be okay. I told you to take a gym class once in a while. You're too young to be in such poor shape."

"At this rate I'll be an Olympic-class athlete in no time," rasped Henry. "If I don't die from a heart attack first."

Boba appeared and his warriors parted to let him pass. He still looked quite angry as he studied the situation. "What is going on, here?" he demanded to Henry in Spanish. "I did not order a stop."

Solaritron edged towards him a bit and delivered Porter's message.

"Silence!" shouted Boba in Spanish, glaring at the machine.

"Maybe now would be a good time to try the gift," said Porter, standing up again. "Is it ready?"

"It is," replied Solaritron. "Would you like to see it?"

"Surprise us," said Porter quickly, worrying too much talk between them might anger Boba even more. "I think we should play it up a bit first to butter him up. Nothing could hurt at this point. Please translate for me." Turning, he gave Boba a deep and reverent bow. "Lord Boba. It grieves us deeply that we were so negligent back at the clearing as to forget to present you with a gift. A small token of good will to you and the rest of your delegation."

Henry, now recovered somewhat, began listening in earnest to his friend's gooey, transparent performance. *Oh, brother*, he thought as Porter laid it on thick. But surprisingly, as Solaritron continued to translate, Boba's anger indeed seemed to ebb away.

"We hope you will forgive us," concluded Porter. "Will you now accept our gift, given with our deepest appreciation of Chief Caguama's gracious invitation?"

At this, Boba put his right hand over his heart and bowed towards Porter and then to Henry. His warriors, reading their leader's sudden change in body language, quickly lined up on either side of him in some sort of ceremonial positioning, placing their right hands over their hearts as well.

Porter spoke quickly out of the side of his mouth towards his grounded friend. "I hope you're strong enough to get up and present Boba with his gift. Play it up. You're supposed to be our chief. He might take offense if I give it to him. It's in one of Solaritron's compartments."

Seeing the situation had indeed reached a delicate point, Henry gathered his energy and struggled to his feet, then bowed at Boba. "Yes," he panted in Spanish, still quite out of breath. "Forgive us. Please accept a small token of gratitude," he added, motioning towards Solaritron with his arm in what he supposed was a regal gesture. The machine responded by slowly advancing towards Henry and turning slightly to reveal the small compartment where Porter's coin had been placed.

Porter crossed his fingers as Henry reached in and gently withdrew a finely woven golden necklace upon which hung the Standing Liberty quarter, now polished and shinning brightly. Porter could barely believe his eyes. He half expected the coin to be hole-punched and hung on a shoestring.

Henry was quite surprised as well, but not so much at the sight of the necklace. Solaritron's human mimicry programming, advanced as it was, certainly didn't allow for the kind of independent decision-making the machine was now apparently capable of. It must have commanded its micro-repairbots to fashion the necklace—no, the work of art—from the robot's gold electrical conductor stores. Had the strange orb affected the robot somehow? If only he had access to his diagnostic equipment!

Porter cleared his throat and nudged his friend with his elbow.

"Yes. Yes. A small token of our gratitude," continued Henry, turning to face Boba and holding the necklace up for all to see.

The nearby members of Boba's delegation gazed at it, murmuring in approval. The warriors on either side of him smiled and sighed with relief. A happy Boba was better than an angry Boba any day of the week.

Boba tried to look unmoved, but his anger was gone. The Spaniards had not slighted him after all and he could now treat them as proper guests of Chief Caguama. He bowed slowly towards Henry, who solemnly placed the necklace over Boba's head. Then, standing erect and squaring his shoulders, Boba held up his arms and called out loudly.

"The Spaniards have properly acknowledged Chief Caguama's generosity! It was all a mistake." He turned to one of his warriors. "Go get Ginhua. Tell her the Spaniards need water and that after they rest Chief Henry shall join me at the head of the procession."

Smiling, the warrior nodded and ran up the path.

Boba turned to Henry. "Rest, please," he said in a voice now filled with concern. He pointed at a nearby fallen tree. "Sit. I have sent for water. The journey with Kulkon must have been tiring. From now on we will proceed at a much more reasonable pace."

"Thank you," replied Henry, sitting down on the tree trunk.

In a short while a young woman appeared holding a hollowed out gourd full of water. She had high cheekbones, sparkling brown eyes, and strikingly beautiful facial features cast over a complexion a bit more olive than bronze. Her shiny, black hair fell neatly over her shoulders and behind one ear was tucked a red and yellow flower. She was wearing a yellow smock of some sort and a knee-length skirt. She smiled and bowed at Henry, then turned to do the same to Porter—where her gaze lingered a bit longer than one might have considered appropriate. She avoided looking at Solaritron altogether.

"This is Ginhua," said Boba, bowing slightly towards the girl. "She and her sister came to your servant Smith's aid last night. Perhaps he recalls?" he asked, pointing towards the lump on Porter's head.

Henry looked over to Porter. "Boba says the girl helped you last night after you hurt your head. Do you remember her?"

Porter fingered the lump gently. His headache was gone, but his forehead was still quite sore. "I don't remember much about last night," he replied with a wince.

"He says he does remember her," lied Henry to Boba, recognizing the young lady from Solaritron's recording. "Smith expresses his thanks to her and her sister."

Boba nodded approvingly and passed the message on to Ginhua, who smiled and blushed deeply before shyly looking away.

What is it with that guy? thought Henry. But before he could dwell on his friend's apparent attractiveness to the opposite sex, Ginhua approached and offered him the water-filled gourd. Henry took it, drinking deeply before handing it back to her. "Thank you," he said in English.

She turned and offered the gourd to Porter, who took and raised it to his lips, draining it with a single, long drink. As he finished water gushed from the sides of his mouth and the girl giggled. "Thank you," he said with a smile, wiping his mouth on his sleeve before handing it back to her. A second water gourd was produced and offered to Solaritron, who respectfully declined a drink with a bow and a wave of one of its metallic arms.

Boba eyed the robot warily for a moment, then fingered the gift necklace around his neck and smiled broadly before addressing Henry again. "You shall join me at the head of the procession, followed by my warriors and then your men. Ginhua shall stay with your servant Smith, as the others are still afraid and she is very concerned about his injury," he said with a knowing wink and a nod at the girl.

"Of course," replied Henry in Spanish. "I'm feeling much better now," he added, standing up from the fallen tree.

"Good. Come with me. Our journey has just begun."

The rest of the way to Chief Caguama's village turned out to be a mixture of frustration and disappointment for Henry and Porter, coupled with wonder and excitement. Their frustration and disappointment lay in the fact Boba refused to speak further of Kulkon or how the three of them had been transported there. All he would reveal was the place where they had miraculously appeared was a seldom used Taino holy center called "Ku'Karaya" or "Holy Moon" which had been constructed many, many years ago by the "Ancients."

Furthermore, Porter's time travel theory was looking less and less farfetched. Despite the boys' hopes, no trace of their prior existence materialized. Never a plane in the sky did they see or hear. Not a single tourist or bike rider along the numerous paths they had traveled. No cars, government officials, or police. Except for Solaritron and the few, seemingly useless items they happened to have with them—wrist watches, wallets, house keys, Porter's radio, Henry's spare portacom, Solaritron's remote control, and some loose change—they saw nothing even vaguely reminiscent of twenty-first century Earth or how they might ever find their way back home.

On the upside, they had never experienced such a beautiful, unspoiled landscape before. Ku'Karaya, which consisted of several square and rectangular ceremonial courts bounded by carefully-placed upright stone monoliths carved with simple, almost child-like, line drawings of animals and grinning or scowling people—petroglyphs according to Solaritron—was located in a small valley surrounded by steep, round-topped mountains draped in tropical vegetation. The whole region, in fact, resembled a giant, green, upside-down egg carton: mountains alternating with lush valleys sloping ever downward toward the island's northern coast and Chief Caguama's village.

The path they had taken—in what turned out to be a two-day trip—was mostly along a narrow river that snaked its way through interconnecting valleys at the bases of the mountains. Every so often they passed by clusters of round, tidy, conical-roofed huts made of wood and thatch whose residents would gather and silently gaze at them as they walked by. On and on they went as the path switched back and forth. Even though their trek was downhill most of the way, the growing heat and humidity in the lower altitudes caused Henry and Porter to tire more quickly than their liking. Luckily, Boba could sense when they were becoming fatigued, ordering numerous stops to rest and drink; helping them acclimate to the tropical climate.

It was during these stops that Solaritron's new, utterly unexpected—and utterly unexplainable, according to Henry—almost human-like personality really started to shine. Without the least bit of prompting, the machine would casually recite descriptions of the flora, fauna, and interesting geological features they had seen, all of which coincided with their conclusion they'd been nearly instantaneously transported thousands of miles to the Island of Puerto Rico by some incomprehensible force.

There were the noisy, green, red-faced Puerto Rican parrots, reportedly near extinction according to Solaritron, but present in vast numbers along the path they traveled. And there were the tiny, fingertip-sized coqui frogs known only to exist in Puerto Rico due to the specie's dependence on nutrients unique to the island's soils.

THE MOON CHASERS

Apart from Solaritron's recitations of these and other facts dredged up from its numerous data files, the real entertainment along the way was provided by Ginhua, a lovely, young Taino maiden who had taken a not-so-subtle interest in Porter. Although he had no recollection of her, she was one of the Taino girls who helped him after being flung out of the strange orb the Taino called "Kulkon." Porter had emerged first that evening: right into an assembly of priests and elders preparing to toss sacrifices into what they believed was Kulkon's gigantic, luminous mouth, where he immediately knocked himself silly by slamming his head against a torch handle one of them was bearing. Luckily, Porter was caught and supported by Ginhua and her younger sister as he stumbled, half-conscious, down the platform's ramp; the girls' quick action certainly sparing him from additional injury.

This chance event seemed to grant Ginhua some sort of proprietary right to interact with Porter, and she wasn't the least bit shy about it. While most of the other members of Boba's delegation gave them a wide berth, all along the way she held his hand, chatting and flirting away endlessly in a language none of them could yet comprehend—chatter which Boba was completely uninterested in translating.

Porter simply smiled, nodding back at Ginhua during intervals he thought seemed appropriate. After a while, this lopsided exchange became a source of mirth to the other members of the delegation and on more than a few occasions Porter's idiotic smiles and nods to Ginhua's never-ending conversation caused open laughter among them. Even menacing Boba cracked a smile when Porter indicated he would indeed enjoy being hit in the head again, this time with a hard, rubber ball: the kind used in Taino ceremonial batey court games. Their amusement with Ginhua and Porter seemed to take the edge off the delegation's initial hostility, as well as their overt wariness of Solaritron, who followed behind Porter and Ginhua as they walked along.

This thawing in relations was *not* shared by the rest of Chief Caguama's village, however. Upon their arrival they were greeted with frowns and what were certainly disparaging remarks from many of its residents. This was not surprising given Solaritron's history on how these people had been treated by the conquering Spaniards, assuming they were one and the same. True to Chief Caguama's word, though, they were never physically threatened and were treated, in all other respects, as guests. They were granted the use of a small, clean, thatched hut furnished with three hammocks at the outskirts of the village in a picture-pretty grove of bushy-topped palm trees. They were told they could come and go as they pleased, so long as they were accompanied by Ginhua and one of Boba's daughters named Lealoa. The two girls were of the same age and apparently had enough family clout to intervene if necessary to keep the boys out of trouble with the locals. Lealoa, who was taller and slimmer than Ginhua—but otherwise very similar in appearance with her smooth, olive skin, intelligent brown eyes, and shiny, black hair—could also speak Spanish and act as their interpreter. The only other rules were that they were forbidden from entering the walled, inner-village of Abacoa until their official meeting with Chief Caguama. The beach was also strictly off limits. Although Boba wouldn't say why, the boys suspected he feared they might attempt to escape, perhaps in a dugout canoe like the ones being constructed from felled trees at a nearby river: the trunks being carefully hollowed out using controlled fires and stone chisels.

After their first day at the village it was clear Henry and Porter, and to some extent Solaritron, had been unofficially adopted by Ginhua and Lealoa. The girls fussed over them, preparing and delivering their morning and afternoon meals, which consisted of various combinations of cooked fish, lizards, or birds, along with papayas, pineapples, star apples, bullock hearts, or other kinds of strange-looking fruit. Each meal was also accompanied by a flattened loaf of cassava bread which—according to Solaritron—was made from the tuberous roots of the otherwise poisonous Yucca plant and kind of tasted like pizza crust.

During the days that followed, Ginhua and Lealoa passed the time by taking the boys to see curious sights such as bat-filled caves, rivers that flowed underground, tall waterfalls, and crystal clear pools used for swimming and bathing. Whether purposeful or not, their excursions tended to be away from the walled center of Chief Caguama's village and the beaches to the north. And while at first Lealoa treated Henry like a sickly, younger brother, after a short while it was clear—at least to Porter—that the two were becoming more and more smitten with each other: taking to holding hands wherever they went and gazing intensely into each other's eyes as they conversed in Spanish while Solaritron translated to Porter in English.

For her part, Ginhua clearly had her sights set on Porter from the outset and didn't try to hide the fact in the least. Everywhere they went she would take up his hand in hers, stopping every now and again to lovingly touch his face in the guise of tidying his hair. And while Porter tried to downplay any attraction he had towards her—considering he already had a girlfriend in Sarah Weston (at least he hoped he still did)—Ginhua was beautiful and effervescent and he found himself unwillingly falling for her like a ton of bricks.

The weather didn't help quell these budding romances, either, as it was almost always beautiful. Days near the coast were warm, but not too warm. In the afternoons there were brief, but at times heavy, rain showers. Nights were breezy and less humid, making sleep easy. After a while it felt like they were on an exotic, rustic vacation. But never an airplane, contrail, or fellow traveler did they see. Time and time again their attempts to use Porter's radio and Henry' portacom proved fruitless. When the morning of the day of their meeting with the Great Chief Caguama finally arrived, and just as Porter was having a vivid dream of Sarah Weston—while in the hammock next to him Henry was dreaming of an equally vivid double cheeseburger and fries—Solaritron beeped loudly a few times to wake them.

"Ginhua and Lealoa are here to see you," it said, standing guard at the entrance to their hut.

Porter slowly stirred to wakefulness as the image of Sarah and his dream of her dissipated into the depths of his unconsciousness like fleeting wisps of vapor. Carefully rubbing the sleep from his eyes, he cursed the machine's dogged determination to implement Henry's standing order they be awakened if anyone came within ten yards of their hut. "Good morning, Sola," he groaned testily in the dim, early morning light. The girls always showed up shortly after sunrise.

By now Henry was awake as well, carefully stretching to twist out his hammock. There was a trick to getting in and out of these hanging net beds without being flung face first onto the ground—as both of them had done on numerous occasions before finally figuring it out. He gave one last strategic twist and sprang forward, landing lightly on bare feet.

"Good morning!" he declared. "I feel like I could eat a horse!" So much sightseeing on foot had turned the boys into ravenous morning persons. His cheeseburger dream hadn't help satisfy his real appetite, either. "Are the girls here with breakfast?"

"Yes," replied Solaritron. "And if it is all right I shall bid them good morning and retire to the clearing for my own. The sun is up once again and my batteries are running low. In the meantime, I strongly suggest that—for the sake of civility—you and Mr. Smith go to the falling water pool and try out my new batch of soap."

Henry looked at his wristwatch. "It has been quite a while since your last recharge. It was so cloudy yesterday afternoon. Let them in and go have your photon breakfast. We may be in for a long day. Who knows when we'll be summoned for our meeting with Chief Caguama? And don't worry; we'll take a bath first."

Rolling outside through the door of the hut, the robot could be seen tipping forward in a bow. "Buenos dias, señoritas."

Ginhua and Lealoa giggled at the machine. "Buenos dias, Juan," they replied.

"What a pity such loveliness shall be wasted on two filthy boys," continued the robot in Spanish. "The both of you, on the other hand, look radiant this fine morning. Such beautiful, green dresses you are both wearing. And the flowers tucked behind your ears: what vibrant reds! Will you be accompanying us to our audience with the Great Chief?"

"Si," replied Lealoa. "You are shining as always, Juan. You may attend dressed in your armor." She pointed at the hut before pinching her nose closed and making a grimace. "We are here to prepare *them*."

Solaritron's main lens turned back towards the door of the hut before swinging skyward in an attempt to mimic a human eye roll. "You certainly have your work cut out for you. Two grubbier boys I have never seen before. You may go in and see what you can do. I bid you both good day, for now I must go to the field to adjust my armor and meditate as I do every morning."

Ginhua ran over and reached up to pat Solaritron on its dome before stretching on tiptoes and whispering where she thought his left ear should be under his clear helmet. "You may go, Juan. And remember our secret," she said in her native Taino tongue.

Solaritron tilted down towards her. "You and Lealoa must tell no one you have taught me your wonderful Taino language," the robot replied lowly. "It shall be our surprise to Chief Caguama and the others when the time comes."

Ginhua stepped back, smiling fondly. *Poor, ugly Spaniard*, she thought; *but he is so very pleasant all the time.* "We shall tell no one, Juan," she confided.

"Good," said the machine, righting itself before turning towards a dirt path leading to a clearing with an unobstructed view of the rising sun. "Until we meet again."

The girls waved goodbye as Solaritron rolled off, then walked into the hut carrying the boys' breakfast: baskets of neatly stacked slices of warm cassava bread, purple star apples, and cooked fish.

"Good morning, ladies," called Henry, hurrying over to inspect the baskets' delicious contents. He bowed at them and they bowed back. Both boys were now well versed in Taino greeting etiquette. Lealoa held her basket up for Henry to smell. Its aroma made his mouth water.

Porter twisted, springing out of his hammock and walking over to Ginhua. "Good morning, Ginhua," he said with a little bow as well. Bowing back, she smiled lovingly at him before raising her basket for his approval. He took a long sniff, which caused his stomach to growl loudly. "Ah. It smells delicious, as usual. Thank you, Ginhua. Thank you, Lealoa."

"You are welcome," they replied in broken English. Both girls had made a game of trying to learn the boys' language and were picking it up quickly. They handed them their baskets and quickly stepped back to get out of the way. They knew that once in hand, Porter and Henry would dive into their breakfasts like starving dogs.

The boys did not disappoint, and as they were thrusting food into their mouths and chewing noisily, the girls disappeared outside and returned a short time later, each one carrying a neatly-folded bundle of cloth. They smiled and giggled to each other, cradling their bundles and patiently waiting for Porter and Henry to finish.

"I wonder what's so funny," said Porter, tearing into his last piece of cassava bread.

"I don't know," replied Henry, wiping residual fish grease he couldn't lick off his fingers onto his trouser legs. "You don't suppose there's more food in those bundles, do you? How I long for a burger or taco or something. I dreamed of a cheeseburger this morning. What I wouldn't give for a cheeseburger and a chocolate shake."

Even though he had nearly finished eating, Porter's stomach growled mightily at the thought of fast food. "Well, I don't," he lied. "I am enjoying the native food. Lots of fresh air. Good, natural food and plenty of exercise. I haven't felt this good in a long time. And you don't look the worse for wear either."

Henry looked down at his belt, which he now had to tighten a couple more notches. For the first time in his life he was starting to look less pudgy. Even his face and arms—he had refused to turn his trousers into cut-offs as Porter had done—were beginning to glow with a tan. "I suppose you're right," he reluctantly agreed. "I do feel pretty good. Homesick and lost, but good."

Porter sat his empty basket down on the mat-covered floor, since their hut was bare of furniture except for their hammocks and meager belongings, before smiling broadly at Ginhua. "Thank you," he said again.

"You are welcome," she giggled back in English. Then grimacing, she pinched her nose closed with one hand and pointing first at Porter's and then at Henry's clothes.

Lealoa giggled and did the same.

Porter and Henry looked at each other. The sight wasn't pretty; but it wasn't that bad, was it? Being bashful and under the ever watchful eyes of the girls, they had tried to keep themselves and their few articles of clothing clean by jumping fully-dressed at least once a day into a small, waterfall-fed bathing pool located in the uplands south of Chief Caguama's village. Without any soap, this modest method of washing was proving less and less reliable. Their shirts, which had been clean and pressed a week ago, now looked like shabby, wrinkled, spotted and stained rags. While Porter's cut-off shorts were passable and Henry was saving his "Robots Rule" T-shirt for the day his button-down was too filthy to wear anymore, their habit of using their clothes for napkins had taken its toll. No amount of breath holding under the tumbling waters would remove the accumulated grime and fish oil stains.

The girls stepped towards the boys and Ginhua offered her bundle to Porter, while Lealoa offered hers to Henry.

Henry set his basket down and both boys quickly wiped their hands off on their shirts before accepting the girls' gifts.

"What's this?" asked Porter. After un-flapping a few folds he found his contained several golden arm bracelets, a green, finely-woven cotton loincloth, an equally green tunic of some sort, a belt made of strings of yellow shell-beads, and a pair of woven slippers.

Henry's bundle contained the same items of clothing, only the neckline of his tunic was interwoven with strands of gold.

"These are what you shall wear to your meeting with Chief Caguama," declared Lealoa in Spanish, pointing at the clothing the bundles had yielded. "If you do not change into clean clothes you will certainly offend his highness and the other Boriken sub-chiefs. Such a meeting cannot be taken lightly."

"You must be joking," replied Henry in Spanish, holding up the loincloth and turning it back and forth a couple of times to look at. "I'm not going dressed in a skirt."

"You shall wear them or you shall be painted and go naked," replied Lealoa. Her tone made it clear she wasn't joking.

"What did she say?" asked Porter. A week on Boriken Island had done little to improve his skills in either Spanish or the native Taino language.

"She says these are our outfits for our meeting with Chief Caguama."

"All right!" exclaimed Porter. "New threads! Get me out of these dirty cut-offs."

Henry looked at his friend in disbelief. "Are you kidding? You'll go wearing a skirt?"

"It's not a skirt, stupid. It's a loincloth. If you haven't already noticed, most of the men around here wear them—or nothing at all, except maybe a little body paint."

Porter spoke the truth and Henry knew it. Boriken Island's tropical climate called for little in the way of clothing, and most of the Taino people wore little, if any. At first, this apparent lack of bashfulness had shocked Porter and Henry. Now it barely fazed them—so long as they didn't have to abandon their own, rather prudish senses of dignity.

"Come, now. You must be properly bathed," said Lealoa. "We must not be late." She grabbed Henry by the hand and started leading him out of the hut. "We are going to the falling water pool."

"Wait!" cried Henry. "Let me get Solaritron's soap." He politely freed himself from Lealoa's grip, wrapped up his bundle of new Taino clothing again and, tucking it under his arm, retrieved a hollowed-out gourd from the floor of the hut. It was filled with awful-looking, ivory-colored gelatinous goo specked with black and brown particles of wood ash. Rejoining her he smiled and took her hand again. "Okay, let's go, Lealoa."

Porter folded up his bundle as well, tucking it under his arm before taking Ginhua's hand. "I'm ready if you are. We'll pick up Solaritron on the way. He has Chief Caguama's very special gift," he added, shooting a subtle glance at his friend."

"Knowledge is power," replied Henry lowly in English as they strolled out of the hut into the pleasant morning sunshine. "And with Solaritron's remote control transmitter woven into it, we should get all the knowledge we need, once the Great Chief himself is bugged."

Solaritron had recharged by the time they reached its clearing, and after exchanging a few pleasantries they proceeded down a secluded pathway to the pool they had taken over since arriving at Chief Caguama's village. The other villagers avoided it altogether now, probably because they didn't want to bathe in water contaminated by filthy Spaniards. That was fine with Porter and Henry, though. It was a wonderful, cool, crystal clear pool fed by a little, noisy waterfall. One edge was lined with sand and some smooth, round rocks that were perfect for sitting. The rest was surrounded by lush, green, tropical vegetation. Upon reaching it the boys noticed some shallow clay dishes filled with red, yellow, and green paint lined up next to each other on a tree stump.

"Body paint?" asked Henry in Spanish, carefully placing his bundle and the gourd full of disgusting goo on the ground.

"Once you and Señor Smith are washed, Ginhua and I will prepare you. The paint must be applied to your faces carefully. Now undress," she demanded, pointing at the pool. "Get in and I shall wash you."

Henry blushed deeply. "We will get in and wash, but you and Ginhua must leave first."

"Why?"

"Why? Well, ah, you see..."

"You and Señor Smith do not possess anything *we* have not seen before," declared Lealoa. She turned to Ginhua and in Taino asked, "Do they possess anything you have not seen before, Ginhua?"

"Of course not."

Porter, oblivious to Henry's predicament, was kneeling next to the pool's edge, dabbing his finger with Solaritron's soap and dipping it gingerly into the water to see if it would lather.

Henry blushed again as Lealoa studied him with her clear, intelligent eyes. She wanted an answer, but he was almost at a complete loss for words. "I, uh, we..."

"Is there something wrong with you and Señor Smith?" pressed Lealoa. "Is that why you will never take your clothes off?"

"No, no, it's not that, it's..."

Solaritron, who had been following along with its newly acquired sense of machine amusement, finally came to Henry's rescue. "Señorita Lealoa," it said in Spanish. "These two boys were raised in a land where taking one's clothes off in front of others is unacceptable in most instances. I assure you there is absolutely nothing wrong with either of them, and by bashfully refusing to do so they are, in fact, displaying their fondness and respect." The robot then deployed a couple of its titanium arms and began hustling the girls back up the path and away from the pool. "Shoo now!" it hallooed, Lealoa and Ginhua laughing and giggling in glee as they scurried away, keeping just out of Solaritron's reach. "After they have washed and dressed I will come for you. Then you can apply their face paint. Buenos dias, señoritas."

When they were gone, Henry sighed with relief.

"What was that all about?" asked Porter absently, continuing to play with Solaritron's soap.

"Nothing, we just avoided a clash of cultures, that's all."

"Oh. Hey. I think this soap works. Solaritron!" called Porter to the returning machine. "It lathers up pretty good, but it sure doesn't look like soap. What happened?"

"The sodium hydroxide solution I made from leaching water through wood ash from the fire pit was too diluted. It would not saponify completely with the acids from the boiled animal fat."

Porter looked over at Henry. "What did he say?"

Henry shrugged and started removing his shirt. "Chemistry stuff."

"It should still work well enough," continued Solaritron. "And I would advise you both to hurry, as Ginhua and Lealoa just informed me that, one way or another, they *are* going to see you both naked. '*Au natural*,' as they say in France. The girls are going to invite you to a village skinny dipping celebration next week and say you cannot refuse attendance."

"We'll see about that," said Henry as he completed stripping. He jumped into the pool with a splash and paddled over to its edge, where he scooped a big dollop of goo from the gourd and started washing his hair and face.

Porter did the same and after a few scrubs the soap began burning his eyes. He plunged and surfaced a moment later, squirting a jet of water from his mouth. "I had a dream about Sarah this morning," he said, swimming over to get more soap."

"Oh, yeah? What about?" replied Henry, splashing water on his face. He wouldn't mind having a dream about Sarah Weston.

"It was more like a vision. Have you ever had a vision?"

"I can't say that I have."

A chill ran up Porter's spine at his recollection of the vivid dream. "It was so real!" He turned to his friend. "At first I was flying through this huge, dark tunnel lined with stars. Then I slowed to a stop and came to rest standing up. I couldn't move my arms or legs and started to get scared. Then I heard Sarah calling out to me in the distance. It was like she and I were alone in the universe. It was so strange, yet it felt so real. I called out to her and after a little while she called back to me. At first she sounded very far away, but we kept calling out to one another and after a while her voice finally drew closer and closer. Then, like a spirit, she emerged from the darkness and walked—no, it was more like she floated—over to me."

Henry dunked under the surface to rinse his hair and emerged with his eyes clenched shut. "She was floating? That's weird."

"Yeah. She kissed me on the cheek and hugged me and started to cry. I tried to hug her back but my arms were frozen."

"What a shame. Why was she crying?"

"She said she had been searching and searching for me and everyone missed us terribly and that we had to try to find a way to get back home."

"She didn't say how, did she? I'm open to suggestions, even if they are from dream phantoms."

"That's the point. It wasn't like a dream at all. She seemed so real. Like I said: a vision."

"What else happened?"

Porter looked thoughtful before grabbing another handful of goo. He started washing his arms and chest. "She said something about a park; something about finding a park on a ship. I didn't hear the rest," he added, nodding towards Solaritron, "because your alarm clock robot over there woke me up."

"A park on a ship?" replied Henry. "Maybe she meant a cruise ship."

"Maybe."

They continued washing in silence and soon the pool was edged with suds. After a deep rinse under the waterfall they emerged squeaky clean again, squeezing their hair and shaking their arms and legs to remove as much water as possible before standing in the sun to drip dry for a few minutes. Then they donned their new Taino clothes.

"I shall get the ladies," said Solaritron, speeding up the path on its roller once the boys were decently clad again—if wearing loincloths could be characterized as "decent."

"Look at those legs," teased Porter, pointing. "They're as white as sheets. You should have had Solaritron turn your trousers into cutoffs like I did."

"You should talk, Tarzan," replied Henry. "I think they sized your loincloth a bit too small. Yikes!"

Soon Solaritron returned with Ginhua and Lealoa in tow. When the girls spotted the boys—washed and wearing their new Taino clothing—they beamed bright smiles and ran over to them.

"There," said Lealoa to Henry in Spanish, running her hands through his hair to slick it back. "You almost look human now. Do you not feel better?"

"Si," replied Henry, closing his eyes blissfully at her touch. "Much better, thank you."

Ginhua took Porter's hand and spun him around, gazing at the young man with adoration. "He looks like a prince," she declared to Lealoa in Taino. Standing on tiptoes she gave him a kiss on the cheek. "*My prince.*"

Porter blushed and quickly looked down at his feet. He couldn't help from grinning broadly and had to fight his sudden, strong urge to grab Ginhua up in his arms and kiss her in return.

"Now we must finish preparing you," said Lealoa. "Sit here. We do not want to be late."

Henry and Porter sat down on a couple of smooth stones as commanded and Ginhua and Lealoa went to work. First, the boys' hair was combed back. Each one had just enough length to tie into short topknots. Next, the gold bracelets were placed between elbow and shoulder on their arms. The tunics were adjusted and the yellow shell-bead belts were tied in elaborate knots. The boys' shoes—which had been cut and trimmed into homemade sandals by Solaritron—were abandoned in favor of woven Taino slippers. Finally, wisps and bars of red, yellow, and green pigment were lovingly applied at strategic facial locations using slender, green reeds. By the time the girls had finished, Porter and Henry almost looked like passable Taino high representatives.

Ginhua and Lealoa were quite pleased with the results and were glowing at the boys' transformation when Ginhua looked skyward. Noting the position of the sun, she looked back over to Lealoa and smiled nervously. "We must go now. We must not be late. Tell them, Lealoa. Tell them how very important this meeting is."

"We will discuss it as we walk," replied Lealoa in Taino.

At this, Solaritron turned on its recorder so anything spoken in Taino by the girls or during the meeting with Chief Caguama could be translated into English for analysis later.

Lealoa pointed at the boys' clothing scattered near the pool's edge. "Leave them. They will be taken back to your hut later. It is time to go." She grabbed Henry's hand and started leading him up the pathway. "I cannot stress to you more how very important this meeting is," she began after a little while. "Chief Caguama and sub-chiefs from every village on the island will be in attendance. Many have come great distances to meet you. Some have traveled for days. Most have lost loved ones to the cruel swords of the Spaniards. Your greeting may be less than cordial."

"What if I told you we're not Spaniards?" asked Henry.

Lealoa shot him a wide-eyed look of disbelief. "Chief Caguama has declared to all you are Spaniards! Such talk will only get you into trouble. Do not be foolish!"

Dear Lord, what have we gotten ourselves into? thought Henry. "I'll try not to be foolish."

"Good. The purpose of the meeting is to help us understand why Kulkon has delivered you to us. If your answers are satisfactory, you and Smith and Juan may be offered a chance to join our people by renouncing your allegiances to the King of the Spaniards.

"That won't be a problem," replied Henry. *We never had any in the first place.*

"You will be invited to live with us in peace and harmony for the rest of your lives. If the Spaniards ever attack us again, you will be called to join on the side of the Taino. Can you fight against your birth people?"

"By then, the Taino will be our birth people," replied Henry diplomatically.

"That is a wise answer," said Lealoa.

"How will we know if things are going well?"

"At the end of the meeting you will be dismissed and sent back to your hut. Afterwards, Chief Caguama and the island sub-chiefs will retire to the Great Lodge of the village. According to our customs they must debate your fate for three days. At the end of the third day, and if you have done well, you will be invited to join the Taino people. To seal the invitation, Ginhua will be promised to Señor Smith as his wife when she is old enough." She stopped and turned to face him, taking his other hand in hers and gazing lovingly into his eyes. "And I have asked to be given to you as yours. Ginhua and I will be old enough to marry next summer."

Henry gasped before choking on his own spit at Lealoa's unexpected declaration of marriage, then his face began contorting oddly as if he was in the throes of some sort of cataleptic seizure. "What did you say?" He could barely breathe past the giant bullfrog which had taken up residence in his throat and the words came out in a gurgle.

Lealoa smiled, looking down shyly. "I know it is sudden, Henrique, but we know each other. I like you very much and a future bride must be selected. Would you rather it was someone else?" she asked, looking back up again hopefully.

"No, of course not," he croaked. "You just caught me off guard, that's all."

"What are you two love birds cooing about?" called Porter. He and Ginhua had fallen behind so Solaritron could remove a thorn that had pierced Porter's foot through his slipper.

"You'll know soon enough, brother," muttered Henry under his breath. "Oh boy, will you ever, but not until *after* the meeting." Even though he could tell Porter was falling for Ginhua in a big way, he still feared his friend might run off if he knew what was in store for them.

Lealoa turned and started leading Henry down the path again. "If you are welcomed into our village," she continued in Spanish, "in three days time there will be an areyto ceremony followed by a great feast and the announcement of our engagement."

"What happens if things don't go well?"

Lealoa frowned. "That is a real possibility, Henrique. If you do not tell them exactly what they want to hear, Chief Caguama will emerge from the Great Lodge three days from now and declare you are still Spaniards."

"Then what?"

Lealoa looked down and Henry noticed her eyes were glossing over in tears. "I don't know, Henrique. Perhaps, in time, if you and Señor Smith and Juan behave properly, you will be given a second chance to join my people. Until then I don't know. My father knows something, but he will not say. That is why you must try to tell them what they want to hear. Lie if you have to. Chief Caguama is Ginhua's uncle and he knows we desire you and Smith, but he will not allow you to join us if it will anger a majority of his sub-chiefs. Do you understand?"

"I think so."

They continued on in silence in the late-morning sunshine, each one introspective and nervous at what the future might hold, and before long the path began sloping downward at a fairly steep angle. Past two tall hills, they found themselves standing before a broad valley ringed with cultivated plantings, followed by neatly arranged rows of huts, and then the tall, wooden wall protecting Chief Caguama's inner-village. Several thin plumes of blue smoke could be seen rising up from its center. The path switched back and forth a few times before they reached the valley's floor. After traveling along a broad curve bordered by long, tall mounds planted with green, leafy yucca plants, they reached a cobblestone-lined road leading directly to a wide, wooden gate in the wall, which was framed on either side by elevated platforms upon which stood several lookouts.

When the lookouts spotted Porter, Henry, and Solaritron, a few raised what looked like conch shells to their faces and began blowing. The loud, deep, resonating sound triggered a flurry of activity as villagers in great numbers began assembling along the edges of the hut-lined road between them and the massive gate ahead.

Henry took a deep breath and clutched Lealoa's hand more tightly as his stomach filled with butterflies at the sight of so many frowning faces staring at them. "Well, here we go. Ready, Porter?"

"Ready when you are," his friend replied nervously. "Solaritron, is the transmitter woven into Chief Caguama's gift necklace working?"

"Transmitter is 100 percent functional. Range is five miles. Three micro-repairbots have been assigned to it to ensure reliability."

"Good. Okay. Let's line up like we practiced." Henry turned to Lealoa and gently pulled her hand away from his. "We are ready, Lealoa," he said in Spanish.

Lealoa looked him in the eye and took his hand again, squeezing it tightly before saying something to Ginhua in Taino.

The girls nodded to each other and Ginhua kissed Porter's hand before they let go of their men, lining up next to each other in front of

Henry in the middle of the road. Porter positioned himself behind and to Henry's right side, while Solaritron did the same to Henry's left. Then, on the count of three, the meager delegation began walking slowly in lockstep towards the gate leading to the heart of Chief Caguama's village.

The Boriken Island sub-chiefs and their delegations began arriving at Chief Caguama's Village of Abacoa a few days ago. The last few from the furthest-flung villages at the eastern and western ends of the island had only just arrived the evening before. Now that all were present, the fate of the strange Spaniards delivered to them by Kulkon could be decided. Or could it?

Sitting alone in his Great Lodge, waiting for his sub-chiefs to assemble in the batey courtyard outside, Chief Caguama's jaw was set in a hard line as he recalled the events since the Spaniards' unexpected arrival one week ago. Unlike the first evil invaders who came to Boriken all those years ago, Chief Henry and his servants Smith and Juan had made no demands upon his people, nor were they arrogant or disparaging. Instead, they behaved politely and had followed his ground rules completely. Most villagers who had encountered the Spaniards said they acted like humans, except for the fact Chief Henry and Smith washed with their clothes on, and Juan never washed at all. They certainly were not making things easy for him, especially since a considerable number of his sub-chiefs were currently in favor of killing and eating them in honor of Kulkon.

Ginhua and Lealoa weren't making things easy for him either. They were supposed to keep an eye on the Spaniards, not fall in love with them. Now the girls' mothers and Caguama's wife, Telanni, were demanding that Chief Henry and Smith be allowed to join the Taino people regardless of the opinions of his sub-chiefs.

"They are just boys!" Telanni had scolded him. "You must make certain they will be invited to join the Taino people. They do not behave like the other Spaniards and Ginhua and Lealoa are in love with them. How can you possibly consider allowing them to be sacrificed? Who cares what the sub-chiefs' think or want? You are High Chief and I am your wife. If you must, have the strange one named 'Juan' killed. That should to satisfy your sub-chiefs."

Chief Caguama loved Telanni and would never intentionally hurt Ginhua or Lealoa: silly girls. He promised to do his best, but island politics, being what they were, clearly trumped the women's desires. He needed to keep all his sub-chiefs unified and in line in case the Spaniards ever came back in force. It was their lack of unity that had nearly destroyed them the first time. If Chief Henry and his men could not win over a simple majority of his sub-chiefs by explaining why Kulkon had brought them here, he would not directly override the majority's decision. That would be too much of an affront after such long journeys. Instead, he would wash his hands of the matter and let the Great Kulkon himself decide three days from now, through Priest Natiao and the cohoba ceremony. That would get him off the hook with Telanni. He had confided this to Boba, who was reluctantly—very, very, reluctantly—in favor of admitting the Spaniards into their village only to please Lealoa and Ginhua, and Boba had certainly told Lealoa. If the Spaniards didn't know how high the stakes were by now, then they were fools.

A drum started beating outside, stirring Chief Caguama from his thoughts as Boba solemnly walked into the Great Lodge. The warrior placed his right hand over his heart and bowed. "The sub-chiefs have gathered in the batey courtyard and await Your Highness."

Chief Caguama slowly rose from his low duho chair, adjusting his red-feathered cape and carved ceremonial club hanging at his side. "What is the latest vote on the Spaniards?"

"Of the twenty sub-chiefs, eight from the nearest villages are in favor of allowing the young Spaniards to join the Taino people. Another seven—the ones from west and south sides of the island where the original Spaniards were the bloodiest—have aligned themselves with Sub-Chief Curreo and are in favor of killing and eating them after we learn what they know."

"I'm not surprised," said Chief Caguama. "The first Spaniard invaders killed Curreo's parents and wife. He has been a trusted and close ally, but his family ruled this island before the Spaniards came. He holds a lot of sway and may ultimately win over a majority. What of the other four sub-chiefs?"

Boba shrugged. "They want to hear what the Spaniards have to say before they decide. They profess to have open minds."

"Well, let's hope the Spaniards tell us what they know," said Chief Caguama as he put on a red, feathered headdress. "I will vote to allow them to join our village to please Ginhua and Lealoa *if* Chief Henry is completely forthcoming as to why they have been brought here. But Boba, as Chief, I must honor the ways of our people. If the Spaniards refuse to tell us why they have been delivered to us, I will not override the majority of sub-chiefs. All I can do is wash my hands of the matter and let the Spaniards' fate be decided through the cohoba ceremony. If I do, and three days from now Natiao wakes and tells us it is Kulkon's will the Spaniards be sacrificed, then they must be killed—even if it means breaking Lealoa's and Ginhua's hearts."

"I know Your Highness. I will support any decision you make. Lealoa and Ginhua are young and resilient. If they must, they will forget about the Spaniards—in time."

"I'm glad, friend," replied Chief Caguama just as a series of horns could be heard blowing off in the distance. "Let us go now, for I must join my circle of sub-chiefs. Chief Henry and his servants have reached the gate and the time is upon us to decide their fate."

The meeting with Chief Caguama and the other Boriken Island sub-chiefs was a complete disaster and Porter and Henry were glad Lealoa and Ginhua didn't have to witness the boys' and Solaritron's self-destruction. It had started off well enough, though. They had been ceremoniously escorted to the heart of Chief Caguama's village—which consisted of concentric rings of large, round huts with tall, cone-shaped roofs—by a contingent of elders and Boba's warriors, where the girls were silently led away. There, they were met by Boba, who took them to a group of men who were assembled in a rectangular, grass-covered courtyard stretching out and away from a large, wood and thatch building: Chief Caguama's Great Lodge. The courtyard was bounded on two sides by carved, three-foot-high stone monoliths—like the ones at Ku' Karaya—and the third by a slightly smaller, oval-shaped lodge.

Boba first introduced them to Chief Caguama, a muscular, handsome, middle-aged man who projected authority and intelligence, despite his gaudy, red-feathered cape and headdress. In turn, they were introduced to each of Caguama's sub-chiefs, all of whom were muscular and bronze-skinned, having their jet-black hair pulled back into topknots and wearing brightly-colored feathered capes, loincloths, and necklaces supporting large, golden disks.

The boys' own Taino clothing and face paint was very well received—Chief Caguama said as much—as was their sneaky gift of Solaritron's remote control transmitter woven into a fine, necklace made from strands of copper sacrificed from the robot's store of emergency wiring by the machine's hardy little micro-repairbots. It would allow them to eavesdrop on Caguama and his sub-chiefs now that Solaritron had secretly learned the Taino language.

After the cordial introductions, the three of them were bid to sit down within a circle the men had formed in the courtyard, with Chief Caguama sitting closest to the door of his Great Lodge on a low, wooden chair: his duho. Once all were seated—Solaritron lowering itself slightly by retracting its ball roller into its saucer assembly—the meeting began in earnest and almost immediately took a nose dive which, try as they might, the boys never succeeded in pulling out of.

Through Boba as translator, a suddenly stern Chief Caguama—at least he and the other sub-chiefs did not possess any sharpened teeth—declared that anyone who spoke or looked like a Spaniard was a Spaniard as far as the Taino were concerned, and that Spaniards and the Taino were mortal enemies. He also made it crystal clear it was only by the grace of Kulkon and the boys' exemplary behavior towards his people that they were being treated as guests rather than prisoners.

Worse, following Chief Caguama's opening remarks, the men sitting around them quickly turned exceedingly grim, and in many instances outright hostile. One after another they shot question after question at Henry, who had no way of knowing how to answer in ways the sub-chiefs wanted to hear. What had happened to the Spaniards who escaped Boriken? Who was now the Spaniards' king? Where were the Taino people who had been kidnapped and taken prisoner? Why had Kulkon brought them? What were the Spaniards' intentions towards the Taino people? Were Spaniard ships in the area? Would the Taino be attacked again?

Henry's professed ignorance of such matters—the young man simply couldn't bring himself to lie above and beyond the white variety—clearly vexed Chief Caguama and his sub-chiefs, serving to solidify their belief the boys were hiding something.

Chief Caguama's answers to Henry's questions were equally as vexing, however. Kulkon was Kulkon. Caguama was not interested in explaining a Taino God to a Spaniard whose people had tried to enslave them and destroy their religion. All that mattered was that the Taino's Great Red God of War had delivered the three of them to the Ku' Karaya for some reason, and that reason was not apparent from the boys' unwillingness to answer Caguama's simple questions.

At one point, Solaritron tried to salvage the meeting by crafting answers based upon historical information contained in its data files. The robot's attempts, well intentioned as they were, met with complete and utter failure. Soon it became clear there was a disconnect in histories: a significant difference in what was contained in Solaritron's information concerning the Spanish conquest of the New World and what had happened to Chief Caguama's people.

After a while, this disconnect served to anger Caguama. "We never believed the Spaniards were immortal!" he shouted at one point. "They did not bring disease to my people! It was the Spaniards who got sick! And who is this King Ferdinand you speak of? The Spaniards' King is 'Cortez.' Why do you declare such obvious lies? Are you mad?"

At this, Henry ordered Solaritron to keep silent and tried to implement some damage control of his own by declaring he and his men were "enlightened" Spaniards who wanted to learn more about the Taino so the former combatants could try to reach some sort of mutual understanding. But by now it was too late, and the meeting turned in a decidedly new direction.

"Since you will not answer my questions, I must ask you to hand over your servant Juan's weapons," declared Chief Caguama.

Upon hearing Boba's translation of this demand, Henry immediately regretted his demonstration of Solaritron's arrow tricks a week ago. Even though the robot was equipped with other devices which would serve equally as well as—or even better than—the compressed air gun and high-speed metal cutter, Henry hated to part with them, as they'd certainly be irreplaceable if Porter's time travel theory proved true. "I assure you, Chief Caguama," he argued, "we would never dream of using Juan's weapons against the Taino people."

"Would not the Spaniards disarm a Taino warrior in their midst?" replied Chief Caguama coldly. "All the people of my village have heard about your servant Juan's terrible weapons. They are afraid. Do you think I would not address the fears of my people? What kind of chief would I be?"

Once it was clear Caguama and his sub-chiefs were becoming impatient on the subject, Henry reluctantly agreed. After taking a few moments to remove the air gun—minus its bullet cartridge—and cutter blade from a couple of Juan's compartments, he bowed at Chief Caguama and handed them over to Boba, who bowed in return before taking them away and setting them aside near the entrance to the Great Lodge.

Nodding at Henry, Chief Caguama motioned towards Boba with his hand upon the warrior's return and then towards the other sub-chiefs. "Boba, do not translate," he began in a grim voice. "These three are quite perplexing and this meeting has not gone the way I expected. They are young and confident and willing to dress as the Taino do: not like the other evil ones who tried to enslave us. They behave as humans and have acted in an exemplary fashion towards my people. My nieces Ginhua and Lealoa vouch for them with their lives, love, and souls—even in longing of marriage. Chief Henry and his servant Juan speak the language of the Spaniards, yet they profess not to know anything about the Spaniards or their plans. They claim no knowledge of Kulkon or why they have been brought here, yet here they are, spat from Kulkon's mouth. They say they want peace, but their knight possesses terrible weapons. Then they speak obvious untruths about our history and of alliances with strange, far-off peoples."

The sub-chiefs grunted lowly and nodded their heads.

Then Chief Caguama pointed at Porter. "And this one, the one named Smith," he said significantly. "He is the quiet one, yet look at his eyes. Clear and bright and knowing: like a Yocoba man-god. He is likely their real chief. See how he studies us like a shrewd, shadow, shark-looker? Boba, do they know what is at stake here?"

"Yes, Your Highness," replied Boba lowly. "Ginhua and Lealoa have told them how important this meeting is. They have been instructed to be truthful."

"They are trying to trick us!" shouted Curreo, pointing at Henry with his polished brown ceremonial club, which was carved to look like a gaping lizard. "Either that or they are mad. Why would Kulkon deliver us three mad Spaniards?"

Chief Caguama frowned again. He could not possibly try to rehabilitate Chief Henry and the other Spaniards now, and no amount of debating over the next three days would change the likely outcome of a vote. Curreo was right. Either these three *were* mad or they were trying to trick him and his sub-chiefs. That or they were still in shock from the trip with Kulkon, just as his wife had suggested. If they were mad, they could be executed or just shunned. If they were trying to trick him and his sub-chiefs, they must die. If they were still in shock, they would need more rest. The problem was any one of these alternatives could apply, based upon the Spaniards' dismal performance. He leaned back and stared skyward in thought for a few moments, considering the situation, then came to his decision. Time to end this before the Spaniards strangled themselves any further with their own tongues. If a vote was taken, even he would have to vote in favor of execution. "Boba, please translate for me. Chief Henry, we thank you for meeting with us today," he began, standing.

The other sub-chiefs stood as well, placing their right hands over their hearts and looking grim.

"You and your men may return to your hut. We will speak again of your situation in three days time—as is our custom."

Upon hearing Boba's translation, Henry and Porter stood as well, while Solaritron rose up again on its ball roller.

"Thank you," replied Henry in Spanish, relieved the dreadful meeting was finally over. "We hope to live with you and your people in peace," he added hopefully.

Porter, reading a series of red flags from the furtive looks of Chief Caguama and the other sub-chiefs following Boba's translation of

Henry's words, quickly reminded his friend of the escape plan he'd cooked up. "Henry," he hissed under his breath in English. "Plan B. Don't forget Plan B!"

"Oh all right," replied Henry. Plan B called for an escape in a stolen Taino canoe. Porter wanted to get to know the local waters a little better first. He also wanted to practice handling the heavy, wooden dugouts so the boys wouldn't capsize and lose Solaritron—the robot would sink like a rock—if they were forced to try to escape. The only problem was Plan B would also result in Henry's quick and certain demise due to his proneness to extreme seasickness. "Boba, my servant Smith is a sailor," he finally said. "He longs to go to sea again, even if only for a short while. Would you please ask Chief Caguama for permission to allow him to go fishing with some of your people? We would be honored to share anything he would be fortunate enough to catch."

It was a feeble, transparent attempt that drew a suspicious look from Chief Caguama following Boba's translation, until Caguama asked whether Chief Henry would like to go along as well.

"Absolutely not!" declared Henry without hesitation. "Boats make me seasick! I will not set foot aboard a boat if I can avoid it."

Chief Caguama could barely believe his ears and made Boba repeat the translation twice. Whoever heard of a Spaniard who despised boats and the sea? Chief Henry must indeed be mad. He mulled over Henry's request for a moment, then decided upon an answer he believed would appear reasonable, yet would prevent access to any Taino canoes or the Spaniards' possible escape. Everyone knew Spaniards couldn't swim. "Boba, remind Chief Henry we are technically still at war with his people and taking a Spaniard along on a fishing trip in a Taino canoe would greatly anger the sea gods. I will not permit the sea gods to be angered. Smith may not set foot in a Taino canoe on pain of death. However, unlike the Spaniards, the Taino are not thieves. Chief Henry and his servants are welcome to reclaim their lawful property: the Spaniards' ship which sits upon the rocks east of the bay to my village."

"Thank you," replied Henry with a bow following Boba's translation. Turning, he relayed the information to Porter in English, who smiled and bowed deeply as well.

My first ship! Plan B is going to be easier than I expected! thought Porter, congratulating himself. But before he could gloat over his good fortune, Boba called out several commands to his warriors and Porter, Henry, and Solaritron were politely escorted away.

When they were gone, Chief Caguama took off the gift necklace Henry had given him and handed it to one of his servants. "Take this and put it with the cloak of the Spaniard Chief I killed," he commanded, before bidding his sub-chiefs to take their seats again. When they all had, he began addressing the concerned assembly. "As you all know, we gathered here today to begin debating the fate of the Spaniards. Based upon their answers to our questions, I agree with Curreo: they do appear quite mad. Either that or they may indeed be trying to trick us for some reason." He looked at Curreo, who nodded back, acknowledging Caguama's wisdom—because it matched Curreo's own. "However, Chief Henry and his servant Smith are very young. They may still be in shock from their journey with Kulkon. I cannot decide which case applies, so I cannot permit a vote to allow them to join our people *or* to be sacrificed. Any debate on the subject would be useless."

At this, Curreo and most of the other sub-chiefs began arguing in favor of sacrificing the Spaniards, if not this afternoon, then certainly tomorrow morning at the very latest. They had come too far to be so disappointed, especially after how the Spaniards evaded even the simplest of questions.

Chief Caguama held up his hand, palm forward, and his sub-chiefs fell silent. "Do you know Kulkon's will, Curreo?"

Curreo shot Chief Caguama an angry look. "Of course I do not! I am not a priest! What of it? They are our mortal enemies and must die!"

Chief Caguama looked thoughtful. "Mortal enemies delivered to us by Kulkon," he finally said. "Do you want to risk angering the Great God by taking the wrong actions towards the Spaniards?"

Curreo, realizing his thirst for vengeance had indeed clouded his judgment, hung his head. "No, Your Highness."

"Do any of you?"

The other sub-chiefs within the circle either looked away or hung their heads as well.

"I too cannot decide what to do with them until I better know Kulkon's will," continued Chief Caguama. "One week ago, shortly after the Spaniards' arrival, I planned for this possibility. Priest Natiao has been fasting in isolation and is prepared to perform the cohoba ceremony three days from now to determine the will of Kulkon. And now that he is nearly ready, I intend to invoke my divine right." He turned and called out for a bowl of water, which was quickly produced from the Great Lodge and ceremoniously presented down to him by one of his servants. Caguama took the blood-red bowl and placed it on the ground in front of him. "In accordance with our ways and traditions, I wash my hands of the responsibility of deciding the fate of the Spaniards," he said, dipping his hands in the water. "That responsibility now falls on Priest Natiao and the cohoba ceremony to be conducted three days hence. Once Kulkon's will is determined, it shall be carried out with swiftness and without further discussion. Do any of my sub-chiefs wish to challenge my divine authority to order the cohoba ceremony to resolve this matter?"

All of his sub-chiefs, including a clearly disappointed Curreo, quickly glanced around at one another, then grunted loudly, clapping their hands in unison before singing, "No! No! No!" No one had ever challenged a call for a cohoba ceremony to resolve a Taino sticky point of contention or important decision.

"Good," said Chief Caguama, standing. "Until then, the Spaniards are to continue being treated as guests, but speak of this to no one until the time comes," he added as his sub-chiefs stood, placing their right hands over their hearts again. Caguama nodded to each man in turn, signaling he was free to take his leave. When all of them were gone, he turned to Boba, who had rejoined him in front of the Great Lodge. "That is the very best I could do under the circumstances, Boba," he said. "The Spaniards still have a chance of survival. Who knows what Kulkon will command Priest Natiao to do?"

"Thank you, Highness," replied Boba. "Lealoa and Ginhua will be heartbroken after they hear how the Spaniards' conducted themselves this afternoon. Although I must admit I prefer they not marry Chief Henry and Smith. I hate Spaniards: *all* Spaniards."

"As for that," continued Chief Caguama in a somber tone, "I don't think it's wise to let Lealoa and Ginhua see the Chief Henry or his servants anymore: at least not until after the cohoba ceremony. If it is Kulkon's will the Spaniards be sacrificed, I want it done quickly and out of sight. If it goes that way, you can tell Ginhua and Lealoa the boys were banished. I don't want to cause my niece or your daughter too much pain if I can avoid it."

"It shall be done, Highness," replied Boba with a bow. "I will have the girls confined within the walls of the inner village for the time being. If it is Kulkon's will the Spaniards must die, then I and my warriors will dispatch them to the spirit world with haste and mercy—and with great pleasure."

Chapter Seven: Porter's Ship

"That didn't go very well, did it?" said Porter as they lingered outside the gate to Chief Caguama's inner village, waiting for Ginhua and Lealoa to rejoin them. Although he hadn't been able to follow along with much of what was being said during the meeting, Chief Caguama's and his sub-chiefs' annoyance with them had been immanently clear from the men's facial expressions and body language.

Henry brushed a little fly away from his nose and squinted. The sun had passed its zenith and was now arcing across the side of the sky owned by the west, beaming its rays hot, bright, and oppressive straight down upon them, cooking each and every area of exposed skin. "I did my best, Porter," he replied, wiping beads of sweat from his forehead. "How was I supposed to figure out what they wanted to hear? I'm not a history buff. Even Sola had a rough time! Right?"

"Either my data files are all wrong or this is not the same early-sixteenth century Earth I once believed it was," replied the robot. "Chief Caguama claims he has never heard of Christopher Columbus or King Ferdinand. This leads me to conclude we have not traveled back in time after all. The orb may have swept us into some sort of parallel universe. Similar, but not an exact match."

"I don't want to think about that right now," moaned Henry, pulling his hair free from Lealoa's topknot string and running his hand across his scalp.

Porter freed his hair as well, then shielded his eyes from the bright sunshine with flattened hands and looked around. The sentries posted on the platforms next to the gate, listless and sleepy-eyed, now completely ignored them, and the villagers outside the wall had disappeared, most having taken to their huts to rest out the midday heat, as was their custom. "Well, we're here, wherever 'here' is," he said, kicking up some dust next to the edge of the cobblestone road in frustration. "But one thing's for sure, we're not going to be invited to join Chief Caguama's village anytime soon. I wonder where the girls are. I want to get going."

"It's probably just as well," said Henry. "I didn't want to tell you before, but if we *had* done well, you and I would be engaged to Ginhua and Lealoa three days from now."

"What?" exclaimed Porter, looking at his friend in disbelief. "Engaged? Engaged to be married? They're nice and everything, but we barely even know them! Besides, I already have a girlfriend. Who told you that, anyway?"

"Lealoa told me while you and Ginhua fell behind to get the thorn out of your foot. She said it's their way. According to Lealoa, they'll both be old enough to marry next summer. Ginhua is going to be quite disappointed, lover boy."

"Me?" shouted Porter, throwing his arms up in the air. "If there's anybody in love around here it's you and Lealoa." He pointed at Henry. "Anyone can see it."

"We are not!" But before Henry could protest too much, the gate behind them slowly creaked open and Boba emerged. The man had shed his feathered cape and other ceremonial trappings, and was now completely naked—except for his loincloth and topknot string. He walked over and bowed at Henry, who bowed back.

"Chief Henry," began Boba in Spanish. "Why are you still here? You and your servants are free to return to your hut."

"We're waiting for Ginhua and Lealoa."

"Ginhua and Lealoa have been detained on other matters," replied Boba, looking furtively away. "Please go now. Good day to you," he added, before turning and walking back towards the massive gate."

Porter shot the man a suspicious glance. "Ask him about my ship, Henry," he said quickly. "Plan B, remember?"

"Oh, all right," grumbled Henry. "You and your boats and schemes." Then in Spanish, "Excuse me, Lord Boba!" he called out to the back of Boba's departing head.

Boba stopped, turning towards them again and smiling like a shark with his sharpened teeth. "Si?"

"Can you tell us where the Spaniards' ship is?"

"Your property—of course!" he replied, chuckling at Chief Caguama's less-than-generous counter-offer to Porter's fishing request. "Follow the river to the sea and go in the direction of the rising sun until you come to three, grand rocks. There you will find your property. And remember, set foot in one of our canoes and you die." He chuckled again before turning and disappearing behind the gate, which closed with a loud and dismissive *thud*.

"What did he say?" asked Porter.

Henry told him as they began retracing their earlier route. Back at the falling water pool, they found their clothes still lying on the ground near the water's edge—where Henry grabbed his pants and put them on over his loincloth.

Porter put his cutoffs on over his as well and both boys removed their shell bead belts and armbands, before exchanging their Taino slippers for Solaritron's improvised sandals. Once redressed, they gathered up the rest of their belongings and walked back to their hut in silence, both boys secretly missing Ginhua and Lealoa already. There, they shed their Taino tunics and took to their hammocks for an early-afternoon siesta while Solaritron resumed its sentry duty at the door to their hut. After a couple of hours, the robot beeped loudly a few times.

"Hi Sola," groaned Henry as he stirred from a hot, fitful sleep. He didn't even try to hide the depression his voice betrayed. Lealoa's presence over the last week had helped relieve his growing homesickness, and without her it was now free to painfully surface: as it was now doing by way of the grapefruit-sized lump formed in his throat to stopper tears from welling up on his face. He had a terrible feeling he was never going to see Lealoa *or* his family again, and the sensation was not unlike two, great gashes slowly pulling open across his heart. "Any sign of the girls?" he asked hopefully.

"No," replied Solaritron.

Henry looked over to Porter's hammock and was about to say something when he noticed it was hanging empty. "Where's Porter?"

"Mr. Smith and I have been discussing our situation. He is out fashioning a weapon. I have lent him one of my spare cutter blades and some copper wire."

"What?" exclaimed Henry, twisting out of his hammock. "Fashioning a weapon? Sola, what's going on?"

"Here he comes now," said Solaritron, backing up a bit to let Porter pass, before blocking the doorway to the hut again. "Ask him yourself."

"Good afternoon, sleepyhead," said Porter with a nod and a determined smile. He was wearing his blue, button-down shirt over his green tunic. "Time to institute 'Plan B!' Come on, Henry. Get dressed. We've got a lot to do between now and Sunday." If Porter was as depressed and homesick as Henry was, he certainly didn't show it. "And put on both your shirts, we might be spending the night on the beach. It might get a little chilly towards morning, but not enough to bother with our leather coats."

"Why between now and Sunday?" asked Henry, stepping into his sandals.

"You told me what Lealoa said! Chief Caguama and his sub-chiefs are deciding what to do with us as we speak. They'll reach their final decision on Sunday. I'll be the one who decides what happens to me," he added, pulling aside his un-tucked shirt and plucking a homemade dagger from a sheath hanging at his belt: one of the Taino slippers Ginhua had given him. Porter had fashioned the dagger by lashing Solaritron's spare cutter blade to a short, thick stick with the copper wire the machine had given him. He brandished it at Henry before returning it to the sheath hidden beneath his shirt. "Tell him, Sola."

"I recorded every word during our meeting with Chief Caguama," replied the robot, its lenses twisting and focusing on Henry. "Towards the end, Sub-Chief Curreo said he believes we all three are either lying or mad."

"So?"

"My data files mention that the Taino, Caribe, and other Arawak tribes of this region sometimes killed their mentally disabled. If they conclude we're mad, we may be done for. If they conclude otherwise, then it is highly probable they will also conclude we lied to them. What do you think the Taino do to their lying, mortal enemies? I would hazard to guess they kill them as well."

"I don't agree," said Henry, pointing at Solaritron. "If those were the only two possible alternatives, we'd have been killed already—and we certainly wouldn't be given access to a ship. What about the transmitter woven into Chief Caguama's gift necklace?" he pressed. "That was the whole point of the bug, after all: to find out what they intend to do with us before we run off half-cocked!"

"That was before our wonderful performance at the meeting this afternoon," replied Porter sarcastically. "The more I think about it, the less I like the body language I saw from Caguama and his boys. And the bug isn't working either, is it Solaritron?"

"It's working," replied the machine. "But it has been placed at some location which renders it useless. Listen."

Turning his head, Henry listened as sounds emerged from one of Solaritron's speakers. He could hear voices, but they were low and deeply muffled; completely unintelligible. "Any way to augment?"

"Not with any reliability."

Henry frowned deeply before turning to Porter. "Since the transmitter isn't working, I agree we need to begin implementing an escape plan, just in case things get ugly come Sunday. But we've got to be discreet, and for God's sake don't be flashing that dagger around! Chief Caguama could have us confined to this hut if he wanted to."

"Agreed," said Porter. "I'll be discreet, but in a determined way."

"Thank you," replied Henry, picking up his neatly folded "Robots Rule" T-shirt from the mat-covered floor and pulling it on over his head. He brushed some dirt off it before grabbing his stained button-down from a stick jammed into the hut's thatched wall, putting it on over the T-shirt.

"Even though I am a robot, I would like to save my skin too, composite though it may be," added Solaritron as Henry finished dressing. "Let's get going; we don't have much daylight left—although I can function equally as well in darkness."

They left the hut and started towards the river leading to the sea, but after a few steps Henry stopped dead in his tracks. "I just thought of something," he said, a look of realization flashing across his face.

"What's that?" replied Porter and Solaritron in unison, stopping and turning to look at their friend.

"If we *do* decide to escape, where will we go?"

"That's easy," said Solaritron.

"Easy?"

"Anywhere, but here, brother," replied Porter, smiling and slapping his friend on the back. "Anywhere, but here."

At the end of the river Henry and Porter finally had their first good view of the sea north of Chief Caguama's village—the Atlantic Ocean according to Solaritron—and it was a beautiful sight. Just past a line of tall palm trees they came upon a broad, white, sandy beach leading up to a relatively calm, natural bay bounded by rising stone hills. The water close to shore was a rich turquoise, which darkened into a patchwork of deep blues further out towards the bay's entrance. Seagulls wheeled overhead in the breeze and late-afternoon sunshine, calling out loudly to one another, signaling the boys' unexpected appearance. Several brightly-painted dugout canoes were beached next to each other on the sand near the mouth of the river, but no paddles could be seen anywhere. A small group of naked Taino men to the west were busily hanging up their fishnets to dry on some sticks. At the birds' sudden commotion, they looked over at the boys, before frowning and quickly returning to their work.

"Friendly bunch," said Porter, watching the men for a few moments before turning his head to look in the opposite direction—eastwards along the shoreline. "I wonder where our ship is? I hope it's not too big for three guys to handle."

"Solaritron, you better deploy your walking legs and solar collector," said Henry. "We may be in for a long evening."

The machine silently complied and they set off along the curving beach until they came to a wide arm of land jutting out into the ocean, forming the eastern side of the bay. They climbed over the arm, once beach gave way to impassable stone, and after traveling along through scrub and thickets of thorn-filled bushes they came upon another. This second beach was unprotected from the waves of the Atlantic, which crashed and bubbled noisily up towards them across the white sand, each one slowly retreating again in turn, only to be rolled up into the next wave clawing shoreward. Further to the east, perhaps a mile and a half away, they noticed three enormous, round-topped rocks snuggling next to each other; rising out of the ocean a short distance from the shore. Each was capped about twenty feet above the waterline with thick, green vegetation.

Porter pointed at them. "I bet those are the three rocks Boba was talking about!" he shouted. "Our ship must be over there somewhere."

Solaritron stopped, looking back at the furthest point of land forming the bay and then over to the three rocks again. "I still cannot confirm our exact location," it said, twisting its lenses to focus on Henry. "The shoreline forming the bay is very similar to that depicted on my geographical maps of Puerto Rico: near the City of Arecibo on the north side of the island, only the bay here is larger and much more protected from the Atlantic Ocean. The shoreline to the east looks like a point of land called 'Punta Caracoles' in modern day Puerto Rico, as well. Again, however, the size and geographical configuration of the three rocks is not exactly the same. Also note the palm trees along this beach are coconut palms. The Spanish introduced coconut palms to the islands of the West Indies from the Pacific in the seventeenth century, over a hundred years after the time of Columbus and the demise of the Taino people. It is all quite puzzling."

"There's the understatement of the year," said Porter. "Hey, Sola. Use your telescopic lens to see if you can spot any cruise ships," he added, remembering his strange morning dream of Sarah and pointing out towards the ocean. God he missed her.

"I already did," replied the robot. "No ships or boats are within my visual range.

"Why am I not surprised," crabbed Henry as they started for the rocks again.

"Although the Atlantic Ocean is quite large, as you know," added Solaritron apologetically, trying not to dash all hopes of rescue.

They walked on in silence, trudging along on the more compact, wet sand near the incoming surf. While the landscape was beautiful to behold—like a living postcard—the periodic crash of the waves against the shore and the hiss of the wind combing through the green, waving fronds of the nearby coconut palms gave everything a lonely and desolate feeling.

"Charging complete," declared Solaritron, its umbrella-shaped solar collector snapping shut and disappearing into a compartment. Then the robot stopped in its tracks, the lenses within its dome focusing and refocusing ahead.

"What is it?" asked Henry. "What's the matter?"

"I see a ship nestled among the rocks," replied Solaritron, its voice betraying a hint of human disappointment. "Chief Caguama is a shrewd, cruel man," it added slowly.

Porter studied the rocks off in the distance, but couldn't see anything yet. "Shrewd and cruel? What are you talking about?"

"It is a ship, all right," said Solaritron. "I can see it with my telescopic lens. At least it *was* a ship. Only now I would more accurately describe it as a 'shipwreck.' Chief Caguama's generosity is not quite as magnanimous as we thought."

The boys had not spotted the Spaniards' ship at first because years of exposure to the elements had reduced most of its wooden surface to the same dull, grayish color as the bases of rocks near which it rested about fifty yards out from shore. It was sitting high in the water, supported by some submerged rise of land or rocks, no doubt, and was cracked almost completely in two near its stern. The ship itself looked like an old Spanish galleon from a pirate movie, only smaller and much more rounded at the front. It was approximately a hundred feet in length, with raised decks at either end. Lines of square ports along its side were closed and a thick rope near its bow hung limply down into the water. And from its three, tall masts dangled a tangled mess of wooden yards, frayed ropes, and flapping scraps of sails streaming out horizontally in the wind. The ship certainly never would have survived the elements for any great length of time, were it not for the three, large rocks to the east and a long reef further out from shore, all of which protected it from the relentless pounding waves of the Atlantic as if it was resting in its own, little, protected bay. As the boys and Solaritron studied the ship from the nearest point on shore, the wind whistled and moaned ghostlike through its old, decaying rigging.

Porter kicked up a cloud of sand in frustration before noticing their lengthening shadows. Looking westward he saw the sun was beginning to redden as it approached the horizon. "How much time do we have before sunset?"

"One hour and ten minutes," replied Solaritron.

"Well, I'm not giving up yet," declared Porter, quickly shedding his shirt and the green tunic Ginhua had given him as he kicked off his sandals.

"What are you doing?" asked Henry, although he already knew the answer.

"Going for a swim," replied Porter, wiggling out of his cutoffs and carefully laying his clothes out on the sand before placing his sandals and homemade dagger on them. "I'm going over to the wreck to see if there's anything we can use. Maybe we can pry loose some planks and lash together a raft. Care to join me?"

"I may get seasick easily on moving boats, but I can swim at least as good as you," said Henry as he shed his shirts, pants, and sandals. "Sola, we're going over to our property to have a look."

"I would advise swimming in from the east," suggested Solaritron. "There may be an undertow towards the stern to the west; observe how it is twisted slightly away from shore. I am water resistant, but I cannot float," it added. "So exercise extreme caution, my friends. If you run into trouble or start to drown, there will be little I can do to assist you, although I would try."

"We know you would," said Porter, starting out into the calmest portion of the little, happenchance bay; wearing only his Taino loincloth. "You're our best pal. Isn't that right, Henry?"

"You know it," replied Henry, stripped down to his loincloth as well and joining his friend in the water—which was much colder than he expected. "Guard our stuff, Sola," he added through chattering teeth. "If anyone comes around, don't tell them where we went. Most sailors of old feared the water and couldn't swim, so Chief Caguama and Boba probably figured we wouldn't even try reaching the ship."

"That's a good point," said Porter, leaning forward once the water had reached his chest, and beginning a slow, plodding breaststroke towards the shipwreck, followed by Henry, who plied along behind him in a sort of weird, modified dog paddle.

Luckily the surf had calmed considerably with the approaching sunset and the added buoyancy of the saltwater made the swim easier than they anticipated. After a few minutes they reached the ship's starboard side, where they turned and paddled towards its bow where the water was almost completely slack.

Once there, Henry grabbed onto the rope. "This must be the anchor line," he said as he started climbing. The young man's stamina had increased dramatically over the last week and Henry was just now starting to get a bit winded. Once he was up out of the water, Porter grabbed the rope himself, helping push Henry up from behind. When his friend was finally out of reach, Porter swam off a short distance to get out of the way in case Henry lost his grip and fell.

Up and up Henry climbed. The deck at the bow of the ship was about sixteen feet above the surface of the water, and it took him several minutes and a couple of rest stops before he finally managed to reach it, where he grabbed onto a big, wooden beam jutting out at an angle. Then with great effort, and several bumps, scrapes, and bruises, he finally managed to scramble and climb through the tangled rigging and up and over a railing onto the ship's weatherworn deck, where he flopped down to catch his breath, panting and rubbing a sore elbow. Once rested, and just as he was about to get up to call down to Porter, his wiry friend bounded over the railing behind him, landing with a heavy thud and a pirate's grin. He didn't look tired or winded at all. "Show off," groaned Henry, frowning as he slowly rose to his feet.

"What a difference a few days of good food and little exercise makes," said Porter, smiling at his friend. "A week ago I'd have bet good money you never would have managed that climb. Good job, Henry."

Porter's words were sincere and Henry's frown flipped into a smile at the compliment. "Okay," he said, smoothing his wet hair out of eyes and looking around. "Let's see what we can use."

The deck upon which they had climbed was directly over the shipwreck's bow. It was practically level and clear except for a few old coils of thick rope. Here and there were piles of white and gray bird excrement, revealing favorite perches on the yards and in the rigging above.

"Be careful where you walk," warned Porter as they started towards the back of the ship. After a few steps they reached an ornate, wooden railing, where Porter turned and pointed to the area from which they came. "We're standing on the ship's forecastle," he said. Looking back again, he nodded past the railing. "That's the waist of the ship down there. That's where most of the sailors worked."

Looking down past the railing, Henry noticed most of the deck below was hidden beneath a tattered, mold-blackened tarp. "Why is it covered up like that?"

"I think it had something to do with heavy weather," replied Porter, starting towards a companionway leading downward. "The sailors on old vessels like this sometimes stretched a tarp drum-tight over the ship's waist during storms to help keep the water out." They stopped at the side railing and looked back towards shore, where they noticed Solaritron wading at water's edge, forcefully plunging a long stick into the surf. "What's Sola doing?"

Henry shrugged. "Beats me." Except for the robot the beach was still completely deserted.

Turning and looking out over the ocean, Porter nodded again. "It must have been quite a storm surge to pick up a ship this size and toss it over that reef," he said, pointing at waves roaring and skidding over a wide, green, slightly submerged area about fifty yards out. "I can't believe this thing wasn't smashed to bits."

"Lucky for us it wasn't," said Henry, waving at Solaritron, who was now looking at them and waving back. "There's plenty of wood and rope here for us to make a raft. We won't have to steal a canoe after all."

"I just hope we have enough time," replied Porter gravely, carefully making his way down the companionway to the ship's waist, followed by Henry. At the bottom they stopped and looked around. Except for tears and holes scattered here and there in the tarp, the entire deck was hidden from view.

Henry reached down and pulled at the tarp's edge, which tore easily: turning into so much dust as he did. "Man is this stuff rotted."

"Hey!" shouted Porter, noticing a big, rounded lump smack-dab in the center of the deck and recalling something. "I think I know what that is!" He started running towards it, nearly tripping a few times over objects hidden beneath the tarp.

"What?" called Henry, carefully chasing after his friend. "What is it?"

Dust flew as Porter began grabbing and ripping away at the section of tarp covering the lump. "Salvation, I hope," he shouted as Henry joined in to help. "Most old ships carried one or more to ferry sailors to and from shore. This might be it!" After a few minutes of frantic tearing, they stepped back and looked at each other in disbelief before smiling broadly at the pretty, little, upside down wooden launch the heavy weather tarp had protected for so many years: a sailboat delivered to them by providence itself.

The ever-resourceful Solaritron had productively spent the time the boys were lowering and hauling their boat to shore—an eighteen-foot-long, copper-bottomed craft painted white with red gunnels and fanciful, gold-leaf-encrusted sea horse carvings on either side of the bow—by building a fire and spearing several little fish that had the misfortune of swimming too close to shore. By the time the nearly-exhausted Henry and Porter had pulled their prize up onto the beach under the fading, red glow of sunset, the robot had already gutted, scaled, and cooked its catch on slender, green sticks jammed into the sand and propped over the fire at angles. It had also cored half a dozen coconuts for milk the boys could drink. Famished and exhausted, Henry and Porter ate quickly before falling fast asleep on the beach next to the fire.

At first light they awoke to find Solaritron sitting quietly in standby mode next to their boat. While they'd slept, the machine had practically drained its batteries dry fixing the little craft's mast and yard into place and freshly caulking the boat's seams with fresh strands of hemp pulled from coils of the best rope the boys had recovered from the wreck. All that was now needed was a sail, and after Solaritron re-activated itself—deploying its solar collector to replenish its batteries—Porter and Henry set out to find one.

"Well, I'm fairly waterlogged," called Porter, trudging out of the surf and up the beach towards the campfire. A chilly morning breeze puffing off the ocean caused him to shiver as he dragged another net full of soggy canvas and rope out of the water behind him. "I think this should just about do it. It's the best I could find. Most of the canvas on the shipwreck is too rotten to hold even a light breeze. Here you go," he added, dropping the net before flopping himself down next to the fire

Henry tossed him his shirt and Porter quickly put it on. "I'm starving. Is there any more fish left?"

Henry stopped his sewing and leaned towards the campfire, grabbing a stick upon which was impaled a little dorado. He pulled the fish from the fire and studied it. "This one looks done. Here you go," he said, handing the stick to Porter.

Porter smelled the fish at its end before blowing on it. "Thanks. How's it going?"

Henry held up an edge of the dirty, old canvas towards his friend, the rest trailing out behind him across the beach, forming a large, rough, triangle. "So far, so good. I just hope this thread holds."

During their continued search of the shipwreck that morning, they had turned up an old, leather pouch filled with long, curved sewing needles, as well as several wooden spools of thick, graying cotton thread. Porter had also found a rusted sword—a Spanish rapier according to Solaritron—with a bronze hilt he claimed for his own. They'd been unable to locate the little boat's own sail anywhere on the derelict ship, so they cut short their search to begin sewing a patchwork one from the best fragments of canvas they could find. Henry's "Robots Rule" T-shirt had gone into the mix as the seed cloth, and now formed a bright red cross practically at the center of the other patches of dirty brown and graying canvass they'd salvaged from the wreck's rigging.

"Good thing Solaritron is a fast sail maker," added Henry. "Hey Sola, how are we doing?"

Solaritron walked over from behind the boat, where it was making adjustments to the craft's wooden rudder and tiller—after carving the name 'Sarah' across its flat, outer rear transom—before picking up the net Porter had hauled ashore. "I believe this is enough," it replied, holding the dripping cloth and rope up to its glass dome. "Thank you, Mr. Smith," it added before trotting over to the other side of the canvas opposite Henry, where it spilled the net's contents out on the sand and quickly began selecting remnants to sew into their patchwork sail. "It should be complete and ready to rig in approximately one hour."

"Good," replied Porter, taking a careful bite of the hot, tasty fish. "Two more days until Caguama and his boys decide what they want to do with us," he continued after a few chews, studying Henry closely. "I don't think we should leave this spot until then. In fact, in my opinion we should take off as soon as possible. We may not have much time come Sunday."

"What about the rest of our stuff back at the hut?" asked Henry, not wanting to risk leaving if they didn't absolutely have to; especially since he'd convinced himself Lealoa was in love with him, and was beginning to realize he was in love with her—if the ache in his heart at her absence was any indication. "If we don't go back this afternoon, Caguama and Boba may get suspicious. And what about Lealoa and Ginhua? They're probably worried sick about us."

Porter stopped eating and eyed his friend. "If Lealoa and Ginhua were free to find us," he began slowly, "they would have done so by now. We're not that far from the village, Henry. The fact they haven't worries me even more. Maybe Chief Caguama doesn't want them hanging around walking dead men."

Henry frowned before returning to his sewing.

"Look, I miss them too, okay?" Porter could tell Henry longed to see Lealoa more than his friend wanted to admit, but that wouldn't change things. He had a bad feeling about sticking around and wanted to get as far away from Caguama's village as they could before Sunday. Henry would just have to get over Lealoa.

"But where will we go?"

"Up the coast for starters. The boat's plenty big enough for all three of us and a good amount of supplies. We'll salvage as much as we can from the shipwreck today, then stow our provisions and take off tomorrow afternoon after all the Taino fishing canoes have come in. We can touch here and there along the coast for provisions and then head west to Haiti. If we don't like it there, it's on to Cuba and then the Florida Coast. If we've traveled back in time, we're bound to run into Spanish ships or settlements somewhere. If we do, we'll know for certain. If this is all some sort of weird hoax, whoever is pulling it will have to show their cards soon enough. No hoax can get any more elaborate than this," he added, waving his arm around at their surroundings.

Henry knew his friend was right, except for Porter's belief someone might still be trying to pull one over on them. Whatever had happened, it was no hoax. If Chief Caguama and his sub-chiefs decided to imprison or harm them, without their bug working how would they ever know before it was too late? Escape in a Taino canoe or a jury-rigged raft was one thing, being equally as dangerous as taking their chances right here—in Henry's opinion, at least. And how would they ever bring Solaritron along on an unstable raft or tipsy canoe? The discovery of the sturdy, little Spanish boat had changed the entire equation! And mathematical equations were one thing Henry excelled in. With Porter's sailing experience and Solaritron as a navigator, he had no doubt they could get just about anywhere they wanted in the West Indies, if that was in fact where they were. He cursed his dismal performance at the meeting with Chief Caguama yesterday and could practically feel the oncoming pangs of seasickness. His heart also ached over the thought of never seeing Lealoa again—more than he imagined possible. "What about water?" he said miserably, solving the equation. They must indeed attempt escape, and as soon as possible. "At the very least we'll need a supply of water."

Porter smiled, knowing Henry was coming around. "Good point. I found some ceramic jars and a couple of small, empty wood casks the last time I went over," he said, pointing towards the shipwreck. "There are bound to be more. I'll retrieve them once we get the sailboat floated again. We can sneak back over to the river tonight after dark to rinse and fill a few. Several gallons should tide us over for starters."

Henry finished his sewing, flapping the canvas back off his lap before standing and dusting himself off. "I wish I could argue with you, Porter, but I can't. Now that we've found a seaworthy boat you obviously can handle, and since we'll no longer have any difficulty bringing Sola with us, I agree we should get going before Sunday. There, do you feel better?"

"Yes," replied Porter, tossing his fish stick into the campfire and standing. "It's settled then," he declared, pointing towards the ocean to the west. "Tomorrow afternoon we sail!"

"Chief Caguama," whispered Boba. "Wake, Highness."

Stirring to consciousness, Chief Caguama sighed, looking over to the door to his Great Lodge. It was quite dark outside, but the fire pit in his batey courtyard was still burning brightly. "What is it, Boba?" he replied lowly, so as not to wake his wife. "It is still many hours before dawn."

"Yes, Highness, but I have just received word from the high priests that Natiao is ready for the cohoba ceremony."

"Ready?" exclaimed Chief Caguama in an incredulous tone, now wide-awake and twisting out of his hammock. "But they said he would not be ready for two more days! Is it too soon? Will not Kulkon be angered?" He pulled on his Chief's tunic and quickly stepped out of his lodge into the ceremonial courtyard outside, where he came upon a delegation of his high priests. They were adorned in their finest feathered capes and headdresses. Two of their attendants were carefully applying more wood to the fire pit, while several others were placing cohoba ceremony torches at their proper locations along the edges of the courtyard. The priests placed their right hands over their hearts, bowing deeply at their Chief as he walked towards them. "What's going on, High Priest Tennehua?" demanded Caguama, bowing back curtly. "The cohoba ceremony is not for two more days. Priest Natiao said so himself!"

"I know, Your Highness, but Natiao is ready *now*." The fasting process usually takes ten days, but he is very devoted and has refused all food. The time of clarity is fast-approaching. If the ceremony is not performed soon Natiao will be too weak and may never emerge from his trance. He may even die if we wait too much longer. Then all will have been for nothing."

Chief Caguama frowned in thought for an instant before making his decision: the only one possible. "Go then. Bring Natiao to my lodge and begin the ceremony!" he declared loudly. "We do not want him to die! That would anger Kulkon greatly. Hurry now and I will gather my sub-chiefs. The Great Kulkon's decision on the fate of the three Spaniards draws near!"

Natiao was weak from hunger and his head spun woozy as the other high priests helped him to his feet in the darkness. "What is it?" he moaned, trying to steady himself.

"It is time, Natiao," said Tennehua. "Time for the cohoba ceremony. We are here to take you to Chief Caguama's lodge."

"Is my duho chair and the cemi of Yocaju ready?"

"Yes," replied Tennehua. "Your cohoba duho and the idol of Yocaju have already been taken there. The batey courtyard is nearly ready and Chief Caguama is gathering his sub-chiefs. Then the drums will be sounded to summon the other villagers."

"What about my vomiting spatula? I must purge myself again."

"No need for that," said Tennehua as they started gently leading Natiao out of the Lodge of the High Priests, which was situated across the courtyard opposite the Great Lodge. "You have nothing left in your stomach to purge. We must go now. Kulkon awaits you in the fifth direction."

Outside, Natiao noticed a flurry of activity: the preparations for the cohoba ceremony. Torches at the edges of the courtyard near the stone monoliths were being lit and drummers had taken up their positions on either side of the doorway to the Great Lodge. Looking skyward as they hustled him along, he finally spotted Kulkon, a bright dot suspended in the heavens: angry and as red as bloodied sand. The sky disappeared and looking down he found he was face to face with Chief Caguama inside the dimly lit Great Lodge. Small oil lamps scattered about the floor cast flickering light and shadows across its neatly thatched walls and roughly hewn support beams overhead, from which hung several large gourds containing the bones of Chief Caguama's ancestors. Natiao could almost feel their spirits reaching out to his. Bowing weakly as the high priests supported him, he placed his right hand over his heart. "Highness."

Chief Caguama bowed back. "They say you are ready for the cohoba ceremony, Natiao," he said in a low and serious tone. "Are you? Are you ready to journey in the fifth direction to the heavens? To determine Kulkon's will towards the Spaniards? They have behaved well, almost like humans, but have also refused to tell us why they have been brought here."

"Spaniards?" asked Natiao. He had practically forgotten about the Spaniards in his weakened state. Of course, the evil ones spat from Kulkon's mouth! The reason for his fast and the cohoba ceremony. A wave of clarity and strength flowed through him as he recalled that dreadful evening all those days ago. Standing erect, he shook himself free of the high priests and adjusted his green, feathered cape. "I am ready Highness. The weakness has become clarity. I am beginning to face the fifth direction. The time is at hand for cohoba."

Chief Caguama placed his hand on Natiao's shoulder, before pointing to the center of his Great Lodge, where a low ceremonial chair had been carefully placed opposite a wooden idol of a squatting Yocaju, the Taino Man-God of Fire and patron spirit of the cohoba ceremony. On Yocaju's round, skull-like head sat a bowl of greenish-brown powder the Taino called 'cohoba.' A powder ground from the seeds of rare trees found only in the jungles of the Great Land to the west and mixed with tobacco to render it more potent. Powder strictly reserved for the high priests. Cohoba powder that would allow Natiao to travel into the heavens in the fifth direction to converse with the Gods at their level: to talk to the Great Kulkon himself. "Sit then," commanded Chief Caguama. "Sit and take cohoba."

The other high priests helped Natiao sit down on the low, wooden chair, directly facing Yocaju, polished and brown, grimacing with teeth of white, bleached bone. Its eyes—inlaid of gold—twinkled back at Natiao in the flickering light cast by the oil lamps.

Chief Caguama nodded towards the other priests before leaving the Great Lodge, where he saw all of his sub-chiefs gathering in the courtyard under a brilliant, star-lit night. The men had taken their proper positions and bowed in unison at him, their right hands over their hearts. Caguama bowed back and, raising his arms and facing skyward, shouted in a great, booming voice: "Yocaju! Cohoba! Natiao! Cohoba! Let the will of Kulkon be known!" At this the drummers on either side of the entrance to the Great Lodge began drumming frantic and loud at first, followed by a slow diminishment to a plodding and somber, low beat. Sitting down, Chief Caguama and his sub-chiefs once again formed a contemplative circle of men, while one after another villagers—solemn and grim—began silently assembling and sitting around their leaders.

Inside, Tennehua reverently approached the idol of Yocaju, spooning the greenish-brown powder from the bowl on its head into a shallow, round dish, which he handed to Natiao, before quickly retreating to watch with the other high priests.

"I seek Kulkon's will through cohoba," muttered Natiao lowly, raising the dish to his face and inhaling the powder deeply. His nose and lungs burned white hot for a fleeting instant as a kaleidoscope of colors burst before his eyes. Dropping the bowl with a deep groan, he convulsed forward—head between legs—as the trance world he was falling into turned upside down. The cohoba ceremony had begun.

Henry was dreaming of home. Home, sweet, home. You never miss it until it's gone, and once it is—more often than not—you can never get it back: at least not the way you remember it. Instead, at the very best it lives on only in your memories and dreams.

And in this case, in his dream—Henry's dream—he was lying luxuriously on his bed back at his folk's house in Kendell, Illinois: head resting on a clean, feather pillow, while the smell of scrambled eggs and hot cakes called out to his empty stomach from his mother's kitchen. He could practically taste the maple syrup. It must be Saturday morning. He loved Saturday mornings! A wonderful breakfast, eaten together with his mom, dad, and little sister Ellen; then on to his dad's laboratory to tinker the morning away. *I can't wait for them to meet Lealoa!* his subconscious mind cried out in joy. "I'm in love with Lealoa."

Fading thoughts and senses—a joyous dream swirling away forever into the depths of his memory—then darkness and the rhythmic sound of surf rolling against shore and the whisper of wind hissing through unseen palm fronds overhead in the darkness. Stirring to wakefulness, Henry groaned miserably after realizing where he was and recalling their predicament. Opening his eyes, the first thing he saw was a sky filled with brilliant stars and the whitish band of the Milky Way. Looking at his watch, he found it was only four in the morning. He tried to fall back to sleep for a few minutes, but instead fantasized a Taino wedding ceremony in which he and Lealoa became husband and wife. It wouldn't be so bad spending the rest of his days here on Boriken with such a lovely woman at his side. What things he could teach her and her people! In time he might even be a sub-chief himself. Henry thought of Lealoa again and was suddenly filled with such a longing for her it overcame his better judgment.

He quietly sat up and looked around. Porter was sound asleep, curled up and snoring quietly next to the crackling, dying embers of the campfire. Over towards their boat he noticed Solaritron: folded up tight and whirring and beeping softly in standby mode. Like the night before, the robot had nearly drained its batteries dry helping make all the preparations necessary for their escape to parts unknown and would not stir again until it detected the rays of the rising sun.

Henry grabbed his sandals, quietly pulling them on in turn. He briefly searched for his red T-shirt before remembering it had been sacrificed to help make their patchwork sail. His button-down would have to do to ward off the coolness of the early morning. Picking it up, he shook the sand from it and quickly pulled it on before standing and starting down the near pitch-black beach: back towards their hut and Chief Caguama's village. "We need our coats, my portacom, and Porter's radio," he rationalized over his real desire to see Lealoa one last time. "I'll just get our stuff and hang around until dawn to say goodbye to the girls when they bring our breakfast. No harm in that," he muttered, looking back over his shoulder at their campsite. No movement. "I'll probably be back long before Porter is awake anyway. He'll never even realize I was gone. Once I tell him I retrieved our stuff, he'll thank me. We may need it someday."

After the explosion of light before his eyes and extreme jolt of pain across his entire being, Natiao suddenly found himself standing alone on a windswept beach bordered by strangely motionless palm trees. Still sensing a drum beating somewhere in his head, he looked about slowly. It was night, but everything he saw was tinged or edged with vivid colors. The sea before him was completely calm, and beneath its flat, smooth surface swam schools of fish that glowed red, orange, and yellow like bright flames of fire. "I am dreaming in the cohoba trance," he realized as a feeling of clarity flowed across his mind. Natiao had performed this divine ceremony a few times before; traveled in the fifth direction to speak with other, lesser Gods, but never the Great Kulkon himself. "Kulkon," he muttered. "I must find Kulkon."

"Here, Natiao," boomed a voice like thunder.

Gazing up, Natiao spotted the Great God, round and red as ocher, rolling high overhead past the Moon Goddess and towards the Milky Sky Snake, which crawled and undulated across a glossy blackness dotted with thousands of impossibly bright lights. "Kulkon!" he shouted, shuddering in fear as some terrible, invisible force began hurling him up into the heavens. Looking at his feet, he gasped as Boriken Island plunged away beneath him as he shot skyward like a great, swift bird. Once the land and the ocean had disappeared below, he raised his head, fixing his gaze upon Kulkon, who was quickly drawing closer and closer.

"Come to me, Natiao," boomed the voice. "Kulkon awaits!"

Faster and faster Natiao flew, his eyes tearing as a cold wind crashed over him; pushing and pressing his topknot against the back of his head; pulling away at his feathered cape. Glancing sideways he saw the Moon Goddess, who waved and smiled at him as he raced past her. Higher and higher into the realm of the Gods he soared and in a short while he was among the sky lights, twinkling and dancing around him, near and yet impossibly far away. Slowing to a stop, he found himself floating before a giant, round, swirling ball of blood: the Great Kulkon.

"What is it you seek, my child?" the voice thundered.

Natiao tried to fall to his knees, but he found he couldn't. Instead, he just floated there in a near paralyzed state: his mind locked somewhere between awe and terror.

"Do not be frightened, Natiao," said Kulkon. "Here, I will assume another form." The ball of blood distorted into five lobes, which quickly shrank, forming a handsome, muscular, ocher-skinned man wearing nothing but a white feathered cape. The man floated over to Natiao and hovered before him. "You are here as part of the divine cohoba ceremony. What is it you seek?" he asked in a deep, commanding voice flowing forth from a mouth of white, pulsating light.

Natiao's fear ebbed away as a misty aura of peace glowed out from Kulkon and over him. "Great One, I am here to determine your will. Many days ago you brought our people three Spaniards."

"Yes," replied Kulkon, a frown of white spreading across his face. "Three Spaniards delivered to help renew the strength of the Taino people. Why have they not been sacrificed? Do the Taino refuse to honor the God who saved them from the evil ones?"

At this Natiao gulped fearfully, sensing Kulkon's aura darken with growing rage. "That is why I have come, Great Kulkon," he replied quickly, his voice trembling. "My people could not determine why the Spaniards were brought. They seem different than the others. Chief

Caguama says they act more like human beings. We did not want to sacrifice them without knowing your will with certainty. After you delivered them to us, I immediately began fasting for the cohoba ceremony. We did not want to anger you."

Kulkon's aura darkened even more. "They act more like humans?" he thundered. "Has Chief Caguama and his sub-chiefs lost their minds! They are Spaniards, Natiao. The evil ones! Mortal enemies of the Taino who must be sacrificed in my honor!"

Natiao buried his face in his hands and clenched his eyes shut in fear, knowing Kulkon would surely strike him dead for such a foolish, unforgivable mistake.

"Look at me," commanded Kulkon.

The invisible force wrenched Natiao's hands away from his face and forced his arms to his sides. As his eyelids were pulled open, he saw Kulkon had resumed its former, terrifying appearance.

"I love the Taino people, but they must obey my will or I will take my protection away," threatened the swirling, red ball of blood. You have allowed the Spaniards to trick you. Where are they now?"

"I do not know," moaned Natiao.

"Listen carefully, Natiao. Listen to the will of Kulkon. When you return, you must tell Chief Caguama and the others I am angered and that a war dance in my honor must be performed immediately. Afterwards, the Spaniards must be captured and sacrificed at dawn. They must not be allowed to escape. One shall be drowned in the sea. Another shall be beaten to death with clubs. The third shall be tied to a post and shot full of arrows. Once all have been sacrificed, Chief Caguama and his sub-chiefs must eat their flesh raw. Only then will the Taino people renew their strength and regain my favor. Do you understand?"

"Yes!" cried Natiao, terror struck again as Kulkon started speeding away. Then he felt himself falling. Falling wildly: head over heels through the heavens. "The will of Kulkon shall be made known to all!" he shouted, tumbling to meet the ground hurling up towards him. "The will of Kulkon shall be carried out!"

Lealoa was hanging miserably in her hammock like a thin, beautifully complexioned, netted fish. Her eyes were swollen with heartbreak and grief as she listened to the muffled sound of the low drumbeat off in the distance. After learning the Spaniards wouldn't be invited to join the Taino people—following their dreadful meeting with Chief Caguama and the others—and upon being forbidden from leaving the walled inner village, she and Ginhua had wept uncontrollably over the loss of their men. *Their men!* Ginhua had wept so much that tonight was the first time in two days she was finally able to take comfort in deep sleep. The poor girl now hung lifelessly in the hammock next to Lealoa, breathing slowly and completely dead to the world.

At first the girls enlisted the help of their mothers and aunts to try to help, but no amount of persuasion could change Chief Caguama's mind. The fate of the Spaniards now rested in the hands of Priest Natiao and the cohoba ceremony, which could mean just about anything—since even high priests couldn't control their trance dreams. Her eyes welled up again at the thought of poor Chief Henry and his men being banished, or worse. *I have always honored my father's wishes, but I must do something*, she decided. *What if Natiao wakes in a short while and declares the Spaniards must die? I could not live knowing my true love was sacrificed while I stood by doing nothing. I must help Chief Henry if I can. I would lay down my life for his.* Both her parents had gone to the batey courtyard to witness the cohoba ceremony. Lealoa suspected most of the other adults in the inner village were there as well: so rare and important was such an event. She had pretended to be asleep when it all started a few hours ago, so now—unguarded—she could slip away. Twisting out of her hammock, she quickly dressed, then started a roundabout path towards the back of Chief Caguama's Great Lodge.

The drumbeat off in the distance grew ever louder as Lealoa quietly made her way though the inner village, behind the backs of silent or snoring huts and around pits filled with the dimly glowing remnants of the evening's fires. The closer she got to her destination, the more her heart began to race. If caught, she would be punished and closely guarded until it was too late. Past another couple of huts she came upon the Great Chief's courtyard. In addition to the Caguama and his circle of sub-chiefs, it was filled to near capacity. Practically the entire village was there, sitting and silently listening to the hypnotic low beat of the cohoba ceremony drummers.

She continued on, crouching low to keep out of sight behind more huts further out from the courtyard. After taking a few minutes to navigate a circuitous path, she finally neared the back of the Great Lodge, where she sank to her stomach before crawling along towards it on her belly. Once there, she sat up and scooted close up next to it, then began tearing away at the thatched wall as quietly as she could, finally making a little peephole near the ground through which she could peer. Pressing her eye against it, she saw an extremely gaunt Priest Natiao sitting before the polished idol of Yocaju. He was hunched forward on his duho chair, drooling from the mouth and muttering lowly in his trance. Several other high priests were standing off to his side, wringing their hands as they silently watched the cohoba ceremony unfold.

Suddenly Natiao's body jerked violently—as if he had just fallen from a great height—and he uttered a loud shriek. At this the drumbeat stopped and the other priests ran to him, gently helping him sit up and offering sips of water from a shallow, red bowl.

After mopping the drool away from Natiao's mouth with a cloth, Tennehua patted him on his cheeks before shaking him gently by the shoulders. "Natiao! Wake up Natiao! Remember! Remember! What is the will of Kulkon?"

"Kulkon?" moaned Natiao in confusion, slowly stirring to consciousness, his eyes rolling lazily around in their sockets. "The will of Kulkon?"

"Yes, Natiao. Yes. Tell us the will of Kulkon," whispered Tennehua close to Natiao's ear. "What does Kulkon want us to do with the three Spaniards spat from his mouth?"

At this, Lealoa turned her head sideways, pressing her ear up against the peephole to listen. The fate of her love was now at hand and she was trembling in dread and hopeful anticipation. Whatever Natiao said would be final.

"The will of Kulkon," muttered Natiao, now awake and shaking the last few cobwebs caused by the cohoba powder from his head. "Yes," he said again, looking up at Tennehua. "I know it. I know the will of Kulkon!"

Lealoa's face contorted into a reflection of pure heartbreak, tears welling up and gushing from her eyes; dripping onto the ground in great drops, as Kulkon's will was recited with urgency and certainty by Priest Natiao. Barely able to keep from sobbing, she sprang to her feet and began running headlong away, retracing her route to keep out of sight, only this time she would continue on to a secret breech in the wall of the inner village only she and her friends knew about. She would run to Chief Henry's hut and warn him. Even though she might be banished herself—or worse—she would warn Chief Henry and his men to try to escape, or she would die trying.

During most of his journey back to their hut, Henry could hear a slow, almost hypnotic, drumbeat off in the distance: emanating somewhere within the walls of Chief Caguama's inner village. Deciding to take a roundabout path to avoid detection once he reached the river, he promptly got himself lost. Finally regaining his bearings after a painful hour of stumbling into ditches and smacking his face into low tree branches in the darkness, he thought he heard a *shriek* just before the drumbeat stopped. Freezing in his tracks, he listened carefully for a while before continuing on. "Whatever's going on in the village must be over now," he muttered, as the chirping of the little coqui frogs around him regained their preeminence over the island's natural, nocturnal serenade. Then, a few minutes later, and just as he was finally nearing their hut, the drumbeat sounded again: only now it was fast-paced; punctuated here and there with loud chants and shouts. Henry's heart jumped and began racing at the ominous sound. Trotting the rest of the way, he poked his head into the hut. "Lealoa? Are you here?" he whispered in Spanish. "Ginhua?"

No reply.

Henry's heart sank in disappointment, but then the drumbeat and chanting off in the distance caught his attention again. It seemed to be growing ever more frantic and aggressive in tone. He went in and let his eyes adjust to the darkness, then quickly began groping around and gathering up their stuff, including the gold arm bracelets the girls had given them, jamming it all into the pockets of their leather coats. Once he had everything, he crept over to the doorway and poked his head outside to see if all was clear and saw someone running straight towards him.

"Henrique! Henrique!"

"Lealoa!" called Henry, dropping the coats and running towards her.

"Henrique," she shouted again as she threw herself into his arms, embracing him tightly and kissing him all over his face before burying hers into his shoulder.

"Lealoa, how I have missed you," he said, returning her embrace and feeling wetness against his neck. He gently pushed her away to look at her. "Lealoa: what's the matter? Why are you crying?"

"Henrique," she said before pulling desperately on his arms and speaking away urgently in her native Taino.

"Wait. Slow down, Lealoa," he said gently, pulling her to himself in another embrace. "In Spanish. Tell me in Spanish."

She sobbed, pressing her warm, wet face into his neck again. "Priest Natiao has completed the cohoba ceremony. Did you not hear the drum?"

"Yes, I heard it."

"Natiao said it is the will of Kulkon that you and Smith and Juan be sacrificed and eaten raw at dawn. Chief Caguama and his men are war dancing right now. They will be coming for you soon and there is little time." Pushing him away, she pointed to the eastern sky, which was beginning to glow with the approaching sunrise. You must try to escape, my love. You must live, or I will go insane."

"Maybe we can reason with Chief Caguama," said Henry, chills of fear running up his spine as the drumbeat and chanting off in the distance started reaching a fevered pitch. "We have done nothing to you or your people!"

Lealoa started backing away from him, shaking her head and trembling uncontrollably. "You do not understand our ways, Henrique!" she screamed in panic, pointing at the growing glow in the eastern sky. "Natiao's word is final! Kulkon has declared you three must die at dawn, and die you will unless you run away! They might kill me too: if they find out I warned you."

"I love you, Lealoa," said Henry, starting towards her. "Come with me. Come with us. We have a boat. There's still time. We can run away together," he pleaded, tears beginning to well up on his face as she kept backing away from him.

"And I love you, Henrique, but I cannot. I will not leave my people."

THE MOON CHASERS

The drumbeat and chanting off in the distance abruptly stopped, ending with a loud chorus of bloodcurdling screams, and both of them froze, gazing into each other's eyes, their souls touching through them in a way they would never experience again with any other. A first love that would never—could never—be repeated.

Turning, Lealoa ran away.

Henry stood there, watching her disappear from his life as quickly as she had entered it all those days ago, and for an instant didn't care whether he lived or died, the gash across his heart now being a permanent fixture of his being. Then his body kicked him in the pants with a rush of adrenaline and he quickly grabbed up their coats and started running as fast as his legs could carry him, tears streaming down his face.

"You didn't see him go?" asked an incredulous Porter, looking westward at the trail of footprints leading off into the distance next to his shadow, which slanted and stretched out across the beach like a long, dark streak in the dim light of a new dawn. "I can't believe it."

"Yes, I did," replied Solaritron, its umbrella-like solar collector pointing at the big, red ball slowly rising in the east. "He left at 4:17 a.m."

"Well, why didn't you say something? Why didn't you wake me up? What kind of guard robot are you, anyway?"

"I have been instructed to warn of approaching strangers, not departing friends. Besides, my batteries were so low I did not want to trigger an auto shutdown. If *that* would have happened you and I wouldn't be speaking right now, unless you and Mr. Dundridge have identical thumbprints: which I highly doubt."

Porter adjusted the Spaniard's sword tucked between his belt and left hip, and checked the improvised dagger slung at his right. In addition to his homemade sandals, which were now more dirty than white, he was wearing his filthy blue, button-down shirt—sleeves rolled up—and black jean cutoffs. He also had the green tunic Ginhua had given him tied around his head like a pirate's scarf, its free-end hanging back over his neck to protect it from the sun once they were at sea. Walking over to their little sailboat, which was beached at water's edge, he looked in.

During the night, Solaritron had neatly packed and stowed their provisions, which consisted of water casks, coconuts, extra rope, folded up remnants of canvas, spools of thread, the leather pouch of sewing needles, a tied up bundle of long, wooden dowels, and a small, heavy swivel gun—most of which had been salvaged from the wreck. They had the swivel gun—a narrow, three-foot-long, rusty cannon mounted on a U-shaped bar—tied to a long rope to use as an anchor. Everything looked shipshape and ready to go. "How long before your batteries are recharged?" asked Porter, turning towards the machine again.

"Thirty minutes tops. It will go much faster once the sun rises a little higher in the sky and its rays are stronger."

"Well, let me know as soon as you have enough energy to walk. You can recharge as we go. We need to find Henry and get out of here," he added, looking back up the beach again, his shadow already much shorter than before. "I bet he went to the hut to get the rest of our stuff. He's so stubborn, he'll get us all killed. He promised he wouldn't leave."

"He probably went back hoping to see Lealoa again. Mr. Dundridge wears his heart on his sleeve, sometimes, I am afraid. He is quite smitten with the young lady."

"I told him he'll just have to get over her."

"That's easy for you to say, Mr. Smith. And in my opinion you should be a little more delicate on how you frame your unilateral proclamations concerning Mr. Dundridge's relationships."

Porter frowned at Solaritron and put his hands on his hips. "How do you mean?"

"You act like it is no big deal or sacrifice for Mr. Dundridge to walk away from someone he is clearly in love with, while you, at the same time, are taking all possible steps to reunite yourself with your own girlfriend. I wonder how quickly you would want to leave this tropical paradise if it meant leaving Sarah Weston behind."

"I'm doing this to save all our necks," grumbled Porter, looking down at his feet.

"I'll grant you that, but the pain of loss would be just as great, necessary though it may be."

"Since when did you get so preachy?" Porter shot back, realizing the robot was right. Unlike Henry, Porter did not wear his heart on his sleeve, or at least he tried not to. And while he would never admit it, he missed Ginhua and her smiles and bubbly laughter terribly, and wondered if it was possible to be in love with two women at the same time. He shook the thought from his head. Ginhua and Lealoa would be better off without them. Their respective cultures were way too different.

A twig snapped somewhere up beyond the line of coconut palms bordering the beach.

Porter turned his head, looking in the direction of the sound.

Another *snap*, and then another—followed by the low *crunch* of creeping footsteps.

Porter crouched low. "Did you hear that?" he whispered, gazing up into the thick, green vegetation to the south. He slowly pulled the sword from his belt, raising it to the ready with a steady and confident grip. "I can't see anything. Can you?"

Solaritron had activated its telescopic lenses and night vision unit and was focusing and refocusing in the direction of the sounds. "Armed men, Mr. Smith. I see many men armed with clubs, bows, and arrows. Boba's warriors, if I am not mistaken. They have spotted us and are approaching as quietly as they can. They appear to be taking up positions to prevent our escape. I do not like the looks of this. I have barely recharged my batteries enough to stand."

"We're sitting ducks out here, Sola," whispered Porter, finally noticing glimpses of movement in the tangle of green and sunken shadows past the line of coconut palms. He quickly turned his head sideways to look back up the beach along line of footprints leading away. "Blast it all Henry! Where are you?"

"Plan B!" shouted Henry Dundridge, crashing headlong out of the jungle, frightened birds squawking wretchedly and soaring skyward around him. He tripped past the line of palm trees and onto the beach. "Porter, Plan B!" he shouted again, his face a red flame of near-exhaustion as he staggered along, gripping a leather coat in each hand. "They're going to kill us!"

"Henry!" shouted Porter, running towards his friend.

They met and Porter quickly tucked his sword back under his belt, then grabbed the coats and Henry's left arm, pulling on it towards the sailboat. "What's going on?"

"Lealoa warned me," gasped Henry, struggling along through the deep sand. "She risked her life to warn me. The Taino had some sort of ceremony last night. She said their priest declared we must be sacrificed at dawn. And it's dawn, brother. We've got to get out of here!"

A blur tore between their heads with a *whoosh* before slamming into the sand in front of them as they ran. They jumped over its polished, brown, feather-capped shaft as another blur grazed Henry's left arm, gashing it and his shirt wide open, warm blood gushing out as a third arrow whizzed just past Porter's left ear. Henry was so tired he didn't even feel it.

Glancing quickly over his shoulder, Porter saw Taino warriors pouring out of the jungle onto the beach further out from where Henry had emerged, trotting along about fifty yards behind them, hooting and hollering at the tops of their lungs. Many had their faces painted—some like demons; others were stopping to take aim, shooting deadly arrows at them. "Come on, Henry!" he shouted, pulling on his friend's arm as hard as he could. "We're almost there!"

More warriors now: running out of the jungle all along the beach around them, screaming and taunting. Solaritron had deployed its insect-like arms and legs, retreating and beating Henry and Porter to the sailboat. Its solar collector had disappeared and one of the compartments on its lower saucer section was open—the robot quickly plucking modular, silver components out and tossing them into the boat one after another.

"Sola!" shouted Porter, an arrow's shaft slamming painfully across his right shoulder and twirling away. "Let's get out of here!" Reaching the sailboat, he flung in their coats, his sword, and Henry as well, then began pushing off as arrows began falling in greater numbers, plunging into the water and thumping loudly into the boat, burying their sharp, metal points deep into its old, wooden hull. "Come on Sola!" he called, struggling to float the sailboat. "Help me push!" Electric motors and servos whined lowly behind him as metal claws grabbed and lifted him into the sailboat.

"Good bye, Porter. So long, Henry," said Solaritron, quickly pushing and floating the boat out into deep water, turning it around and giving it a good shove away from shore into the smooth water of the little bay.

"Good luck to you both and may you find your way back home. Don't forget me."

"Sola!" shouted Henry, scrambling into the rear of the sailboat, tipping it to and fro violently, the blood from the huge gash in his left arm gushing and smearing crimson as he crawled over their supplies and the robot's folded up solar collector and other tossed in parts. "Come back! We need you!"

"Get down!" shouted Porter, pushing Henry into the belly of the boat as more incoming arrows fell around them like angry hornets; plunging into the water and slamming into the sailboat with loud, vicious, *thump-twangs*.

Once Henry was out of the way, Porter sprang over a thwart like a sure-footed monkey and grabbed a line, pulling on it hand-over-hand as fast as he could. *We're not going to make it*, he thought, trying to set sail as the boat slowed and started losing way; stalling momentarily before lazily turning and drifting shoreward again. *We're not going to make it.*

Then they heard Solaritron calling out loudly from behind them in a language both of them recognized, but neither could understand, and all the hooting and war screaming stopped, as did the terrible rain of deadly, hateful arrows. Looking back, they realized they were still quite close into the beach, which now was crowded with Taino warriors. Many had surrounded the robot. Others had waded out into the water and were not more than several yards away. All were silently staring at the machine, practically frozen in fear at what they were hearing.

"Fools!" thundered Solaritron again in Taino, its arms waving through the air and claws snapping loudly. "We are the messengers of Kulkon!" As it spoke, a smooth section on its upper assembly faded to a milky white as the recording of its passage through the strange orb at the old field house started playing—buzzing loudly. "The Mighty Kulkon is angered! Look upon his face: the face of your death," it shouted, turning around slowly for all to see. "He will rain fire down upon you now!"

At the sight of Kulkon's shimmering, white light, most of Boba's warriors fell terror-stricken to their knees on the beach, while others began running away and screaming loudly.

"Kulkon is angered!"

"We all shall die!"

"Sola is buying us some time!" shouted Porter, watching the mayhem the robot was playing upon Boba's warriors. Collecting himself, he took to setting their boat's sail with renewed determination, which he did quickly and smoothly with a practiced hand. After a short while their patchwork canvas caught a stiff breeze and billowed out, heeling the sailboat over with several creaks as it started picking up speed and pulling away from shore; Porter manning the tiller and steering clear of the shipwreck before looking back over his shoulder. "If it wasn't for Sola, we'd be dead now," he muttered lowly—reverently—as they sailed out of range of those dreadful, deadly arrows. "God bless him. God bless Solaritron."

"He must be nearly out of power," groaned Henry, now on his hands and knees next to Porter, looking shoreward with tears streaming down his face—which was beginning to turn green around the edges with the early pangs of seasickness. "This is all my fault." He rose up on his knees, cupped his hands around his mouth and shouted in a raspy, grief-filled voice. "Sola! Turtle at five percent power reserve! Protect yourself, you can do it! We'll come back for you! I swear it!"

At the sound of Henry's voice, the lenses beneath Solaritron's dome—weak with dwindling power—slowly turned and focused on the miraculous machine's two best friends, who were now sailing away forever. It was the last thing the robot saw as its batteries ran dry; the last thing it wanted to see as it shut itself down for good, folding up its arms and legs before lifelessly toppling over sideways onto a beach filled with anger and rage.

Seeing this, Boba's warriors realized they'd been tricked. Standing and crowding around the fallen robot, they cursed and shouted at it, beating violently on Juan's armor with their clubs to make certain he was dead, while others began running as fast as they could towards the bay to the west to launch their war canoes. The will of Kulkon *must* be carried out and the pursuit of Chief Henry and his remaining servant Smith was far, far from over.

Chapter Eight: The Moon Chasers

"Sail ho!" cried Morgan Landon—lookout assigned to the second watch. The wiry, young man was balancing precariously within the ropes and cordage converging near the foremast top of the *Moon Chaser*. He brushed his long, sandy-brown hair out of his eyes and began shifting from rope to rope, gazing intensely into the distance as he crawled out and along the foreyard on his belly like an overconfident lemur. Even from his vantage point sixty feet above the sea, the small sail appeared as no more than a light-colored spec peeking out ever so often between the tops of low waves rolling off in the distance. Waves that chopped one after another as they marched upon the white band of beach edging the green, mountainous island looming before them. He gripped the yard tightly and twisted around to call out toward the ship's stern: its rear. Except for the forecastle directly below, most of the deck was hidden from view by the billowing canvas on the mainmast behind him. "Sail ho!"

Captain Gordon Parks and his second in command, Kinshasa Mahn, were on the *Moon Chaser's* poop deck discussing the miserable vagrancies of wind and weather—and yet another lost opportunity for Gordon to get back to his strange, far-off home—when the lookout's call rang out. It was a beautiful, cloudless morning and the sea was a striking patchwork of deep blues abruptly turning into turquoise before bubbling into foam as it skidded against landfall. The two men were wearing comfortable work clothes suitable for tropical weather—white, cotton shirts unbuttoned at the neck and trousers made from sailcloth dyed blue—and sitting at a small table beneath a stripped awning set up on the highest deck at the stern of the ship. At the sound of Landon's call, they looked at each other in disbelief for a moment, then bolted to their feet and stepped over to the poop's railing.

Most of the seamen on the second watch and idlers who couldn't sleep were already gathering at the larboard railing in the waist of the ship, looking southward towards the island they had been reconnoitering for the last couple of days—Boriken Island.

Gordon surveyed the situation and, looking aloft, cupped his hands around his mouth to call out towards ship's foremast—located just aft of its rounded bow and narrow forecastle. "Where away?" he shouted. "Is it the *Hound* or the *Jackal*? Where away, Mr. Landon?"

They hadn't seen a sail west of the Canasta Islands and didn't expect to see any either, except perhaps the dreaded *Hound* or *Jackal* galleons: Spanish warships assigned to enforce the quarantine of all lands of the so-called "New World." Anything west of the Canastas was off-limits to all, including the *Moon Chaser* and her crew, and the Boriken Islanders didn't use sails, only large, well built and highly manned seagoing canoes.

"No sir," shouted Landon. "It's not the *Jackal* or the *Hound*—thank God. It's a small launch, sir. She's two points off the larboard bow, between us and Boriken. She's clearing the passage to Abacoa Bay and heading west. Just east of the bay I can see a large shipwreck near the beach. Looks like an old Spanish carrack that's been cracked in two amidships. She probably broke her back when the tide went slack." Landon's famous ability to turn a phrase brought a few stifled laughs from the seamen below.

Gordon shook his head at Landon's droll humor as he started down the steep companionway leading from the poop followed by Kinshasa. "The wreck is probably from the doomed Spanish occupation fleet of 1511, but the launch? A sailed launch after all these years?" He sprang from the last step and landed on the wooden quarterdeck with a *thump*. "Where's Mr. O'Farrell? Where's my steward?"

"Here, sir!" called a seaman down in the waist of the ship; standing with the helmsmen at the ship's wheel near the forward most edge of the quarterdeck. In addition to being Gordon's personal assistant and guard, one of Daniel O'Farrell's numerous duties was to prepare a written account of the effectiveness of the many sailing innovations their ingenious captain had made to his beloved *Moon Chaser* over the years. This morning it was the peculiar spoke wheel helm installed to steer the ship. It had replaced the cumbersome whipstaff and below-decks tiller relieving tackles used before this most recent voyage and the helmsmen could not now imagine life without it. It actually allowed one man to control the ship's rudder—one man! Danny jammed his parchment book under his arm with a well practiced flip and ran to the edge of the quarterdeck to salute his captain—palm forward and two fingers extended; touched quickly to brow. "Yes, sir!"

"Mr. O'Farrell. I pray you're finding the new helm wheel system satisfactory."

"Yes, sir. If I didn't I would so note. Your standing order, sir." He plucked the parchment book from beneath his arm and held it up towards Gordon. "No negative comments from the helmsmen, only Mr. Thomas thinks the spokes could be a tad longer to help increase leverage in heavy weather: to prevent the helm from going alee in the hands of weaker men."

"Excellent!" replied Gordon. "Make note of it and give Mr. Thomas credit. But now I want you to take those hawk eyes of yours up to maintop to see what all this 'sail ho' fuss is about."

A boy suddenly appeared; running across the waist followed by Matey, the ship's scrappy—and much beloved—red and white spotted king spaniel mascot. The boy was wearing black, knee-length trousers, a baggy, white shirt several sizes too big, and, like most of the crew, preferred bare feet to buckle shoes in such pleasant weather.

"Mr. Jared Kinnel!" shouted Gordon.

The boy skidded to a halt, like he'd just run into a brick wall, then stood erect and saluted the quarterdeck's railing. "Yes, sir!"

Matey skidded to a halt as well and sat down next to the boy, assuming a silent, statuesque pose of deference as they faced their captain.

"Cease that horse playing at once or I'll be forced to put you on report. Now run to my great cabin and fetch Mr. O'Farrell my best telescope—the one in the leather case hanging next to my pistol locker. Understand?"

"Yes, sir!" shouted Jared. "Best telescope, it is. To Mr. Hawks, er...Mr. O'Farrell, sir."

"And bring me my binoculars. They're in the bench beneath the starboard stern windows."

Jared touched two fingers to brow again. "Aye, aye, sir." He turned and started trotting towards the rear of the ship, Matey springing to its feet and following closely behind; playfully nipping at his heels."

"Oh. And, Mr. Kinnel," called Gordon after the boy. "God save the man who drops my binoculars and jars its prism loose again. It's the only pair like it in the entire world."

Jared stopped in his tracks and looked back at his captain. "Yes sir," he replied with a gulp. "Care it is, sir." Matey jumped up on the boy's chest and yelped loudly as if saying, "Let's go!" before they sped off again, disappearing through the wooden, watertight doors leading to the officers' quarters nestled between the ship's main and quarter decks.

When Jared was gone, Gordon turned to Kinshasa. "What do you think, friend? A sailed launch? At Boriken Island, of all places?"

Kinshasa looked out over the expanse of blue sea between them and the island. "It could mean one of two things," he replied.

"Pray tell?"

"Well, it could mean the Taino and their Caribe allies have finally taken to sails."

"Doubtful. And God save us if they have."

"Or maybe there are still Spanish survivors on Boriken. Perhaps they spotted our sail and have decided to make good their escape by seeking asylum aboard the *Moon Chaser*."

"Survivors? After all these years? The Taino believe they gain strength by consuming the flesh of their adversaries. Ritualistic cannibalism, I believe it's called. I would've guessed any Spanish survivors would have been sacrificed and eaten long before now, especially after such a bloody occupation and war. There's no love lost between the Taino and the Spaniards, you know."

Kinshasa shrugged. "So I've heard. But if it's a sailed vessel, and the Taino don't use sails, then someone is helming her. The question is who."

Gordon signaled Kinshasa with a discrete look and the two walked back towards the companionway leading up to the poop deck. When they reached a distance out of earshot of the others, they stopped and Gordon continued confidentially under his breath. "Well if they *are* Spanish survivors they'll find no refuge aboard my ship if it means offending the Taino. Even though we've missed the 'event'—blast that heavy weather—I still intend to parley with Chief Caguama, assuming he still rules these islands. We're going to stand into the bay at noon on

Tuesday, wearing full dress uniforms and with banners flying. We'll be fit for a king's review with plenty of gifts for the Taino, as well as great tales of our own hatred of the Spaniards."

"You intend to impress Caguama and win over his friendship even though we're a week past the ley node expansion?"

"Yes. I'm going to arrange for an expedition to see where the node is located. According to Mr. Pulilu, it's well up in the mountains: a ceremonial place called Ku'Karaya near the village of Otoao. Caguama may know when the next occultation of Mars will occur: the date of Kulkon's next visit. If these islands are as close to paradise as the Spaniards claim, then I for one would not mind spending a few leisurely years here before I return home—my real home, that is. I'm getting old, Kinshasa. I'm tired of chasing the Moon. If things look promising I may cut you and the others loose to trade for gold and pearls like we planned, then return to Fodo Island to carry on the work we've started. With or without me, the abolition of the slave trade is still a costly endeavor."

"Caution, sir," replied Kinshasa, his ebony face reflecting a look of deep concern, as he looked seaward again. "Don't forget. We've quite a few Spaniards aboard who were seamen with the original occupation fleet. We might risk an uprising if we refuse to rescue some of their compatriots."

"A mutiny? Aboard my ship? Nonsense!"

"Bringing the Spaniards along was a necessary evil—you said it yourself. We needed them to help us locate Boriken Island and Abacoa Bay, which they've done as promised. Your necessary evil may turn into an intolerable risk if we turn Spanish survivors away. Look how Diego and his men have gathered in the waist of the ship to see what's happening."

Gordon glanced towards the larboard railing, where he saw Diego Colón—the boisterous leader of the Spanish contingent of the *Moon Chaser's* crew—gathered with several of his black coat-clad men. All were taking turns pointing and talking excitedly amongst each other. A ship's boy ran up to Diego and tugged on the man's shirtsleeve to get his attention, before offering up a brass telescope. Diego grabbed it away and rudely pushed the boy aside, then turned and trained his eye through it towards shore. Gordon shook his head before looking back at Kinshasa and grunting in disapproval. "I'll have them all clapped in irons. They can spend the rest of the trip in the hold."

Kinshasa shrugged his shoulders and sighed. "Captain, permission to speak freely?"

"Of course, Kinshasa. Speak away."

"Why do you persist in this quest of yours? This Earth is your home world now, and in it you've accomplished great good—more than most men. Destiny brought you here all those years ago and it won't let you go. Can't you see that? How many times have you tried to get back, only to end up at the wrong location, or miss the Mars occultation by days or weeks, like we've done once again? Would you even recognize *your* Earth after all these years?"

"We've had this discussion time and time again, Kinshasa," replied Gordon. "If there's ever a chance for me to get back, I'll take it. It's as simple as that. There's something about being away from the place you consider your home: an emptiness that never seems to go away. It's hard to explain, but I..."

"Here you go, sirs!" shouted Jared, cutting Gordon's sentence short as the boy trotted back out of the officers' quarters—followed by a yelping Matey—and over to Danny, the tubular, leather case holding the best telescope the ship possessed tucked under his left arm while he clutched Gordon's binoculars in both hands as if they were made of gold. "Best telescope it is to Mr. O'Farrell."

Danny ran over to meet Jared. "Thank you, Mr. Kinnel," he said with a nod, quickly grabbing up the telescope case before the boy could drop it. Turning, he stepped over to the ratlines strung amidships from the top of the mainmast to the larboard railing below, slinging the case's strap over his head and shoulder as he went. Once his burden was safely secure, he started climbing with the ease and swiftness of a man born to be at sea.

After saluting Danny's back, Jared quickly strolled to the companionway leading to the quarterdeck, climbing it carefully to present the binoculars to Gordon. "Your binoculars, sir," he said in the most serious tone he could muster, considering there was a playful and excited dog yapping at his heels. He walked over and handed them up to Gordon, then saluted. "Sorry about Matey, sir. He's quite spun up all of a sudden. Maybe he can smell them sailors Mr. Landon has spotted. Shall I have him taken below?"

"That won't be necessary, Mr. Kinnel," replied Gordon, fondly studying the battered, old pair of binoculars. They were one of his few remaining possessions from his former existence: a gift from his Aunt Dottie. They had survived his passage through the Mars Beast orb in Guatemala all those years ago and, miraculously, had never been lost or stolen—at least for any great length of time. Battered and old, much like himself, but still quite functional. He wondered which one of them would survive longer. He looked down at Jared before gazing shoreward again. "Perhaps Matey does sense something. He's quite a perceptive dog. But now I want the both of you to jump up to forecastle to help keep watch, but tie Matey to his leash first so he doesn't get near those confounded Spaniards."

"Yes, sir, but you needn't worry about that, because Matey steers clear of 'em. The Spaniards kick at him when they can."

"I'm aware of that, Mr. Kinnel. They've been warned the next time one of them does, the grate will be rigged and the whole lot of them flogged in turn, starting with Diego. Now off with you."

"Yes, sir!" replied Jared before he and his noisy shipmate ran down into the ship's waist again.

"Come on, Kinshasa," said Gordon, starting up the companionway leading to the poop deck. "Let's have a look." There, they stepped over to larboard railing and Gordon raised the binoculars to his face, peering through them in the direction the lookout had called out. After a few focuses and searching around a bit, he finally spotted it: a small sailboat pitching along close into shore. Its canvass looked dirty and old. "Well look at that," he muttered, offering the binoculars over to Kinshasa. "It *is* a sailboat."

"Taino war canoes!" shouted Danny from his perch high atop the mainmast. "Captain! War canoes are chasing the sailboat. I count six so far. They've just cleared the passage to the bay. They're manned to the teeth and paddling like their lives depended on it, sir."

"Kinshasa?" asked Gordon.

"I can't make out any canoes yet, sir. I can see the sailboat, though. There's a red marking of some sort at the center of her sail."

"She runs beneath the Red Cross of Cortez!" shouted Diego in a thick, Spanish accent. "I can see it! I can see it! They must be fellow Spaniards! Go, lads, go!"

A cheer erupted from Diego's men as they began waving their hats or handkerchiefs towards the shore, hooting and hollering like madmen.

"Go, lads, go!" shouted Diego again before returning to his animated narration of the events he was witnessing through his telescope.

"Looks like them Taino cannibals are trying to re-catch their breakfast!" shouted Morgan Landon from the foretop, followed by an emphatic laugh.

"Silence on deck!" roared Gordon from the poop's railing. "Mr. Mahn, take down Mr. Landon's name for punishment. And the next man who speaks out of turn will have his name taken as well!"

The deck fell silent and grim as Gordon glared down upon them with the giant, frowning Kinshasa at his side. A punishment from Captain Parks was rare, but certain and swift once declared. And Jack Deeth, the boson's mate, was a lively and spirited sailor who took his flogging responsibilities quite seriously. Deeth was also a firm believer in *practice makes perfect* and wasn't all that fond of Mr. Landon or the young man's quaint ability to turn a phrase, either. Landon's back would be flogged bloody for sure.

Once the matter was settled, Gordon shouted up to Danny again. "Mr. O'Farrell, please call out an accurate accounting of what you can see. Call out for all to hear!"

"Yes, sir!" replied Danny. "The launch is still running close into shore and maintaining her distance from the war canoes. Wait...she's changed course a bit to the north...and she's adjusting her yard closer in to her starboard railing, I think."

"Have they spotted us?" called Gordon.

"No sir. I don't think so. I don't think any of 'em have. The war canoes are turning as well. Look at those buggers paddle...sorry sir."

"Excuse me, Captain Parks," said an apologetic Lieutenant Paison Hullings, coming up the companionway and saluting Gordon. "The word has just been passed that Mr. Colón would like to speak with you."

Gordon glanced down into the waist and saw Diego and several of his black coat-clad men standing near the companionway leading to the quarterdeck—all were glaring up at him expectantly. Gordon ignored them as he took back his binoculars from Kinshasa to gaze out at the sailboat again. "Mr. Hullings, remind Mr. Colón he's not an officer aboard this vessel. Tell him I'm indisposed right now and may put his request in writing—for consideration at my time and choosing, if at all."

"Yes, sir."

"And gather the officers of the watch on the quarterdeck."

"Aye, aye, sir," replied Paison with a nod, before stepping down the companionway again.

"Mr. Mahn," continued Gordon in a casual tone. "Discretely summon your pistoleers and station them fore and aft—along the railings to the quarterdeck and forecastle. If Diego or any of his Spaniard thugs dares set foot on that companionway, I want you to have them clapped in irons immediately. If they resist, your men are free to shoot them."

"Yes, sir," replied Kinshasa with a grin. The large man disappeared from the poop deck and in a short while more muscular, ebony-skinned men—armed with bulky-looking revolver pistols holstered and slung across their chests—began trotting and lining up next to each other along the railings as ordered; staring down cold-eyed and bloody-minded serious at the sailors in the ship's waist.

With this, Diego and his men—all unarmed and frowning—slowly retreated from the companionway one after another before gathering at the larboard railing again, Diego's jaw set so hard in anger his cheeks could be seen twitching through his coal-black beard.

"We're starting to close with the launch, sir," called Danny from the maintop again, his eye trained through the long, brass telescope. "I can see her sail much better. It looks like a patchwork of old rags and I believe it's starting to fray apart. The Taino canoes are shifting to fresh paddlers. Once that sail goes, God save whoever's aboard that launch."

"She runs beneath the Red Cross of Cortez!" shouted Diego, now at the threshold of the companionway again; glaring up at Gordon and pointing seaward. "I can see the Red Cross on her sail. I lost many men to the Taino. We have a chance to rescue a few from those cannibal devils! You may flog me if you like, but I insist you do something Captain Parks. Those are citizens of the Crown!"

"You're in no position to insist on anything, Mr. Colón," replied Gordon coolly. "I understand your frustration, but as a Spaniard, you of all people understand the code of slavery. Even if they are Spanish survivors, they're also the lawful property of Chief Caguama and he has every right to retrieve them. Neither I nor this vessel is under any obligation to the Spanish Crown or her citizens—prisoners or otherwise."

"How can you be so heartless?" shouted Diego.

"Heartless?" laughed Gordon. "Oh, the irony! The sick, twisted irony. Have you forgotten the pain and suffering the Spanish inflicted upon the Taino people? How many innocents were killed because they refused to succumb to your country's slavery? How many have you yourself knocked around simply for daring to look a Spaniard in the eye? I would wager the number is legion. Now I'm the heartless one?"

"There's something written on the cross, sir!" cried Danny O'Farrell. "And it's written in English, sir, not Spanish."

Gordon's face snapped skyward towards the maintop. There were no Englishmen in the Spaniards' occupation fleet. "English?" he shouted in disbelief. "That's impossible. English? Can you read it Mr. O'Farrell? What does it say?"

"It looks like nonsense, sir. Right in the middle of the cross is written: 'Robots rule.'"

"Repeat that, Mr. O'Farrell," shouted Gordon. "What does it say?"

"Robots rule!"

Kinshasa, who was back on the poop deck, looked at Gordon questioningly. "Robots rule? What in God's name is a 'robot?'"

"It's a word I've not heard uttered in thirty-five years," replied Gordon lowly, looking out towards the sailboat again through his binoculars. "Good God, Kinshasa," he continued under his breath after mulling something over in his head. "Whoever's in that launch must be from *my* Earth; swept here through the expanded ley orb portal we just missed! I can barely believe it!" He turned and ran over to the poop's railing. "Mr. Watkins," he shouted down to the ship's master, who was now gathered with the other officers on the quarterdeck below.

"Yes, sir!"

"Make for the launch with all possible speed! I've decided to save those poor devils if we can."

At this a cheer rang out from Diego and his fellow Spaniards. "Silence on deck!" shouted Gordon. "Mr. Colón, I'm going to overlook your clear insubordination just now, but just this once. These are uncharted waters, at least to my crew. I want two of your most experienced men from the Spanish occupation fleet heaving loglines from the larboard and starboard catheads, calling out depth soundings as fast as they possibly can. If we strike a reef we'll be stuck here. And you know how much the Taino like Spaniards."

Diego, now beaming, saluted Gordon with a gaudy flourish—in the custom of the Spanish Service in which the man trained. "Aye, aye, sir!" he replied loudly in his thick accent.

At the same instant the ship's master began barking out orders from the quarterdeck. A moment later the ship's coxswain ran up to the forecastle's railing and began a loud series of beats on his drum—some fast and rolling, others stilted and staccato—signaling sailing orders in well-known codes. At the sound of the drum, men in great numbers began scrambling up ratlines and heaving on ropes and tackles: quickly raising or unfurling more canvas fore and aft on the ship's three masts. Soon the *Moon Chaser* was blossoming sail after sail and picking up speed, kicking up a bow wave as Diego's men, stationed out over the water on the catheads at the ship's bow, heaved their log lines—long strings weighted with lead slugs at their ends and knotted at fathom intervals to gauge ship's speed and water's depth—calling out their Spanish-accented soundings in turn.

"No bottom with this line!"

"By my mark, no bottom!"

"What's going on now, Mr. O'Farrell?" shouted Gordon, looking up towards the maintop again as the *Moon Chaser* heeled over slightly in the wind, steering directly towards launch off in the distance.

"I don't think we're going to make it, sir. Their patchwork sail is all but ripped to pieces and the Taino war canoes have just shifted to fresh paddlers again."

Porter had been so busy tying up a canvas tourniquet around poor, seasick Henry's left arm to stop the bleeding from the arrow's gash, he hadn't noticed the Taino war canoes pursuing them at first. It wasn't until after propping his green friend on a thwart near the starboard gunnel—so Henry could vomit freely out over the water *with* the wind—when Porter finally spotted them as he stepped aft to man the sailboat's tiller.

There were six, long war canoes in all, crammed with so many men that tired paddlers would take turns swapping out with fresh ones. This procedure appeared to take place at regular intervals through a well-orchestrated maneuver in which paddlers would rise and change places in unison, not so much as tipping their crafts or loosing any speed. Porter could barely believe such heavy canoes could travel so swiftly, and for a while it looked like they were gaining on the sailboat, and that's when he made his fatal mistake.

In order to pick up speed and outrun the canoes, Porter adjusted the boat's yard nearly perpendicular to its keel and turned to run directly with the wind. This gave him an extra surge of speed, but it also placed a greater pressure upon their patchwork sail, which slowly began pulling apart at its seams. Porter, obsessed with gauging the distance they were gaining by watching the war canoes behind them, didn't notice at first, and when he finally did—after hearing some sickening, long, tearing sounds over Henry's periodic dry-heaves—it was practically too late.

Porter did what he could, pulling the yard closer to the boat's starboard side and maneuvering north a bit to relieve the wind's pressure, but by now whole patches had already ripped wide open and their sail was beginning to look like an old, gray piece of Swiss cheese. Soon the Taino war canoes were gaining on them again and after a while Porter gave up praying their Olympian paddlers would tire of the chase. "Henry?" he finally asked in a resigned tone, beginning to hear the cadence drum and unified grunts of the canoes' paddlers slowly creeping up behind them; now certain they wouldn't escape after all. "How are you feeling, buddy?"

"Not so good, Porter," gurgled Henry, weakly raising his head. "I want to go home. I wish I would wake up from this nightmare already."

"Me too," replied Porter, deciding not to tell his friend their minutes were numbered. And then for some, unexplainable reason he felt warm pressure against his right cheek, like someone had just given him a kiss. He reached up to touch it as a vivid memory of Sarah flashed into his head. He glowed at it, then just sighed and looked wistfully skyward. "I remember my first kiss from Sarah," he said absently, recalling the play rehearsal not so long ago, but feeling a universe removed from it. "My first and probably only kiss from the girl I was meant to be with. Did you kiss her? Lealoa, I mean."

No reply.

Looking over, Porter noticed Henry was now hanging limply over the gunnel, his left arm dangling into the water streaming along its side. "Henry? ... Henry!" He bolted forward and knelt down, gently shaking his friend's shoulders, but Henry wouldn't wake up. The young man's face was strangely pale; projecting a serene look of inner peace. He studied Henry's blood-drenched shirt and then glanced into the belly of the boat, where all the crimson puddles and splatters across their supplies were already browning in the sun. *He's lost too much blood*, Porter suddenly realized. *He's dying. Oh, my God, Henry is dying!* He looked about helplessly for a moment, then back at their relentless pursuers, who were now maybe a hundred yards away and closing fast.

A man in the bow of the lead war canoe stood and brandished a polished, wooden club at Porter, then grinned with a mouth lined with shark teeth.

The sight of his dying friend, the grinning Boba responsible for their certain doom, and his feeling of helplessness suddenly combined like an explosive mixture, filling Porter with uncontrollable rage. He grabbed his sword and leapt up to the boat's stern thwart, raising and twirling the blade over his head like a mad, bloodthirsty dervish. "Rotten murderer!" he screamed. "Come and get it, Boba! I'll take you with me!" No longer caring for anything except at least one blade stroke of vengeance against Boba, Porter jumped around and with a smooth, forceful, blow chopped through the line tying their patchwork canvas to its yard, which quickly pulled free and billowed away: streaming and flapping loudly in the early-morning wind like a big, dirty flag unfurling from the mast. Jumping up on the thwart to face their pursuers again as the sailboat slowed to a crawl, Porter twirled his sword over his head with such adrenaline-pumped anger he felt the strength of ten men. "You want me? Come and get me, Boba! I'll carve your cold, bloody heart out!"

Boba, still grinning, brandished his club at Porter a second time, before raising it to his mouth like a leg bone, tipping it to and fro as he pretended to rip flesh from it in big bites.

"Oh yeah?" shouted Porter. "We'll see who gets who, you devil!" And just as he started twirling his sword again, imagining it was cleaving Boba's viscous head from his neck, a black ball came whistling and streaking downward in an arc from the sky; falling between the sailboat and lead war canoe to the loud, crashing report of a canon off in the distance. The ball plunged into the water not thirty yards away from Boba's now shock-filled face, sending up a huge waterspout as it exploded; raining water down upon the Taino paddlers and tossing their vessels violently in its wake.

Porter turned, looking seaward in disbelief, and for the first time noticed the big, wooden ship off in the distance and bearing down upon them. Its sails billowed pearly white, like beautiful clouds against a blue sky—the wings of a rescuing angel. A jet of crimson flame and a puff of gray smoke mushroomed from its bow and a second black cannonball raced up, over, and down in a wide arc; finally plunging into the water in front of the Taino war canoes. Next to the discovery of their little sailboat, it was the most beautiful sight Porter had ever witnessed in his life.

The cannonball disappeared beneath the waves and another waterspout erupted, this time even closer to Boba's canoe, pitching it high out of the sea as men aboard it began screaming in panic, torrents of salt water falling down upon them.

"How do you like being shot at?" cried Porter, jabbing his sword in near maniacal glee at his pursuers again, who were now struggling to escape; shouting and paddling as fast as they could; slowly maneuvering their canoes through the waves back around towards the safety of Chief Caguama's bay. "Ha! Ha! Not so fun, is it?" But when the rain of water from the second cannonball explosion finally subsided, he saw Boba on his feet. The grim warrior was now holding a bow and nocking a long arrow as he struggled to maintain his balance at the curved bow of the war canoe.

Finally steadying himself, Boba looked over and caught Porter's eye glaring at the young Spaniard in pure hatred for a moment: a moment in which mental clarity in carrying out Kulkon's will seemed to make time stop for a purpose. Then, with a parting grin of divine certainty, he quickly braced himself—muscles and tendons tensing like piano wires under his bronze skin as he mightily drew back the bow; raising and aiming it at his adversary. Exhaling, he released his bowstring, knowing his arrow would strike its mark.

Porter's jaw dropped in disbelief as a growing blur whistled and raced towards him at an unbelievable speed, a serpent striking out from Boba's bow and exploding like sledgehammer against the young man's chest. Crying out in pain and shock at Boba's lucky shot, Porter reeled back at the impact before crumpling and rolling sideways into the belly of their sailboat, sprawling over their bloodied supplies as the world around him spun lazily away into a tingly, muffled darkness.

"Porter Smith!" shouted Sarah Weston. "Wake up this instant! You have a lot of work ahead of you, young man. This is no time to sleep."

Porter slowly stirred to wakefulness—at least he thought he was awake—and found himself sitting in the front row of Kendell High School's theater, facing its stage. He was still dressed in his ragged Boriken Island clothes and his chest itched and ached strangely. Noticing pressure on his hand, he looked down and saw it was being held by another wearing an emerald ring he recognized. "Sarah?" he croaked weakly, turning to see her radiant face smiling lovingly back at him, which was edged with a blue, velvety aura. "Sarah! What happened? How did I get here? Am I having another vision?"

"Hello, my love," she replied, quickly leaning over and pressing her lips to his.

Their kiss was long and tender, and Porter resisted when she finally pulled herself away. "Oh, Sarah," he murmured in longing and confusion, gazing into her beautiful, green eyes. "I love you. I swear I never tried to kiss Kelly Martino. That Mephisto video was a fake. You've got to believe me."

"Shush," replied Sarah, gently stroking her hand across the green tunic tied around his head. "I know that now. Everyone does, thanks to Henry's dad and the police investigation over your and Henry's disappearance. You should have seen Robby Lee cry when they kicked him out of school last Friday. They all cried after being expelled for what they did to you: Kelly, Larry, and the rest—all expelled for good. And I'm certain Kendell High will be a much more pleasant place as a result, except for the fact you and Henry won't be there—at least for a while. I'm dreadfully ashamed I didn't believe you."

The ache in Porter's heart suddenly surged into a dagger stroke of pain and he pitched forward, groaning at it.

Sarah placed her hand over a spot on his chest from which protruded the dark, shadowy shaft of a phantom arrow. At her touch it dissolved into a puff of smoke. "Peace, Porter. I will not allow you to die at the hands of Boba. His wicked, misguided arrow is gone. You must listen to me carefully now," she continued, pointing towards the stage, which was now filled with twinkling stars surrounding a pyramid covered with strange markings; above which floated Elizabeth Weston, sitting cross-legged with her eyes closed and arms held out to her sides—apparently in some sort of deep trance. "Time is short and the celestial alignment which has allowed us to contact and protect you and Henry is drawing to an end. We will not be able to visit or assist you again for some time to come."

"What's going on, Sarah? How can I be speaking to you right now?"

"Through my mother's powers projected through me. I can't explain things yet—I can hardly believe what's going on myself. I...We—my mother and I—are very, very special beings, Porter. I cannot reveal any more right now, but you must trust me."

"I do."

"In a short while you'll find yourself aboard the *Moon Chaser*." She pointed at the stage again and one of the stars hovering above it twinkled, then shined brightly—bursting towards them as it expanded into a broad, round disk showing a vivid, moving image of a large, ancient-looking sailing ship with three masts. Billowing white sails were quickly being taken in on its masts and yards as the image lazily spun about, creeping forward towards a little sailboat drifting along nearby.

Closer and closer the sailboat came into view and soon Porter could see Henry again: passed out and pale; hanging limply over the starboard gunnel. Then he spotted himself, crumpled over sideways near the sailboat's mast; the long shaft of Boba's arrow sticking out of his chest but quickly dissolving away to vapor and dust. The little boat gently bumped into the *Moon Chaser's* hull with a lazy thud. At nearly the same instant men were scrambling down into it, shouting and gently lifting Porter and Henry out and up the ship's side.

The image pulled back again, focusing on the *Moon Chaser's* deck where the boys were being handed aboard. It was crowded with concerned sailors—and a little yapping dog—who parted quickly to let a muscular-looking man with long, graying-brown hair pulled back into a ponytail pass, followed by an even larger, more muscular, black-skinned man. The image pitched forward and settled on the man with the ponytail.

"This is Gordon Parks," continued Sarah. "He is the captain of the *Moon Chaser*: the ship in the process of saving you and Henry. You both owe him your lives. What he will tell you when you awake a few days from now will sound fantastic and strange, but you must believe him. He knows the locations of the cosmic doorways which can get you back home."

"Cosmic doorways?" asked Porter, watching this man named "Gordon Parks" pointing and calling out muffled-sounding orders Porter could just make out in his head somewhere.

"You and Henry were accidentally swept through one which opened briefly next to the altar at the old Kendell field house: the orb you saw. Gordon Parks was swept through a similar doorway in Guatemala years and years ago. All swept though into an alternate universe: a nearly identical Earth 500 years out of step with our own. My mother said she tried to save you, but arrived at the field house too late."

"I don't remember any of it," replied Porter, watching himself and Henry being loaded onto canvas stretchers and hustled away quickly, all the while being surrounded by the sailors, some of whom were now nodding their heads and smiling. It was like he was having one of those strange, out-of-body experiences he'd read about. Then the image star hovering before them on stage contracted into a point of light again as voices—strange, yet friendly and comforting—began bubbling up all around them; echoing across the theater one after another.

"You'll be all right now, lads. You'll see. We can use a couple of fresh hands around here."

"Be still. Be still. We've got the best surgeon in the world aboard."

"Easy, son, don't try to move."

"Make way there! Make way for the young lion!"

"Did you think you could take on two hundred Taino warriors single-handedly? Young lion? I call it misguided bravery. Lucky for you we happened along when we did, forsooth!"

"I think this green one here will be okay. He's looking around now. He's lost a lot of blood, but he's mostly just seasick. Doc Rosa's got a sure-fire cure for seasickness lad. Don't give up the ship, yet. Heh! Heh!"

Sarah waved her hand and the voices quickly faded and ebbed away to silence. "How you arrived where you are doesn't matter now, Porter," she said. "What matters *is* that you get back home. Unfortunately it will not be easy. While Gordon Parks knows the locations of the doorways between our universes, he cannot accurately predict when they will open. Lunar occultations of Mars are not that common."

"What should I do, Sarah?"

"You must encourage and protect Henry. He has the mathematical skills necessary to predict when the orbs will appear—the cosmic doorways home—using tools that will be provided. He is vulnerable now, so don't let him lose hope. And when the time comes, you must tell him to use the levels. The levels are the keys."

"The levels are the keys."

"Remain strong and vigilant, Porter. There are people—evil, ruthless people—who will try to stop you. Gordon Parks has made many enemies over the years in his quest to stamp out slavery in the alternate Earth universe you're now trapped in. By befriending him, as you and Henry must do, Parks's enemies shall become your own." She reached over and gripped his right hand tightly.

At her touch Porter felt a strange, tingling sensation pulsing into his palm and up into his shoulder like a low, electric current flowing through his veins and into his nerves.

"There," said Sarah. "The energy I have delivered to your fighting arm will help protect you. In addition to the Kendell High fencing team you are now the finest swordsman aboard the *Moon Chaser*." Finally letting go, Sarah leaned over and kissed Porter on his cheek. "And forgive you for your fondness of the beautiful Ginhua, but let not your eye wander again, *my* love," she whispered.

Porter blushed and started to say something, but Sarah put her finger to his lips. "No need for explanations, my darling. I must leave you now." She pointed at the stage, where they saw clusters of stars and bright planets slowly shifting and pulling apart as the image of the pyramid and Elizabeth Weston began to ripple away. Facing Porter again, Sarah began wiping away tears that were now welling up on her face. "I love you, Porter. You and Henry shall awake strong and healthy in a few days time, seemingly pulled from the jaws of certain death by the *Moon Chaser's* surgeon. Remember what I have told you and return to me as swiftly as you can. You can and you must. We are soul mates now." Throwing her arms around his shoulders, she pressed her lips to his again, kissing him deeply as the theater lights slowly faded into darkness, filling Porter with the strength and courage he would need to get back home.

◆ ◆ ◆

Printed in the United States
1348500001B/83